Never After

Never After

ALEXIS HALL

This is a work of fiction. Names, characters, organizations, places, events, and incidents are either products of the author's imagination or are used fictitiously. Otherwise, any resemblance to actual persons, living or dead, is purely coincidental.

Published by Montlake, Seattle

www.apub.com

EU product safety contact:
Amazon Media EU S. à r.l.
38, avenue John F. Kennedy, L-1855 Luxembourg
amazonpublishing-gpsr@amazon.com

ISBN-13: 9781662509414 (paperback)
ISBN-13: 9781662509407 (digital)

Cover design by Hang Le
Cover image: © Miguel Sobreira / ArcAngel Images; © Gorbash Varvara / Shutterstock

Printed in the United States of America

Though nothing can bring back the hour
Of splendour in the grass
Of glory in the flower
We will grieve not, rather find
Strength in what remains behind.

"Ode: Intimations of Immortality from Recollections of Early Childhood" by William Wordsworth

Volume I

London

Chapter 1

1

Please darling, he says, give yourself to me.

He says, there is no sin in this.

He says, I will always love you. I will never leave you.

And I believe him. I believe him, and there is only beauty beneath his touch. Love and desire, paradise in prefiguring miniature, all the ecstasies of faith transubstantiated into skin until we are stars.

~

"Micha," snapped Madame Defleur, as he stumbled over the threshold, "you look about as fuckable as a hole in the wall." She ran a modest house on Church Lane, at which Michael Dashwood—when he was so inclined—made a modest living. "Mary's tits, what's wrong with your eye? Are you bleeding? And on my new carpet."

"There are some clients," he slurred, "who would likely pay extra because of it." But he let himself be hustled downstairs into the kitchen, where none of the customers would see him.

"Well, I don't trade in damaged goods."

A laugh, harsh as blue ruin and utterly mirthless, rolled out of him. "Of course you do, dear Madame."

"Are you drunk?" Madame Defleur glared at him through her paint-thick eyes.

"No, I am not drunk." He had a surprisingly refined voice, and the diction of an educated man. It was incongruous with his general manner, his threadbare clothes, and the tawdry cosmetics that defined his eyes and darkened his lips.

She snorted. "Poppy-addled?"

He smiled at her, all sudden charm and blank eyes.

"Oh, clean yourself up," she growled. "And then piss off."

His lashes swept down in a look of practised submission. "Yes, Madame."

She swept out in a rustle of scarlet skirts.

The room was shabby. But it was familiar and warm. Better than outside, where it was raining. Or so Micha thought. It was hard to tell through the drug haze. He put a hand to his coat sleeve and pressed it against his skin until he felt the damp and the cold seep through the fabric. Yes, it must have been raining. Then he touched his fingers to his mouth. They came away bloody. The pain would be later, if at all.

In the middle of the kitchen was a rough wooden table, flanked on either side by long benches. It was a style of furnishing better described as "cheap" than "rustic." Sometimes he waited here with the other whores, listening to their laughter, swapping stories filthy and ridiculous. As much performance as everything he did upstairs, among the velvet and gilt, promises and lies.

Micha swung his legs over the nearest bench and sat down. A cough took him by surprise, erupting from a red centre of agony in the middle of his chest, stealing breath and thought alike as he fought to subdue it. He was left gasping and trembling, the weakness of his body cutting sharply through the opiates that usually shielded him. He hunched his shoulders, curling in on himself, dragging in painful breath after painful breath until, at last, the instinctive physical fear was gone. He thought it strange the way the body struggled on, when all else was lost and gone. He watched the shadows dancing in the corners of the room. They made the shapes of monsters.

Then he folded one of his elbows on the table, cushioned his head on it, and fell asleep.

In his dreams, the shadows kept dancing, drifting sometimes into men who had known his body, the one who had known his soul.

"What the fuck are you doing?" Madame Defleur shook him roughly awake. "This isn't a fucking church."

Micha blinked phantasms from his eyes, trying to remember where he was. He ached. He was tired. Shivers chased each other across his flesh like ripples across a fetid pond. He put fingertips to his lips and winced as the skin cracked, flakes of dried blood falling in rust-coloured petals onto the tabletop.

Madame Defleur dragged him to his feet. He was tall but far too thin, and she had the build of a prizefighter. He stumbled, his knee catching sharply against the bench. The pain troubled him less than the realisation that he'd felt it in the first place. He thought he had long dispensed with feelings of any kind.

This hazy awareness brought with it other realisations. He had no money and, as of tonight, no lodgings. How had that come about? Ah yes. The money, put aside for rent, he had instead given to the proprietor of a particular house in Tiger Bay, a gentleman who arrayed himself in robes of gold-embroidered silk and styled himself Johnny Wu, though he was as Chinese as Madame Defleur was French. Nevertheless, his skill in the toasting of opium was such that his customers were rumoured to include dukes and marquesses. And, on this occasion (as on many others), Micha had fully intended to replace the money. But time and opportunity had somehow got away from him. And he had made similar promises before.

Until this last incident, he had shared a miserable set of rooms in Raven Row with another whore called Nettie. He had known her for a year or so, a long time by the standards of a life which rendered fleeting everything it did not soil. She thought herself his friend, but Micha had little use for friendship. He could, however, be winning enough when he chose, though increasingly the effort of it (when he was not being paid for it and sometimes even then) wearied him. Nettie was softhearted enough that she would have forgiven this lapse, as she had all the ones preceding it. Unfortunately, her fancy man, upon whom she had prevailed to cover the shortfall, had been less tolerant. The black eye and the split lip were his parting gifts, along with the avowal that Micha had got off lightly.

Micha had no opinion on the subject. Mere brutishness touched his flesh as transiently as water.

"I don't want to see you around here," Madame Defleur was telling him, "until you're cleaned up and ready to work."

He briefly considered seducing her. He had done so before, and it would be a warm room, a bath, and a bed for the night. But he felt too bleak and too distant to be able to play the lover, which—unlike his preferred clients—she would want. Stripped of her bawd's splendour, she wore her years heavily, and Micha would see his future in the flesh he strove to satisfy. After, she would want to talk of lost things. Youth and faith, love and happiness, and the daughter who had fled her.

So he bade her farewell and slipped out of the back door into the cold, mist-sodden night.

His circumstances were troubling, but they were far better than when he had first found himself homeless and penniless on the streets of London. This time, he had no pride or hope to lose, and he had long since abandoned any qualms he might have entertained about his profession. As a young man of some beauty and limited education, with no connections, no references, and no other talents, it was quite simply all he was good for. An understanding he had learned, somewhat painfully, to accept without judgement or self-censure. When he had been in a position to make choices, this was where they had brought him. And he had found ways—one way, specifically—to make existing bearable. Unfortunately, without money, there was little likelihood of that either. Johnny Wu had stopped allowing him to punt on tick a long time ago.

As he stepped out of the dingy alley that oozed between Madame Defleur's and the slop-shop next door, Micha caught sight of one of the establishment's regulars coming down the street the other way. He knew very little about him, only that he was employed as a graver down at the docks and that he usually visited Philip—a pale-faced, yellow-haired waif of a Mary-Anne—although his eyes had occasionally strayed speculatively to Micha. Madame Defleur's patrons were encouraged to sample the varieties of the house, but poaching each other's customers directly was discouraged, as it was bad for business.

Micha plunged his hands into his pockets and walked briskly towards the client, keeping his head down as though he was protecting himself from the chill bite of the prevailing wind. His shoulder brushed against the other man's as they passed each other.

"Oh, I'm terribly sorry." Micha managed a fair semblance of being startled. He was sober enough that his voice shone like glass amongst the crawling alleys of Whitechapel.

"Nae worries, man." Philip had mentioned this particular client came from one of the Northern cities. He had no family in London, and few friends. It would be a lonely life, even had he not been a sodomite.

Neither loneliness nor sodomy troubled Micha anymore. He did not speak, but he leaned a little closer, letting the heat of his body mingle with that of the stranger's. His finely chiselled lips curled into a hint of a smile, his dark eyes shimmering with promise.

"Y'off then?" The client had a strange, almost musical lilt, roughened by burgeoning lust.

"I could be persuaded to stay," Micha murmured. He turned his head so that his breath grazed the client's cheek. "For a little while."

And there it was.

Silver, pressed into his hand, like pieces of the moon.

659

Open your mouth, he says. And I do. His thick fingers taste of tar and sweat and skin. He tells me I'm beautiful. At least I think that's what he means. Bonny, he says. A bonny lad.

I moan suggestively around his fingers. He fucks my mouth until I gag. My cock stands on reflex alone. But he likes it, paws at me and, somehow, I'm responding.

I shove myself to my knees, a blank dark pain as the bones crack sharply against the flagstones.

Alreet, he says. I've no idea what it means but he sounds worried.

I suck him off. He mumbles about my pretty mouth and my posh voice.

He's rough but not cruel. I only realise my lip has split open again when I see there's blood in the drool and semen I wipe from my mouth.

~

Micha walked briskly towards Bluegate Fields with the surety of a ship following its star. Money gave him his destination and something that was almost pleasurable—anticipation. The rain persisted, coming slantwise through the yellow fog and speckling his face with its chill, bright needles. A heavy weight, damp as the weather, had gathered in the centre of his chest, and no amount of coughing would ease it.

He moved fearlessly and as quickly as his laboured breathing would allow through the dank and tangled alleyways that led him towards High Street, Shadwell. The air was as stagnant as an open sewer, heavy with the stench of poverty and human filth. The painted tigresses, from which Tiger Bay derived its name, lolled in doorways or leaned from open windows, gin-soaked fantasies in rotting finery. Pickpockets, cutthroats, and cash carriers lurked sullenly in the wretched courtyards formed by the close-packed tenements. But nobody troubled Micha. Some even called out his name in greeting. Familiarity had rendered the squalid horrors of the slum an everyday banality. He stepped carefully over a slumped, tattered body that lay—dead or insensible—in the street, and thought nothing of it.

"Ahwight, Micha?"

A boy stepped from the shadows between two bawdy houses and fell into step beside him. He was bird-thin and bone-pale, his age impossible to guess. Fifteen? Thirteen? Younger yet?

Micha was not in the mood for conversation. He felt cold and ill. His mouth stung and tasted sour, the realities of the world and his life crashing too hard against him. But still. He slowed his pace. Just a little.

"Good evening, Alfie." A mockery of courtesy coloured his voice, but it was not entirely without warmth.

The youth grinned up at him. "'Ow's tricks wiv you, then?"

"Well enough, thank you."

Alfie nodded. In the uncertain light, his eyes were the same colour as the rain. "Going to see ol' Johnny?"

Micha nodded.

"You shouldn't. I seen what too much smoke does t' men. It's like sumfink's eating away at 'em but from the inside out."

"And you shouldn't listen to so many penny dreadfuls."

Alfie's hip suddenly grazed Micha's. "If you wanna feel good, maybe, I'm 'ere. Better value 'n' all." Micha recoiled, which made Alfie stumble and then glare. "What?"

The question *How old are you?* lodged in Micha's throat, but he was too tired, too selfish, and too afraid to ask it. "We're in the same business. Why the fuck would I pay for it?"

Alfie shrugged. "Dunno why anybody would." Again, his eyes sought Micha's, tugging at him like a hand upon his coat sleeve. "I fought it'd be ahwight wiv you. And everybody knows you're a mandrake for real."

Micha shocked himself by laughing, though it was not a happy sound. It echoed eerily between the houses and through the muffled noises of bartered pleasure and smothered misery. "Once maybe."

"You ain't a pervert no more?"

"I'm not anything." As soon as he spoke the words aloud, Micha knew them for truth. He was a body or the façade of a body. A convenience for the desire and shame of others. And, as for his own—nothing. Lost, shed, forgotten, like so much else, leaving behind only the faintest residue of humanity: a bestial compulsion to survive and a base craving for a fleeting approximation of a higher form of happiness.

"I fought you liked me." Alfie flared with unexpected rage. "You talk to me."

"Only because you talk to me."

"Yeah, 'cos I fought . . . ah, forget it. Fuck you. Smoke yourself to hell." Alfie made an obscene gesture and turned away.

This is hell, thought Micha. *Nor am I out of it.* But he did not believe in hell. Or heaven, for that matter. He sighed, dully annoyed. "Alfie," he called out.

"What?" The boy turned, one hand resting on a jutted hip.

Micha flicked him one of his coins.

"What's this? Charity? Ooh, lah-di-dah." Despite the scorn in his voice, the boy showed no inclination to return the money.

"Call it whatever the fuck you want. I don't fucking care."

Micha walked on. From behind, he felt the impact of spattering droplets that were not the rain. A new coldness. He reached up and wiped Alfie's spittle from his shoulder.

19

The first thing he does is hit me. I've never been struck before. It's the shock more than the pain that sends me sprawling at his feet. Then he's hauling me up and I think he's going to hit me again—maybe he's going to kill me, I've heard stories. But all he does is shove me onto the bed. His hand on the back of my neck pins me down. Dust, and the stench of strangers, rushes up my nose from the tawdry velvet coverlet. He's rough enough that it hurts but it doesn't last long. He sputters obscenities with every broken breath and tears himself away afterwards, spilling himself over me as well as in me. My body is trembling. The pain has gone but my skin feels as thin as parchment. I get up. Find him on the floor. He has his head in his hands. I think he's crying. I kneel down beside him. I don't know why but I try to tell him it's all right. He looks at me, shame stark in his eyes, then hits me again. When I come to, it's only moments later, but he's gone.

~

Finally, Micha turned into an arched alleyway, as dark as a yawning, toothless mouth. He had to stoop beneath the dirt-smeared, weed-webbed brickwork. It led him into a tiny square of hunched and dilapidated houses, leaning against each other like drunks. The reek of sewage intensified. Occasionally light would move behind the fractured windowpanes, squeezing between the cracks like bile from an infected wound.

He approached one of the hovels and pushed open the door. The rotten wood felt spongy beneath his fingers, and from within came the faintest suggestion of vapour, the sweet-sickly essence of a scent as transitory as the promise of pleasure. He stepped inside and made his way up the narrow, filthy staircase, knowing better than to touch the handrail, which was coated with a damp, strange dust.

Inside the public smoking room on the first floor, he found Johnny Wu crouched before the fire in his filthy silks and curling-toed slippers. He was tending to a saucepan of simmering water, over which was hung a finely woven sieve containing shreds of raw opium. There was only a handful of customers tonight. One was just leaving—pushing past Micha on his way out—another was slumped in one of the three wooden chairs provided, and the last was sprawled, barely conscious, on the sagging four-poster bed that was the room's most significant article of furniture. The mattress was bare but for some Chinese matting, the counterpane rolled into a thick bolster that lay lengthwise across it. Pieces of tattered silk in some oriental design were slung from the frame, the original colour and pattern long lost to dirt and grease. The walls and ceiling were blackened with smoke and smeared with a greenish damp that spread across the flaking plasterwork like pox. The only window had no glass and was covered over with pieces of brown paper, but even so, it was almost suffocatingly warm from the fire.

Johnny Wu rose from his haunches and performed a grotesque semblance of something Micha thought was meant to be a bow. "Neen how, good sir, neen how." He bobbed up and down. And, then, seeing it was Micha, he went on in a completely different voice: "Oh, it's you. You better 'ave the cash this time, my buff."

"I do." Micha handed over his shillings. "And that should cover what I owe you."

Johnny Wu nodded, and the coins disappeared somewhere into his robes. "Molly," he bellowed, thumping one of his feet on the floorboards.

The man on the bed made a soft, indistinct sound but did not otherwise stir. After a moment, a woman, frail as a ghost, came into the room. Unlike her husband (at least, Micha presumed Johnny Wu was her husband), she wore a threadbare gown of English cut. Her skin had a yellowish, unhealthy tinge to it, and the hair that brushed her sharp-boned shoulders was as brittle as old straw. He nodded at the saucepan and she took his place, coughing softly, the same scent that permeated the house drifting from her clothes and hair.

Micha settled himself onto the bed, propping an elbow on the bolster as he waited for Johnny Wu to begin the ceremony of preparation. The first time he had come here, in company with someone he no longer remembered, he had been as repulsed as he had been fascinated. It had struck him as a new, and peculiar, indignity to lie so close to a stranger, both helpless in pursuit of private shadows. But he had soon forgotten everything but the pleasure. There was little for Micha's clients to recognise in the cold, blank-eyed man who trod the weary circuit of his life beyond their sight and care. But here, at last, was an eagerness they might find familiar, though, on this occasion, unfeigned.

Johnny Wu sat down on the edge of the bed next to Micha and laid out cloth, an oil lamp, a pipe, and a small pot of cooked opium. From his box of tools, he produced an opium needle, dipped it into the treacle-thick opium, and held it to the flame, turning it carefully until the droplet had swelled and crystallised into a perfect, amber-coloured jewel. A jewel that was worth more to Micha than all the treasures of Christendom. The process continued until Johnny Wu had toasted enough opium to fill the pipe bowl, at which point he passed it to Micha.

Micha's fingers trembled upon the bamboo stem as he held it over the lamp. Then he took it deep into his mouth and sucked, the pipe gurgling its sweet seduction as he swallowed down the smoke. A few threads of yellowish vapour drifted up from the bowl, dissipating to nothing in the fetid air and taking with them time and truth and everything Micha wanted to forget. He fell back against the bolster, eyelids flickering, the stupefaction of bliss easing the harsh, cynical lines of his face.

In a little while, the pipe was done, and Johnny Wu made him another and then a third. Micha would have smoked all night had his funds allowed it. But, for now, he was content, surrendering himself, moment by moment, to the spell of opium. Like falling into feathers. The room was beautiful. The shadows spun mysteries from the corners. The wind played symphonies on the paper that covered the window. The mould that wound its intricate labyrinth across the ceiling was the colour of the Chartreuse he had drunk in Paris with Isidore.

Oh Isidore.

In this wavering light, he looked like an angel of alabaster and gold. Micha gazed at him, full of loss and the habit of wanting, knowing a chimera when he saw one but stripped of the ability to care. He opened his arms, and Isidore came into his embrace. He was as insubstantial as ashes and the promises he had made, slipping through Micha's clutching fingers like a sinner's hope of paradise.

Memories swirled through him with the smoke. Here, they could not hurt him. He could live them, again. With Isidore, on the wide, quiet streets of Oxford, when the wisteria and the magnolia were in full bloom, and the bells sang out their love songs over the gabled rooftops. Come with me, I love you. Paris in the spring, its flower-strewn days and sparkling nights, where sin was not sin, and kisses did not always have to be stolen and all touches covert. I love you, I'll never leave you. The hushed marble severity of Rome, the dazzle of sunlight on the canals in Venice, the pale white-gold streets of Vienna. And then, Dover, grey cliffs, grey sea, grey sky, the newly unfamiliar English cold, where everything was broken.

I believed you.

But Isidore only kissed him with the ghost of his mouth.

And then Micha followed him from the room, down the stairs and into the night. The huddled houses sighed and stretched in the arms of the misty dark. His mind expanded to fill the empty spaces of the city.

He walked. Westwards. Into the light. Isidore, always slightly ahead of him, slightly out of reach, gleaming through the gloom, pristine as a pearl.

The rain came down in earnest now, slicing through the fog, coating Micha in the silver of fallen stars. He held up his hand so he could watch the way the water streamed over his skin, making him shine, as though he could be cleansed. Miniature rivers spilled down his fingers, mingling and parting, crossing each other sometimes and then breaking away, cutting their own paths across his palm. He was a tear in a flood of tears, travelling the furrowed landscape of his own hand. But he was still watching too, each and every drop a diamond, and the city watched him, with a thousand gaslight eyes, and he watched the city, and he was the city, and he was the raindrop. He was everything and nothing and saw everything and everything saw him. And though he could not predict the course of the water over his palm, the chaos of it was so swift, so lovely, that it felt directed, part of the same pattern that bound him to the city and the city to him.

Tiger Bay lay behind him. The Thames curled languorously at his side. Even opium could not make it beautiful, but now the smog was thin enough that Micha could see the moon. It was a pale, distant thing, half-smothered in mist and shadows, but its light gilded the rough brown waters like a crown. In the tobacco-stained sky, the stars were tiny, cravat-pin promises.

He wandered through Cheapside. Unlike Bluegate Fields, which stirred itself like some nocturnal monster only as the sun slipped away, these thoroughfares were quieter. He saw the reflection of the cloud-chopped sky in the rut-riven road. In every puddle, a universe gleaming. Whole cities unfolding themselves in half-glimpsed corners.

The doors of the world lay open. Everywhere was horizon.

He turned his face into the rain, into the light, into the possibility it promised. He was shuddering uncontrollably with the ecstasy of hope. He felt, perhaps, there was some meaning, some grandeur to his life, that he did not walk always straight and narrow streets, in darkness and in shame. If only it did not die in the dregs of morning, this certainty, this connection, this faith. He did not call it God, for Micha had given up belief with everything else. But, for a too-swift moment, he felt alive and as if, in some way, it mattered that he was.

Even though he knew that with every passing day he fell a little deeper, mattered a little less, suffered a little more. He was buried, in flesh, in brick, and the sky was a coffin lid.

And Isidore was growing as faint as the moonlight.

Don't leave me alone.

Micha began to run. His limbs were leaden, his heart felt tight and hot, like a piece of coal. His breath clogged his throat.

Distantly, he realised something was wrong.

He was still shaking, not as he had thought, in joy, but in weakness. And though he did not feel cold, his sweat was mingling with the rain and the moisture that leaked from his eyes.

Isidore was gone by the time Micha staggered onto Drury Lane.

The world splintered into pieces of light.

He couldn't breathe.

And he couldn't stop trembling.

People jostled into him and then recoiled. They came spilling from the theatre like coloured beads. And he was falling with them.

Into a smear of darkness.

And nothing, and nothing, and nothing.

121

It's been a long night. A party of gentlemen, slumming it. I just want to sleep but Madame Defleur tells me someone is waiting. Two of them have already shared me. Apparently it isn't sodomy if you do it with friends. I clean myself and struggle into my clothes. My value tends to decrease if I look too used. When he comes in, I enact the usual sad pantomimes of desire but when the moment comes, he rolls away from me.

Like this, he says.

It's the only words he's spoken. I've heard there are such clients. Philip says they often come to him because he does not threaten them. But I am too tall, too dark, too much a man, whatever that means, and so I am mastered, not master. When surprise wanes it leaves me with only annoyance. This requires performance more than acceptance, and I am tired, tired of everything. I try to use my anger, to take from his flesh the price so often wrung from mine, but I am only ashes. I prepare him with oil, ready a sheath. He is so tight. I could hurt him so easily. He gives me nothing but the changing rhythm of his breath. And when I have him, he drops forward onto his elbows, sweats and shakes and muffles himself in the silk pillows on the bed. It's strange to see the effect of my usage upon his body. Only strange. Release comes as though from the bottom of a deep and silent well. Afterwards, he turns onto his back and lies unmoving. His eyes pass back and forth across the canopy like ants. Why won't he leave? We do not touch but the heat that radiates from his skin is like a thread of fire that runs the whole length of my body.

Today I am to be married, he says, as he leaves in the grey dawn.

~

A stranger's voice, refined, impatient: "For God's sake, Thomas, come away."

Micha was lying on the ground. A man in evening dress was leaning over him, apparently heedless of the mud and filth upon which he knelt. He was peering down at Micha, and his face was neither beautiful nor kind.

Micha tried to sit up, tried to say something. It took all his strength just to open his mouth, and when he did, he felt like he might vomit. He collapsed onto his side, struggling to breathe. And suddenly he was choking, coughing, painfully and helplessly, blood, spit, and mucus spattering the ground and the backs of his hands. The protective haze of opium was faltering. The world closing in again. He felt wretched and mortified, locked into a body he hated and a world that despised him.

"Come away. This could be any manner of contagion."

But the one who knelt would not be moved. "This man is ill. He needs help."

"Then he may go to a workhouse."

"I-I . . . am quite well," interrupted Micha, dragging his voice from his raw throat. He made another attempt to stand, which brought him to his knees in short order. Dark smudges filled his vision, like the burned-out afterimages of suns.

"You are not." An arm caught him about the waist. Micha tried to pull away, but the man first addressed as Thomas was too strong for him. "Who are your friends?" he was asking, with consideration rather than warmth. "Your family? May I see you to them?"

Micha realised that his accent had misrepresented him. They must have believed him respectable. "I have none." And before the stranger who held him could react, he added with a sneer, "Nor do I wish any."

There was a moment of silence at the heart of a busy street. Pressed as he was in the crook of his arm, it was hard for Micha to avoid

Thomas's eyes. They were brown, plainly brown, but arresting in their warmth, and all the more so in his austere, patrician face.

"You heard the fellow." Thomas's companion shifted from one foot to the other. "I'm due at the club."

"Then you must go to your club."

The man made a sound of ill-repressed frustration. "Must you make Christianity an affliction, brother?"

The stern mouth quirked into what seemed its more natural shape, a smile touched by a hint of whimsy. "'And now abideth faith, hope, charity, but the greatest of these—'"

"Oh be quiet." His brother turned up the collar of his greatcoat and strode into the mist.

Micha shoved Thomas—with his deep eyes and gentle mouth—away from him. Oxford had been lifetimes ago. He had nothing but pieces of Greek, fragments of Latin, and a thousand memories of Isidore. But his tutor had been a patient, learned man who had not laboured entirely in vain. The words tangled around his tongue as he tried to speak them. "'The righteous is more excellent than his neighbour: but the way of the wicked seduceth them.'"

Micha delivered his rejection and did not look back. He took a few faltering steps, away from Thomas, away from the theatre, back towards the East End. And then weakness overtook him, darkness snatched at him, and he discovered he was on the brink of fainting for the second time that evening.

Thomas caught him before he fell. "Whether you are wicked or not, I think I must insist that you bear me company."

Micha struggled on some combination of principle and instinct. "I won't go to the workhouse."

"No, of course not. Come with me, and I will see you safe."

Safe? Micha tried to laugh, tried to push the man away, but shards of glass were breaking in his chest and his mouth was thick with blood and all he did was fall into the stranger's arms.

64

The usual mechanics, body to body, skin to skin, in and out, in and out, making the noises he wants me to make. Behind my eyes, nothing but blank darkness, sour and solid as a wall.

~

The man called Thomas had access to a carriage. Micha drifted in and out of awareness as he half-sat, half-lay in the velvet gloom.

He was cold, then hot, then cold again.

He shivered and sweated.

When he coughed, it felt like he was dying, as though it was the remains of his own heart's blood he was bringing up.

Occasionally, moonlight would fall hazily through the window across the stranger's face. Strong features, cold lines, like something from the portrait of a bygone age, a living testament to English breeding: centuries of pride and privilege rendered in cold stone.

512

Wanting coins for the dragon, I let a sailor have me against a wall for a shilling. I scrape my palms raw while he ruts and I shake with need, though not for this. Never anymore for this.

Chapter 2

3rd September, 1864

Influenza, is the doctor's verdict, possibly brain fever. Malnutrition certainly. If he does not die, I am to give him laudanum. Beyond that, there is little I can do for him. Pray, of course. But who am I—a mere man, a servant of men—to intercede with the divine on behalf of a stranger whose name I do not know? Do I pray for his sake or for my own?

I have sat often at the bedside of the ill and the dying and felt the clutch of desperate hands on mine. I would so ease the terror of those final moments but I am a beast of duty, a poor bearer of grace. I should have been born a puritan. Perhaps that would have been a father's love I could more easily have made manifest in the world.

I should not write these wild and wandering things. The thinking is itself a sin. How may I guide others, if I cannot control myself?

My guest is lost to fever, calling out for Isidore. I have tried to calm him, but without success. The doctor suggested I might speak to him. I tried that also, conscious of the absurdity in gravely introducing myself to an insensible man. I doubt he heard and my presence does little to soothe him. I know that suffering is not merely a consequence of but endemic to free will. I know that. But sometimes all I see is pain.

How helpless I am. Here is one man, and I can do nothing for him. I should—I must—trust in a power greater than my frail self, and I long to abandon myself to the promise of such comfort, but I am a creature of reason. I was made so, presumably by His hands and His will. Faith must be more than a feeling, otherwise we believe in God only as children believe in bedtime stories. Perhaps that is sufficient for the field-hand, the factory worker or the chimney sweep but I do His work. I am, somehow, to bring His love to the field-hand, the factory worker and the chimney sweep. But how, how may I do that if I do not feel it?

This was, after all, an alliance of convenience.

I am the Lord's reluctant wife. And, on nights like these, His widow.

~

Thomas Mandeville, or more properly the Reverend Thomas Edward Mandeville, wiped the sweat from his patient's face with a cool, damp cloth. His movements were careful and efficient, but his touch was not naturally tender. He searched in vain for a sign he had brought some relief to the suffering man. Then he tried to make him take some water, again without success. Finally, he pulled a hard chair from the corner of the room, placed it next to the bed, and simply sat down to wait.

He was tired but it did not trouble him. He preferred action to idleness, but his profession had taught him patience. The silence of his father's house dragged at him like manacles. In the hollow corridors and empty staterooms, dust hung in the air, heavy as jewels in a crown. It had been shut up for little more than a year, but it felt like a tomb. And, though the whole place should rightly have been George's, his brother had kept to his bachelor's rooms instead.

The man on the bed gave a sudden, convulsive movement. His eyes snapped open but they stared at nothing. "Isidore?"

Thomas hesitated, torn between mercy and truth.

"Isidore?"

"No." Thomas tried to soften his tone. "My name is Thomas."

"Don't leave me."

A clammy, fever-hot hand flailed for him, so he caught it and held it. "I'm here. I will not leave you."

The stranger quieted a little and fell back against the pillows. He began to cough again, but brought up no more fluid. Thomas watched him anxiously and tried, once again, to make him drink. Finally he wet his fingers in the water and put them to the man's pale, cracked lips. It was peculiar to feel the shape and texture of another man's mouth. The damp heat of his breath. Drop by drop, he coaxed his patient to take nearly half a glass of water, and then sat back. His hand was still a prisoner.

"O, Father of mercies," he whispered, "and God of all comfort, our only help in time of need. We . . . I . . . humbly beseech thee to behold, visit, and relieve thy sick servant—" He did not know the man's name. Presumably God could work it out. "Look upon him with the eyes of thy mercy. Comfort him with a sense of thy goodness; preserve him from the temptations—"

He stuttered to a halt. There was nobody to watch him, except the one to whom his prayers were directed, but he felt self-conscious. His gaze was drawn afresh to the stranger in the bed.

Even sick, sweating, possibly dying, he was—Thomas hardly knew where that thought ended. His nature, he had always believed, was inclined to the ascetic. His education, first at the hands of tutors and then at Cambridge, had been exceptional, but no one had taught him about beauty, nor had his life disposed him to seek it. He was, partially by disposition and partially by expectation, quiet, grave, introspective, and dutiful, a pale shadow of the boisterous, reckless brother who had preceded him into the world by a mere handful of minutes. And so he had gone meekly enough into the church, as a third son ought to do.

His existence, he told himself, could not have been an accident. For we are His workmanship, created in Christ Jesus unto good works, which God hath before ordained that we should walk in them. And so on and so forth.

But, perhaps, an afterthought? That felt so much easier to believe.

He tried again to pray, but the words were as ungainly as pebbles in his mouth.

As a youth of eighteen, he had read *Paradise Lost.* He understood, with his rational mind, the wretchedness and iniquity of the fallen angel, the sheer folly of his rebellion and the hollow core of his disobedience. Even so, some wicked corner of his heart had entertained not only an appropriate Christian pity for he who was once Lucifer but secret admiration too. He had attributed this impulse to the power of literature, rather than personal corruption, but it had nevertheless stayed with him through the passing years.

And now he recognised the echo of his Satan in the stranger whose hand he held, while the prayers dried on his lips. Thomas did not know if the man was beautiful. If it was right to think another man was beautiful. But he was striking, somehow, gaunt and fierce, and as wary as a wild thing. His eyes were closed now but Thomas remembered them well enough, that hollow, burning gaze, dark as a starless night, to match the coarse black curls that clustered damply at his brow and clung to his neck. A gathering of hair roughened the line of his jaw, though, in repose, his mouth had a dreamy, incongruous tenderness to it. There had certainly been no trace of that when he had pushed Thomas away from him on Drury Lane. There had only been defiance, despair, and a terrible, terrible pride.

It suddenly became imperative to Thomas that he liberate his hand. His palm was sticky with the other man's sweat, his fingers cramped from having been crushed. And the other man uttered the most piteous moan at parting.

"Perhaps," Thomas said, a little desperately, "I should read to you."

He looked about the room. Like the rest of the house, it had been designed to impress—or, possibly, oppress—but, being a guest chamber, it lacked even the most rudimentary of personal touches. The bed had been hastily made up, the furniture only partially unmuffled from the heavy sheeting that covered it. It was testament to the dedication of the housekeeper that the air was fresh and clean, untainted by dust.

There was probably something to be found in his father's study, but he was reluctant to leave his patient. He was equally reluctant to disturb the servants any more than his unannounced arrival already had, but he realised he had little choice. He crossed the room, easing some of the stiffness from his joints, and rang the bell.

In a few scant minutes, there was a gentle tapping at the door, and he went to answer it. The house was maintained only by a limited staff, and it soon became apparent that the housekeeper was the only servant in residence who dared answer the summons of the son of the Marquess of Montrose, even if he was only the third son. Thomas, who had grown up accustomed to the rigid hierarchy of a grand estate, was accordingly flustered to be attended upon by a person of such exalted belowstairs status.

"I am so sorry to have troubled you." He tried to conceal his awkwardness and did not succeed.

The housekeeper was surprisingly young for her role, with cool grey eyes and a crown of lustrous dark hair wound into austere braids. She had handled Thomas's unannounced arrival, and his unorthodox guest, with quiet composure. She seemed equally unperturbed now, despite the early hour and Thomas's rumpled, weary appearance.

She dropped a curtsy. "I'm here to serve, my lord."

"Please don't call me that. I left behind such titles. But I was wondering, Missus . . . ah . . ."

"Clark."

"I was wondering, Mrs. Clark, if you would be so kind as to fetch me a book from the library."

"Of course. Was there something in particular?"

The patient had started coughing again, and Thomas glanced helplessly over his shoulder, distracted. "I . . . er—" He cringed internally at the hesitation. The marquess had instilled into all his sons certain principles for handling the lower orders. They required neither kindness nor cruelty, simply clarity and consistency, as with other trained animals. But, at that moment, still unsettled by his own reactions and preoccupied by the afflictions of the other man, Thomas was utterly incapable of articulating his needs.

Thankfully, Mrs. Clark seemed to possess an instinct of understanding, and—rather than force him to struggle towards precision—she simply said, "I'll do what I can."

He murmured his gratitude and closed the door.

She returned about fifteen minutes later with a tray and a stack of books tucked beneath her arm. He went to relieve her of the tray, which contained some cold meats and a pot of tea. He had not realised he was hungry, but the sight of food was unbelievably welcome.

"You are very kind."

She offered a careful smile. "You must take care not to fall ill yourself."

"Oh, I am never ill."

"Perk of the job, Mr. Mandeville?" He thought he caught the trace of an East London accent, carefully subdued, and a gleam of wickedness in her eyes, also quickly banished.

He smiled. "Perhaps, but the Lord helps those who help themselves, so I thank you for the consideration."

"It's nothing, sir." She turned to leave. Then paused. "If I'm presuming, do you know this man?"

"Er, no. He seemed in need of assistance, so I rendered it. Or tried. I do not know if he will survive the night."

She cast a look at the figure in the bed and seemed about to say something.

"Do you know him?" asked Thomas.

"I'm not acquainted with him."

"But you know him?"

Her eyes slid away from his. "There aren't many who'd stop to help a stranger for no reason but goodness."

"There is"—he offered one of his shy, whimsical looks—"a fine precedent. But I am not accustomed to London. There are so many who suffer here that it challenges me. I try but I simply cannot imagine so many souls, afraid, alone and overlooked."

"Nobody can, sir. Maybe that's the problem."

"'The eyes of the Lord are in every place,'" he said, rather doubtfully. "It seems a kind of pride to believe the salvation of the world is one's personal responsibility. So what remains but to do what we can?" He folded a fresh cloth and dampened it, adding softly, "Though it seems but little."

"Sometimes little can be enough." Mrs. Clark gestured towards the bed. "I can sit with him, when you need to rest."

"I couldn't possibly ask you to do that."

"You didn't. Good night, sir." She slipped out, closing the door with barely a sound, leaving Thomas to his patient.

The man showed very little sign of improvement, but at least he was no longer crying out frantically for a stranger who would never come to him. Thomas poured himself a cup of tea, which had gone slightly cold by the time he came to it, but he drank it gratefully enough. He also devoured the food Mrs. Clark had brought him and sorted through the stack of books before settling on one.

"I'm afraid I do not know what you would find pleasing," he told the unconscious man, shyly. "But perhaps . . . perhaps this will do." He turned to the opening chapter. "'Chapter one,'" he read, "'The One Thing Needful.'" He paused, faintly smiling. "You will have to forgive me. My oratory—such as it is—is better fitted to the pulpit than the theatre."

Perhaps it was the safety of knowing he was unheard, but some of Thomas's anxiety eased, and he found himself speaking with a freedom he would never have otherwise permitted himself. "My eldest brother, Edward that is, used to read to George and me when we couldn't sleep, which, I will confess, was often. I was a little afraid of the dark, you see. But he used to do the voices quite wonderfully. His Lordship—the marquess—found out, of course, and it stopped after that. It was coddling, you know." He cleared his throat. "Anyway. I apologise. I promised you reading, not idle recollections. But I thought it important to warn you against expecting too much from me. I, ah, I should commence, shouldn't I?"

He smoothed his fingers over the page, with a touch of his former self-consciousness, and, at last, began to read. "'Now, what I want is Facts. Teach these boys and girls nothing but Facts. Facts alone are wanted in life.'"

He read through the grey dawn and through the morning's watery gold, his words threading between his patient's uneven breathing and the frequent bouts of coughing and delirium. He stopped often to tend and soothe the man, but he read until his voice was hoarse. He read until, at last, exhaustion claimed him, and he fell fitfully asleep, his head resting half on the book and half on the bed, his fingers tangled with a stranger's.

5th September, 1864

The man's fever broke and then returned, perhaps worse than before. He seems to get no better and I am at a loss. I sent again for the doctor, but he merely repeated what he told me on the previous occasion—influenza, general poor health—and rebuked me for wasting his time. Of course, since I was paying for his time, I could have made the argument that it was mine to waste. Unfortunately, I was too polite. Oh, who am I pretending for? I was too cowardly. And I should not sit here, impotently resenting a professional, for simply wishing to perform his job efficiently. But what else am I to do, when I am so powerless in the face of whatever ails my patient? He suffers convulsions, sweats copiously, brings up bile and blood and whatever sustenance I can induce him to take, and seems racked by terrible pains.

I think often of my conversation with Mrs. Clark. I wonder if I am abruptly, some might say hypocritically, grown so concerned with the problem of human suffering because I am, in truth, consumed by the suffering of a single man. It is foolish, irrational, perverse even, to lump the entirety of human pain into a vast, unimaginable sea and then childishly question the benevolence of the Lord the moment the matter becomes non-abstract. Whenever my parishioners lament in this fashion, I tell them God never afflicts us with more than we can endure. It seems to bring them comfort but I know the words are hollow. What, after all, of Edward. What was the affliction he could not endure? Or do I ask the wrong questions? Perhaps the affliction is mine. This knowledge, this ignorance, this helplessness.

I must remember: Strait is the gate and narrow is the way. For men such as I, born to the security of rank and fortune, it is only fitting that we must enter the Kingdom of Heaven on our hands and knees, crawling in the dust of the world. We are God's creation. In His power and wisdom, He made us. And in His power and wisdom, He may break us also, to better be worthy of His Kingdom. More hollow words. I sometimes think I am composed of them. Nothing but them. Did He make me this way? Why? Why?

And what of this stranger? What am I to do for him? I should know that salvation lies solely with the grace of God. That it is not for me to take upon myself the ills of the world as I perceive them. Nor to question the burdens and the losses placed upon me or upon others. But I wish—I hardly dare write it—in my pride and foolishness, I wish to save this man. I could not begin to understand why. In truth, I feel some danger in it. As though it is rooted not in kindness or charity but in some selfishness I cannot articulate. That I think not for him, but for myself. That I think him . . . beautiful. A most peculiar preoccupation of mind, for the man lies ill and helpless, and I have never been troubled by such notions before. I had convinced myself that my distance from earthly passions was a further indication that the path laid out for me was the correct one, though now such an idea seems hubris of the wildest, most sinful kind. Why would I, of all people, be blessed with a nature resilient to the temptations that challenged other men? At last, I see my restraint for what it truly was: a veil of self-love, now torn away. And I must be ashamed. Though even that feels like a kind of indulgence when I have more practical concerns to, well, concern me.

My occupation of the townhouse, for example, has already attracted attention. The other day, I was importuned for some time by two unsavoury gentlemen who claimed that George owed them considerable sums of money.

He has his army pension and I know my father makes him a generous allowance so I was not inclined to believe them, despite their insistence. They even attempted to extort funds from me, but I cannot imagine what they thought I would be able to give them, since I surrendered all claim to my family's wealth on first entering the Church.

Nevertheless, I am worried for my brother. Since Edward passed away, I have heard rumours of behaviour—

~

"Still here, old boy? What are you writing? Sermons?"

Thomas jerked awkwardly, smearing ink across the page of his journal as he slammed it closed. "Oh, ah, yes." As George leaned over him, he caught the sourness of alcohol upon his breath. "Have you been drinking?" he asked. "It's not yet noon."

"Of course I have. Just got back from Devon. What else is a fellow to do?"

Thomas shuffled his papers around, lest George prove curious about the journal. "How is the marquess?"

"Dying, still dying. I wish he would bloody well get on with it. He didn't ask after you, by the way."

"Well, no. Why should he?"

George glared. "How can you always be so damned calm?"

"Why are you never?"

George flung himself into a chair. He was still in travelling clothes and his boots were muddy. Although it was a simple matter to trace a familial resemblance between the brothers, there was no denying George was the bearer of Nature's felicity. There was a luminous vivacity to him and a pronounced sensuality in the generosity of his mouth and the brightness of his eyes. At present, however, he looked tired, and lines of dissipation were beginning to mar his fine-cut features.

"He's on at me to get married," he said finally.

"I thought you might rather like to be married."

"I would but not at his instigation."

"That's just churlishness. You would not deny your own happiness simply to thwart His Lordship's."

"Damn right, I would." George dug around in the pockets of his overcoat for his cigarette case, plucked a cigarette from amongst its fellows, and lit it with clumsy fingers. "It's the only choice he's ever given me."

"That's simply untrue. And what of your duty—"

"Fuck duty. My duty was to die nobly in a pit in Balaklava."

Thomas gave him a horrified look.

"What? It's true. I sometimes wish I was back there, to be honest. And what a bloody terrible thought that is. The best years of my life were spent in a hole in the ground, watching all the men around me fall to disease, neglect, and gunfire." For a moment, something softer than bitterness touched George's features. Sadness perhaps. Or regret. But then his expression shifted, and the moment was gone. "It's a bloody joke."

"I'm sorry, George."

He gave a harsh laugh. "Is that really the best you've got? That's the word from Above, is it? 'Sorry, old chap, your life was all a bit of a blunder.'"

"No," said Thomas sharply. "No, I was speaking as a man, as your brother. Not in any sort of official capacity. But it was still a facile excuse for an answer."

George's mouth twisted into a sneer. "I suppose I shock you?"

"You could never shock me, George. Should I have some coffee sent up? You seem . . ."

"I seem what?"

It turned out, there was no good way to tell your brother he was inebriated past the point of self-control or circumspection. "Perhaps you aren't . . . thinking clearly?"

"Oh, I think all too clearly. At least I was doing something back then. And what am I now? Stupefied with idleness. Our father's puppet."

"Let me see about that coffee."

Thomas went to the bellpull, and they waited for the summons to be answered in a silence that was not quite comfortable. Mrs. Clark slipped into the room a minute or two later. Her gaze flicked momentarily to George, and Thomas experienced the painful revelation of seeing his brother through someone else's eyes. A man careless, spoiled, and intoxicated at eleven in the morning. But whatever Mrs. Clark might think, her composure did not falter, and she departed to see what could be done about the coffee.

Thomas had been about to say something understanding, if not reassuring—for George would not have thanked him for an attempt at consolation—but his elder brother spoke before he had properly assembled his thoughts.

"Well. She's a fine piece, make no mistake."

Thrown by the abrupt change in conversation, Thomas grew flustered and finally managed, "She's been very kind."

"Hah. I know you're a clergyman, but you can't say you didn't notice."

"Notice what?"

"Fucking hell. Did the marquess make you a eunuch as well as a priest?"

"I own," offered Thomas uncertainly, "she is a handsome woman?"

"She's a stunner, man. Even in that ghastly grey thing she's wearing. Those eyes. That hair. And her body. Like iniquity made flesh." George gave his brother another provocative look and crossed himself flamboyantly in the Catholic fashion. "Oh, forgive me, Father, for I have sinned. Or I'd very much like to."

Accustomed to this style of baiting and not disposed to see malice in it, Thomas simply smiled, shaking his head in mock chagrin.

Evidently recognising that teasing his brother was a lost cause, George grinned. It banished the cynicism of his eyes and made him look younger. "How's your mongrel?" he asked.

"Please don't call him that."

"What do you expect if you take waifs and strays off the street? What's next, a plucky urchin? An honest doxy? People are starting to talk, you know."

"Let them talk, if they must. I can't imagine what they might find to say."

"His Lordship won't like it."

"Perhaps he need not find out?"

George laughed without mirth. "He will. He always does. Even figured out I'm in queer street. Read me a bloody lecture, can you believe? Didn't give me a clipped copper, mind. Says I have to cut loose the divine Lady Montague before he'll bail me out. Miserly son of a whore."

"How can you possibly be in debt, George?"

"I don't know. I don't fucking care."

George fell silent, staring sullenly at nothing, just as Mrs. Clark entered with coffee. He roused slightly at the sight of her, but she studiously avoided his gaze and then fled. With his attention still fixed speculatively on the spot she had last occupied, he went on, "Maybe I will do what he wants. Lady M's a bore, anyway."

"Then why must you"—Thomas folded and unfolded his hands—"consort with her?"

"Because it's the fashionable thing to do. And because His Lordship doesn't like it."

Once again at a loss for anything more useful to say or do, Thomas handed his brother a cup of coffee, the rich bitter smell of it mingling with the musty room. "Here, drink this. It will steady you." He paused, trying to find the right words. "And I hope you will not behave badly towards Mrs. Clark."

There was no reply. Just an apathetic glance, as mistrustful as a wounded animal's.

"She is under our protection," Thomas persisted. "She is not for your . . . entertainment. I know you're angry and frustrated and, for that matter, intoxicated, but you've never been cruel."

"And you've always been a prig."

Thomas nodded. "I know." He gave a faint, apologetic smile. "I don't mean to be."

Disregarding this small attempt at conciliation, George climbed to his feet and strode to the window. He pulled the heavy velvet drapes aside, stirring up a column of dust motes, and stared down into the pristine green haze of the Grosvenor Square garden. "I hate this house."

"You could probably improve it," suggested Thomas. "If you tried."

"Edward was supposed to do that. Do you remember?"

"Of course I remember."

Edward had said he would fill the rooms with light and the halls with laughter. Thomas caught his breath against a sudden twist of pain.

"I can't believe he's gone," muttered George. "A hunting accident. He didn't even like hunting. Damn fool way to die."

"Yes." It was all Thomas dared to say.

George half-turned. The sunlight gleamed upon his tangled hair. "Tell me again. How did it happen?"

Thomas swallowed the taste of sickness as he repeated the lies his father had taught him. "His gun discharged. It was an accident. A stupid, tragic accident."

His brother gave a weak smile. "Well, at least you were there, eh? Got him winging his way to heaven ahead of the crowd."

"Yes," said Thomas, in barely more than a whisper.

There was a long silence. Thomas poured himself some coffee in order to have something to do with his hands, which, unaccountably, he could not hold still.

"If the dead go to a better life," asked George, at last, "why do we mourn them?"

"We mourn ourselves. Our own loss."

"Bit selfish, don't you think? Should we not be celebrating everlasting happiness instead?"

Thomas could feel the gatherings of what would surely turn into a stormy headache. "Is there a point to this?"

"I just think if we truly believed everything we say about death, then grief would be different. I don't think we'd be so afraid. I don't think it would feel so final."

"I do not wish to talk about this," said Thomas in a stifled voice.

"Why not? Isn't it your area of expertise?"

"You know it isn't."

"I want an answer, Thomas. Don't forget, I've seen a lot of fucking death."

"I don't *have* an answer," cried Thomas, pushed beyond endurance. "Not to this. Not to any of it."

"At least you got to see him. I just waved him off on his honeymoon, and the next thing I heard he was dead." George said nothing for a moment, still gazing out of the window, at the world beyond. Then his shoulders slumped. "It wasn't supposed to be like this. I wanted to be an uncle. I had every intention of being a doting one."

Thomas sank into a chair, fingertips idly massaging the bridge of his nose. "What do you want from me, George? I've already told you, I can't help." He sounded so very weary, even to himself. "I wish I could. But the mysteries of the universe are as mysterious to me as they are to everyone else. We simply have to trust in . . . in a plan, the workings of which are too subtle, and too vast, for us to discern them."

"So it's submission to someone else's, one way or another."

"Is that so terrible?"

His brother stared at him. "Yes," he said. "You grovelling charlatan. It's fucking terrible." Then he threw his coffee cup against the wall. It shattered: pieces of white porcelain and a dark stain.

And when George stormed out, a few seconds later, Thomas did not try to stop him.

He simply sat there, a little dazed, feeling not unlike the broken cup. What had he been thinking? What sort of priest would have said such a thing? *Is that so terrible?* He should have explained that God only wanted His children to flourish. That He did not want their submission. But, truthfully, it was far easier to believe in a patriarch who expected obedience than one who offered love, and somehow he had allowed himself to speak aloud what he felt, instead of what was needed. And with that—with a few selfish, heedless words—Thomas had failed his brother and his God. Yet again.

He crossed the room, lowered himself to his knees, and used his handkerchief to gather up the remains of the cup, doing his best not to catch himself on the sharp edges. Suddenly, the door swung open and Mrs. Clark came over the threshold with something less than her customary care.

"I . . . I heard a crash." She, too, looked flustered. Her colour was high, and a lock of hair had been shaken loose across her cheek.

"Mrs. Clark, are you quite well?"

Thomas heard the distant slamming of the front door.

"Yes, yes, quite well."

"There was an accident," he explained, politely disregarding the fact that she sounded far from well, *quite* or otherwise.

"There's no need for you to do that, sir." She sank down beside him. "I can see to it."

He sat back on his heels, noticing that the sleeve of her dress had been torn. "What happened here?"

"Oh, I caught it. It's nothing."

Thomas frowned, suspicions he did not wish to entertain, let alone acknowledge, clouding his mind. "Did my bro—"

"Forgive me, but may I make a suggestion?"

"Of course."

"It's about the man upstairs. I wondered . . ." She hesitated. "I wondered if you might try him with laudanum."

"The doctor told me not until the fever had broken."

"I see." Again, she hesitated. "I am not a doctor, and speak only from my limited experience, but I believe it may help him. I believe he suffers from the lack of it."

He turned his head to look at her. Her grey eyes were steady on his.

"I do not believe it could make him any worse," she added.

"I suppose there can be no harm in trying."

To his surprise, her fine, pale skin flushed. "You have only my word for it. I . . . I did not think you would listen."

He pressed her hand lightly. She was cold, her fingers stiff under his, but she did not pull away. "You are clearly a woman of superior sense and kindness, Mrs. Clark. Why would I not?"

The flush deepened, but she spoke with a sharpness he found quite charming. "I have not found those qualities any guarantee of consideration."

"Well." He stood, dusting off the knees of his trousers. "You may consider yourself considered."

He had surprised her into laughing, and the sound rippled through the stillness of the room like a stone thrown into a stagnant pool.

Chapter 3

5

Do you like this, he says.

His thrusts shove me forward onto my elbows. It's all a mess of sweat and skin. Nowhere to go. His fingers will leave bruises on my hips like a chain of dark roses.

I don't know what he wants me to say.

Do you like this?

I tell him no. The hands of strangers smudge the memories of Isidore that once gleamed upon my skin.

Laughing, he drags me against him. His fingernails leave bloody trails down my chest. A hard hand encloses my cock.

But you want it, he says.

I shake my head. My hair clings to my neck, heavy, damp and itchy.

He frigs me while he fucks me. He makes me gasp for him and cry out.

Then he makes me spend.

~

Consciousness came back to Micha in jagged pieces. Slowly, in the darkness behind his eyes, he taught himself to recognise anew the borders between dreams and reality, past and present, memories and nightmares.

He felt weak beyond reckoning, to say nothing of ill, but the worst of the pain had departed with the phantasmagoria of delirium and the torments of opium withdrawal. There was a familiar haze in his mind, a softness to the world. He tried to remember what had happened or where he was, but he found only fragments. A night that could have been any other night. Smoke. Shadows. And a name. Thomas?

Slowly, he became aware of a voice. The voice seemed familiar to him, but that was impossible.

Words washed over him.

"'But the sun itself, however beneficent, generally, was less kind to Coketown than hard frost, and rarely looked intently into any of its closer regions without engendering more death than life. So does the eye of Heaven itself become an evil eye, when incapable or sordid hands are interposed between it and the things it looks upon to bless.'"

He pushed open his eyes and was immediately dazzled.

The voice stopped abruptly. And then there was a cool hand on his. Micha tried to shake it off, but he was unable to move. He opened his mouth, but all that came out was a dry croak. Immediately a glass of water was brought to his lips. The first few droplets were cool as diamonds and tasted sweeter than anything he could ever have imagined. He jerked forward, eager for more, and choked almost immediately. The hand steadied him, and a second gathered the water as it trickled from his mouth.

"Careful." The strange-familiar voice had a peculiar, pleasing timbre to it, the cut-glass vowels of privilege softened by calm, careful rhythms. It was as unexpectedly lovely as the water.

"Don't," Micha rasped. "Don't touch me."

There was a swift, clumsy withdrawal. "I'm terribly sorry. But you should drink, if you can."

"I can do it."

With an effort that was as much will as physical strength, he tried to enfold his fingers around the glass. His nails were ragged and rimmed with dirt, his hands inelegant and wasted by illness, a wretched reflection of the white, long-fingered, and gentlemanly hand that supported the other side of the glass. Micha hardly dared contemplate what had happened to the rest of him. Without his looks, he had no profession, and with no profession he had no money, and without money, there would be no opium. And without opium, his world was nothing. He was nothing.

He tugged impatiently away from the stranger who had tried to help him, taking sole possession of the glass, though his perspiring fingertips smeared the clear surface. His whole arm began shaking. He fastened his spare hand over his forearm to steady himself, raising the glass inch by inch towards his mouth. The surface of the water seemed to shine from a great distance, and he could have wept for wanting it. It was almost within reach when his fingers betrayed him. The glass slid from his grip, and there was nothing he could do to catch it. Water soaked the bedsheets.

"Fuck."

There was a sharp intake of breath from beside him. And Micha looked up, furious and mortified, only to careen headlong into the forgiving gaze of the deepest eyes he had ever seen. A shudder ran through him, for, across the breadth of human weakness, he could not abide kindness.

The man caught the empty glass before it rolled off the bed and refilled it from a nearby ewer. "Please, permit me to help you. There is no shame in frailty."

Micha tried to laugh, but the air just scraped harshly across his vocal cords until he began to cough instead. And then he had no choice but to accept the water that was held to his lips. He clamped a pathetically feeble hand about the stranger's wrist, exerting what little control he could. The man seemed perfectly willing to be guided, his slight movements as smooth as a quiet stream beneath Micha's fitful directions. Under his palm, Micha could feel flowing heat and the steady throb of a pulse, pristine skin and slender bones. If he had possessed the strength, he would have left his thumbprints behind like footsteps upon fresh snow, anything to ruin the serenity of such uncomprehending, careless beauty.

But the effort of trying to drink, then drinking, had apparently exhausted him. He fell back against the pillows, his eyes closing of their own volition. His last conscious thought, which was really little more than a blurred sensation, was of an endless, unchanging warmth beneath his hand.

73

There is a pale shadow of Isidore in this youth. In his golden hair and his apple green eyes, rose leaf lips and sun-touched skin. But he is not Isidore. He is uncertain. Rapt, he undresses me, touches my well-touched skin. His breath is warm, his tongue is light. He is the explorer of a land with no secrets left. He says he wants to watch my face. I try to give him a performance of pleasure but, as he sinks into me, his eyes look through me to some private paradise I have long since forgotten how to find. He squanders care on me as though I am precious. Afterwards, he asks, was it all right, was he pleasing, did I like him. I tell him, get the fuck away from me. Before he sees me weep.

~

"Isidore?"

Micha tumbled into wakefulness, roused by his own cry. For a moment, he was utterly disorientated, wrapped in unfamiliar sheets, surrounded by unfamiliar walls. An oil lamp, turned low, wove about him a net of shadows. Then he remembered. He lay in a stranger's bed, in a stranger's house, under a stranger's care.

He struggled to sit up and just about managed to prop himself on his elbows. The man was still at his bedside, as if he had not moved all the time Micha slept.

"You were dreaming," he murmured.

Micha glared. "I noticed."

The man lowered his eyes apologetically. Such soft eyes, with lashes so thick and dark Micha could have counted them. Not that he would have wanted to. "May I have him brought to you?"

"What? Who?"

"The man for whom you call. Isidore."

It was strange to hear Isidore's name on another's lips, as though he were some private ghost summoned suddenly into reality by a spiritualist. Micha's fingers curled into his palms, little pricks of superficial pain against a deeper one.

"He is a friend? A brother?"

Micha shook his head. "Not a brother." His lips curled into a sneer. "Nor a friend." He was seized by a sudden, savage impulse to tell the truth. Just to split this man's compassion open like rotten fruit. Shatter his calm into pieces. Show him he had a heart just as capable of hate.

"Oh yes," said the stranger, with a look Micha could not read, "you did tell me you had no need of friends."

He had a vague memory of saying something like that before he fainted right into the man's arms. "I suppose," he snapped, "you expect my gratitude for this?"

"Of course not. One does not give aid to make others feel beholden."

"Right."

The man tilted his head curiously. "Do you think I want something from you?"

"I've nothing to give you, so you're doomed to disappointment regardless. But I don't believe something for nothing exists in this world."

"I hope only for your well-being."

"Then you're deluding yourself."

To Micha's surprise, the man flushed. He had a stern, angular face, not handsome but expressive somehow, full of subtleties. "What may I call you?" he asked, after a moment of flustered silence.

"Michael. Dashwood. Most call me Micha."

The man smiled shyly, as though he'd been given a gift. "Micha then. My name is—"

"Thomas."

His smile turned radiant. "Yes. Thomas Mandeville." He seemed to hesitate. "The Reverend Thomas Mandeville."

Micha threw back his head and laughed himself breathless. "A priest. I should have fucking known. Oh, does my language offend you, Father? I am to call you 'Father,' yes?"

The man—Thomas, Father Thomas—was folding and unfolding his fingers. "I am not accustomed to such forthright speech," he admitted, before adding earnestly, "Though I will grow accustomed. And I do not usually go by 'Father.' Thomas is fine, or Mr. Mandeville if you must grant me a title."

"I think I can probably bear not to."

"I did not mean . . . that is . . . some people are uncomfortable to address a priest as they would any other man."

"Well, can't have the wheat muddled with the chaff, the righteous with unrighteous, is that not so, Thomas?"

"No. Not at all. I would simply not wish any to confuse the man with the message. There is already a Father in Heaven who guides and loves us."

"Oh, yes, Him." Micha fell back against the pillows, dizzy, tired, and, as he was beginning to notice, laudanum-deprived. There was no pleasure in tormenting this man. He took everything so seriously and seemed disposed to give even Micha's weakest, most unjust barbs fair consideration.

"My brother," offered Thomas weakly, "calls me Thom. Or, you know, 'prig' or 'arse' or things along similar lines, as brothers are wont to do."

"And what do you call him?"

"Er . . . George."

Micha turned his head. His voice was little more than a whisper now. "That's the best you can manage? Pathetic."

The Reverend Thomas Mandeville smiled suddenly, a wicked, gleaming smile. "On the contrary. George absolutely hates it when I turn the other cheek."

"Does Our Lord and Saviour mind you using His teachings to piss off your brother?"

"Our Lord and Saviour had brothers too."

Micha gave a sputter of weak but genuine laughter.

"You need to rest." Thomas's hand moved as if to touch Micha's, but then he clearly thought better of it. "You are far from well."

Micha closed his eyes. "I was an only child. Still am, I suppose."

His body wanted rest, but his mind would not lie still. Images of entwined bodies and twisted flesh swirled sickeningly through the darkness until he had half-convinced himself he was seeing visions of hell. And Isidore, like a revenant angel who would not leave him alone.

A hand touched his brow, and he knocked it away.

"I'm sorry." Thomas. Of course. "I thought you were feverish."

"Talk to me." The words escaped Micha's lips before he could seal them in.

"Of course." He heard the hint of a smile in Thomas's voice. "I will lull you to sleep with my tedious reminiscences of childhood."

There was a brief pause.

"Get on with it, then. Start lulling."

"I was gathering my thoughts," returned Thomas, calmly. "Perhaps I could tell you something of my brothers?"

"Don't ask," Micha growled. "Just talk." *Please.*

"Well, um, my eldest brother—Edward—used to call George 'Topper' because he said he was like a spinning top. I can remember once, rather cruelly, explaining to Nurse that it was because George was always running in circles, but Edward meant it kindly. George never stopped moving, you see. He had endless energy and was—as I am sure you can imagine—endlessly in trouble."

"What," slurred Micha, "did Edward call you?"

"'Skittle.' Because George was always pushing me over, one way or another. We were born just minutes apart, you see. Edward said it was probably because I waited politely for George to go first."

Thomas's words seemed to come more easily the more he spoke, and it was frighteningly easy to listen to him. To let another man's remembrances serve as distraction from his own. And how sweetly they were offered up, these gifts of the self. Then again, Micha reflected bitterly, it was easy enough to be generous when you knew nothing of lack.

"I don't think the marquess ever forgave our mother," Thomas was saying. "He had ordered two sons, you see, not three, and she died before she could give him a daughter." The gas lamp was turned too low to reveal much of his expression, and Micha was too weary to try, but the shadows seemed to soften him. Sadness and secrets revealed by the dark. "I don't remember her very well at all. I think I only saw her once or twice. I remember having to wear my very best clothes and recite the Lord's Prayer to her, so I was naturally quite resentful. And—this may seem a peculiar confession for a priest—but when I was very young, I found it almost impossible to memorise the Lord's Prayer correctly. Nobody had ever tried to explain it to me, so it was nothing but obscure and meaningless sounds. Once I think I said, 'Give us this day our daily trespasses,' and His Lordship thought I was being wilful and had the butler beat me for it."

Thomas's voice rolled over him like velvet until, at last, Micha slept.

Chapter 4

7th September, 1864

Oh God. Michael Dashwood sees right through me and knows me for a hypocrite and a fool. He has practically called me such and I could not deny it. I do not understand how a piece of kindness, enacted in good faith, could have become twisted into something . . . else. *What have I done? Is my heart so corrupt?*

I am lost and I cannot even begin to fathom how I came to be lost. Less than a week ago my path was as straight and clear as a bridge across calm waters. But nothing is as it was before, and I cannot trust my footing or what my eyes perceive. It is as though I have worn blinkers my whole life, but now they are gone and all I understand is how close I am to a sin from which I believed myself remote.

Perhaps I have always been astray, walking in the Devil's footsteps, not the Lord's, in thinking myself better than other men. I am not. I am worse and I simply did not know it. My iniquity is of such magnitude I do not even have a name to call it, nor knowledge of how it may be practised. I think it must be a form of idolatry. For when I look on Michael Dashwood, I think not on God. I think nothing of God. Only of him. I think him beautiful. Illness has left him pale and weak and his eyes are as black as hell and reflect nothing but bitterness and pain. Yet, still, I am—

I am what? Entranced. I pursue his rare smiles like the promise of paradise itself.

He speaks harshly, his words are cruel, I find no kindness or compassion in his gaze, no sense of a higher self. But he is like some magnificent, ruined thing, a piece of stained glass, still vivid and no less beautiful for its cracks and rough edges. I ask myself, how is he brought so low? Who in the world beheld such splendour and chose to break it?

I do not think he will tell me. He will never trust me. And it is right that he does not, for I do not trust myself. How am I to untangle this—whatever this *is—and find my way back to righteousness? I try to imagine that my patient might be a woman and I might feel such things. I think this must be a common struggle for priests, for are we not men, as well as servants of God? But, of course, he is not a woman and I have never felt anything for women beyond what was appropriate for my role, so I am clearly* not *like other men, and I have nothing to compare against. Besides, were he a woman I could woo and wed him in all honour and goodness.*

Have I looked thus upon other men before? Not to my recollection but perhaps I deceive myself?

Then let me imagine, for the safety of a moment, that I am a priest, a priest like any other, with a problem, like any other. There are many who would hold the thinking, in itself, a sin—ill thought, the brother to ill deed, whether it is carnality or doubt that preoccupies the wayward, imperfect heart. But I cannot believe that. I believe it is freedom of thought and deed that lends validity to moral choice and action. Though, writing this, I must not think too much upon my own life for, like my brothers, I never chose, and I have no certainty that God chose me. But if we felt no struggle, if we resisted no temptation, of what worth would be our capitulation to moral law? To God's love? For what benefit free will, if we have not the mind to exercise it?

Or perhaps I write these things, which stand upon the brink of heresy, because I do not know how to feel God's love. I have no worldly analogue that would teach me how. This need not necessarily be a lack of faith. Nor even necessarily a lack of God. One should not need to feel a thing, to understand that it may be there. That higher consciousness, the ability to reason, gifts from God, surely? Distinctions between man and beast. Nonsense, then, to conclude that the universe is a cold and unloving place, chaotic and empty. It is surely right, it is surely logical, to believe that there is order and goodness here. Even if it is unseen, sometimes, unfelt.

I can *trust. I* will *trust. On thought alone.*

Chapter 5

303

His desire is a flickering candle flame, shame and frustration, want and fear, and it leaves me exhausted, sweating, and a failure. He does not pay.

~

Days and nights slipped away in an indeterminate haze as Micha gradually recovered. There seemed to be a never-ending supply of soup, which he initially had to suffer Thomas's aid to eat and left him pathetically exhausted. There was also a supply of laudanum, but, unlike the soup, that was very much finite, and he slipped through his supply at an alarming rate. Thomas had commented only once, though with concern rather than censure, which had led Micha to decant most of the medicine into a stolen glass, secrete it under the bed, and top up the bottle with water. His thoughts tended to drift rather than cohere, but he was plagued by constant, almost unbearable anxiety about what would happen when the laudanum was gone.

That Thomas suspected his dependence on it he was certain, and yet the thought of Thomas knowing the depth of his dependency was unbearable. Not because he had any good opinion of Thomas, or gave a damn what Thomas thought of him, but because he was nursing a nasty little dislike that made him resentful and protective of his own weakness. He had already shown Thomas far too much of that. Lying in a borrowed nightshirt, upon scrupulously clean sheets, he was horrified to think of the particular care Thomas had taken with his person when he had been helpless and insensible. And perhaps it was easier to dwell furiously on imagined indignities (ironic, surely, that a whore would have any concern for dignity) than the other truth: how close he had come to death and a pauper's grave.

None would have been more surprised than Micha to learn it had frightened him. He could have slipped through the fabric of the world, and no one would have noticed, no one would have cared, if not for the care and notice of a stranger. It was a paradox impossible to reconcile, hating life and yet fearing death, and it left him with no choice but to despise Thomas instead. What was the alternative? Gratitude? And he could hardly teach himself to like the man. Micha had lost those habits long ago and there was no use trying to recall them now. Besides, once Thomas knew the truth—that he harboured beneath his roof a renter, a bugger, and an opium eater to boot—there would be no more kindness for Micha. No more interested looks and shy smiles. Not, he told himself, that he needed or wanted those things. From anyone. Thomas least of all. But his life was, for the moment at least, comfortable. And he would just have to hope his health improved, either before Thomas learned who, and what, he was, or before the laudanum ran out.

His strength came back only slowly but sufficiently that he was bored and restless most of the time, while still unable to do anything. Thomas brought him books and newspapers, but Micha had always been a half-hearted reader. For the past year, his sole pleasure had been opium, and, while laudanum kept the cravings at bay, it was a poor substitute. While it smoothed out the rough edges of his mind, it showed him no beauty, brought him no sense of hope or belonging. It just made him numb. Some days he resolved he would not take any, except the resolution never lasted.

Thomas sat with him often, sometimes talking, sometimes silent. Micha welcomed him indifferently, if at all, and still Thomas came. Micha sometimes wondered what he would have to do to drive the man away—if Christian kindness had a limit—but he found he lacked the will to try, and that worried him. He could no more depend on Thomas's visits than he could depend on his hospitality.

"You know," Thomas began, one afternoon, "you must be so tired of listening to my ramblings. I have drowned you in the minutiae of my life, but I know nothing of yours. Will you not tell me something of yourself, your past, your family? Anything you care to share?"

"There's nothing to tell."

"There's always something to tell the sincerely interested listener."

"Perhaps the sincerely interested listener can fuck off and mind his own business."

There was a long silence.

Then Thomas flushed with shame and embarrassment. "I'm so very sorry. I deserved that. I shouldn't have pried."

"No, you shouldn't have."

There was another long silence. Thomas had poured himself some tea earlier and was sitting with both his hands wrapped around the cup, soaking up the heat with a certain unconscious sensuality. "May we then," he tried, "speak of your interests, your pursuits, your hopes and dreams? I fear you must find your convalescence here rather dull. I would alleviate it, if you'll let me."

"Interests?" repeated Micha, his lip curling into a sneer. "Pursuits? Hopes and dreams. I have none."

Thomas drew in a sharp breath, and faint furrows appeared across his brow. His face seemed all the more angular and irregular in distress. Micha watched him, surprised into momentary (and later regretted) curiosity.

"Micha." Thomas's voice was strange and tight. "Please tell me what has brought you to this? I ask not because I wish to interfere, or because I expect you to answer me, but it . . . it breaks my heart to hear you speak like this. I have long wondered of the circumstances that . . . that . . . the circumstances in which I found you."

Micha opened his mouth to say something cutting, then closed it again. Thomas had put his tea aside and was leaning towards Micha, one pale, elegant hand clutched upon the bedspread, his eyes wide in some mute and luminous appeal. Micha stared, swallowed, and tried to look away. But Thomas drew him like a lodestone. He looked so sincere, so naked somehow, and so utterly unafraid of being either. Given Micha's behaviour in general, he could not have expected anything but the harshest rejection. But, still, he had asked.

And Micha had thought himself so safe. Everything that had once made him vulnerable, made him stupid and made him human, he had sewn up inside his too-used flesh where even he no longer knew how to find it. But, just then, for one awful, annihilating moment, he wanted to believe again. Believe in Thomas, as he had once believed in Isidore. Had life taught him nothing? Had he changed so little? Was he the very same fool who had given up his entire self and future for a flimsy promise of love?

"I . . ." Micha managed finally, his attention flicking with some poor shadow of irony to the book they had just finished reading. "I have fallen upon hard times."

If Thomas had pushed him, Micha might have crumbled into pieces of dust and bone. Instead, he accepted the evasion. "I know. But things will get better."

"Right." Micha mustered something of his usual harshness. His eyes narrowed. "What are your dreams, then, Father?"

"Oh." Thomas gave a nervous laugh. "I suppose I should like to fulfil my duty to my family. And live always with honour and integrity. And serve God to the best of my ability."

Micha snorted. "Those are your dreams? They sound like a shopping list."

"Well." Thomas's hands waved agitated patterns in the air. "Obviously one's dreams are constrained by the . . . by the expectations of the world in which one moves and the necessity of living a full and useful life, dedicated to higher principles than . . . than. Oh dear. You're quite right. I appear to have absolutely terrible dreams."

Micha spoke without thinking, forgetting far too easily that he disliked Thomas. "What if you weren't . . . what was it . . . constrained by whatever you said you were constrained by? What if you could do anything you wanted?"

"I've never thought about it."

"Think now."

"I am thinking. Um, could I be Richard Burton?"

"No, you can't. Everyone wants to be Richard Burton. Women want to have him and men want to—" Micha stopped, horrified at what he had been about to say, which was *be had by him*.

Thomas, however, didn't seem to have noticed. He was either the most oblivious or the most forgiving man Micha had ever met. "If I must be myself," he said softly, "may I still travel, perhaps?"

"They're your dreams. I don't know why you're asking me for permission."

Thomas gave one of his sweet, self-deprecating smiles. "Force of habit, I fear. But very well." He pressed a closed fist decisively into his other palm. "I would travel. How is that?"

"Where would you go?"

"Anywhere, Micha, everywhere. France, Italy, Spain, and far beyond. To the places we cannot even imagine. I would like to see other skies. I would like to see deserts."

"Deserts?"

"Oh yes, I sometimes dream of deserts. The harsh, searing emptiness of infinity. The silence of eternity. And God in every grain of sand."

There was a long silence. Thomas blushed.

"I . . . I've travelled a bit," offered Micha abruptly. "Nowhere special or exciting. Grand tour stuff, you know."

"You went on a grand tour?"

"In a manner of speaking."

"My brothers did. I had to study. How wonderful it must be, to know a little of the world beyond our shores. 'Broadening the horizon,' I think they call it."

"My horizon is as narrow as the eye of a fucking needle. Just because you can see through the bars of a cage doesn't make it any less of a cage."

"None of the memories bring you pleasure?"

Micha could not bear the hope in Thomas's eyes. "I liked Venice. It was"—he paused—"very beautiful. It was as though the light itself was made by some magician. Whatever it touched, it made lovely, even the slimy marble steps and faded brocade furnishing of the palazzo we took that overlooked the Grand Canal." He fell silent for a moment. "The sunlight, there, in the mornings, gleaming on the lagoon, was the brightest I'd ever seen."

"How much beauty in your world."

Micha suddenly tasted bile. "Beauty is only a commodity." And, before Thomas could reply, unravel him, and expose him further, he snapped, "I wish you'd leave me the fuck alone."

Thomas nodded and climbed to his feet. He was not graceful, but his movements had a carefulness about them that gave him a certain fluidity. "I have imposed upon you more than enough."

"What does that mean?" asked Micha sharply, convinced he had finally pushed Thomas too far, and that he was going to be thrown out into the street, as he deserved. He hardly knew why he persisted in these childish, self-defeating games. It would have been far better for him to play the perfect, grateful guest. He had taken far more demeaning roles. But Micha, a man who displayed himself for strangers as a matter of course, simply could not bring himself to do it. He was half-consumed by the need to make Thomas hate him before Thomas found his own reasons to do so and, at the same time, terrified to think he might succeed.

"It means"—Thomas smiled—"that I shall leave you to rest."

"But you're coming back?"

The smile grew faintly bewildered. "Of course, Micha, if you wish it."

"What do my wishes have to do with it? You show up anyway."

Thomas gave him a long, steady look. "You know you may stay here as long as you need."

"And then what?"

"That's up to you."

"That's not good enough."

"What would be good enough?" Thomas spread his hands in a gesture of invitation. "What do you want from me, Micha? You refuse my help when I offer it, but I can see you're worried about your future. You need not fear I would abandon you."

"But you don't know who I am."

"Perhaps one day you will tell me. Perhaps not. I fail to see its relevance."

"What if I am not worthy of your help? I could be a criminal."

"And are you?"

Micha flinched from Thomas's eyes. "I . . ."

"It's not my place to judge you."

"No, but you will."

Thomas only shook his head, leaving Micha to a tangle of unformed thoughts and restless slumber.

104

His wife stares into my eyes as he readies himself. Between them, I shiver in my nakedness. And when I turn my head away she puts a cold, gloved finger beneath my chin and holds me there. Her gaze slips past me to her husband. Her lips form a red crescent.

I feel something sour and unfamiliar. I think it might be envy. For I know this twisted, ugly thing is love, as true as any I once believed in.

Use him, she murmurs. Use him as a woman. Make him bleed. I wish to hear him scream.

~

The laudanum was done. Micha had knocked back the last of it two days ago. Which meant he was completely and utterly fucked.

He tossed the empty glass aside and stared blankly at the far wall of the bedchamber. While he was not particularly enjoying his lengthy sojourn in one room, it was infinitely preferable to the alternative, which, as far as he could tell, was dying in a gutter. Though it had now reached the point that dying in a gutter might be his only remaining option. He ran through his extensive repertoire of obscenity but it brought him only scant relief.

Regret, he knew, was a fool's game. Still, his feelings were awkward and conflicted. It did not please him to admit it, but this had been the closest thing to peace he had known for quite some time. He lived what was left of his life at the extremes of experience: the utter, sordid misery of selling his body and the wild, artificial ecstasies of opium. And, before that, he had known only the banality of his middle-class existence and then the dizzying joy of Isidore's love. Here, life was simply quiet. Micha had been bored, resentful of his dependence, tormented by his reactions to Thomas and the driving need to keep his kindness at bay but, somehow, he had not been unhappy.

It had taken him a long time to recognise it. The strange, calm state of being not unhappy. Like a man expecting to drown, discovering he could float.

And now it was over.

It was time to move on before his truths caught up with him.

He pushed back the bedcovers, horrified at how much effort it took just to move the sheets around. Then he got out of bed. Then he fell over. Then he swore for a while.

Sweating and panting, he wrapped an arm about one of the bedposts and dragged himself first to his knees and finally back to his feet. He stood there, swaying, while the room lurched around him as moorless as a drunkard looking for somewhere to vomit. Micha closed his eyes and dug his fingernails into the wood until the world stopped spinning and he could breathe again.

On the other side of the room, out of sight of the bed, was a free-standing mirror in a wrought iron frame. Doggedly, step by step, pausing frequently to rest and even more frequently to curse, Micha pulled himself towards it.

The stranger who watched his halting progress with dull black eyes was not a pretty sight. Micha touched disbelieving fingertips to the glass. And the figure within did likewise. He put a hand on his hip, took a swaggering pose. Fuck, there were cadavers with more game. He shrugged the nightshirt off his shoulders and let it slip slowly down his body. His chest was a grotesque patchwork of bony ridges and sallow skin, and he hastily covered himself up. He was not vain, for vanity required some shadow of pride, but he was accustomed to having—or rather being—something other people wanted. Right now, he couldn't imagine anyone wanting him. Even if he was the one who paid.

He turned away from the mirror. He didn't enjoy looking at himself at the best of times. It was like staring into a well, at his own corpse, blurry through deep water. He sometimes imagined he didn't have skin at all. That he was just a paper man, hollow and heartless, upon whom other men left a muddle of rough handprints.

What was he going to do? He stumbled back towards the bed, gave up and crumpled to his knees, too tired and too full of hate even to weep. Nothing ever changed. It was just another form of dependency, another form of powerlessness. If nothing else, he had chosen his own downfall. Twice. How many men could say that? It was a freedom of a kind, when all else was trammelled.

His two lovers, equally treacherous. Isidore and opium.

A painful shiver ran through his body. He really wanted—make that needed, although, at this stage, there was no distinction—some laudanum. He dragged himself across the floor to the bottle on the bedside table and chased the dregs with his tongue. How was he to get more? Even if he found the strength to dress and leave with some trace of dignity, he had no money, no possessions, nothing he could sell, not even himself. He looked around for something to steal, but there was nothing either small or valuable enough to make it worthwhile. His room (no, not *his* room, *the* room), though far grander than anything he had experienced since his time with Isidore, was clearly neglected. Not in the sense of uncared for, so much as unlived in, unwanted. This was a house of silent days and cold nights. But surely it had silverware? Trinkets. Anything. Somewhere.

He pushed himself to his hands and knees and, from there, back to his feet. He was drenched in sweat—from effort, exhaustion, or lack of laudanum he could not tell. And the memory of the monster in the mirror haunted him, as though he had finally become the thing he truly was, as wasted, ugly, and corrupt on the outside as he was in his heart.

His conscience, however, he did not let trouble him. If it was wrong to repay kindness with selfishness, kindness was itself little more than a whim, changeable and ephemeral, whereas basic human selfishness was very dependable indeed. There seemed little point in allocating behaviour to moral categories. There was simply folly and common sense, and Micha had indulged in enough folly to last him a lifetime. For which he had surely paid his dues.

His course resolved, he was about halfway towards the door when fatigue and weakness overcame him, and he passed out.

2

I'm so hungry, so utterly weary, that when the gentleman offers to take me to dinner, I agree. I am about ready to agree to anything. He calls me his panther. And later his kitten. He smiles indulgently as I eat, and eat, and eat, though the richness of the food almost sickens me. I'm not innocent in this. I know what is to come.

The truth is, I simply lack the courage to die.

The hours drag. The man eats and talks and drinks and talks and talks and talks. My mouth tastes of sickness. Eventually, he takes me to a hotel. They know him there. It's a copper and sawdust place, I can still remember the faded sunflowers on the quilt blurring with the tears I make sure he doesn't see.

There is nothing of Isidore in him, even that part all men share, swaying between his white thighs like some bulbous, sap-dripping flower. He is a squalid devil, a vile toad of a man, but I let him have me anyway. His soft hands touch me everywhere.

I wake to find him leaving.

I smell his body on my skin. I am beyond mortified but I mutter something about payment.

My dear boy, he says, wide-eyed, if you expected remuneration you should have said before, not after.

I sit there wrapped in soiled sheets, full of an unspeakable hate, for him, for me, for everything.

Something makes him relent. He touches my cheek. Calls me a sweet, silly kitten. Leaves me his cigarette case, which is silver and engraved with his initials. I pawn it and do not die.

~

When Micha opened his eyes, he was cradled in Thomas's arms and there was a woman crouched next to him with a bottle of smelling salts. The acrid scent rushed over him, forcing him into a harsh, painful consciousness. He choked, sneezed, and sat up, spluttering, trying to push them both away. But, for once, Thomas was not to be pushed. He was surprisingly strong for his slender form. Perhaps this was what they called Muscular Christianity. The thought might have amused Micha, once upon a time.

"I thought you were supposed to be resting." Though Thomas's voice was too gentle to be chiding, Micha resented it anyway.

"I'm sick of fucking resting," he growled, to cover a rising sense of panic. He hated being helpless. Yet it seemed the world and his own body were constantly conspiring to remind him that he was. He told himself it could have been worse, for at least he hadn't fainted in the silver cabinet, but the need for laudanum was a brand in his mind, and the possibility of actually acquiring any was disappearing over the horizon like the sails of a tall ship.

"I'm sick of looking and feeling like I'm already dead," he went on, angry, stubborn, doggedly careless of his own best interests. "I'm sick of pissing in a pot." He suddenly remembered they were not alone, and, though he had no scruples in haranguing Thomas mercilessly in private, some vague, deeply buried sense of shame made him hesitant to do it publicly. Besides, he had not been so long in the company of whores that he thought it was appropriate to talk about his cock, or any of the fluids that came out of it, in front of a respectable woman. "Fuck. Sorry," he choked out. "I didn't mean to—sorry."

"It is quite all right." Thomas smiled down at him like the sun. "I know how frustrating you find being bedbound. And if your frankness on the subject has startled Mrs. Clark, we are already supplied with hartshorn to revive her."

Micha had been idly aware of Thomas's housekeeper, but this was the first time she had impinged upon his notice. "Oh please." She actually sounded amused. "I would not faint for mere words."

"Are you reserving your swoons for something special?" asked Thomas, in a tone so full of affection and laughter that it went through Micha like a shard of ice.

He twisted his head in time to catch a look of real sympathy pass between them, as though they were old friends, not master and servant. Or more than that, perhaps. Was the priest fucking his housekeeper? Micha hoped he was, for hypocrisy was something he could understand—could work with—and the mysteries of Thomas's nature infuriated him. But whatever satisfaction he expected to derive from learning that Thomas had feet of clay, just like everyone else, was spoiled by something else. Something he could not name, a bitter-tasting thing, as sour as old tears and as sharp as arsenic. How dare Thomas look softly on someone else. How dare he smile with such ease. Share those secret flashes of humour Micha had begun to believe were his alone. As if these were everyday gifts. As if anyone could have them.

He cast a swift glance towards the woman who had captured Thomas's interest, and most likely more than that. Of course, while he was ghastly, haggard, and feeble, it was only fitting she would be extraordinary. A lush, classical beauty, raven-haired, with eyes like the wild sea. And then he recognised her. Their gazes snagged and held for a long moment, and he saw she knew him too. Then she sat back on her heels and looked away.

There were few worlds smaller, Micha thought, than the world of a whore.

Plain clothes and pinned-up hair couldn't disguise the woman who had once had punters queuing round the block to sample her wares. She'd been little more than a legend by Micha's time, the subject of an explicit mural in the most expensive room, and the source of Madame Defleur's anguish and indignation. He'd heard the story many times. He'd even listened to it, at first.

A twisting, poisonous hope curled itself around his heart. Under different circumstances, he would have cared less than nothing for the fate of a prostitute he had barely known, but the prospect of a little power was as sweet to him as opium smoke. Perhaps it was no longer necessary to leave. At least, not yet. Not until he had regained more of his strength. And the silver would still be there. If he played his cards right, he might not even have to be the one to steal it.

Once upon a time, stealing would have been alien to the point of unthinkable to Micha. But he had taken up petty theft almost without noticing—a few coins, here and there, from gentlemen too drunk to notice, a cigarette case, a silk handkerchief, then a few more coins, not always from those who could afford it. It had been such a gentle slide, there was never an opportunity for it to feel wrong. Rather the opposite, in fact. By the time he was desperate enough to do it, he mostly believed his clients as good as deserved it. A reciprocal indignity for the ones they practised on his body. Even so, his thieving had always been personal and small-scale, and ransacking Thomas's house would be a noticeable escalation. It was use or be used; he knew that well enough. And his mind was already turning through all the ways he could turn the situation to his advantage.

He might even be able to take some pleasure from it, as much as he was capable of finding pleasure in anything not directly derived from the poppy. "Mrs. Clark," as she styled herself, so clearly enjoyed Thomas's admiration. It would do her good to remind her of her place. She was, after all, no better than Micha. Worse, in fact, for he was born a gentleman. It could be her punishment for this moment, a scrap of vengeance for having to lie here and watch them smiling at each other.

"I'd quite like to go back to bed," Micha snapped, interrupting whatever playful observation Thomas was making about the things he supposed worth fainting over.

"Of course you do." Thomas was instantly contrite. "I am so sorry. Here, let me help you."

The housekeeper excused herself and fled. Whatever she had seen on Micha's face had made her turn pale. And that was good. Well, good for him. The more anxious he made her, the easier it would be to get what he wanted. Thomas, of course, would have stayed with him, but Micha waved him off imperiously. He wanted to be alone with his cravings and his scheme. At last, he was somewhat in control of the situation. It made even the aches, sweats, and shivers just about endurable. Soon he would know relief, and that was enough. After opium, cessation was one of Micha's few remaining bodily satisfactions. He rarely expected, or wanted, to feel anything, but there was a certain private solace in afterwards, when things stopped, when the client was gone, when he was once again his own. Opium was like that too. It brought him cessation from the world as a whole.

And Mrs. Clark would be back. He knew it. He had nothing to lose and she had too much.

442

Fuckingwhorecuntslutdoxyfuckingmandrakecocksuckingpricklovingsodomitewhore.

He comes, yanking off the sheath to spatter my back and arse with his clammy spendings, and it's over.

~

It was nearly midnight when Mrs. Clark tapped softly on his door and glided inside.

"I came to bring you some fresh pillows." She hovered on the threshold, clutching a bundle of sheets protectively to her chest.

Micha hauled himself upright. "No you didn't."

She hung her head, and the heavy coils of her hair made her look like a flower in a storm. After an awkward moment, she tumbled what she was carrying onto the nearest chair. "I thought we should talk."

"Then, let's talk, Mrs. Clark. Or should I say, Mademoiselle Defleur."

She flinched visibly. How satisfying it was to wield, for once, the petty blade. To be the one to cause the hurt instead of feel it. Fair payment for her careless smiles, though Micha would never have admitted they had wounded him.

"That was never my name," she said, at last. "And I go by Mrs. Clark these days."

"And whose name is that? Not Mr. Clark's, I'm sure of it."

She shook her head. "As I'm sure you're well aware, there is no such person, nor has there ever been. I needed the respectability of widowhood."

"Call yourself whatever you want, you're still a whore and the daughter of a whore."

He waited, so he could watch her react, but this time her composure did not falter. She met his gaze calmly. "I kept your secret."

"For now," he sneered.

"Forever. We come from the same place. I would not betray any who tried to escape it."

"Actually, we don't. I fell to the gutter. You were born to it."

"If that distinction matters to you, then yes."

He curled his lip. "Oh, you're worse than he is. Are you two fucking?"

"He has been kind to me."

"Kind. Hah, he's kind to everyone. I bet he spurts the milk of human kindness when he comes."

If Micha had expected to shock Madame Defleur's daughter, he was doomed to disappointment. "He has only tried to help you," she murmured.

"Yes, and now you're going to help me too."

She folded her hands primly in front of her. "Why should I do that, Michael Dashwood?"

"Because you know what will happen if you don't. I don't know how you landed this job, but it can't have been through honest toil and merit. Generally, women who open their legs to all comers don't get to run respectable households."

"My place is held through merit, but you are correct. I did not win it honestly. I was desperate. Surely you can understand that."

"I'll be as understanding as you like when you do what pleases me."

There was a long silence.

"I will not sleep with you," she told him, in a choked voice.

"What? Fuck, no. What in God's name made you think I'm interested in sex?"

"I'm sorry." She seemed genuinely embarrassed. "I . . . old assumptions, I suppose. It tends to be what men wish of me."

And of me. Though Micha did not appreciate the parallel. "Trust me, I have absolutely no desire to sleep with you. What I want is for you to bring me a bottle of laudanum. First thing tomorrow."

"Is that truly what you want?" The wretched woman was actually looking at him with pity.

"For now."

She perched on the far edge of his bed. Her movements were so decorous and restrained, it was hard to imagine she had once been the toast of Whitechapel. "You know, you could break this dependence."

He glanced up sharply. "Does he know?"

"I'm not sure. He would help you, though, if you wished."

"I don't wish."

"I know you dislike accepting aid, but you could use this opportunity to—"

"You don't understand," he interrupted. "I don't want to break my dependence, as you put it. Opium's my only pleasure. The only thing that makes this filthy fucking world bearable."

"Oh Micha, I'm sorry for it."

The softness of her voice, the understanding in her eyes, acted on him like salt rubbed into an open wound. "Don't be. It's my choice."

"How can it be, when you no longer have the power of choosing?"

"I'm not going to talk about this with you. You'll bring me a bottle of laudanum, and you'll say nothing of this to His Reverence."

"Absolutely not." She shook her head. "I won't do it. I won't deceive Mr. Mandeville, and I will certainly not be coerced."

Micha snorted. "You're already deceiving him. Everything you are is deception. You're just like me, worse than me, and you'll do as I damn well say."

"Or what? You'll tell him who I am? And reveal yourself as well."

"I'll say I used to fuck you for coppers. Men always believe other men over women. Even the supposedly decent ones."

"You can't prove—"

"All I need him to do is look into your references. Even if he doesn't believe you're a whore, he'll know you're a liar."

"Are you sure," she asked weakly, "it's worth the risk?"

"I'm a charity case he scraped off the street. When he tosses me out like so much refuse, I'm no worse off than I was before. But you, Mrs. Clark"—he threw the name at her like an obscenity—"you have your position to consider. You have something to lose."

She closed her eyes, tension visible in the lines that gathered at the corners. "More than you can possibly imagine."

"I doubt that. Loss has had his way with me like anyone else."

At last, she looked at him again. The shadows in the room danced starkly upon her face. "I have a daughter. For myself, I don't care what happens. But I wish to give my child some chance at life beyond the gutters of Church Lane." Her voice rose in sudden passion. "Please, don't ruin that. Please."

That was unexpected. As was the direct entreaty. It was strange to be pleaded with, thrilling and discomforting at once.

Isidore had begged Micha to love him once. The scene was a vivid memory among so many tattered ones. The glass-smooth river and the overhanging willow, the golden haze of summer and the endless blue sky. Isidore had been brighter than the sun. Micha had trembled beneath his hands, as if his body had only newly learned how to live. *Please. There is no shame in this.* He could remember the scene and the words. Even the smell of the grass beneath them and Isidore's skin. But whatever it had made him feel, the power, the wonder and vulnerability of trust, had been irretrievably lost, devoured by time and pain, and everything he had since become.

"Is that why you ran away?" he asked, pushing aside the daggers of memory.

Mrs. Clark just nodded.

The rumour at the brothel was that she had found herself a rich patron. As for Madame Defleur, she had dwelled more on treachery and broken trust, and Micha had never been interested enough to ask questions. "Throw you out, did she?"

Perhaps she hoped that his questions implied some sympathy, for she gave a slightly twisted smile and said, "Oh no, my mother was delighted. Seeing the success she had made of me, she was more than happy to raise my daughter." Her hands curled into tight fists against the bedclothes, her eyes gleaming knife-pale through the dim light. "But I couldn't do it. I couldn't deliver another human being—whether of my body or no—to a fate like mine."

"How maternal of you," he drawled.

"Not really." She gave an odd, graceless shrug. "At first she was nothing but an obligation thrust upon me. It's one thing to make a rational choice to do what you believe is right, another to commit to it emotionally. Love does not come easily to me, I think. I'd never known it, never felt it, never wanted it. But, in time, she changed . . . everything for me. And she changed me too. I was twelve, you know, when my mother sold my virginity." Again, her lips curved into a smile, as dark as Micha's, but tempered by warmth, softened by hope. "I know she will only be the child of a widowed servant, but better than the grandchild of Madame Defleur. And perhaps, by the time she has grown . . ."

"I wouldn't hold my breath."

"Oh, but I am. I was never a devout woman, but I pray. I pray there may be a place for my daughter in a better, different, fairer world. And I will do whatever it takes to build even the tiniest fraction of that future for her. If I have to lie for the rest of my life." Suddenly Madame Defleur's daughter slipped from the bed, until she was kneeling on the floor, her hands spread in supplication. "If I have to plead with you, now, tonight. Is that what you want? Do you want me to beg? Because I will. It would cost me nothing, Micha. You can have no idea how little this costs me."

He stared down at her, hating her for how little pleasure her subjugation had brought him. Love, that faithless whore, had vanquished him again, and he felt not powerful, but sickened, worthless, and utterly alone.

"I want," he said, "for you to stand up, shut up, and bring me a bottle of laudanum tomorrow."

"You don't have to do this." God, why did she keep *trying*? Hadn't she learned that Micha had no better nature left to appeal to? "He will understand, I am sure of it."

"I don't care what he thinks of me. I just want some fucking laudanum."

"I've seen the way you look at him."

"Oh? How's that?"

"Like he's a miracle you dare not believe in."

"Right, and you look at him like you want to wrap your lips round his cock."

"You can be safe here, Micha. I promise."

He watched her through narrowed eyes. "Is that so? Is that fucking so? Well, how about I make you a deal? You tell him about you, and I'll tell him about me. And then we'll see how safe we both are."

She climbed to her feet, her movements suddenly heavy. She paced back and forth across the room, her head bowed in thought. "I can't. I can't take that risk. For myself, I would. But I need to think of my daughter."

He barked out a laugh. "So you want me to keep your little secret while I spill mine? Either you think this man is God's gift to the world or you don't. Get me that laudanum. You sanctimonious cunt. And don't talk to me again, because I don't give a fuck about you, or your fucking daughter."

"I understand." She left the room as silently as she had entered it.

And the next day, she brought him a bottle of laudanum.

Chapter 6

15th September

I have tried to pray but I cannot find the words, and I do not know for what I am praying. I do not know what I want. Though I do know what is wrong, and what it is wrong to want. And I cannot beg forgiveness because I have not repented. After all, I have not erred—unless I accept the position that thought itself is sin. But these thoughts, these thoughts that many would call iniquity, come from some part of me that, though only freshly discovered, seems inviolable. How can I repent that which I know to be wrong, yet does not feel wrong? If I am made in God's image, then surely he made this also? Or does that part of me belong to the Devil?

Why is this done to me? I am nothing but His poor servant. I have striven all my life to fulfil my duty, to my family, to my God, to His teachings. Is this some punishment or some test? How can I believe that God is love, as Saint John would teach us, in the face of what seems arrant and arbitrary cruelty? Am I unfit, immoral, corrupt, simply because I look upon a man as other men—other priests—may look upon women? Deed, intent, everything, rendered irrelevant simply by the existence of the thought. The truth.

I am sickened. I am betrayed. By myself? I do not know.

I am come to Carthage burning, burning.

And I ask: am I the graver sinner, though I do not act, than he who lies with women and yet repents? And I find no answer. I am like a child, crying in the night. This is unfair. But mine must necessarily be a limited understanding. Is there not some plan, as I have often claimed to others? Some deeper meaning? But, oh, what is it? What is it? I can find no sense in this. And I cannot see the harm.

How can it be harm? Idolatry, I have confessed. Covetousness? I do like to look at him, but I do not covet him. He is not my possession. He is his own self, so very much his own self, it bewilders and bewitches me. Porneia, then? Unlawful desire, selfishness, an act that debases another. It crushes me beyond expression to believe that simply by their existence, my . . . what must I call them? . . . my preferences are unlawful, unnatural, and degrading. But what nature? What laws?

And likewise also the men, leaving the natural use of the woman, burned in their lust one toward another; men with men working that which is unseemly, and receiving in themselves that recompence of their error which was meet.

Has God turned away from me? Or have I turned from Him?

No. I cannot accept this. The sin in porneia is the use of others without care, for the fulfilment of the basest, most self-centred lusts. It is not a particular desire, it is not a particular act—it is simply the perversion of love into something that harms someone else.

I would not harm him, for all the world. I wish I could please him only half as well as he pleases me, but I fear that is beyond my power.

Some days ago, I found him insensible upon the floor, I believe trying to escape the confines of his room. Of course, I promised him liberty, shamed that my care of his body had paid so little heed to his mind. It was no wonder he was bored, restless and stifled. Not long after, I helped him dress. My clothes do not fit him well. He is too thin, too tall, but he holds himself with such pride, and glared at me so fiercely, I could not laugh. My king of shreds and patches.

Such an expedition, from his bedroom, down the stairs, to one of the drawing rooms. He had to rest so often, yet still he insisted. While I admire his will, I fear for him. A broken reed is one who never bends. He thinks he hides them but I see his wounds, ill-knit bones and scar tissue. I would protect him from all the world's brambles, if only he would let me. I would never see him hurt again.

Finally, we staggered across the threshold. It was not an edifying sight for the culmination of such a journey. His eyes travelled across the faded furnishings, the covered furniture and the heavy curtains. "O brave new world," he said with magnificent scorn, and fainted.

Oh my heart, my heart. I have never felt such things.

I have had the room aired. We sit there fairly often now. It grows easier every day to get him there. I think his strength returns. He has certainly been calmer since the day I found him on the floor. I am glad for him. The time will come that he may want to leave—I dread it and anticipate it, with almost equal fervour. When he is gone, I will be free. I will no longer fear myself and my sins. I have duties in my parish that require my attention. But it does not feel like liberty. It feels like loss.

~

"This is a stupid game," announced Micha, having lost at chess, yet again. He batted over his king with such a dismissive gesture that it toppled most of the other pieces.

Thomas, observing the carnage, covered his mouth with his hand to conceal a smile.

"And stop laughing at me, you smug prick."

"I'm so terribly sorry."

"Then, why are you still laughing?"

Taking a deep breath, Thomas just about managed to compose his features into something suitably solemn. He had grown accustomed to Micha's harsh responses, finding at their heart a strange contradiction, for as much as he complained of Thomas's mirth, he also seemed to court it. And Thomas was glad, more than glad, to give it. Somehow, they had found an odd equilibrium between Micha's moods and Thomas's care. Though Micha was no more inclined to be amiable than he had ever been, Thomas thought he had been calmer lately, not precisely at his ease but softened, as if he felt himself protected in some subtle, private way. Thomas was not self-important enough to attribute it to his own influence; he was simply happy for Micha's happiness.

And for his own, since he simply enjoyed Micha's company, difficult though it could be sometimes. He was like no one Thomas had ever met before, so careless of the opinions of others, direct to the point of cruelty, and, to Thomas's untutored perception, freer, somehow. As for Thomas's equally untutored heart, he was still sufficiently innocent of the sin in which he believed himself now utterly steeped that he drew as much pleasure from Micha's simple presence and his growing good health than he did from any more carnal meditations. He accepted Micha's beauty, and his response to it, as a mere part of something in every way as delightful as it was mysterious.

"You," he said, "are a terrible loser."

Micha slumped back in his chair. "Well, who likes losing?"

Thomas began to gather up the scattered chess pieces and arrange them in their little wooden box. The hand-painted scene on the lid had faded long ago. Thomas could just about make out a pale splodge of sun, a few splashes of green. It had been a gift from Edward, when they were all young. There had been one for Thomas and one for George, but whatever their brother had been trying to portray was lost to time. Thomas could not even remember if George had kept his. "You make a good point. But would it be unbearable of me to remind you that this was your idea?"

"What else am I supposed to do? Stare at the ceiling until my eyes bleed?"

"We could play a different game. I am entirely at your disposal."

Micha looked unimpressed by this prospect, and there was silence for a while. "A friend taught me," he offered abruptly, looking not at Thomas but at a thread that had come loose at his cuff and at which he was picking distractedly. "A long time ago. I've always been terrible at it."

Thomas suspected this was the mysterious Isidore. Micha spoke of him often, but never directly, and Thomas knew better than to ask questions or Micha would only grow impatient and refuse to say anything at all. "You refuse to consider the broader strategy," he teased instead. "You just shift the pieces around because you can."

"As though you're any better. You agonise over the fate of every pawn."

"I still won." Thomas paused meaningfully. "Twice."

"Only because I let you."

"By being—to use your own words—terrible?"

Micha tapped the side of his head. "It's my broader strategy."

Thomas was laughing again, helplessly. Micha, of course, glared at him, but the more he glared, the harder Thomas laughed. There was something different in the other man's eyes, a trace of warmth and a hint of pride, as lovely as it was unexpected.

"I'm not your fucking jester," he snarled, but the words lacked conviction.

"Your friend should have taught you better," replied Thomas, gravity finally returning.

A flash of pain quenched the brightness of Micha's eyes, and Thomas wished he could have cut his tongue out rather than have spoken so carelessly. But before he could apologise, Micha went on, his voice very soft, "I was not attentive. And he was . . . he was a master at it. He knew my every move before I made it. An astonishing mind, really. Fuck knows what he saw in me—I mean, why he would have sought my friendship."

Thomas put the box aside and folded his hands on the tabletop. This flicker of uncertainty was unusual. Even in his physical frailty, there was something invincible about Micha, but Thomas suddenly realised how young he was. Perhaps not even three and twenty. Yet he spoke, and acted, as though centuries hung on his shoulders. A lot of the time, he made Thomas—who had passed his thirtieth year—feel callow and ignorant.

"Are you truly in doubt?" he asked.

A strange shadow crossed Micha's face, his lips twisting cynically. But whatever had inspired the thought, he did not utter it. "Well." He shrugged. "I'm not clever, I'm not learned, I'm not rich, I'm not anything, really. No wonder he tired of me."

Once, when Thomas was quite young, he had been walking with Edward somewhere in the lands beyond Montrose, past the ordered loveliness of its widely admired gardens. Edward's idea, he seemed to recall. There had been wild lavender tangled among the hedgerows, and then a storm of sunshine-yellow butterflies. One had alighted, in the confusion, on Thomas's nose. "It has mistaken you for a flower," Edward had said, laughing. And Thomas had stood there, barely daring to breathe, afraid for the transience of the moment, yet knowing the transience was part of it. He felt rather like that now. "Any man would be honoured to have your friendship."

"Right."

Thomas was learning to hate that word. Never had he heard it imbued with such utter scepticism and such utter despair. He leaned across the table, trying to catch Micha's eye, though Micha was rather practised at looking anywhere but at Thomas except when he chose. "You have a . . . lustre," he said, earnestly.

"A what?"

"I don't know. Something remarkable. It draws the eye and fixes the attention, as though you bring light to a room just by being in it." Micha's expression had grown, if possible, even more scornful, so Thomas went on, in a more playful tone: "And, besides, there is more to merit than wealth and more to cleverness than being able to play chess."

Micha's whole cuff had practically unravelled, and he was still not looking at Thomas. "Rubbish," he muttered. "Also, between having merit and having money, I'd rather have money."

"Surely merit can readily produce money."

"I wouldn't know."

Micha glanced up, frowning, a flash of anger in his eyes as though Thomas had somehow tricked him into confidences against his will. Thomas was, however, tolerably accustomed to this too and quickly sought for a way to turn the conversation to something frivolous. As much as he pretended not to, Micha seemed to genuinely enjoy it when Thomas amused him. And that dreamy, shyly tender mouth of his seemed made more naturally for laughter than for scowls and sneers. "So much for merit then. And you said yourself that chess was a stupid game."

"It is. Who rides their horses in an L shape?"

"For . . . flanking?"

"And why do bishops barge up and down, diagonally, always stuck on their starting colour?"

"Ah, now that, I think you must agree, is a startlingly accurate portrayal of an English bishop in action."

Micha raised his eyes slowly, and the corners of his lips twitched as though he was trying to suppress a smile.

And Thomas gazed at him, smiling too, enchanted. "You can laugh," he whispered. "I won't tell a soul."

"I'm not giving you the satisfaction." But Micha's face betrayed him. He smiled with everything except his mouth. "You've already won at chess. Twice. What more can you want?"

"I think . . . I think I'd like this better."

"All the more reason not to give it to you."

"'And now abideth faith, hope, charity, these three; but the greatest of these is charity.'"

Micha spluttered, his expression a wonderful tangle of surprise, amusement, and outrage. For someone who hid behind scowls and indifference, he could be very animated when caught unawares. "You said that when . . . when you found me. The way you use scripture, I sometimes think"—he drew in a slow breath—"that beneath your façade of virtue you might be a very wicked man."

"I sometimes think," returned Thomas, "that beneath your façade of wickedness, you are a good one."

Micha pulled back, and the moment shattered like a mirror. "I wouldn't count on it."

There was what Thomas thought must have been a mutually bewildered silence, and then the door burst open, and George came striding in. He looked better than he had the last time Thomas had seen him, though not by much and, once again, travel-stained. Stripping off his overcoat and tossing his hat aside, he threw himself down in a nearby chair.

"Please." Thomas smiled. "Don't stand on ceremony on our account."

George cast a disparaging glance in Micha's direction and then said to Thomas, "I see he's still here."

Thomas fully expected Micha to come back with something cutting, but when he tried to catch his eye, Micha was staring fixedly at his hands. What Thomas could read of his expression, which was little, suggested some scalding combination of fury and mortification, and seared him as painfully as if he had been the subject of George's discourtesy. "He's my guest. And," he went on, striving for a way to resolve the tension peaceably, "he's sitting right there, fully able to witness your abominable manners."

George still refused to acknowledge Micha, and Micha still refused to show any sign of being alive—it was, in short, a rather awkward situation all round. Thomas knew George was best confronted directly. His heart was stubborn, though, Thomas believed, generous in its way. And it was not like Micha to be cowed by mere bluster. But perhaps it was difficult to be reminded of dependency. Like most things too fiercely protected, Micha's pride was a fragile thing.

"You don't know anything about him," George was saying, at his most blustersome. "Who is he? Where has he come from? Rather convenient for him, isn't it, being able to latch on to you?"

And, again, Micha was uncharacteristically silent, though his eyes were burning coals beneath the shadow of his lashes.

"His name," said Thomas, as patiently as he could, "as I have told you, is Michael Dashwood. He is a gentleman who has fallen upon hard times, and he is my guest here while he recovers. That is no concern of yours. I only ask that you treat him as you would anyone else—with respect."

"Respect?" repeated George, turning the word into something more exclamation than question.

"Yes, respect. It is not easy for any man, let alone a proud one, to accept aid from a stranger. Mr. Dashwood has been gracious enough to allow me to help him, and I am grateful."

Micha cleared his throat. There was a feverish flush standing out upon the jutting bones of his still-gaunt face and, as familiar as Thomas had grown with his humour and expressions, this was the first time he had seen him in something like real distress. "Don't pretend I'm better than I am," he whispered, so softly that Thomas barely caught the words at all.

But before he had a chance to answer him as he might have wished, George had swung himself to his feet and Thomas's attention was distracted. His brother had that sullen, resentful look Thomas had always disliked and was beginning to witness far too often. "And if I don't meet your exacting standards of civil behaviour? What then?"

Thomas stifled a sigh and also stood. He was, by disposition, self-effacing, but birth had made him a brother before life had made him a priest, and nothing in this world or the next would induce him to sit still and uncomplaining while George loomed over him and acted the bully. The worst thing to do when George was in one of his moods was yield. "Are you trying to start a fight with me in the drawing room? What nonsense."

George swaggered a step closer. He had strength, but Thomas was taller, something he suspected had always annoyed George, who put great store in the scant handful of minutes between them as though, in being older, it was his right to be bigger too. Up close, Thomas could see the fine lines that had gathered at the corners of his brother's eyes and the deep shadows beneath. "I doubt you still have it in you," sneered George.

Thomas was deeply conscious of the ludicrous picture they must have presented to a stranger. Grown men acting like children. But he could not back down. Not in the face of Micha's stifled silence. "Then try me."

George laughed, the harsh sound reminding Thomas unexpectedly of Micha. "Is that what you preach on Sundays? Brotherly love."

"The Bible says honour thy mother and thy father. Not thy brother when he is being a . . ." Thomas cast an uncertain glance at Micha, his tongue tripping slightly over a word he had never found occasion to utter aloud: ". . . a prick."

"Oh, a hit," returned George, with a theatrical stagger, "a palpable hit. Is that the best you can do?"

Thomas's patience, often believed to be unassailable, finally broke. "Why," he said, with evident frustration, "are you trying to provoke me? If you want to strike me, then do it. If you don't, sit down, be quiet, and try to be courteous."

There was a long silence.

"You sound just like His Lordship," muttered George.

And it seemed to Thomas, in those few fleeting moments, very likely that his brother would hit him. It was something he would have preferred to avoid, but, all things considered, it was easily borne. While Thomas could defend himself if necessary, he lacked the will—or perhaps the need—for violence that sometimes seemed to take hold of George. His time in the army had hardened him, and his personal frustrations had few outlets while he lived beneath the marquess's eye. It had also been their preferred measure for solving disputes when they were young, and the marquess had encouraged it. Usually it had been left to Edward to pull them apart before anyone got really hurt—though, in general, Thomas tended to receive the worst of it—but now it was Micha who suddenly interposed himself between them.

"Lawks," he drawled, flipping his hands into the air in a ludicrous gesture of affronted modesty. "Good sirs. Pray do not fight over unworthy little me."

George, who, for all his faults, had a pronounced appreciation for the absurd, gave a startled-sounding laugh. His eyes slid, almost unwillingly, to Micha. "You have to understand," he said, "sometimes my brother needs someone to beat the seven hells out of him."

"Now who sounds like His Lordship." Thomas sank, with some relief, into a chair. He was surprised to find Micha's eyes on him, though his expression was bland to the point of unreadable. Thomas tried to communicate his gratitude, and Micha immediately looked away. "And forgive George, will you?" he added. "I think in his own way he's trying to care for me."

George, too, took a seat. The anger seemed to have drained out of him. He looked tired again. "Somebody has to."

"He probably thinks you're taking advantage of me."

"Well," said Micha to the rug, "aren't I?"

"Oh Micha, you're supposed to be on my side, not his."

"I'm on my own side. Always."

Thomas turned to George. "He is, at the very least, honest."

"Oddly enough," returned George, "I'm not reassured by that. But it's moot, anyway. I come bearing a message from the marquess."

"Oh?" Thomas's brows went up.

It was very rare for their father to communicate with him about anything, for, unlike George, he did not go out of his way to challenge His Lordship's will, which was the surest way to garner his attention. His life had largely slipped past the marquess, except when he had been required to fulfil some duty or obey some directive, as in the case of Edward's death. When the marquess had succumbed to infirmity, Thomas had, of course, gone immediately to visit, only to be told, in no uncertain terms, that His Lordship wasn't dead yet and would call his own priest when the time was right.

George's mouth pulled tight. "Don't look like that. You make me feel like a beast."

But, even so, Thomas could not suppress the hope and pleasure that made his heart expand like a hot air balloon. "Does," he asked, eagerly, "does he . . . does he want to see me? I can go to him. At once, if necessary."

"Of course he doesn't." George's tone was not unkind. "What would he want to see you for?"

Thomas looked away. Again, his unanchored gaze landed upon Micha, and, for once, the man did not shake him off like a moth. There was something strangely steadying in his attention, warm somehow, like a hand on his shoulder. "I . . . have no idea," he admitted. "I merely thought that he might."

George shook his head in despair. "How old are you?"

"The same age as you, almost to the minute."

"Exactly. And when, at any point during that time, has His Lordship given a fuck about you? Why do you still expect something from him?"

"I'm not expecting anything from him. I merely wish he might expect something of me. Someday." Thomas laughed, self-consciously, far too aware of his own foolishness. But, for once, there was no censure on Micha's face. "What is his message?"

George reached into an interior pocket and produced a letter, sealed with thick red wax, imprinted with the family crest. Thomas took it from his brother's outstretched hand and opened it. There were a couple of lines, the script too weak and wavering to be decipherable. Even the marquess's signature was little more than a fading line, the peaks of the *M* of Montrose rising weakly from the blur like the turrets of a sinking castle.

"I'm sorry," said Thomas, finally. "I can't read this at all. I have no idea what he wants from me."

"He made me memorise it." George took a deep breath and then intoned, "'Mandeville, do not think it has escaped my notice that you have turned my home into an alms-house. Depart at once.'"

And, with that, Thomas lost Micha. Neither of them moved, but it was as though whatever fragile bonds had been spun between them snapped, and Thomas felt dizzy and peculiar, as though he had been cast over empty space and was about to fall.

"I should . . . take my leave," said Micha, somewhat unsteadily. "I've already imposed—"

"No. No, you must not."

"Look, I do have some fucking pride."

"This has nothing to do with pride." Thomas sighed. "But the marquess is right. I have taken too much for granted. We shall both take our leave."

Micha nodded. His eyes were sharp and bleak.

"Come home with me." The words came tumbling out of Thomas in a messy pile.

"What?" barked George.

"Wh-what?" asked Micha.

Thomas glanced from Micha to George and back to Micha again, bouncing between looks of utter incomprehension. "Well," he blundered on, "if there is, as you say, nothing and no one to keep you in London, why not?"

Micha stirred restlessly in the chair, his hands clasping and unclasping. "What . . . well . . . I mean . . . how . . . where is home, I mean your home, anyway?"

"I have a small parish in Oxfordshire. The village is called Nettlefield."

Micha spluttered out a laugh. "Nettlefield? Well, that sounds lovely."

"The name does not do it sufficient credit."

"I'd hope not. Nettlefield, in the county of Cesspit."

"Cesspitshire," said Thomas, smiling.

There was a moment of silence that hung in the room as heavy and inevitable as a raindrop about to fall.

"Nettlefield," murmured Micha. "Nettlefield."

Thomas had no idea what he was thinking. Micha's face, for once, was open, but his expression was so strange and so uncertain, it offered no insight into his mood. "Just while you recover," he babbled, into the quiet. "If you wish. And, of course, I would not keep you stranded in Oxfordshire. I would have asked you before, not sprung the idea upon you like this, but I was afraid you were not strong enough for travel. The rectory is far too spacious for a man of my habits, and the doctor said country air would improve your health . . ."

Micha looked up, a soft, brittle light glowing in the depths of his eyes. "I've been in London so long I've almost forgotten what the rest of England looks like."

"Thom," expostulated George, his voice cutting over Micha's, "you can't just invite anybody to live with you."

Thomas turned to his brother, though he was unaccountably reluctant to look away from Micha in case it broke whatever spell had momentarily gentled and bewildered him. "Why? There is no impropriety in it. I don't believe he is a danger to me. And we can claim him as a distant and removed cousin if it troubles you."

"I don't want him for a distant and removed cousin. I don't know who the bloody hell he is, and neither do you."

"No," said Micha, suddenly. "No. I . . . can't. I'm . . . I'm . . . I don't know what I am. I can't accept anything more from you. I'm a stranger to you. And I have nothing but the clothes I was wearing when you found me in the street."

"Oh." Thomas gave an embarrassed cough. "About those."

Micha gave him a look.

"As a matter of fact, you no longer have them. I'm afraid we burned them. They were filthy, Micha, and the doctor thought they might have carried your sickness."

Micha's lips curled into a smile both savage and mirthless. "Right. Wonderful. Very well. Then, I have literally nothing, not even the clothes on my back. I cannot repay you. I have nothing to give you."

"I want nothing from you." Heedless of his brother, heedless of anything, Thomas impulsively reached out a hand. His fingers curled lightly over Micha's wrist, over his frayed cuff. The skin was cold and very tender, smooth as eggshell and just as fragile. "Please. To turn you onto the streets now, if you are truly as friendless and bereft of means as you say, would be a death sentence."

"Please," repeated Micha, as though Thomas had spoken in some foreign tongue. "Please?"

"Yes. Please. I beg you, accept my invitation. Grant me your faith, if not your trust."

Micha was ice and stillness, as though the light pressure of Thomas's fingers was a harpoon through his flesh. "I . . . I . . ." He swallowed. "You would . . . truly do this? You want to do this?"

"Of course."

"For me? For a stranger? A stranger like me?"

"Of course."

"You would take me away from here? Away from London?" Micha's voice cracked on some terrible mixture of hope and incredulity.

"Of course."

He tore himself away from Thomas and dropped his head into his hands. The words drifted, muffled, from between his fingers. "I can't tell if you're a saint or a Bedlamite."

"I agree with you," said George, staring at his brother as though he no longer recognised him.

"I'm just a man, Micha," said Thomas. "If you cannot believe in my goodwill, then accept it simply as a gift from God. I am His servant, after all."

"No." Micha shook his head. "I'd rather you than Him."

"I'm not sure there is really such a choice."

Another of his harsh laughs. "Believe me, there is."

"If you insist." Thomas paused. "What do you say, Micha?"

"I . . . I suppose I say . . . yes."

"Jesus Christ." George's voice seemed too loud for the moment. "Are you trying to kill the marquess? Because I'd applaud you, but—"

Thomas interrupted, not sharply, but quite firmly. "This has nothing to do with our father." He glanced back at Micha. "Now, if you will forgive me, I shall go make preparations for travel."

Chapter 7

631

I could do anything to you, he says.

Yes, I tell him, because it's the answer he wants. Yes you could.

I don't say, it's what you pay for. I normally don't let my clients restrain me but I'm too drugged to care, too drugged to feel anything as he arranges me and then immobilises me. I should be afraid. I should be vulnerable. I should be ashamed.

But I'm nothing, nothing, nothing.

And I like it.

My body is a soiled thing, miles away, a tarnished trinket given to a stranger's keeping. He does what he will. And it responds, oh yes, it puts on the required show, feels pleasure, feels pain, feels violation and disgust.

But I am dancing in the dust motes, in the velvet hangings, in the candle flames. I am the gleam in the cheap gilt mirror. I am in the stars I cannot see. I am everywhere and nowhere.

Nothing.

~

With the click of the door closing behind Thomas, silence enfolded the room once more. Micha's mind, however, was carnage. What had just happened? What had he been offered? And what had he accepted? He would leave London? This sprawling, festering harlot of a city, between whose thighs ran a river of filth and upon whose blackened breath was always the reek of death. But she had sheltered him when Isidore was done with him, sheltered him, shamed him, and helped him survive. Made him who he was. A whore like her, a fitting reflection. Drowned him in her ugliness until he could no longer tell where he ended and she began. Until he was just another piece of nothing, lost among eight million other nothings, labouring and suffering and living in vain. Micha hated London, and yet she was still his only friend. At his side, glittering in the corners of his eyes, through the long opium-saturated nights, all their secrets bared in a spill of yellow-grey smoke.

To leave would be like leaving himself.

And there was nothing he could imagine wanting more than that.

"Who the hell are you?" George's voice sliced through Micha's whirling thoughts.

He started, only now remembering Thomas's brother was still in the room. "What?" And then, "I'm nobody."

"Everybody's somebody."

Micha shook his head. And, though it was beyond humiliating to have to justify himself to a man like George, he made the attempt anyway. For Thomas's sake. For even the hope of a different tomorrow. "I don't mean him any harm."

Though he knew it was a lie. He was a thief, a whore, an addict, and a sodomite. He could bring nothing but harm to someone like Thomas. Had he been a better man, he would have refused him. Left. But he was too selfish for that and far too desperate.

"And I'm just supposed to believe you, am I?"

George was on his feet. And a moment later, leaning over Micha, hands splayed on the arms of the chair that held him.

Micha was accustomed to yielding whatever of his body was required, but George's abrupt proximity and the sense of being trapped made him flinch regardless. George's hand shot out and caught him roughly by the chin, and Micha swallowed a sound of instinctive protest. He willed himself to calm. It was nothing. Just skin and bone. Nothing. He was something else. Somewhere else.

"I may not know who you are," said George, his eyes burning into Micha's, "or what you think you're going to get out of my brother, but you may be damn certain I'm going to find out."

The part of Micha that was currently capable of being rational very much doubted that a gentleman of rank and privilege would think to look for his answers among the rank and file of male renters. And, even if he did, the likelihood of unravelling Micha's sordid history was slight.

But, nevertheless, he panicked. And, on some level, he was irritated with himself because George was clearly trying to make him panic. On the other hand, since life had—in a moment of apparently arbitrary kindness—decided to show him a glimpse of, even temporary, improvement, it did not surprise Micha that it was now trying to pull it away from him. He felt like a street cur fighting for a scrap of rotten meat: a ragged, cornered, starving, frantic thing. In a typical act of foolish naivety, it had simply not occurred to him to choose a different name when Thomas had asked.

His nerve broke beneath that slight, unwanted touch, and his hand came up, knocking George's away with an uncontrolled, agitated motion. He would have said anything, betrayed anyone, whatever would convince George to leave him alone.

"You condemn me," he said, hardly knowing what was going to come out of his mouth, "but a whore keeps your house. Was she your mistress? Is this how you paid her?"

Bewilderment flashed across George's face, but he was not easily deterred from his purpose. "Look, I want you gone. How much do you want?"

It should have been a familiar question—it *was* a familiar question—but somehow, in a room where he had sat so often with Thomas, it startled Micha, and seared him, like the crack of birch on skin. And he could find no answer to it.

"A hundred quid?"

There was a sickly rustling of paper, and five rather tattered banknotes landed in Micha's lap. He jerked his hands away, driven by an instinct he did not know he possessed. There was enough money there to buy him anything he wanted. A decent room, someone to suck his prick, for a change—though he could not imagine wanting that—and all the opium his body could bear. He could smoke himself sweetly to death with £100.

"Two?"

Another sheaf of soiled papers. Falling on him like spit.

"It's more than you're worth."

I used to have pride, Micha thought. Yet, here he sat, silent and ashamed, because George was right. It was more than he was worth. Far more. His hands shook a little as he gathered up the notes and smoothed them into a pile. He should take it and leave. Men had paid him far less for far greater mortifications. Oh, but Thomas. Thomas. And the promises he had made. Micha dragged up his head and managed to sneer. "Then why pay it?"

George's eyes flared. "For my brother, of course."

"I don't want your money."

"Be reasonable, man. You won't get more from him. I'm the heir to one of the oldest marquessates in England. He's a rector."

Micha held out the notes. He wished he had the courage to throw them at George's feet. "Take your fucking money. I said I don't want it."

George glared at him so furiously that, for a moment, Micha thought the man might strike him. But then a strange smile unfurled across his lips. He plucked the notes from Micha's hand, folded them neatly, and leaned in. And, once again, Micha flinched from him, but he had nowhere to go. He turned his head away helplessly, hating himself and hating George and hating Thomas, too, for abandoning him to this. George peeled open Micha's coat and slipped the notes into the inside pocket.

"Keep it, you little parasite." He smiled, sharp-toothed, falsely sweet. "And when you finally realise my brother has nothing to give you, come and find me, and I'll double it, just to keep you away from my family."

Pushed beyond endurance, Micha shoved George away and leapt to his feet, his arms folded tightly across his body to try and control his shaking.

"But don't wait too long, old man. Because if there's anything out there about you, I'll find it. And then I'll destroy you."

And Micha ran. Like a thief, like a whore, like the broken coward he was.

He dragged himself up the stairs, as fast as he could manage, barely able to breathe by the time he stumbled into his room and half-fell onto the bed. As soon as he had the strength to move, he curled himself up tightly. Fuck George for frightening him. Fuck himself for being frightened. Fuck Thomas for discovering—after all this time—something Micha still wanted. Fuck everything.

In a little while, he dipped a hand beneath the bed and dragged out the bottle of laudanum Mrs. Clark had brought him. He sat up and mixed himself a draught. It helped still the trembling in his hands, but it could not quiet the turmoil of his thoughts.

I want nothing from you.

Thomas's voice seemed to echo endlessly through his mind.

What did it mean? Was he supposed to believe it? Everybody wanted something. It was simply the way of the world.

And Thomas was wrong, regardless. He did not ask for nothing. He asked for faith, hope, trust, all things that Micha had long since forgotten how to give and, even had he not, would never have readily surrendered to another's care again. Trust was an invitation to betrayal. Hope an opportunity for disappointment. And, as for faith, that was a fool's virtue. Why give anything, or anyone, that sort of power over your heart or happiness?

But Thomas's words and careless promises had nudged something in Micha. Leaving London was a prospect so remote that he'd never even allowed himself to think of it. He preferred opium's painless, artificial dreams to impossible ones. And had always thought the city would be his tomb. But perhaps Thomas would take him to green places. He would see stars again. He could pretend to be some other man and live some other life. As though his body was not a desecrated shrine to the basest lusts, his soul a nest for worms. As though his heart was more than just red meat.

He could almost have wept with longing and fear. But, of course, he did no such thing. He had lived for so long with nothing to lose, with opium as his sole desire, that wanting anything else felt like weakness. A restless tingling gathered in his fingertips. This was unbearable. He was utterly powerless. That was the problem with kindness. Sincere or otherwise, it stripped you of yourself, left you vulnerable and dependent. It was easier to be fucked for money.

Easier, yes, but not preferable.

Micha told himself it was simply another sort of usage and that he could learn to endure it. But even another measure of laudanum could not calm him. His thoughts kept springing back to Thomas like a compass needle to a magnet. What did the man want? What did he truly want? What lurked behind his earnest eyes and shy smile? It was not, in truth, that Micha believed Thomas had some unpleasant or sinister purpose. But he burned with the sudden need to find some secret sin or piece of darkness, a moment of cruelty or selfishness, anything that would prove he was as human, fallible, and self-motivated as everyone else. Something Micha could hold over him, even if just in the privacy of his own mind. Since he was sure he bore Thomas no *real* malice.

Did he?

Tangling his fingers in his hair, he pulled until he felt a distant, muted pain and swore softly. He had, of late, touched by small gestures, self-conscious confidences, and quiet mirth, been forgetting his dislike. It was the laughter that had undone him. Thomas smiled like a man without fear of pain.

Micha had no real plan, and only the vaguest of intentions, as he hauled himself upright and left the room. The house, as ever, was silent. The place was vast, and there were so few servants it was rare to even catch a glimpse of them moving around. It reminded Micha, in his more whimsical moods, of a cursed castle from a fairy tale. He knew only his bedroom and a handful of staterooms below, but he set off resolutely down the corridor, pushing open door after door, searching for the other occupied room and hoping Thomas was still busy with his travel arrangements. If not, Micha could easily attribute his wild wanderings to boredom and curiosity—an explanation considerably more plausible than the truth.

Eventually, through luck and determination, he found what had to be Thomas's bedroom. It was no less neglected than his own, and Thomas lived a neat, austere existence. There was a travelling bag at the foot of the bed, one of his plain black coats flung across a chair, a copy of the Bible on the bedside table, and what looked like a half-written sermon on the dresser. Otherwise nothing, either illuminating or incriminating.

Micha dropped to his knees and went shamelessly through the travelling bag. Still nothing. Thomas was less a man of mystery than a man of no discernible personality whatsoever. It would almost have been laughable, except Micha was too frantic, and he knew it wasn't true. Thomas was a creature of light and subtlety, like colours shifting over the surface of a pearl. And Micha blamed the laudanum for allowing him to form such a ridiculous thought. He was here to learn Thomas's secrets, not sit around making fanciful comparisons.

He stopped rifling through Thomas's unmentionables and cast his eyes over whatever Thomas had been writing. Dull. Finally, he picked up the Bible, just in case a note or a letter slipped out from between its pages, and that was when he saw the slim leather-bound volume that had been partially obscured beneath it. At last. Micha seized it and flipped open its covers to reveal page after page of dense handwritten text. The first entry was dated over a year ago: *Edward shot himself today*. God help him, Micha was reading the private thoughts of a man so utterly naive it had not even occurred to him to hide his fucking journal.

He glanced over his shoulder towards the partially open door. He didn't have time to read even a fraction of these words. He fanned the pages, letting phrases and paragraphs jump at him at random.

Why? Why would he do it? A newly married man with everything to live for. I never knew him to be unhappy, at least no more than anyone else. Why? The question is relentless, like a red hot iron held to my flesh. Why? I pray for peace, not answers. I find neither.

Lies attract lies like flies to a carcass. How many must I tell? Surely the Lord does not count untruths, like a miser hoarding gold. And the marquess is right. It is my duty. It is all he has ever demanded of me. For my brothers' sake.

It soothes my soul to be back in Nettlefield.

His Lordship has fallen ill with apoplexy. He does not wish to see me.

This was no use. Micha turned to the final entries.

I think him beautiful . . . Entranced . . . No sense of a higher self . . . But he is like some magnificent, ruined thing . . . How can I repent that which I know to be wrong? . . . I am come to Carthage burning, burning . . . I cannot see the harm . . . It bewilders and bewitches me . . . Unlawful desire . . . An act that debases another.

The journal slipped from between his fingers and landed heavily on the floor. And, after a moment, Micha followed it down, crumpling into a heap at the side of the bed.

Well. He had found what he had sought.

Beautiful. Entranced. Magnificent, ruined thing.

It was not what he was expecting. But perhaps it should have been. He knew what the world wanted from him. He knew what he was good for. He thought he knew shame, too, but this was its own unique and awful mortification. Reflected in another's eyes, held inescapably in the bondage of another's words: beautiful, ruined. Everything he held inside—and tried to hide—as visible as scars. As though he lay on a dissection table, his soul pinned open, for any to see.

I want nothing from you.

Liar. Fucking liar.

Unlawful desire. An act that debases.

Micha covered his face with his hands and gave a sobbing laugh that hurt the back of his throat. He tried to gulp back further sounds lest he betray his presence, but, having started laughing, he found himself unable to stop. He locked his hands over his mouth, but that made no difference either. The strange laughter bubbled out of him like vomit. Being right had never tasted quite so bitter.

Still, what did it matter? What did it matter, really? Thomas offered more than most of his clients and treated him far better. And when he was done, Micha would be no worse off than he had been before. He had been a fool to believe he could leave anything behind. He was who he was. He did what he did. And Thomas was no different, no better or worse, than the rest of the world.

He told himself this was preferable. It was a transaction he understood. It was less challenging to his expectations than Thomas's behaviour so far. Much easier to go on thinking as he had always thought, believing as he had always believed, than change. Thomas had been an intriguingly shaped puzzle piece with nowhere to fit. But now he had his place: 660.

Micha dashed the stinging moisture from his eyes with the back of his hand. Just in time because, at that moment, the door was pushed open. He froze, but it was not, in fact, Thomas.

"What are you doing in here?" asked Mrs. Clark sharply.

"N-nothing."

"This is Mr. Mandeville's room."

He bared his teeth in something not very like a smile. "I know. What are you going to do? Tell him?"

"Are you going through his things?" He saw the flash of frustration in her eyes.

"And if I am?"

Her hands curled into fists, only partially hidden in the folds of her dress. "Get out. You have no right."

Slowly, he climbed to his feet. He picked up the journal and put it back where he had found it before laying the Bible on top of it with a theatrical flourish.

"It's been rather interesting." He strolled across the room.

Mrs. Clark said nothing, merely waited for him in the doorway, a prim shadow in her black dress.

"Yes," he went on. "Turns out, he's not all that taken with the idea of fucking you." Again, he was met only with silence. He slid his body past hers, rustling the folds of her gown, pausing for a moment to look down into her cold, pale face. "He's more taken with the idea of fucking me."

Their eyes locked. Her expression reflected neither surprise nor censure.

"Well," she murmured, "there's no accounting for taste."

Volume II

Nettlefield

22nd August 1854

My dear Topper,

I hear tell you are bound for Sevastopol, which I understand gets ferociously cold in winter so I enclose with this letter some socks. Well, a sock. More of a tube really, as I had no idea how to make the heel. But it is in a very manly shade of lavender and I hope you can find a use for it. Now I consider the artefact in question, it crosses my mind I may be some kind of hitherto unrecognised genius for it occurs to me that it could provide valuable insulation for a particular and intimate region. I think I shall call it the Gentleman's Muff, it will come in a range of tasteful colours to suit all tastes and inclinations, and perhaps I shall not have to marry an heiress after all.

The Season has come to its close and I am at last released from social bondage to be myself again. I think I may seize my freedom and escape to Cambridge to see our brother. I have barely spoken to him since the Regatta, which I think he only attended to please me in the first place, and I am half-convinced he has not left a library in the last year. He grows paler than a ghost, though he does not seem discontent. But then, he never does, does he? I cannot tell if that is his curse or his blessing, while we rail foolishly and flutter our wings like sparrows on birdlime.

The marquess, as usual, is not best pleased with me, for I made something of a spectacle of myself at Lady Cavendish's fancy dress ball and some of the details got into the scandal rags and, really, far too much has been made of the matter. It could have happened to anyone. You see, our father made the profound strategic error of leaving the matter of my attire in my own hands, which was such an unprecedented degree of liberty that it quite went to my head and, well, the long and the short of it is, that I resolved to attend dressed as a crocodile. A feat that required an extraordinary unification 'twixt tailoring and engineering. History in the making, old boy, history in the making. And, honestly, it gave me more to think about than the rest of the Season taken end to end. Since His Lordship does not permit me to distract myself with painting, I confess I sometimes fear some kind of private, soul-deep atrophy but my dear crocodile awakened me like Galatea. I had such tremendous fun. I only wish you could have been there.

The ball was much as any other. They all said I was terribly original, but with that edge of censure in their voices. The marquess was furious, naturally, but there was nothing he could do about it, not unless he wanted to shout between my teeth. It made me wish I could wear a crocodile suit every day. Eventually, he calmed down sufficiently to introduce me to some nabob's daughter which was, of course, the whole point of the evening. It is quite abominable of me, but

I cannot recall her name, only that she was wearing a vast, pink concoction, with more tiers than our hostess's chandeliers and as frighteningly wobblesome as a poorly prepared blancmange. The newspapers later reported that it had no fewer than, oh I don't know, eighty-seven thousand real diamonds sewn into it. Completely lost for what to say to her other than "argh my eyes, my poor eyes," I asked about her costume. She suggested I guess and, not wanting to respond with "you have come dressed as a monstrosity," I went with Marie Antoinette, which turned out not to be too far wrong, as she explained she was (wait for it, old boy) a shepherdess. I then enquired if she herded golden fleece, a remark which endeared me to neither our father nor hers. At this point, there was little left for our families to do but glare at each other in silence. Given my crocodile (oh brave crocodile, crocodile the saviour) I was in no position to ask her to dance but, desperate for any escape route, I offered to bring her some lemonade.

This would, I am sure, have been terribly gallant of me but, in the awkwardness, I had quite forgotten my tail. It had been quite the trickiest part of the whole operation, after the mouth, and I had been forced to rely on the reinforcement provided by a light steel girder. I had the misfortune to catch the young lady shepherdess behind the knees and she had the misfortune to topple into the champagne fountain. Of course, being a gentlemanly crocodile, I tried to go to her aid, but crocodiles do not flourish upon highly polished marble floors, so I went in also, taking with me two footmen and a dowager.

You see. It is as I said: it could have happened to anyone.

I am, once again, unworthy of the Montrose name, a blot on the escutcheon, a worthless son and a less than worthless heir. But Cambridge will hold out her golden arms and welcome me. And I will paint, I will paint until my heart is the blank canvas. Come home soon, George, come home safely. I miss you, and the world is waiting. As is your pretty Rosa with her summer golden hair. Do not, please do not, you absolutely must not, fall upon some distant battlefield to sate our father's damnable pride. Live, dear brother, and I will too. We will both learn to live.

I remain your loving brother,

E.

Chapter 8

It took them two days, at an easy pace and stopping often to change horses, to travel from London to Oxfordshire. Micha had not known the luxury of a private carriage since his time with Isidore, but his strength was not what it had been and he spent most of the journey sleeping fitfully. Sometimes he would rouse to find himself braced against Thomas, tucked against his arm, or—on one particularly unfortunate occasion—half in his lap, while one of Thomas's pale gentleman's hands had moved almost absently through Micha's tousled hair.

Micha had seen very little of Thomas in the handful of days preceding their journey. Not enough to miss him—because why would he?—but enough to feel his absence, in spite of what he had read in the journal. And that made no sense at all. Micha half-suspected Thomas had to be a servant of the devil, rather than the Lord, since knowing what he did of Thomas's intentions and distinctly profane desires had made less of a difference than Micha would have hoped. Some part of him still wanted to respond to Thomas's warmth, the mischief in his smile, the concern in his voice. In short, to the lies. But then, who knew better than an opium addict just how worthless truth could be?

Maintaining his supply of laudanum had, in fact, been Micha's dominating concern. There would likely be a druggist in, or near to, Nettlefield, but getting through the journey was a problem in and of itself. He used laudanum more than he had ever smoked opium, but previously his intake had always been controlled by his finances. Now, tucked safely away inside his coat was more money than he had ever held before in his life. The idea of using it nauseated him, but the idea of going without laudanum hurt him still more. It was no longer even a matter of pleasure. He was merely staving off the misery of going without. But, like so many other things, it mattered little. Micha had no reason to think life would be any better without laudanum than with it. And, if nothing else, it deadened pain and kept the tigers of memory at bay. For travelling made him think too easily of Isidore. How wide the world had seemed at Isidore's side. And now its horizon was Micha's own flesh. He dosed himself heavily each morning and let the two days slip away in a dull haze of drifting thoughts and bodily weakness.

"Micha?" Thomas's voice stirred him at last.

"Mm?"

"We're here."

"Oh. Right. Right." Micha shook himself and tried to ease the stiffness from his limbs as the carriage door was opened by the coachman. Darkness washed in from outside, and silence as deep and thick as a blanket.

Shaking off Thomas's assisting hand, Micha stepped down, the crunch of his boots on gravel resounding in his ears. Shadowy gardens lay all round him and, in the distance, the inky silhouette of a church tower. He could just about make out the curve of a hill, leading into a speckle of golden light from the village below.

Thomas had disembarked behind him and was giving quiet instructions for the unloading of their meagre luggage. Micha, meanwhile, turned a slow circle. Thomas's home, what little he could see of it, suggested Georgian symmetry, all canted bay windows and gabled parapets. It felt suddenly quite impossible that he was here.

He drew in a breath of the crisp, cold air, and it felt like the first breath he had ever taken. His heart was thudding hard, as if the cage of his chest had expanded to let it truly beat. He took a few steps into the darkness, and it embraced him like silk. His soul expanded into the vast and beautiful emptiness of the universe like it did after a pipe of opium, but here there were no urban geometries to shape and limit him. He tipped back his head to see a sky infinitely black and full of stars. Silver burned his eyes like tears.

He lost track of how long he stood there.

Then came a light touch on his arm, just below his elbow.

"Micha? Would you like to come inside?" In this softer, wider, more lovely world, Thomas's voice was honey-sweet.

"Look at the sky."

"Pardon? Oh . . . er. The sky?" Thomas, obliging as ever, glanced up.

"The stars look like someone spilled them."

"I have never stopped to think about it but—yes, yes they do."

"I had forgotten there existed so many."

There was a line of broken heat running the line of Micha's body where the edges of Thomas met the edges of him.

"There is a generosity to it, isn't there?" offered Thomas, finally.

"Or carelessness."

"I know very little about beauty, Micha, but I think to be heedless is not necessarily to be careless. It seems, I don't know, free somehow."

Micha extended his arm, his gaze following his finger into the sky. "They look so close. As if I could reach them if I only stretched a little further."

Thomas's fingers closed lightly around Micha's wrist and turned his palm upwards. "There. Now it looks as if you hold them."

The starlight spilled over his hand and down his wrist like pure, bright water. Unexpectedly, Micha shuddered. He dropped his arm, breaking the contact, and Thomas did nothing to prolong it. "That constellation"—he gestured half-heartedly—"the one right above us, is called Cygnus."

"I can't see anything that looks much like a swan."

Micha traced the lines between the stars. "There . . . those are the wings, see, outstretched, and there's the neck."

Thomas tilted his head. "If you say so."

It should have been enough. But Thomas made no further move to touch him.

"Portly Man with a Cigar," he said, instead.

Which was really not what Micha had expected. "Uh?"

Thomas's smile was close now, close enough to kiss. He pointed. "There, look. Those three bright stars close together. And there's the man, holding the cigar."

"That's the Warrior, you stupid man. Those three stars are Orion's Belt."

Thomas shook his head. "I don't see it."

"Then take it up with Ptolemy."

For a little while, they said nothing more. Micha edged a step closer. Thomas's head turned ever so slightly, his breath cresting, warm and sinuous, against Micha's lips. Micha's pulse was fluttering as frantically as the wings of a captive lark. He felt confused and sick and wanting all at once. *Just do it,* he thought. *Get it over with. While it may not feel like too great a debasement. While I am so close to something like happiness.* But Thomas did not respond. His attention was fixed on the heavens.

"The bright star in Cygnus," said Micha, finally, desperately, "that's Bessel's Star. It's actually two stars close together, the primary star and its companion, but when we look at it from here, we only see one."

"What a lot of things you know."

The admiration in Thomas's voice seemed genuine, and it threw Micha into confusion and resentment. Why did it matter what he knew or didn't know—it made no difference to what Thomas wanted. "I don't really. I just picked it up from Isidore. He told me that Bessel's Star is ten and a bit light-years away from us—they measured it using parallax or something, but I have no idea what that actually is—which means we're looking at something out of time."

"What do you mean?"

"Well, what we see is not what's there. It's what was there ten years ago. It could be changed or gone or anything."

"How very remarkable."

Again, that burgeoning sense of wonder, while Micha had only scorn to cast into the dark. "Remarkable? Really? We could be standing here, admiring the beauty of a dead thing."

Thomas was silent for a moment, and then he offered hesitantly, "It seems to me rather fitting that beauty transcends time and that lost things still have the power to touch us. Besides, there is nothing to say that Bessel's Star is lost at all. Perhaps it shines on, with its companion at its side."

Micha needed laudanum. The conversation was scraping him raw. "You are so fucking sentimental," he choked out.

"You just said I was deeply unromantic."

"Well, if a star can be alive and dead, I'm sure you can be both unromantic and sentimental."

Thomas laughed. "Come, you must be cold standing out here, and it's been a long journey. Shall we to bed?"

That, at least, dispelled the uncertainty of the moment. Micha stepped back abruptly. Starlit delusions faded rapidly in the harsh glare of truth. What choice did he have? "Yes. Yes, all right then."

He followed Thomas inside, trying not to fidget restlessly as the hall lights were lit. The interior of the house seemed as effortlessly, comfortably charming as its exterior. The generous golden glow from the lamps illuminated the graceful curve of a broad Georgian staircase and flickered upon rich wood-panelled walls. A clearly adoring housekeeper had left them a cold supper of meats, bread, and cheeses.

Thomas ate with obvious relish, but Micha had utterly lost his appetite. He was irritated with himself—he was, after all, a hardened street doxy, not a virgin sacrifice. And Thomas was young and moderately attractive and showed no signs of harbouring any particularly challenging perversions. Although Philip used to say it was always the quiet ones, so who knew what Thomas might want to do, or have done to him. Micha shuddered, in spite of himself, and Thomas asked if he felt quite well.

"I'm fine," he answered, with what he hoped was a placid and inviting smile, though it felt stretched and peculiar on his lips.

"Well," drawled Micha, "what happened to your sense of romance? Would you rather they called it 'the one with the pointy downwards bit and the two pointy sideways bits'?"

He caught the glimmer of Thomas's smile in the darkness. "I fear I'm a poor stargazer. Nobody has ever named them for me before."

"Isidore knew them all." From nowhere, a piece of memory: lying with his head against Isidore's shoulder on one of Oxford's glass-smooth lawns, gold and silver spun into a tapestry of light for their pleasure. Micha swallowed. "And that one . . . the long one with the square tip, that one is Draco."

"That is not, by any means, a dragon. It's a wiggly line with a dot on the end. If anything, it is a kite."

"For fuck's sake, that's its tail. And that's the curve of its neck. Are you laughing at me?"

"I am certainly not laughing at you. I think it's lovely that you know these things, and I'm touched you would share them with me."

"Oh shut up. That one there, with the three lines radiating outwards from the square, that's the Bowl of Peonies."

"What?"

"And that one, just next to it, with the three small stars and the cluster, is known as the Cheese Board and Fish Knife."

"Now you're just making it up."

"Yes."

Thomas's laughter rang out, as clear and joyous as bells on a summer morning. "You wretch."

And, for a moment, Micha forgot to care that Thomas had only brought him here to fuck him. He almost wanted him to do it, here and now, amid the silence and the beauty. It seemed almost like a price worth paying. Thomas's body would cover him like moonlight and Micha would live amongst the stars, in the distant depths of the sky, far away from everything below. He turned, quite deliberately, pressing himself to Thomas, and the line of heat became a lake of fire.

He realised, then, that it was not the use of his body that troubled him. He could have borne to be fucked by Thomas, as he had borne so many others. It was everything else. Fingers in his hair. A hand in his hand. Thomas laughing. The way he had almost taken a strike from his brother, not in weakness, but in strength. It was flaying Micha like a sandstorm. He was bleeding from a thousand cuts of kindness.

Laudanum would dull the pain. Perhaps Thomas would give Micha some moments alone that would allow him to take some.

Finally, eventually, Thomas led him upstairs. "I was going to put you in the front guest room. I'm afraid it's not the largest, or the grandest."

"Whatever you want," said Micha, listlessly.

"But it's one of my favourite rooms in the house—it catches the light quite beautifully in the mornings. Edward used to work in there sometimes. I'm afraid his paintings are still on the walls. They can be a little startling, I'm told, but I can have them removed if they trouble you."

"I don't think I'll be looking at the fucking walls," snapped Micha, his nerve breaking completely.

Thomas gave him an odd look and said nothing more until they came to a door at the end of a corridor. Thomas handed Micha the lamp and pushed it open. The room inside was neat and well kept. The case containing Micha's meagre possessions—most of which Thomas had purchased for his comfort—had already been placed by the bed.

Fuck, thought Micha, his gaze locked on the floor, I'm a fucking kept man.

"I hope it goes without saying that my home is your home," Thomas went on. "Do whatever makes you most comfortable."

Micha put the lamp down on the dresser. He peeled off his coat and waistcoat, let them fall to the floor, and pulled his shirt over his head. Though better than it had been, his body was still—in his estimation—far from lovely, but if Thomas wanted it, he could have it. He had, after all, paid for it.

"Oh." Thomas's eyes were wide in the dim light. "That is more comfortable than I anticipated. I shall leave you to rest."

And, to Micha's boundless surprise, he did.

What the fuck had just happened? Had the sight of him killed Thomas's ardour? Except Thomas had tended him through sickness, so he must have known what he was getting. Feeling suddenly absurdly naked, Micha put his shirt back on. Then he took some laudanum. And that helped. He sat on the edge of the bed, which was covered by a quilted coverlet that looked handmade, and he floated peacefully through nothingness.

If not tonight, tomorrow. Thomas could fuck him tomorrow. Or the next day. Whenever. However.

After a minute or so, or perhaps more than that, Micha stood, picked up the lamp again, and directed its light towards the walls, which were, indeed, hung with paintings—heavy oils, the colours as rich and vivid as stained glass, though shot through always with the suggestion of shadow. They were all abstract, depicting a mood or a sense of place rather than any particular image, but, in Micha's drugged state, they seemed to drag him into their depths. He thought he saw lone figures, devoured by darkness, lost among landscapes of light and colour, bars and chains and the bodies of men, intertwined in acts of pain and passion. He looked and tried not to look, and a terrible despair, painted jewel-bright, conquered even the laudanum.

He took more.

Mostly dressed, and still in his boots, he rolled on top of the bedcovers. Colours spun themselves into cages. Scarlet and violet and green, twisting like serpents behind his eyelids and, when he opened his eyes, twirling and flickering over the walls, as though they had slipped from the paintings to undulate among the shadows.

But, at last, he slept. And it was empty, deep, and dreamless.

Chapter 9

Parish life reclaimed Thomas as though he had never been away and kept him too busy to see much of Micha, who lived in his house so quietly he might as well have been a ghost. Thomas almost suspected his guest was avoiding him, but that would be absurd. What reason would he have to do that? And Micha had seemed to respond positively to Nettlefield, at least initially. His face, turned to the star-filled sky, had been about as content as Thomas had ever seen it, and so beautiful, starkly silvered like some pagan etching, that Thomas had barely dared to gaze upon him. It had been an experience unlike any Thomas had ever known, to stand in the darkness with a man like Micha and speak of the stars. It had made him as dizzy as wine, as though some distant, silent part of him had learned, entirely unexpectedly, how to sing. Through Micha's eyes, he saw a different world, one filled with beauties he would never have imagined, let alone noticed. It felt hedonistic, almost wicked, to be so captivated by stars, by falling leaves, by the changing landscape of the sky, as though he moved through not the everyday places he thought he knew so well but some enchanted garden, made for him by Micha, like a secret they shared.

Micha had spoken then with such remarkable candour that Thomas had half-believed he might truly have won his trust, if not his liking. A hope proven to be entirely unfounded the moment they had entered the house. Micha had been, frankly, strange. Defiant and uncertain at the same time, a question and a challenge in his eyes that Thomas had been unable to answer. Perhaps it was simply being in an unfamiliar place. Perhaps he regretted leaving London. Thomas had no way of knowing, and, in truth, it was a baser matter that preoccupied his thoughts.

He had been too startled to react when Micha had carelessly shed his clothes on the night of their arrival. But afterwards, oh afterwards, the sight had haunted him, burned into his eyes like Icarus's final vision of the sun. And how could he feel anything but shame because of it? Nothing could be more natural than a man naked with another man. He had seen the unclothed bodies of his compatriots often enough at university, and anything he might have felt then, he had lacked a framework to understand and had, therefore, dismissed.

For that matter, he had seen Micha's body before, when he had cared for him. But this had been different, utterly different. An insensible form was mere clay. Micha, standing there stripped to the waist, his eyes burning in the darkness, like some fallen angel, had been fire given shape. A masterwork, carved by an artist's loving and particular hand. And, where Thomas's desire had previously been of an abstract sort—a deep burning, devoid of focus—now images held him like inescapable vines. The shadowed column of Micha's throat, rough with stubble. The deep slashes of his collarbones. The slope of his shoulders, which seemed made to fit the clasp of hands. The dark hair that dusted his torso. A man's body undeniably, hard planes and sharp angles, the promise of strength and savagery, and still no check to Thomas's wanting. He wanted to . . . touch. With his fingertips and his mouth. With his skin to Micha's skin, as though the whole of him could become an extension of his yearnings, an act of worship.

It horrified him that something Micha had done so casually, so innocently, had been twisted by the deep corruption of Thomas's nature into something carnal. Thomas prayed that night, and the nights that followed, wordless and helpless, just a single idea: *Make me good, make me good, make me good. For Micha's sake.*

A few days later, he arrived home from a visit to a sick parishioner to find Micha curled up on the window seat in the garden room. Despite the hour, he was fast asleep in a pool of autumn sunlight, his cheek cradled against his hand and his hair falling wildly across his brow. He looked absurdly young. Even a little fragile, with his naked, tender mouth softened in sleep. Pushing aside such thoughts, Thomas murmured his name softly and, when Micha did not rouse, shook him until, at last, he stirred.

He woke with a start, his eyes blurs of shadow beneath his lashes, his lips forming their customary frown. "Wh-what? What the fuck?"

"Do you often sleep through the day?"

"In case you've forgotten"—Micha's voice was slurred to match his gaze—"I was ill. I nearly died."

Thomas tried to cover his confusion. Micha had complained so bitterly when he had been bedbound in London, it seemed actively perverse that he would idle away his time now that he was in somewhat better health. In truth, Thomas would have been happy for Micha to do anything he wanted, but he had not thought Micha the sort of man to enjoy indolence. Perhaps he was less well than Thomas had thought. He certainly looked a little strange, pale and blank-eyed. "Would you not," he suggested, "prefer to be doing something to help you regain your strength?"

Micha's brows arched lazily upwards. "Why? Bored of me already? If you want me gone, just say."

Thomas sighed and took a seat on a nearby chair. It had sometimes crossed his mind these past nights, when his body had felt like a crucible, heated hellfire-hot with desire and shame, that it would be easier for him if Micha was far away. But he would not allow his weakness to hurt the object of it. And, besides, there was yet another part of him that dreaded the day of Micha's leaving, when the world would turn back to its older, greyer self and there would be nothing left but the interminable march of his duties. "You know I don't want that. You may stay with me as long as you wish. I'm very glad to have you here."

"Oh are you?" said Micha, with another of his strange looks. "I wish you'd get on with it, then. The waiting fucking kills me."

Thomas was starting to feel as though he was an inadvertent participant in a different conversation, though its meaning entirely eluded him. "Pardon? What are you waiting for? There's no need for you to wait."

Micha laughed harshly. "Down to me, is it? You're one of those. Fine, if you want me to have the illusion of choice, then you can wait. I'm not in the mood right now."

Thomas put a hand to Micha's brow, only to have it knocked roughly away.

"What the fuck are you doing?"

"I thought you might be feverish. You do feel slightly clammy." Thomas leaned forward and peered into Micha's face. "Your eyes look very strange."

Micha turned his head away. "I'm fine, Mother Goose."

"As you wish." Thomas made a gesture of surrender. "But you need occupation, I think, to engage your mind and your body."

"I've had occupations. I didn't enjoy them much."

"Micha, there must be something you do enjoy."

"I told you, no. I have no skills, no talents, no accomplishments."

Micha was clearly in one of his darker humours, sour and obstinate, his capacity for cruelty turned inwards, upon himself. He reminded Thomas of a lion with a thorn in its paw, striking out at others in its own pain, incapable of alleviating its own distress. He did not like to bear the brunt of Micha's bitterness, but the wounds it left upon him were shallow enough, and he would willingly have endured worse to protect the other man from the claws of all that self-directed hate. He risked a smile and a mischievous look. "Accomplishments? Well now, I should like to see you try your hand at needlework."

Some of the bleakness faded from Micha's face, and he gave an amused splutter. "Fuck you."

Thomas smiled at him, unrepentantly. "Pianoforte?"

"Shut up."

Sensing victory, Thomas grew solemn again. He reached across the space between them, his hand pressing close to Micha's, though he did not dare to touch him. "Please, Micha. Before you fell upon hard times, there must have been something that gave you pleasure?"

"Oh there was." He was sneering again. "But it's not easy to find, believe me."

"Something else then? Anything."

Micha huffed out an exasperated breath. "I used to sketch a little, all right? Happy now?"

Thomas was, as it happened, delighted, but, knowing Micha was unlikely to react well to it, he asked with a tolerable display of indifference, "What did you sketch?"

The words came haltingly, as though it was a confession wrung from deep inside Micha's heart. "People . . . a person. Sometimes architecture. When we were in Italy. Landscapes, maybe."

Thomas was smiling again, unable to help himself. And, to his surprise, Micha's lips twitched, just a little in return. "I shall have some supplies sent from London at once."

Micha immediately shook his head. "Don't bother. I wasn't very good."

"What does that matter, if you enjoyed doing it?"

"But what's the point?"

And, thus, it seemed they were back to stalemate. Micha rested his head against the window, his gaze sweeping the shadow-smothered gardens as restlessly and apathetically as a lighthouse illuminating only empty seas.

"Perhaps," tried Thomas, "I shall send for some materials anyway. When they are here you may feel moved to use them?"

"Do what the fuck you like," returned Micha, sleepily.

Thomas watched him, feeling like a fly crawling over glass, helpless and ignorant. Whatever ailed him, a few days in the country had not been enough to ease it.

"You know"—Thomas burst suddenly, and a little desperately, into speech again—"I think I might have some of Edward's things somewhere. I'm sure I saw some paints and a sketchbook, if I haven't thrown them away."

Micha cast him an indifferent glance. "You want me to use your dead brother's stuff?"

"Well." Thomas smiled faintly. "He is in no position to use it."

There was a long silence. Micha's hand twitched with what was surely an idle reflex, the tip of his little finger inadvertently brushing the edge of Thomas's, where it still rested close by. The gentle, careless pressure of his nail sent a silver-cold shiver running all the way to Thomas's wrist. And suddenly he felt every breath he took as it moved between his lips.

"Your brother was . . ." said Micha, eventually, ". . . quite talented. His pictures give me nightmares."

"Do they really? I can have them moved."

"No, don't." Micha shook his head. "I like them."

Thomas tried to laugh, but it came out thin and shaky. A tiny patch of skin, never before heeded, had become a pinhead upon which hosts of angels danced. "That seems a rather peculiar sentiment."

Micha's eyes slid away from Thomas's and, a second after, his hand did as well, leaving Thomas wildly, impossibly bereft. "I feel like they're saying something I understand, even if it isn't something I like hearing."

Thomas was quietly in pieces. He grasped for words, like a miser after banknotes scattering upon a breeze. "Edward was the only one of us with any great talent." He knew he was babbling and yet was utterly unable to control himself. "Though George did rather well in the army, we are told. Since he rarely speaks of it, however, I do not think it is a talent he is happy to own. And I'm afraid I know nothing of art at all. I always thought Edward's paintings were rather beautiful. The colours, perhaps? But even if they weren't, I would want to have them anyway.

Death is very . . . devouring. It takes so much. And all you have left to show for a life is a small pile of things."

"Your funeral sermons," drawled Micha, "must bring the house down, Father."

Micha's words spun Thomas from one state of agitation to quite another. He remembered the lion and tried to compose himself, but this wound was not glancing, and he flinched visibly, pulling away from Micha as though he had, indeed, been struck. Once again, with heedless thoughts and a lack of faith, Thomas had betrayed himself—revealed all the messy doubts and fears that should have had no place in the heart of a priest and yet grief had planted there, a bloody-fanged harvest. "I . . . I speak of those who are left, not those who have departed."

"Look, I'm sorry," Micha blurted out. "I didn't mean to say that. It was cruel."

"No, it was fair." Thomas rose, feeling older than his years and unspeakably weary. His hand was ordinary again, flesh and blood and bone, without grace or magic. "Let me see if I can find those things for you."

As he opened the door, Micha called out his name. Thomas stopped, half-turning back. "What is it?"

Micha just looked at him.

"Is something troubling you?"

Micha shook his head. "It doesn't matter. Nothing."

And Thomas had no wish, that night, to press him.

He owned few enough of Edward's possessions. Just some paintings and whatever his brother had left at the rectory on his occasional visits. Most of that had been bundled away and disposed of, but, eventually, after some diligent searching through cupboards and desks and dressers, Thomas managed to unearth an untouched sketchbook, some pencils, brushes, and a few slightly sorry-looking tubes of watercolour paints. The oils, however, were quite beyond rescue. They had all congealed into muddy brown paste and flaking rust.

Thomas left his offerings out for Micha, but he did not expect he would use them. Miracles, after all, belonged in the Bible.

However, when he came home the next day, he found Micha tucked into the window seat with the sketchbook open on his knees, a paintbrush moving rapidly over the paper. He looked better, too, less dreamy and distracted.

"I'm terrible," Micha said, by way of greeting. "Truly terrible."

"I'm sure that's not true." Thomas stepped quietly across the room. "May I see?"

"Why not?" Micha shrugged and turned the page to face Thomas.

"It's . . . um . . . it's . . . what is it?"

"It's the gardens, what the fuck do you think?"

"Oh, yes, I . . . um . . . see that now. I think the apocalyptic vortex in the sky rather confused me."

"That's the sunset."

"And the . . . camel?"

"That's a duck."

"Of course it's a duck. I'm so sorry. I did warn you I had no understanding of art."

Micha sighed. "No, no, it's me. I said I was terrible."

He seemed resigned, rather than bitter, but nevertheless Thomas rushed to reassure him. "Please don't think that. I'm sure there's a great deal of merit to be found here." He quickly scanned the image, looking for something. "This firepit, for example, is beautifully detailed."

"That's the flower bed. Fucking hell." Micha snatched the book back, ripped off the top page, and scrumpled it into a ball. "I told you." He glared accusingly at Thomas. "No skills, no talents, no nothing."

Thomas went to pull over a chair, hesitated, and then perched instead on the other side of the window seat. Micha shifted slightly to accommodate him, tucking his feet out of the way, the movement so casually and instinctively intimate that it flustered Thomas. The window framed them like a mirror, but they could not have looked less like reflections: Micha, sprawled but graceful, Thomas, prim and neat, each of them close enough to touch the other, though neither did. "I thought you were painting because you enjoyed it, not because you wanted to be Botticelli."

"Well, I'd like the option" came the sulky reply.

Thomas reached out, his hand closing around Micha's clenched fist until it relaxed beneath his fingers, and he was able to tug the paper free. "Perhaps, we are simply looking at it wrongly. It is, after all, a startlingly challenging and original piece of work."

Micha's lips twisted reluctantly in something like a smile. "Startlingly bad, you mean."

"As a depiction of the rectory gardens, I will agree, it leaves something to be desired. But as a picture of a camel emerging from a wound in the sky, it's quite magnificent."

"Oh fuck off." But now there was no concealing the amused glitter of Micha's eyes. "I suppose I should name it something terribly queer that has nothing to do with the picture, like . . . *Glass Carrot & Moonlight*."

"It's perfect. You may inspire a movement. Now, let me preserve this masterpiece."

"As you will." Indifferent as ever, Micha flung the sketchbook between them.

Thomas caught for it clumsily, and the pages fanned open to reveal the pencil lines of an earlier sketch. "You drew something else?"

"It's nothing," said Micha sharply. "It's not finished. Leave it alone. I said—oh fuck."

"Oh my. Micha."

Micha was scarlet. "Seriously, give it back."

"Is this—"

"You were the only model I had. Now give it back."

"I don't know what to say."

"You don't say anything, and you give it back."

Thomas looked up with a shy smile. "I don't really look like this, do I?"

"Not remotely. We've already established I'm very bad at drawing."

"You're bad at watercolour painting. You're not bad at drawing. But we must get you a proper subject."

"You'll do for now." Micha gestured dismissively. "As it happens, you spend most of your time with your chin in your hand, staring at nothing, so you're easy to do."

Thomas glanced again at Micha's drawing. It was faintly sketched and obviously incomplete, but, sure enough, there was the outline of a man sitting with his chin in his hand, his expression at once intense and abstracted. He was not handsome, for his features were too angular for beauty, but the artist had been generous, catching the intelligence of his eyes and the paradox of a mouth at once whimsical and stern. "I'll have you know that I am not staring at nothing, I am thinking deep thoughts about life and God and faith. And things."

And so Micha was laughing, truly laughing, as he reached over to reclaim his sketchbook.

Chapter 10

Micha woke to a golden haze, rolled over, and reached for his bottle of laudanum. It would send him, if not back to sleep, at least into a state that was almost the same. The bottle felt slick and familiar beneath his fingers, but he hesitated, wanting out of the habit of wanting but also not wanting, which was an entirely new sensation. It was not, however, any sort of choice. He mixed up the laudanum and took enough to make the wanting fade, though it never really stopped.

He lay there for a while, feeling nothing but a painless, thoughtless calm, not quite floating, not quite dreaming, just cushioned by a softer world. It was tempting to take more, make the world softer still and fall into it, like angel feathers. But Thomas kept scratching at the edges of his peace.

You should do something, Micha. You need occupation, Micha.

Damn Thomas. Damn him.

And Micha didn't need anything. Well. Nearly anything. The bottle slid from his slackened grasp and rolled across the covers.

Would nothing rid him of this turbulent priest?

Finally, he crawled out of bed, tugged on a dressing gown, and staggered across the room. The light came gentled through the window and embraced him, stroking warm fingers over his face and throat. The world outside was deeply green, tipped with scarlet and yellow, curled around the blue-grey horizon.

Perhaps . . . perhaps he would go out. Fade into a fall of autumn leaves.

Or he could take that damn sketchbook. Try to draw the world as it was, rather than drug-fuelled phantasms of what it could be. Except he preferred the latter. At least there was a place for him in it.

Half an hour later, dressed, with the sketchbook (the damn sketchbook) under his arm, Micha was standing at the edge of the rectory gardens, wondering where to go and feeling like a man at the edge of a precipice, though this part of England rolled away smoothly in all directions, as serene as the surface of a lake. After a moment, he turned away from the village and began to walk. His steps were slow, and he rested often, but, for once, it did not trouble him. The world kept pace with him, speckling him with slow-dropping sunlight and sending little eddies of red-edged leaves to dance around his feet as he walked.

He came to a meadow, mingled with wildflowers, and sat awhile upon a stile to sketch. It turned out rather poorly. He had misjudged the perspective, and the whole thing ended up looking like a strange, multicoloured sandwich. So, he flipped the page and worked a little on his drawing of Thomas, deepening the eyes, adding detail to those expressive, perfect hands. How would they feel when they took possession of Micha's body? Would his touch be gentle? He could not easily imagine violence from such smooth palms or cruelty from such tender fingers. But perhaps he was only deceiving himself. Sex was power, desire was shame, and Isidore had been the illusion all along. Though his lips faintly remembered Isidore's kisses—and perhaps, somewhere beneath the noise of other hands, his body still bore the imprint of his touches—such things were for another time, another world.

Micha put his pencil away and closed the book. He had lost interest in drawing. He climbed down into the meadow and kept walking. The tall grasses bowed like mocking courtiers as he passed through them. Then came another stile, another meadow, this one studded with bloodred and tiger-black butterflies that flickered from flower to flower like pieces of flame. He was the serpent in paradise, and the loveliness sliced his heart to ribbons.

A small stream cut a swathe of silver through the green, here and there overhung by the branches of a weeping willow, spun Rumpelstiltskin-gold by the season. Two ducks paddled along placidly, the undersides of their wings flashing emerald. It was a scene far beyond Micha's paltry watercolours. The world had decked itself in brilliant gemstone hues until it was almost luminous beneath the sun-bright sky.

Unable to bear the beauty of it, Micha was turning to leave when something enormous, red-brown and quite extraordinarily hairy, went barrelling past him, almost knocking him over. He had a jumbled impression of a joyously lolling tongue and streaming ears, and then came a voice, far too genteel for the words it uttered: "Ruff, get your arse back here, right now. I said 'Heel,' you mongrel son of a bitch."

Micha spun. Climbing over the stile was perhaps the tiniest woman he had ever seen.

Ruff, halfway across the meadow, hesitated. One paw still raised, he cast a guilty look over his shoulder. Then his nose twitched. Then he went rigid, even to the furthest flying feathers of his tail. His head snapped forward. In those fleeting seconds, he was quite the pointiest dog Micha had ever seen, a long, lean canine arrow.

"Oh no you don't," bellowed his owner. "Leave those fucking ducks alone."

Ruff was practically vibrating with indecision.

Then one of the ducks rose up from the water, its wings fluttering, bright as banners.

And Ruff was off.

"Fuck," said the woman, who had to be sixty if she was a day. "Fucking fuck."

"Er . . ." Despite his time on the streets of the London slums, Micha was still enough a child of the middle classes to instinctively respect his elders. Even if his elders were swearing like a sailor on shore leave. "Don't worry, I'll get him."

He put down the sketchbook and ran off after the dog. He thought he heard the woman call something after him, but he could hear very little beyond his own laboured breathing and pounding heart. Maybe Thomas had been right. He did need to do something to regain his strength, because this was ridiculous. A week-old kitten would have outpaced him, let alone a vigorous dog the size of a small elephant.

By the time Micha caught up with him, Ruff seemed more interested in chasing the ducks in circles than hurting them, and Micha joining the fray only contributed to the excitement. Such was Ruff's joy in this new and thoroughly entertaining game that all remonstrations went unheeded, and Micha was obliged to make a wild grab for Ruff's collar instead. His fingers closed around it, but he had considerably overestimated his own strength. Ruff—assuming this was all part of the fun—bounded onwards. Micha lost both his footing and his hold on the dog and went arse over apex, face-first into the stream.

The squelch of mud and the shock of cold water.

Coupled with mortified dignity and searing personal outrage.

Spluttering and swearing, Micha pushed himself to his hands and knees, just in time to see the ducks flapping lazily off into the sky. Ruff plonked himself down on the bank and tilted his head curiously at the foolish human who had unaccountably jumped straight into the water.

"You—" began Micha. But then his hands, inadequately braced on silt and pebbles, slid out from under him, and after a second or two of unseemly flailing, he went down again.

When he resurfaced, it was to the sound of someone laughing and an arm extended to help him.

"If you weren't old enough to be my grandmother," he grumbled, while the woman steadied him and got him back onto his feet, "you'd be in here with me."

"I tried to warn you." She dabbed at her eyes with her free hand. "Dear me, that was the funniest thing I've seen all year."

Micha scrambled onto dry land and collapsed onto the grass in a sodden heap. “Dull year?”

“Rather a sublime downfall, dear.”

“Nice to know I’m good for something.”

She eyed him, not unkindly. “You poor boy. You could catch your death of cold.”

Micha could already feel the chill seeping into his skin. “I’ll be all right.” It was typical really. This was what you got for trying to do a good deed. Thrown into streams and laughed at by old women with monstrous dogs. He crawled to his feet and lurched off to retrieve his sketchbook.

“That will never do,” said the old woman, keeping pace with him easily. “You’d better come along with me.”

“Is that so?”

“Yes.” She clicked her fingers, and the dratted animal—miraculously obedient all of a sudden—came bouncing over. “Come, Ruff, come.” He pushed his nose apologetically into Micha’s hand, nearly knocking him off his feet again. Micha glared at him and then, somehow, found himself scratching the dog behind his silly flyaway ears. Ruff made a deep happy noise and drooled on Micha’s boots.

“Is this some kind of convoluted kidnapping racket?” he asked. “Using your dog to lure helpless young men into streams and then you whisk them off to who knows where?”

The woman’s eyes, which were very blue, twinkled at him rather charmingly. “Do stop making a fuss and come along, dear.”

Micha gave an aggrieved sigh but, not knowing quite what else to do, he fell into step beside her. Finding his way back to the rectory in wet clothes was not a pleasant prospect, and besides, she was . . . she was . . . nice?

“It’s Michael,” he offered, “Michael Dashwood. But—” He had been about to say that most people called him Micha, but then he stopped. Micha was a name that had once glittered gold upon Isidore’s tongue, before it became a common thing, passed between the mouths of strangers, spit-tarnished. It had been many years since he had been merely Michael. His mother's son.

"Esther Dawes," she told him, with a smile. "And I believe you've already had the pleasure of Reginald Ruffington's acquaintance."

"I . . . what?"

Esther pointed at the dog, who was gambolling around them in wide, gleeful circles. "My late husband's notion. He had the oddest ideas about what was amusing."

"Oh, right, yes, because watching some poor fool fall face-first into a stream is the epitome of wit."

She chuckled. "We deserved each other."

There was a pause. Micha frowned, trying to remember how ordinary people spoke. How you conveyed the right sort of things, how you cared and showed you cared. What was too much and what was not enough. It had been so long since conversation had not been imposition or transaction. "Sorry for your loss and . . . all that."

"So am I, Michael, so am I."

"Uh, you want to tell me about him or something?"

"You're a sweet boy. But no. I wouldn't bore either of us with that."

"I wouldn't be bored," he lied. In that, at least, he was well practised. "And I'm twenty-three and a half, nearly twenty-four, you know, so you can stop calling me 'boy.'"

"My heavens. Twenty-three and a half? Ancient. Practically dead yourself."

"I should have let you chase your own damn dog."

"Take some advice from an old, old lady, Michael." She smirked up at him. "If you want anyone to take your claims of maturity seriously, don't calculate your age in fractions."

She had led him through the other side of the meadow and down a narrow lane, edged by clusters of yarrow and teasel, pink and white pockets amid the fading yellow-green. The first of the village cottages lay just beyond—he could just about make out sunlit stone and thatched roofs, the occasional tangle of ivy and climbing roses. It was so fucking picturesque Micha would have scoffed had he not been feeling quite so drenched and shivery.

"Nearly there, dear. We'll soon have you right as rain again."

"I've been ill." Micha scowled. "That's the only reason I—" He gave a violent sneeze.

"Yes, yes, Michael."

Esther hustled him along until they came to a simple square cottage in the same elegant slate-and-ironstone style as the rectory and wreathed in dark-yellow wisteria. As soon as they approached, a door popped open across the street and a woman came flying towards them, like a frigate under full sail. Panting a little, she came to a halt, glancing expectantly from Esther to Micha and then back to Esther again.

"Michael," said Esther, in rather dry accents, "this is my dear friend Ada Stanton. Ada, this is Michael Dashwood."

She was about twenty years younger than Esther, with a comfortable peaches-and-cream prettiness. "How thrilling." Her eyes roamed over him with avid interest.

"Ruff was so disobliging as to pull him into the brook," explained Esther.

"I shall lend my assistance!" cried Ada immediately.

They hurried him into Esther's house, and Ada peeled him out of his coat while Esther made up the fire.

"Um," said Micha awkwardly, "I can—"

"Oh, do stop getting in the way, Ada." Esther tugged at her friend's arm.

"But we should get him out of these damp things at once."

"For which he does not need your assistance."

Ada put a hand to her heart and heaved a deep sigh. "But one sees so few drenched young men these days."

"Well, find your own and push him in the stream yourself."

Micha, who thought himself far beyond such things, actually blushed. The truth was, he was unaccustomed to the attentions of ladies, and he had no idea how he was supposed to react.

"Look what you've done to the poor dear." Esther shooed Ada away. "Go and make tea. There should even be cake." Ada scampered off down the hall, clearly determined to miss as little of the drenched young man as possible. "Now, Michael, come with me."

Esther took him upstairs and wrapped him up in towels, while he stood there dazedly, his hands crossed with absurd modesty over his chest, for the material of his shirt was clinging to him in an unseemly manner.

"You must not mind Ada," Esther told him. "She's a giddy kipper and means no harm."

She crossed the room and began rummaging in the wardrobe. "I'm sure something in here will do." She pulled out a double-breasted frock coat, about two decades out of fashion, and threw it onto the bed, along with a pair of dark trousers, a matching vest, and a fresh linen shirt with a low standing collar. "Well, you won't be cutting a dash, my dear, but you won't freeze to death either."

Then she left him alone, in what was clearly the bedroom she had once shared with her husband. It was a lived-in room, faded and familiar, full of memories. Micha stripped off his ruined clothes, bundled them into a ball, and began towelling himself dry. Fortunately, the more intimate elements of his attire had mostly survived the drenching. He perched in some embarrassment on the edge of the bed as he fastened the shirt and did something slightly haphazard with the cravat, as he had no idea what he was supposed to do with such a low collar. He wondered what it would be like to share the same bed with the same person every day, and for the rest of your life. To have that certainty of warmth.

He was feeling a little better now he was inside and out of his wet clothes. Gradually, he was able to control his trembling, though lights were flashing, sharp as pinpricks, at the corners of his eyes, and when he stood up, dizziness rushed over him so abruptly he had to sit down again. What he really needed, he thought, was some laudanum. That would ease everything and stop him thinking such strange things.

Eventually, he was able to stand, steady himself, and go downstairs. Ada said that he looked as dashing as Heathcliff, and Esther pointed out that comparing him to a murderous commoner was hardly flattering. Then they insisted on rewrapping him in towels, and he found himself pressed into a chair by the fire and plied with tea and plum cake. Ruff, perhaps feeling guilty for having caused the whole mishap, lolloped over and collapsed protectively over Micha's feet. Micha liberated a hand from deep inside his towel cocoon and reached down to scratch the dog's ears.

"So." Ada, having supplied herself liberally with cake and settled onto a sofa, addressed him with obvious excitement. "You must be new to Nettlefield?"

Micha, who had fallen into a peculiar state of semi-oppressed contentment, between the dog and the fire and the tea and the plum cake, was pulled sharply back to reality, with all its complexities, compromises, and falsehoods. "Uh . . . yes. I'm staying with . . . with my cousin."

"Oh?" Ada cast him a sly, gossip-hungry look, but it was not malicious.

Esther shook her head, as if she was far above this sort of thing, but there was no hiding her interest either.

"Thomas," said Micha. "Mandeville. The rector."

"We all know who the rector is, Michael." Ada laughed rather wickedly and tossed her buttercup-yellow curls. "We all know everything. You must be used to city life."

He nodded. "Yes. Manchester originally, then Oxford. And then I moved to London." He paused, frowning. Why was he telling them this? This pathetic patchwork of truth and lies. Maybe there was something in the plum cake. Or maybe it was just pleasant to sit in someone's parlour, to talk of unimportant things with incidental acquaintances, and pretend to be the nice young man they thought he was.

"And you say you're Thomas's cousin?" asked Ada, who clearly had the tenacity of a bulldog.

"Distant cousin," he said quickly. "Twice removed. It's very kind of Th-Thomas"—it felt so strange, suddenly, to speak his name aloud to strangers—"to take me in."

"It's just like him," agreed Ada, with what Micha considered a rather squishy look. "He's such a lovely man."

"Pish," said Esther. "The company will do him good, I'm sure. He's far too serious."

"Essie! I think a sober bearing and a certain . . . distance is very fitting for a priest. I suppose you would have him fat and jolly and worldly? Like something out of *The Canterbury Tales*."

"I would have him happy. His weight is entirely his own business."

"Is he unhappy?" Micha asked, carelessly, his eyes fixed on his teacup.

There was a long silence.

"He's a dutiful fellow," said Esther, finally. "And we think the death of his brother hit him hard. But you surely know more about that than we do."

Well, now he was fucked. He was just about to chance a general remark when inspiration came. "I was out of the country at the time. I mean, I heard but—"

"I know!" cried Ada. "It was awful. A hunting accident. And straight after his honeymoon. His poor wife. Poor Thomas."

Suddenly, a line from Thomas's journal unfurled before Micha's eyes, as clearly as if it were in front of him again: *Edward shot himself today.*

"Yes." He covered his confusion as best he could. "A terrible misfortune."

"He was a fine man," said Esther. "Not like his brother." She coughed. "Not that Thomas is, in any way, unfine. But they're quite different sorts."

Micha knew curiosity to be dangerous. It implied, if not led directly to, caring. But it was strange—alluring in some way—to see Thomas through someone else's eyes. "How so?"

"Oh, well, Thomas is . . . that is . . . Edward wasn't the sort to hold himself aloof."

Aloof? Thomas? The man who had plucked a stranger from the gutters of London? Who had whispered his childhood secrets and shared his undared dreams?

"But," Esther went on comfortably, "let us not mix tea and tragedy. What are your plans, Michael? Will you be with us for long?"

Micha, who had been close to settled, nearly dropped his teacup, struck by the question as if by an unexpected blow. He had always known his leaving would be inevitable, but damn Thomas, and damn these kind, charming ladies, for giving him something to lose. How could he go back to Church Lane now? Turn his body over to strangers. Walk always through tangled streets, beneath a grey sky and the eye of a pale, indifferent sun. For a helpless, furious moment, he genuinely hated Thomas for bringing him here. For returning to him so many little pieces of humanity he had long since thought taken or abandoned. And for reminding him what the world could be like, when it believed you were good. "I-I don't know. I should not outstay my welcome."

"Nonsense," protested Ada. "Amiable young gentlemen will always be welcome wherever they go."

"Wet or dry," added Esther.

Micha flustered visibly, much to their amusement.

"I suppose"—Esther seemed to take pity on him—"you will just have finished at Oxford."

"Oh . . . er . . . I didn't finish." He waited for pity, confusion, or condemnation. None came.

"Was it awfully boring?" asked Ada, sympathetically.

"Just not the right place for me, I suppose."

"Did you have to do Latin and Greek and things like that? My husband is terribly clever when it comes to useless languages and terribly stupid when it comes to everything else. I blame too much university. Do you know, just the other day, he climbed into the bath still wearing all his clothes. He said he was thinking about a book."

"Dangerous habits," observed Esther. "Men should not be allowed to challenge their delicate minds."

"It must have been a very important book." Micha was finding it difficult not to laugh.

"So you would think. But I checked, and it was *The Woman in White*."

"Oh, I love that." Esther took another slice of cake. "William is to be excused, even applauded, Ada."

Ada wrinkled her nose. "If you say so. I have not read it, so I cannot judge."

"Nor I." Micha's conversational skills may have tarnished over the years, but he had quickly realised that his best strategy with these two ladies was to murmur his occasional assent.

"This," declared Esther, "must be rectified. With winter on the horizon, perhaps we should see to the reinstatement of the Nettlefield Reading Group?"

Ada nodded eagerly. "A wonderful idea. And you will come, will you not, Michael?"

"What? I mean . . . forgive me . . . pardon?"

"To the meetings. Every Friday."

"I don't think—"

"So, it's settled. How marvellous."

"But—"

"My advice"—Esther smiled at him—"is simply to surrender. And come to the reading group."

Micha's palms were sweating against what was probably Esther's best porcelain. He was a fraud, a cuckoo, and he had no right to be here, accepting tea and cake and invitations. "Can I bring Thomas?" he heard himself say. As if dragging along the man who wanted to fuck him would somehow make the situation better.

There was a small, tense silence.

"Well, of course you may," said Esther, finally. "If you think he would care to."

Oh, what had he done?

Micha had always thought he was a fairly competent whore. It was not a career path he would have chosen, nor was it one he relished, but he took what was given and gave what was wanted, and his clients went away—in general—satisfied. Many returned. But since his arrival in Nettlefield, the whole arrangement, the whole concept, seemed to be unravelling around him. Thomas had brought him here to fuck him, but there had been no fucking, just conversations that haunted Micha through the deepest of his laudanum hazes, small considerations and unwanted gifts, fleeting touches that left him hot and cold and endlessly on edge. But he was still a prostitute, paid for his body, not his mind or his company. He was not a friend. Nor a lover. Theirs was—or should have been—a straightforward narrative of usage and barter. How the hell was he supposed to invite Thomas to a book club?

Belatedly, he realised Esther was talking to him, asking what had made him leave Oxford.

"I fell in love." Micha hadn't planned on telling the truth, but it was the only answer he had. "And I had some half-formed idea of being an artist."

She patted his hand gently. "I take it neither worked out?"

He shook his head. "I was not quite good enough. For either."

"You have your whole life ahead of you. There will be other loves and other opportunities. You will find something else to inspire you."

No, he wanted to tell her. *My whole life is behind me.* But Esther had been kind to him, and, in turn, he wanted to protect her—even from himself—so he just smiled and nodded, as though he believed her.

Then came a knock on the door, and Esther went to answer. He caught snatches of the conversation as it drifted into the parlour. Something about a vase that had been borrowed, now being returned.

"Why thank you, Sophie." Esther came back into the room accompanied by another lady a few years her senior. "I believe I lent this to you in the summer of '43, but I'm very gratified to have it back."

"Oh." Sophie threw her hands into the air in great surprise. "I am so sorry, my dear, I had no idea you had company."

"How very shocked you must be. Do have a seat. May I introduce Michael Dashwood? Michael, this is Sophie Butterworth."

Sophie beamed at him, clearly delighted. "I heard Thomas had a cousin staying with him at the rectory. And so when I saw you with Esther in the village, I was sure you must be him. I am so happy to finally meet you."

"I thought," murmured Esther, "you had no idea I had company."

"And plum cake too," cried Sophie. "How lovely."

"You had better give Sophie some plum cake, Ada." Esther took her seat again. "Sophie"—she turned to Micha—"is responsible for the sprawling of flowers that threatens daily to engulf our little chapel."

Sophie scowled. "Esther, you are a puritan."

"And you, my dear, are positively pagan."

"Michael?" Sophie ignored her friend quite magnificently. "Have you seen my lovely flowers?"

"I . . . I'm afraid not, I haven't visited the church."

"A heathen," whispered Ada. "Could he be any more thrilling?"

"I promise you," Sophie continued, "there is nothing sinful or . . . or . . . papist about flowers in churches." She paused and then added rather smugly, "I asked Thomas. And he thought about it for a while and said flowers were 'the fairest and most unblemished among the remnants of paradise.'"

Micha had to hide a smile. He could so easily picture Thomas considering the matter, dreamy-eyed and stern-mouthed, his chin propped in his palm.

About ten minutes later, there was another knock.

"Why, no," Micha heard Esther say, from the hallway, "the meeting of the Nettlefield Knitting Circle is tomorrow. But, please, Laura, come in. It seems I am hosting a party."

Laura turned out to be a young, lanky-limbed woman, with rather direct manners, a tangle of red hair, and a lot of knitting. She pulled a chair up close to Micha and threw herself down in it without ceremony. "I say, do you mind if I borrow you, old chap? Turns out it's not knitting day, but I'm in a spot of bother here and I need about six or seven extra pairs of hands."

"Good heavens, don't do that." Sophie glanced up from her teacup in alarm. "We'll never get you out again."

"Don't even like bloody knitting," whispered Laura, stabbing him in the arm with a needle as thick as a sabre. "But got to keep the old girls out of trouble, what?"

She decanted an enormous snarl of thread onto Micha's knees and then proceeded to tie him up.

"Don't panic," she told him, half an hour later. "I know it looks bad right now but bound to get darker before dawn, right? I'm sure I'll find the end in a minute. Bally stuff."

Later they were joined by Captain Cartwright, a retired officer with formidable side-whiskers who just happened to be passing by, a shy young woman with a faint stammer Micha was sure he heard introduced as Miss Violet Mouseworthy, Jennifer Ryan, who had brought a lemon drizzle cake and her husband, and a handful of others he was simply too overwhelmed to remember. The parlour filled up with people, the babble of conversation, and the scent of brewing tea. Groups formed and broke up and formed afresh. It was like watching pebbles drifting in a stream, and Micha drifted along too, quietly and contentedly, feeling—however fleetingly, however undeservedly—part of something. Miss Mouseworthy, whose stammer intensified in the presence of Laura, helped untangle him. He noticed the brief, trembling contact of two sets of fingers amidst the coloured strands, thought of Thomas and his pale, beautiful hands, and shivered.

Micha returned to the rectory in time for laudanum and then dinner. The day, for all its unexpected pleasures, had taken its toll on him. He was wrapped in lies, like climbing ivy, stricken to the roots. As much a part of him now as whatever was left of the truth. He did not know if it had been the exercise, the drenching, the socialising, or the lack of laudanum, but he was exhausted. And, released from the charmed sphere of country life, he was annoyed that he had allowed himself to be so easily bewitched by a group of foolish villagers. How quickly they would turn on him, if they knew who he really was. How eagerly they would condemn him. A thought that should not have hurt, for Micha was immune to hurt. Like a man accustoming his body to poison, take a little every day. That was the secret. Oh, why had Thomas brought him here? He could have fucked him in London and left him no worse off.

"Good Lord." Thomas looked up from his book as Micha took a place at the table. "What are you wearing?"

"I fell in a stream. Don't ask."

Thomas's expression communicated that he very much wanted to ask, but he kept his peace, as Micha had known he would. The day would come, soon enough, when Thomas would have demands to make, but in the meantime, Micha contented himself with petty tyrannies.

He reached into the pockets of his borrowed frock coat and began to pull out the neatly wrapped packages that had been pressed upon him before he left Esther's home. "Look at this." He laid them out on the table. "The way they carried on, you'd think you weren't feeding me."

"You are a little thin," observed Thomas dryly. "Perhaps your benefactors consider you the victim of my Christian austerity."

"There's plum cake, lemon drizzle cake, apple loaf, peach cobbler, and some sort of bun affair I can't remember. You'll have to help me. Seems a shame to waste all this."

"Well . . ." Thomas shifted uncomfortably.

"It's cake, Thomas, not Sodom and Gomorrah."

He blushed. "You're right, of course. The lemon cake looks lovely."

Micha pushed over the little parcel, and Thomas unwrapped it with careful fingers. He ate carefully too, popping neat squares of cake into his mouth, almost as if he feared enjoying them. But Micha was not completely oblivious to the way his eyes and his lips softened very slightly in pleasure. The pink curl of his tongue as he chased an errant crumb.

"I see," Thomas remarked, apparently unaware of—or untroubled by—Micha's gaze, "that you've been meeting my parishioners."

"They didn't give me much choice."

"No . . . no . . . they probably wouldn't." Thomas looked briefly crestfallen. "They did not trouble you, I hope?"

Micha could not have explained his discomforts, even had he wanted to. "It was fine. But I'm not sure I ever want to see another cake again."

"They did the same to me when I first arrived."

"But not anymore?"

Thomas licked lemon-sugar from his thumb. "I asked them to stop. It felt . . . I felt . . . oh, I don't know what I felt. Uncomfortable."

"People bringing you cakes made you uncomfortable?"

"It's not as if I've done anything to earn them." Thomas's lips twitched into the suggestion of a smile. "One would think I was selling indulgences for baked goods."

Though he had made many resolutions when it came to Thomas, Micha still had trouble, sometimes, resisting his playfulness. He smiled faintly. "Well, there has to be something wrong with you underneath all that godliness."

Micha had only meant to tease, but to his surprise, the other man flushed. "None are without sin."

"You don't know what sin is," Micha told him, taking refuge in scorn. There was no reply from Thomas, which meant he was obliged to break the deepening silence. "There was talk of a book group or some such thing on Friday. They wanted me to go."

"You should."

Micha squirmed with incipient mortification. "They"—he couldn't even meet the other man's eyes—"I mean. That is. You should come too." There. Barely a request at all.

"I don't think that's a good idea."

"Why not?"

"I'm here," Thomas said, rather primly, "because I have a responsibility to these people."

"So? What? That means you can't read a book with them?"

"I'm their parish priest. They feel morally obliged to invite me to everything, much as they feel morally obliged to shower me in cakes or heed my thoughts on flowers for the church. If they invited me, Micha, it was most likely out of politeness."

This was surely the crowning irony of Micha's day. That the Reverend Thomas Mandeville was anything but utterly confident in his role had simply not occurred to Micha before. Whatever Thomas's unnatural desires, his outward virtues had always seemed so implacable that Micha had believed him a man utterly assured of his worth and his place in the world. Perhaps, at some other time, he might have found this hint of personal vulnerability just a little bit charming. But, today, it was simply cruel. The shreds of acceptance and crumbs of affection that Micha's deceits and obfuscations had stolen, Thomas had rightfully earned. He had everything, and Micha had nothing. And that was how it would always be.

He opened his mouth, intending to say something sharp yet fairly measured, but all that came out was a roar. "Are you fucking blind?"

"Pardon?"

"Can't you see what you have here? You could be part of something. Part of people's lives. Part of a community. You could be . . . loved." The word hung between them: ungainly, somehow, and unlikely. "So you might as well attend their stupid fucking book group."

Micha sagged in his chair and put his head in his hands. His outburst—that nonsense about being loved—had come from nowhere, and he was regretting it already. The way Thomas had chosen to live his life wasn't Micha's business. If he wanted to take it for granted, then . . . so be it.

After what felt like forever, Thomas nodded. "If you think I should go, then of course, I shall."

"I don't care what you do."

There was another endless silence.

"Micha," Thomas said, very softly. "Micha, I just want you to know—"

But Micha was in no mood to listen to platitudes.

"Shut up," he cried. "Shut up and leave me alone."

And, dignity be damned, he half-ran from the room.

Chapter 11

The next day, Thomas woke Micha early, something he protested against vociferously, though he eventually came down to breakfast, looking bleary-eyed and rumpled. Thomas's fingers itched to smooth his wayward curls. He wanted to ask him about last night, but since Micha did not mention it himself, it seemed kindest to let it go.

"This better be good." Micha picked at a piece of bread. "It looks suspiciously like morning is happening out there."

"Not merely morning." Thomas smiled at him. "A beautiful morning."

"No such thing."

"You might change your mind. I'd like to take you to meet someone."

Micha actually recoiled. "Oh no. I met enough people yesterday. I'm done with meeting people for a good long time."

"You will like each other, I promise."

"No." Micha shook his head. "Absolutely not. And nothing you can say will make me change my mind."

"What about . . . *please*?"

Micha's mouth quivered with reluctant amusement. "How old are you? Eight? 'Please' is not a magic word."

"I know. But I thought it might appeal to your better nature."

"I don't have a better nature. You should know that by now."

A few days, or weeks, ago this might have discouraged Thomas. But he was learning to read Micha, and the hint of a smile suggested he might be more amenable than his words, or his manner, conveyed. Thomas was not a man to ever think of his looks, but he had found that a certain expression had a strange effect on Micha's resistances. He assumed it now. "Please, Micha. It will not take long."

Micha frowned, though he seemed far angrier at himself than Thomas. "All right, all right, don't make eyes at me," he snapped. "Though if I faint from exhaustion and fall ill again, the blame will lie entirely with you."

"Come now, you survived both a drenching and the ladies of Nettlefield. You will be quite well."

Micha made a sceptical sound, but he pulled on his coat and hat without further complaint and followed Thomas out of the house into the brightest of autumn days. The sun came down, as thickly abundant as treacle, and Thomas—far too aware of everything Micha did—noticed the shudder of pleasure that rippled through him as he stepped into the light. Before Micha, Thomas would have walked heedless through the beauty. But today, everything seemed blessed with gold, from the glowing ironstone of the rectory to the dappling that came through the russet-crowned trees and spun like coins upon the gravel. And Micha, of course, careless, scowling, and sun-gilded. He was looking better, still pale, still too thin, but his features had found again their natural harmony. Deep eyes, strong bones, generous, masculine lines.

They walked along in silence, at Micha's pace, passing between strips of smooth green lawns and borders that blazed with a tumult of autumn colours. Riotously orange daisies, scarlet and sunshine dahlias, tall pink and rust-dark sage, woven through with a delirious haze of purpletop vervain. The sky arched high and endless, swirled blue and white like willow pattern porcelain.

"Don't you live well here?" Micha gestured sardonically at the gardens and the gardeners that surrounded them.

"Yes. I have been very fortunate. Much of the land hereabouts still belongs to the church. I lowered the rents on the whole glebe when I became the incumbent, but . . . yes . . . I confess, I have too much for my needs."

"What a trial for you."

Thomas hung his head, his fingers twisting together. Micha, of course, was quite right. It was bad enough to have so much, and still worse to make an ordeal of it.

"Oh come on," said Micha, after a moment, his shoulder brushing clumsily against Thomas's, sending a jolt of heat between them. "God wanted you to have it, right?"

"Actually," whispered Thomas, admitting rather painfully to a source of private shame, "my father wanted me to have it. He knows the family in whose gift is the living. I did nothing to earn this."

Micha had been so openly disdainful of Thomas's easy life, with his gardeners, his cook, and his housekeeper, that he expected nothing but condemnation for this latest confession. Whatever Micha said, however scathing, would have been nothing he had not often thought himself. But, to his surprise, Micha was silent a moment, his eyes locked on Thomas, and then he shrugged. "Well, I suppose they call it 'preferment' for a reason."

Thomas gave a startled laugh. "How can you go out of your way to make me feel terrible and then go out of your way, not two seconds later, to make me feel better?"

"I'm a complicated man. Now where are we going?"

"We're here actually."

"The stables?" Micha put a hand on his hip and struck a pose, at once ludicrous and oddly brazen. "You certainly know how to show a fellow a good time."

Thomas found himself faintly flustered, though he hardly knew why. "Do stop being difficult and come inside."

"How do you know I even like horses?"

"I don't. I am merely hoping that you might."

Micha sighed heavily and trailed after Thomas into the cool interior of the stables. Thomas kept only three horses, though he could easily have afforded and accommodated more. But, unlike his brothers, he was not a natural or enthusiastic horseman, and he did not think a country priest had any place maintaining an extensive stable. He took off his hat and coat and flung them onto a nearby hay bale, and then led Micha over the cobbled floor, through a spiral of dust motes and the scents of clean straw, leather, and living things.

"This is Brimstone," he said, stopping before a fine English thoroughbred with a coat as black as tar.

After a moment, perhaps in spite of himself, Micha reached out a hand and smoothed it over the sleek, strong neck. "He's a handsome beast," he said grudgingly. "Interesting choice of name."

Thomas gave him a wry look. "They say if you can ride the devil, you can ride anything. But he belongs to George. He's resting here for now. His half-brother Hellfire is still in London. I thought, perhaps, you might like to ride him?"

Micha pulled his hand back abruptly. "I can't imagine George would appreciate me pawing at his horse."

"George wouldn't care. He half-killed him not so long ago, just to win a bet."

"What?" Micha gave him a mocking look. "Is that disapproval I hear in your voice, Father?"

Thomas glanced away, wanting to hide his anger and slightly ashamed of it. When he spoke, it was with real passion. "It's simply wasteful, to hurt another living creature for vanity. I think carelessness can sometimes be the worst sort of cruelty."

"Cruelty is the worst of cruelty," retorted Micha. "And don't you think it's a bit off to get all self-righteous about the mistreatment of animals when there are people you could be wasting your worry on?"

"Oh Micha, it's the same, don't you see? It is not our place to divide the world into deserving and undeserving. What would be the value of my kindness, if I believed it gave me the right to treat animals with disregard?"

"I don't know, it might mean quite a lot to someone who was starving to death, for example. I don't think the people at the bottom of life's cesspit really care why you're doing what you're doing, or if you're good, or bad, or basically indifferent. Morality only matters if you've got enough to eat."

"'A righteous man regardeth the life of his beast,'" murmured Thomas.

"'But the tender mercies of the wicked are cruel,' yes, yes, I know that one. Interesting, isn't it, the way you were saying we don't get to carve up the world, but this is basically saying an act is only worthy if the right person is doing it."

"Not at all. It's saying that the wicked will always have other reasons for performing acts that may initially seem virtuous."

Micha folded his arms, his eyes catching at Thomas, sharp as fishing hooks. "Now that *is* curious," he drawled. "So if a man does something that seems like a kindness, it could very well be wickedness if he happened to have, say, an ulterior motive?"

Thomas wanted to look away, but he couldn't. Silence stretched between them, sticky as spider's silk. His heart felt like quicksand. Then he nodded. "Yes," he said softly, "that man would be wicked. And his act would be worthless."

Confusion crossed Micha's face, and he was the one to flinch. He swung away and peered into the next loose box. "Who's this, then?"

"That's my horse. Slug."

Micha did not look very impressed by Slug, but Thomas could not blame him for that. Slug was not an impressive animal. "Did you just say 'Slug'?"

"His real name is Sammy, but George has been calling him Slug for so long that he answers to it. I'm rather an indifferent rider, and Slug suits my needs. He's . . . slow and docile. Like me. You're welcome to make use of him. I just thought you might prefer Brimstone."

Micha took up a pose of studied apathy. "I'll think about it."

"As you will." Thomas was conscious of an unworthy flicker of irritation, which he partially blamed on the unsettling exchange that had just passed. As much as he believed he'd accepted his own iniquities, having to confront them directly had shaken him. Even the fact that Micha could not know the depth of them offered scant comfort. All the same, and personal corruption aside, he found himself ungraciously wishing that Micha would just . . . like something. Anything. For once. Then again, maybe it was better that he didn't. Thomas's wish to please Micha was too entangled with his own pleasure for it to be an uncomplicated impulse.

"You think too much," Micha said, suddenly.

Thomas, who had indeed been lost in his reveries, started.

"It's all air and philosophy and reason with you."

"I was taught that way. I don't know how else I might bring the Lord to His people."

"Eating their cake might be a start."

Thomas laughed before realising Micha was serious. "What has that to do with anything?"

"Well, how are you supposed to bring the Lord to His people if His people think you're a prig?" But before Thomas could even begin to frame an answer, Micha turned and walked away. His boots echoed on the cobbles as he strolled over to the final, occupied stall. "And who—" he began. "My God. What a beauty."

"What? Oh." It took a moment for Thomas's head to stop spinning. "That's Edward's old horse, Bucephalus." Even the words hurt a little, though it had been over a year. "I'm afraid he's not quite the prize he once was. And please be careful, he's rather wary. He can bite, if you catch him in the wrong mood."

Micha held out a hand, murmuring softly under his breath, words Thomas was standing too far away to catch. There came a stirring from within, and Bucephalus's head appeared over the top of the door. Micha stroked his nose with calm assurance. Bucephalus tossed his mane nervously but otherwise stood still and endured it.

"He's Arabian stock, isn't he?" asked Micha.

Thomas kept his distance, not wanting to startle either of them, and nodded. "But he damaged his knees. He'll never race again."

"How?"

A blank, cold syllable that hung in the air like gun smoke. Thomas felt a little sick.

"We don't know. He limped home after Edward's . . . accident, like this. Perhaps he stumbled when the gun was discharged. I don't suppose we'll ever know."

Micha half-turned, his hand still stroking almost hypnotically and Bucephalus quiescent beneath it as though bespelled. "Is that how your brother died?"

Not for the first time, Thomas felt the truth surge hotly inside him, as though it wanted to force its way out of his throat. But he had given the marquess his oath. It was not his secret. It was Edward's. It was the family's. "Yes," he managed. "As I said. A hunting accident."

Micha's eyes were very dark in the half-light. They looked like pits into which Thomas could fall and never be found again. "A hunting accident," repeated Micha, in a strange, harsh voice. "Right."

Thomas nodded. "They brought him back to the house, but it was too late to . . . do anything. And they found Bucephalus wandering afterwards."

It had been a question that had long troubled Thomas, one he clung to, perhaps, so he would not have to think about the others. Suicide was, after all, a sin. What did that mean for Edward's soul? But if Edward had, indeed, shot himself as the marquess had said, what would have caused Bucephalus to break his knees? Did that mean someone had maimed him, simply to support the lie of Edward's death? How much pain could one life cause? "George wanted to shoot him," Thomas heard himself say. "But I would not allow it."

"Let me guess," Micha sneered, "you threw yourself between beast and bullet."

Thomas said nothing.

"Did you really? For a horse? What if George had shot you?"

"He would not have shot me. He's impetuous but not fratricidal. And we can hardly blame Bucephalus for what happened."

Micha shrugged. "What's the use of a horse with damaged knees?"

"Edward loved him dearly. For that I am grateful."

"You know it's a horse, right? I don't think it really cares if you're grateful or not."

"I care. And you said yourself, he's beautiful."

Micha stepped away. "He's ruined. He'll never be worth anything to anybody."

"Except me."

Micha snorted.

"He can still be ridden," said Thomas. "He just needs to be treated with a little consideration."

"Words to live by."

Thomas had run out of things to say. All the talk of Edward and Bucephalus had been unexpected and had left him feeling rather bruised. Micha's mood was clearly settling into bleak and unhappy, and Thomas felt incapable of handling it. It had been such a beautiful morning, shadowed now by an impending storm of death, lies, and sin. He had always said—maybe even believed—that he wanted nothing from Micha. But that, he was beginning to realise, was just another lie. Though he would never have sought gratification of desires he knew to be wrong, he still selfishly wanted Micha's smiles. His gratitude. His joy. Gifts, in short, he had no right to expect. "Will you excuse me? I have duties to attend."

"Of course." As ever, Micha showed no sign of caring whether he was there or not.

Thomas broke into the sunlight, breathless and panicked, as though he had been deep underwater, and strode rapidly away through the gardens. It was not until he had been walking for about five minutes that he realised he had left his hat and coat behind, and reluctantly turned back.

He entered the stables with apologies ready on his lips, but Micha was standing in front of Bucephalus's box, his face resting against the proud arch of the horse's neck and his fingers curling through the animal's mane.

"That's my beauty," he was whispering, in a voice sweeter and far gentler than Thomas had ever heard him use before. "You're all right. Everything is all right."

And knowing he was an intruder on this scene, Thomas crept away.

Chapter 12

Micha, however indifferent he pretended to be to Thomas, went riding the next day. Isidore, of course, had taught him, because all freedom, all pleasure, had both its origin and its ending in Isidore. Isidore, who was nothing now except a habit of thinking, a piece of memory and a half-forgotten dream. Once, Micha had wondered where Isidore was, what he had done, who he had become, but then he had decided it did not matter. Not while, poppy-fettered, Micha had dreams instead, though they drowned in daylight, like the shadows of childhood monsters.

He took Bucephalus, not Brimstone. They were both cautious and he went carefully at first, past the village and down twisting country lanes until the world rolled at his feet like a green velvet beast and the sky flared as wide as angels' wings. Micha knew better than to push his mount, but he gave Bucephalus his head and soon they were travelling at an easy canter. While they did not fly as they might once have done, it was a taste of lost things, and it was enough. The thud of Bucephalus's hooves was as steady as a second heartbeat, more real, somehow, than his own. The wind ruffled his hair and swept the surface of his skin, like hands that could not touch him. He did not think of Isidore and he did not dream of anything. Creeping through the cracks, like a gleam of pale light, came the suggestion of pleasure.

Somehow, he forgot Thomas's evasions and lies. They were whisked away on the wind. And he remembered, instead, his laughter. His gentleness. The hope in his eyes. His kindness may have come with a price, but it came with other things too. Like this. A gift Micha would never have thought he wanted. Perhaps even fallen leaves could soar again sometimes.

Later, after they had gone about as far as Micha dared and turned again for home, he heard the sound of hoofbeats behind him, and a strident voice called out, "I say, tally-ho."

He peered over his shoulder, and Laura—mounted on an enormous bay hunter—came thundering down the lane after him. She was dressed in a green riding habit of rather military design and a tall hat with a plume, from which most of her hair had already escaped. But the air and exercise became her. There was a flush on her sun-freckled cheeks, her eyes were bright, and she seemed far more at ease here than she had at Esther's.

He slowed Bucephalus to a walk, and she manoeuvred her horse alongside his. He felt an edgy, snappish uncertainty travel through Bucephalus's body at the sudden closeness of these strangers, but he calmed beneath the touch of Micha's hands.

Laura touched the brim of her hat. "Fancy meeting you hereabouts."

"Fancy," returned Micha dryly.

She rolled her eyes. "Oh, all right. Truth is, I saw you from across the field, gave chase, and, well, here we are. Thought you might like a spot of company on your way back to the village. But don't fret if not—just say the word, and I'll push off again."

Micha opened his mouth and then closed it. He could not entirely resolve how he felt on the matter. Something about being cordially invited to tell someone to go away rather took the fun out of it. "Why not?" he said at last, not precisely warmly, but then, he had long lost the habit of friendliness.

"Splendid." She reined in her stallion so that his long strides would not draw him too far ahead of Bucephalus. They advanced for a while in this companionable fashion, and Micha wondered—rather fretfully for a man who insisted he had no interest in the opinions of others—whether he was supposed to be responsible for making conversation.

Conversing with men was straightforward, but young women were dangerous and unpredictable, and he had little experience of them.

"How's the knitting?" he tried, at last.

"Utterly buggered, but nil desperandum."

"Are you making . . . well . . . anything?"

"Thought I'd try for a scarf. Seemed a fairly simple proposition. I mean, start at one end, stop at the other, but it seems to have gone all over the bloody place."

Micha made what he hoped was a sympathetic noise and crashed headlong into silence again. What on earth did women like? "That's a nice . . . outfit?"

"What? This? I say, it's bloody awful. I absolutely loathe riding sidesaddle. I actually had a tailor in London run me up some trousers, you know, such as you fellows wear. Unfortunately, Ada saw me and it gave her such a fright she walked straight into a wall and the doctor had to be called. Complete carnage."

Micha suspected he had an understanding of "carnage" rather different to the residents of Nettlefield, and he was just hiding a smirk when he caught a glimpse of Laura's sparkling eyes and realised she was laughing too. "Poor Ada." He managed a tolerable approximation of sincerity.

"She had a bruise the size of a shilling," confided Laura. "A shilling. Can you imagine?"

"It hardly bears thinking of."

"I know."

Wonderful. Now he needed a different topic. Clothing had clearly been a false lead. Micha tried to remember if he had ever been fit for company or whether life had simply accommodated his deficiencies by throwing him to the bottom of the pile, where nobody would care about them. Perhaps he had been in the right profession after all. His education had included the rudiments of Latin and Greek; his secondary education had taught him what it meant to love, to truly love, another human being. And, finally, when all other lessons had been lost to time and circumstances, he had learned how to efficiently bring a man to completion. At no point had he wondered how one talked appropriately to young ladies, nor felt the lack of such knowledge.

"Um," he said, finally. "Nice horse."

Laura became suddenly quite animated. "Marvellous, isn't he? We call him Gulliver."

"Yes, I can see that. He's very . . . large."

"Only thing I ever learned. 'Ride a really big horse.'"

"I see." He gave her a confused look. "Is there more to that story? Or is it just a family motto? Uh . . . something . . . 'Equus magnus'?" (Thomas, he thought, Thomas would know. And Isidore, of course, who flowed through languages like water.)

She gave a wild shout of laughter. "It should be, dash it, it should be. But I used to have this awful governess called Miss Wheezle, one of a long line of awful governesses, actually. They were always coming and going, trying to get me to sit still, be a lady, hold a teacup, embroider a cushion. Who has the time, really? To embroider a cushion. In any case, I managed to get rid of most of 'em, thank God, but Wheezie was like a burr under a saddle blanket. Couldn't shift her. Got quite fond of her, in the end, truth be told. What else can you do with someone like that?"

Micha tried to sort through this anecdote, in search of its relevance. "And she told you to always ride a really big horse?"

"It was in a book, as a matter of fact. I can remember it almost exactly: 'The most honourable exercise, that beseemeth the estate of every noble person, is to ride on a great horse.' And I thought, 'Why bloody not.'"

Micha surprised himself by grinning. "Why not, indeed?"

"Better than all that Italian rubbish. 'Be feared, if you can't be loved, but don't be hated; try not to employ mercenaries, and always wear your own armour.'"

"Was Miss Wheezle trying to raise you to be a lady or to invade Europe?"

Laura was silent for a moment. "Oh, you don't know, do you? I sometimes forget there are people who don't know everything about everyone else." She gestured at the manor house, which was a blur of golden stone against the horizon. "I'm actually, well, Lady Chalfont. I'm the only child and there's no entailment, so all this is, well, mine. Bit embarrassing really."

"Oh good God."

"Don't worry about it or anything," she added, fervently. "We don't stand on ceremony here in Nettlefield."

"Yes but—"

"Shush. And that's an order from your social superior." Micha shushed, and Laura went on abruptly: "Listen, you seem like a decent chap. I'm sorry I haven't been completely square with you. I mean, about who I am, or why I'm talking to you now. The thing is, I sort of wanted to ask you something. You know, as a man of the world."

Micha choked. "As a what?"

She eyed him appraisingly. "You are, though, aren't you? A man of the world."

"I don't know what that means," he said faintly.

"Oh, you know, lived a bit, had your heart broken, and all that?"

"I suppose . . ."

"Good. Yes. I knew it. So, let's say, hypothetically you were, say, interested in, you know, some ah, well, in my case, fellow, obviously—let's say you were me and interested in some fellow, how would you go about making that known? To the fellow?"

"Um." Micha had even less experience in courting women than talking to them.

She looked at him expectantly. "Well?"

"I think," he hazarded, "it might be rather a matter for the . . . fellow."

"What if the fellow was . . . shy? I'm not talking about ravishing . . . the fellow . . . in the bushes, Michael, I just want to find out if he was by any chance interested in me."

He stared at her blankly. "Who is this fellow?"

"Violet."

"Violet?"

There was a long silence.

"Um . . . well . . . that's sort of a nickname, really. It's what we call, um, Fred."

There was another long silence. Laura had gone pale, then pink. And Micha, against his better judgement and all the bulwarks he had constructed against the world, felt for her. He had known this kind of love well, once upon a time, a universal thing made specific, and enacted hastily, shamefully in the corners of other people's lives. Making thieves of those who did not steal. "And this Fred is a shy gentleman?" he asked.

She nodded vigorously.

"And you have no idea how he might feel about you?"

"Not at all. I mean, let us just say I am aware that I would be an unconventional choice for . . . for . . . Fred."

"I see your dilemma."

"Sticky, isn't it?"

"Perhaps you should try to be honest with Fred and see where that leads you?"

"What if he's disgusted?"

"That's always the risk."

She sighed. "But then I'll have lost even the friendship of someone I care about."

"That, too, is the risk."

She thought about it. "What a bugger," she concluded.

Micha nodded.

They rode on in subdued silence.

"Maybe I wouldn't want to be friends with someone who was disgusted with me," Laura muttered. "I mean, if someone cares for you, even if it's only as a friend, it shouldn't matter who you love."

Micha could remember, with the sort of clarity that only ever preserves the most painful of memories, saying the same sort of thing to his parents. His weeping mother, the father who would no longer look at him. They probably remembered the day he left with Isidore as the day he stopped being their son, but he knew it as the day he realised he never had been. "I don't know. I really don't know."

She mustered a smile. "Not one for false hope, are you, old chap?"

"I've lost track of what's hope and what's falsehood. But if Fred has any sense at all, he'll at least listen to what you have to say."

She nodded. "He's the most wonderful . . . man . . . I've ever met. It's all inside, you know. Like those caves you read about with lakes and crystals in them that nobody would know about if they didn't go looking. And properly accomplished too. Not like me." Her voice had gone soft and dreamy. "Such delicate hands on the harpsichord."

Micha coughed.

"I mean—oh dash it all." She turned pink again. "Anyway, I should get off home. Thanks for talking to me, Michael. I really do appreciate it. Come over for tea, won't you?"

"Oh, right, thank you."

"Enormous house on the hill, can't miss it." She smirked at him. He gave her a sour look in response, and she laughed. "And if you like riding, you should see the white horse."

"The what?"

"The white horse."

"I've already got a horse."

"Not like this one. Ask Thomas." And with that, she urged Gulliver into a trot and struck out across the fields. Soon, she was galloping. He heard her curse as her hat went flying. And her hair unfurled behind her like the rays of the sun.

Micha went home at a more measured pace. Of course he had no intention of asking Thomas about the white horse, whatever that was. But when he came through the door, he found him sitting on the bottom of the stairs, his arms folded across the top of his knees. The position made him seem more than usually rangy, like some scrawny, black-feathered bird.

"Something the matter?" Micha lounged against the doorframe.

Thomas looked up, tried to smile, and shook his head. "No . . . I . . . Forgive me, this must look quite peculiar."

"Well, yes, a bit."

"Mrs. Greenlie passed away this afternoon."

After a moment, Micha pushed himself away from the wall and went to sit beside Thomas. His upper arm, from elbow to shoulder, fit against Micha's. "Oh, sorry."

"It was very peaceful. The family are sad, of course, but it was a shock to no one."

Micha realised he had heedlessly mirrored Thomas's pose, so he turned his head so he could watch the other man's profile. There was something a little forbidding about Thomas from this angle. Although he was not handsome, there was a degree of hauteur to his features, a gift of his lineage rather than his character. "If it was all angels and hallelujahs, why are you sitting on the stairs?"

Thomas visibly crumpled. "Because I lied to you."

"Everybody lies."

"I know." Thomas closed his eyes. "But I hate this lie. I hate it more than anything. And I have to tell it, over and over and over again."

Micha shifted uncomfortably, accidentally banging his arm into Thomas. He had, after all, already plundered Thomas's secrets and only yesterday used what little he knew of them to torment him. It had been the pettiest of impulses, but Micha had indulged it anyway, all because Thomas had tried to give him something that had the power to make him happy.

"You don't owe me anything." He shrugged. "Truth or lie, it makes no difference to me."

Thomas leaned a little, just a little, into his shoulder. "I don't want to burden you with this."

Micha wondered if he would still have touched the journal if he had understood the context of those four carefully written words. Probably. But now he knew the extent of his trespass. "I'll manage. Tell me, if you want to tell me, or don't."

"My brother Edward," said Thomas, his voice cutting strangely through the silence, precise as a razor blade, "did not die by accident. He shot himself."

Micha suddenly realised his acting skills were largely sex-based and he had no idea how to plausibly sound surprised. "He must have been very unhappy."

"Yes." Thomas's voice wavered. "He must have been. But Micha, I had no idea."

Micha tried desperately to think of something comforting. "Well, how much can we know about each other? I mean, really."

Thomas sat up, his fingers twisting together. "He was my brother. How long and how deeply he must have suffered. And I am still no closer to understanding than I was the day the marquess summoned me to help him cover up the scandal."

There was a long silence. Micha saw himself, two years ago on the docks at Dover, those monstrous cliffs standing at his back like sentries, while Isidore left him. Stopped Micha's life like a finger upon a compass and disappeared into his own. It should not have been unexpected. Had Micha been Isidore, he would not have chosen differently. "Sometimes knowing something doesn't make it any easier to understand."

Thomas turned his lips up into something like a smile. "I suppose you must be right," he murmured. "But I feel so very far from any understanding."

"What was he like?"

"Edward? Oh, he was the best of us, and I do not say that simply because it's convention that the deceased must be sanctified in memory. He had George's looks and spirit, but he was kind, so very kind. It was as though nothing was ever beneath his notice. And when he spoke to you, or looked at you, he could make you the centre of the world. I always felt less dull when I was with him."

Micha lowered his head onto his hands. "I don't think you're dull," he muttered, resenting the admission even as he offered it.

But Thomas went on as though he had not heard. "The marquess is, well, he is who he is. We Mandevilles can trace our line back to 1066, you know. This seems to mean something to him. But I think he truly loved Edward. George was simply insurance. And I, of course, was unforeseen, inadvertent, and unnecessary. At least to His Lordship." He paused and then added, in a rather brittle tone, "Let us hope this wayward course is part of some greater plan, its intricacies both unseen and unknown."

Micha had long ago abandoned all belief that life was anything but utterly, and carelessly, arbitrary, so he had little comfort to offer. There might have been a time when he would have offered touch instead, but that was no longer a simple thing, nor an innocent one. He knew incalculable ways to make a man shudder and spend, but he had forgotten how to ease loneliness or pain.

Suddenly Thomas stood. He paced across the hall, his steps ringing loud across the flags, his coat a blur of shadow. "But how can it be?" Rage and sorrow were thick in his voice. "How can it be part of a divine plan that my brother die alone and afraid and damned? Self-murder? A sin?" His hands came up, long fingers twisting through his hair. "No, no, He is not supposed to burden us with more than we can bear. But if we buckle, then we are forever cast out? If our lives are truly His, then our deaths must be too, even the ones we believe we choose for ourselves. Or does He abandon us, then? In our deepest need? Why should we trust in a God so cruel? Why should we venerate Him?"

"Thomas," said Micha helplessly from where he still sat, frozen, on the stairs. "Thomas."

"Even His own son despaired of Him. His own son. What kind of father—" Whatever Thomas had been about to say was lost in a rush of tears, and he sank slowly to the floor. "Oh God, forgive me. What am I saying?"

"Just words."

Thomas raised his head. Pale face, drowned eyes. He might as well have been miles away, he was so far beyond Micha's reach.

"It's just words," Micha said, again. And then, "I'm sure Edward's fine. Sitting on a little cloud with little golden wings. Or something."

Thomas made an odd sound that was not quite a laugh. "Oh Micha. I know you're trying to help but—"

"What? It's no less plausible than a great fiery pit where you burn for all eternity."

"Hell isn't a place. It's simply the absence of God."

Despite Micha's carefully nurtured apathy, the words were chilling. Or perhaps it was the certainty in Thomas's voice. Too much loss, tangled up like fraying yarn. "Then maybe we're already in it."

"Please don't say that." Thomas shuddered. "I can't bear the thought of it."

"Sorry."

"No, I should be the one to apologise. What a dreadful scene for you to witness. I don't know what . . . what happened to me."

"It's fine." Micha could hear his own harshness as it echoed in the stairwell. "Don't worry about it. Really. I'm not one of your parishioners, and I don't have much love for this God of yours, so you don't have to put on a show for me."

"No but . . ." Thomas covered his face with his hands. "What must you think of me?"

"I think you're grieving. That's not a crime."

Thomas was silent.

Micha tried to think of something he could say. "Th-Thomas," he tried at last, stumbling when he realised how rarely he used the man's name and how much he had said it during this single conversation.

"Yes?"

"What's the white horse?"

Thomas looked briefly startled by the question. "It's . . . well . . . you sort of have to see it, really."

"Oh." Micha swallowed. All he had to do was ask. But it was utterly beyond him, the words caught in his throat like a fragment of bone. He had what he had told himself he wanted: Thomas, as frail and flawed and lost and human as everyone else. And yet, it brought Micha no satisfaction. He could not feed his own pride on the dust of someone else's. He wanted to say something, or do something, that would ease the pain and shame he could see etched across Thomas's features. Yet the price was too high.

Thomas rose slowly to his feet, dashing the moisture from his eyes with the heel of a hand. "I could take you," he offered hesitantly, "if you wish. It isn't far. Perhaps tomorrow afternoon?"

Micha shrugged, as though it didn't matter to him that, even in weakness, Thomas was still the stronger man. The better man. "Yes. Yes, all right."

Chapter 13

They rode out together the next afternoon, Micha on Bucephalus, Thomas on Slug. The weather held fine for them. The sharp autumn breeze was temporarily banked, and a faint warmth touched the air instead, like the trailing fingertips of summer. It soothed Thomas's bruised heart. Speaking of Edward had been like lancing a wound: necessary but painful. He had not thought his soul so full of poison. And, even now, he had no way of telling how deep the corruption went. Or if it was permanent. If he could be saved.

More than anything, he wished it had not been in front of Micha. The man thought little enough of him already. But, at the same time, Thomas could not have imagined saying those things to anyone other than Micha. There had been no shock, no disappointment, and no false reassurances either. And, though he was deeply embarrassed, Thomas was grateful too.

And, most surprisingly, it had led to this. It was the first time Micha had intimated that he might want to spend time with Thomas other than incidentally. Thomas did not entirely know what had changed or if Micha had just begun to feel more settled in Nettlefield, but it was a question he was content to leave unanswered. He was simply happy to ride quietly alongside Micha—who had a careful, graceful way about him on horseback—as though they were, or could be, truly friends.

In this unstirring, sun-washed afternoon, yesterday seemed a long time ago. The grief was still sharp inside him, like a blade plunged deep, but it seemed, at last, possible to bear it, to grow around it, new skin over raw flesh. Everywhere he looked, the world was beautiful, as though it put on new colours and took up new forms in Micha's presence. Or perhaps it was his eyes that had learned to see differently. Greener greens and bluer blues. The secrets of all the little things: calligraphy in the waving of the grass, constellations in the falling of the leaves.

"Where are we going?" asked Micha eventually.

Thomas pointed into the distance, where a blur of white was just about visible as it cut across the hillside.

"I can't see anything."

"You will."

Micha frowned, though his eyes gleamed with amusement. "This better not be some local joke at my expense. I'm wise to that sort of thing. Isidore took me to see the hand of a buried giant once. And what did we find? Five carved tree stumps."

Thomas laughed. "It's nothing like that, I promise."

They rode on.

"What's wrong with that hill?" Micha squinted into the distance. "It looks like the chalk is . . . Oh wait, that's the horse, isn't it?"

"Yes, but it's hard to really see the scale of it from down here. I wish I had a way to take you up into the air."

"What, no hot air balloon in your pocket?"

"In my other coat, I'm afraid."

Thomas led the way to the top of a small, flat-topped hill, from where they could see the stylised, bone-pale outline of the white horse as it swept over the escarpment. It gleamed against the hillside, timeless as the moon.

"Is it better than five carved tree stumps?" asked Thomas as Micha regarded it in silence.

He nodded.

"It's Bronze Age, I think. Or possibly Iron Age. Either way, it's the largest in England, perhaps the oldest."

"You seem very proud of it." Micha sounded a little sardonic.

"I do feel a touch of ownership," Thomas admitted. "Every seventh Midsummer, we join with some of the neighbouring parishes to weed and scour it so that it will never be lost to time."

Micha barked out a laugh. "Always on your knees, Father."

"But is it not a wonderful thought? Like linked hands reaching back through history. And then everyone gets terribly drunk."

Micha shivered, though the day was warm, but when he spoke it was only to ask who had first carved the horse.

"Nobody knows. Hengist, possibly, because his standard was a white horse. Or Alfred, perhaps, as a memorial of his victory over the Danes at Ashdown. Or maybe it was just to honour pagan gods, I don't know."

Micha, frowning again, his expression otherwise unreadable and his eyes distant, said nothing.

"We call this Dragon Hill," Thomas continued. "Legend has it that this is where Saint George slew the dragon."

"You do like to stake your claim to history around here."

"We like to feel important." Thomas smiled. "But you see that piece of exposed chalk? No grass has ever grown there, and they say it's because that's where the dragon's blood was spilled."

Micha snorted. "Any other local legends I should know about? Did the Battle of Hastings actually take place in the next village across? Was Excalibur plucked out of that stone there? I suppose they signed Magna Carta in your front parlour?"

"Be careful," said Thomas, mischievously. "You don't want to give us ideas. But, now you mention it, the Spanish Armada did come up the Cherwell."

Micha's lips betrayed him, quivering with the slightest hint of mirth.

"Although," Thomas added, "here's a real piece of local superstition. They say if you stand on the eye of the horse, it's meant to grant you a wish."

"Is that so?"

Thomas nodded.

"Well, what are we waiting for?"

Micha urged Bucephalus into a brisk trot and set off down the hill, with Thomas and Slug wheezing after him. At the bottom of the valley, Bucephalus broke into a gallop, and Thomas, with no hope of keeping up, let Slug slow before the poor creature had some kind of aneurysm. Micha's laughter caught on the air like cherry blossom in spring.

By the time Thomas made it to the top of the next ridge, Micha had already dismounted and was standing on the chalk circle that represented the horse's eye.

"Are you sure this is a horse?" He stared at his feet. "Looks more like a dog from this angle."

"You shouldn't insult an animal about to grant you a wish." Thomas, out of breath, clambered awkwardly down from Slug.

Micha looked up. "I don't know what to wish for," he said, in a strange, strangled voice.

"You mean, there's nothing you want? Then you are truly blessed."

"There's too much I want. And it's all fucking impossible."

"Tell me?" asked Thomas, softly.

"Someone to love me. Everything I've already lost. To be different. Maybe I want to be scouring this damn horse next Midsummer. Maybe that's what I want."

"That's not impossible."

Micha stubbed his toe angrily into the ground. "And what about the year after that and the year after that? History doesn't want to hold my hand, believe me. I'm a man out of time. No past, no future."

"No." Thomas shook his head. "Whatever your past, you always have a future. Here, if you want it."

Unthinking, he held out his hand, as though, with a single touch, he could somehow bring Micha back to the world he seemed so sure would reject him. Micha's cold fingers closed around his wrist hard enough to bruise and yanked him forward until they were standing, close as lovers, in a circle of white dust. Suddenly, Thomas could barely breathe.

"And what do you wish for?" Micha asked, his eyes blazing hellfire-dark.

So Thomas, unable in that moment not to, told him. "You."

The world did not reel. The sky did not crack. Lightning did not strike them apart. And, before Thomas could even begin to feel afraid or regret what he had done, Micha nodded. "Not here. Come on."

They remounted in silence and began their journey back to Nettlefield. Finally, they came to the outskirts of a small wood, where the trees were crowned red-gold and the sunlight fell thickly through the baring branches. Micha reined in Bucephalus. "Let's walk."

They left the horses tethered and stepped between the trees like princes in a fairy tale. Their footsteps rustled upon a multi-hued carpet. Thomas was uncertain what was expected of him now, and Micha's face was shadowed, and as stern as ice.

Thomas stopped walking and opened his mouth to speak—hardly knowing what he was going to say—but then Micha took a step towards him. On instinct, rather than with any intent to evade him, Thomas took a step back. Micha took another step forward. And Thomas found himself against a tree, a rough tortoiseshell of bark pressing through his coat, while the newly woken breeze stirred a fall of bright leaves around them. Micha's body enclosed him, the hard pressure of his chest, the sharp angles of his hip bones, the thunder of his heart. His face came closer still. The edge of his cheek met Thomas's. His hair tickled Thomas's nose. The heat from his lips travelled all across Thomas's skin like a magic spell.

"What are you doing?" Thomas's voice sounded peculiar, faraway even to his own ears.

He felt the movement of Micha's mouth as he spoke. "I'm giving you what you want."

Thomas had never really imagined something like this would happen. Could happen. He had thought his desire a private monster, to be locked away and ever unspoken. His secret sin. But here was Micha, reaching fearlessly between the bars of the cage Thomas had so diligently fashioned. Thomas tried to turn his head away, just so he could think, but Micha was everywhere. Warmth and strength and subtle mysteries: the thickness of his lashes and the softness of his lips, the places where his body met Thomas's body as though they had been designed to stand thus interlocked. Everything he had learned about right and wrong, lawful and unlawful, natural and unnatural, was flying away, chaff upon the current of Micha's breath. None of it seemed to matter now. Mist and shadows and pieces of words. All he felt was gratitude and wonder. And no shame at all.

Thomas swallowed, his eyes closing as though they could protect him from too much truth. "You knew?"

"Of course I fucking knew."

He opened his eyes again. Micha had not moved. Slowly, Thomas lifted his hand. With a single steady fingertip he traced the line of Micha's jaw and the other man trembled slightly, for all the strength of his body. Micha's lashes swept across his eyes and then he bowed his head, leaning into the touch, as though inviting it, surrendering to it. It was the tiniest, fleetest of movements. And it was, without question, the most beautiful thing Thomas had ever seen. It gave him courage. He was a pilgrim, on the road to revelation. He found Damascus at Micha's lips—rough-smooth, almost like a scar, breath-warmed. They yielded beneath his fingers.

Micha exhaled, half-sigh, half-gasp. "Oh, kiss me." His voice was so hoarse it was barely audible.

And so, Thomas did not fall from grace. He opened his heart and jumped, without hesitation, without regret.

He put a hand upon Micha's hip and drew him in, letting Micha's body shape his own, until there was nothing between them, not even air. The sheer intimacy of holding someone, the mixture of the familiar and the strange that was another man's form, was shocking and exhilarating at the same time. And Thomas unravelled, utterly. His heart went wild against Micha's, his breath crested in a gasp. And before he could start weeping with pure physical joy, he pressed his mouth to Micha's. It was a kiss without knowledge and without elegance, but it was the first and truest kiss Thomas had ever given. And, to it and into it, Micha made the softest of noises, stunned and fragile.

Thomas was praying without gods, entwined with Micha, like some perfect sacrament. He had been, at first, preoccupied with what to do. How he would know what was right, whether he gave pleasure or overstepped the boundaries of his wanting, but with that sound—that impossible, lovely sound—and the parting of Micha's lips beneath his, all thoughts that were not *Micha*, and *Micha*, and *oh Micha*, dissolved into nothing. Micha's body was the only tutor Thomas needed. His lessons in the involuntary clutching of Micha's hands upon his shoulders and the broken murmur of his breath. Thomas might not have known how to kiss, but he knew how to kiss Micha. How to learn his lips, how to take the offered chalice of his mouth with gentleness, how to gather the taste of him with his tongue, how to make him shudder and moan and fall against him, helpless.

Thomas would have liked to keep his eyes open, for that way he could hold Micha and be held by him, kiss and be kissed, and look at him still so that he could truly believe that they did this thing together—this thing called sin that felt like paradise—but it was impossible. The pleasure of Micha's mouth was simply too intense, and Thomas kept falling into a soft interior darkness that built a world from Micha, and Micha alone. He thought perhaps it was a defence mechanism—like the instinct to draw away from pain—as it seemed beyond his body's earthly limitations to see so much beauty and feel so much joy all at once.

He could not have said who broke the kiss—and "broke" was the word, for pulling away felt like shattering—or if it was a mutual parting. But when Thomas drew back, just enough to breathe and open his eyes, he felt as though he would have fallen if not for Micha and the tree. He let out an unsteady breath and sagged within the circle of Micha's arms, hiding his face in the curve of the other man's neck. For a long moment, Micha was absolutely rigid against him, and then his hand came up to stroke through Thomas's hair, lightly but surely, as though he touched the strings of a harp.

Thomas pressed into him, still and silent. The kiss was done but everything had changed. Where once he had given himself to duty, and duty had demanded he give himself to God, he was Micha's now. Circumscribed by fingers in his hair and the body that demarcated the edges of his own. Strange, unimagined pleasures ran up and down his spine, and through his shivering skin, just to touch and be touched like this. His breathing steadied slowly. He could taste Micha's pulse beneath his mouth, a hard and steady beat that made Thomas feel closer to him than he could have believed possible. As though it would be the rhythm of his own heart now.

Suddenly Micha's hand tightened in his hair and pulled Thomas's head back, until Thomas met his wild, burning eyes. There was a slash of red across each of Micha's cheekbones. The mouth that had succumbed to Thomas's kisses was set in a strange, harsh line.

"Down," growled Micha. "Lie down. Now."

And then he was pulling Thomas with him into a flurry of leaves that crackled beneath them like applause. Thomas landed on his back, startled and breathless, his hands flung wide across the forest floor. Micha came after, stretching across his body, strong and supple as a panther in pursuit of its prey. He pinned Thomas by the upper arms—hard enough to hurt, though Thomas would not have thought to fight him—and kissed him, with a deep, deliberate carnality. Thomas made a noise, less of protest than of surprise, but the insistent thrust of Micha's tongue soon stole all words, all breath.

To lie beneath a man, so completely possessed, brought a host of new experiences, no more or less intimate than standing within the circle of his arms, but different. There was such an unabashed physical audacity to it that it made Thomas flame with intense, if unfocused, wanting. He could feel the shape of Micha's pelvis and the flex in his thigh muscles. And then, quite suddenly, the hot, hard outline of his cock. Thomas's hips came up of their own accord, nudging clumsily at this evidence of Micha's desire. It seemed a profane, impossible miracle that Micha wanted this too.

Another sound, lost in Micha's brutal kiss, and Micha pulled back, staring down at Thomas, his expression tight and unreadable, almost angry. His mouth looked red, like the interior of some poisonous fruit, and slightly bruised, in stark contrast to the darkness of his eyes.

The sun broke unexpectedly from behind a bank of cloud, half-dazzling Thomas and gilding Micha's tousled curls with transitory gold.

"I'm sorry," said Thomas, feeling he must have crossed some line without knowing it. "I'm so new to this."

"You don't touch me," Micha told him.

If this was strange, Thomas had no way to judge its strangeness. There was already too much for him to feel and think. Knowledge that he had always known to be forbidden, revealed to him, in all its beauty, like a vision of heaven itself. To be like this, with another man, crowned in falling leaves and sunlight, seemed a blessing beyond any earthly reckoning. His heart over-spilled on the loveliness of it, and happiness—pure and clear as water—ran through all his veins, as riotous as spring after the longest of winters. Thomas made a sound he barely recognised as coming from himself. "Kiss me again."

Micha glittered above him, as hard as a diamond, though he was breathing heavily. "Ask me. If you truly want it."

"I do. I want you to kiss me. Please."

"Fuck." Micha suddenly sounded almost on the verge of tears. "Oh fuck."

He dipped his head and Thomas pressed up against his mouth and they were kissing once again. Thomas had been kissed twice now—he was counting—once with tenderness and once with wantonness, but this was different again. Micha was neither compliant nor deliberate. He was just clumsy. And the kiss itself was deeper, somehow harsher. It tasted of desperation and the stinging salt of Micha's unshed tears. Thomas parted his lips, clinging to the heat that poured from Micha's open mouth, until they were both ragged and frantic and lost.

Finally, Micha tore himself away. His fingers tangled with Thomas's simply tied cravat and pulled it aside. And then his mouth came down afresh on Thomas's exposed throat. Thomas felt his pulse leap, his body arch, involuntary responses that tipped his head back against the leaves and canted his hips once more up to Micha's. And, this time, Micha did not stop him.

Thomas was not entirely a stranger to sexual desire, though he had not previously associated it with other men. He had, during his adolescence and occasionally after, granted himself physical release. Over time, the need for it had lessened. He hardly thought of it, certainly did not miss it. It had never occurred to him that he had given anything significant up. But the inexpert solipsism of his own hand was as different to this as a candle to the sun. If he had known of this—God, *this*—the hard pressure of another's body atop his, a mouth moving against his burning skin, rough, demanding hands that held him down and held him close, he would more readily have abandoned breathing.

He gave an awkward gasp, and it shuddered in his throat, as if Micha's mouth had drawn it directly from the skin. He was undone by a scattering of kisses. His body—made in the image of God, to have dominion over all creatures, redeemed by His son's sacrifice—surrendered wholly to the most earthly of caresses. And Thomas did not even think to struggle. He was conscious of no conflict, no concern, not even the faintest stir of guilt. It was like he had somehow gathered up the sundry threads of his physical being and brought them together into this bright-woven tapestry of perfect, sinless desire.

Micha's hands released his arms—blood returning in a pricklish flood—and then he was dragging apart the fastenings of Thomas's shirt, and Thomas was shipwrecked all over again. At first, it felt almost an assault, just heat and pleasure in near-unbearable waves, Micha's mouth and hands sweeping over Thomas's untouched body, claiming and inflaming. And Thomas writhed and shuddered under him, each panting breath a shallow moan, as he gave himself to Micha, piece by piece, gasp by gasp, until the other man suddenly muttered something inaudible, tumbled down against Thomas, and kissed him hard enough that Thomas tasted copper.

The urgency of Micha's body driving against his was such a new and raw kind of sensation that Thomas actually cried out—loud enough to startle a bird from where it must have been resting in the branches of a nearby tree. It took to the sky in a rustle of wings, streaking across his vision, the moment Micha took his mouth. Eventually they broke apart, and Micha shoved him back down amongst the leaves. His kisses spilled from Thomas's lips, down across his neck and torso, scattering bliss wildly and unbearably in their wake. And Thomas felt . . . unlike himself, transformed beneath Micha's touch into someone desirable and desired, and he thought he might be just about dying with the need for Micha, and for this. Thomas's fingers curled heedlessly, clutching at nothing but crumbling leaves and grass. He feared he could run mad on the sheer rapture of it all.

His body, at least, seemed to understand, on some ancient, fundamental instinct, how to surrender itself, to lips and hands and the promises of pleasures to come, as he had once surrendered all his dreams to duty. Life had taught Thomas control. Now he was learning how to abandon it. Not a dignified lesson, but perhaps the most joyous. For Micha, he came apart, everything he was and everything he knew transformed into panting desire and frantic urgency, and, with the shreds of reason he had left to him, he called it paradise.

"Oh God," gasped Thomas, the words flying from him, as heedless as swallows in springtime.

Micha froze. "Don't say his fucking name." A pause. "Say mine."

"Micha." Uncertain what Micha wanted from him, Thomas had left his arms spread where they had been pinned. He was desperate to reach out to his lover, but Micha had told him not to touch. So, instead, he tried to put it all in his voice, all the yearning and all the wonder. All the unleashed wantings he was only beginning to discover. "Oh Micha."

Crouched over him like this, Micha seemed an extraordinary being, a wildling of shadow and fire, mercurial, cruel, tender, and beautiful. It struck Thomas as rather incredible, incredible and humbling, that he—the youngest, dullest, and shyest of all his father's children—could be wanted by such a man.

Micha, clumsy again, made an abrupt, convulsive movement. His hand pressed downwards, beneath the waistband of Thomas's trousers and, fumblingly, beneath his drawers, until it curled around Thomas's stiff and straining cock. Thomas's body ignited into shuddering ecstasy, and he babbled out Micha's name, repeated like the most heartfelt prayer he had ever uttered. It was a searing kind of bliss, too beautiful and too terrible for shame, and that was all it took. The embrace of Micha's hand.

Thomas threw back his head, the distant sky, bluer than any sky had ever been, the purity of it filling his eyes like tears. "Oh Micha . . . I . . . can't . . ." His back arched, he thrust his cock against Micha, and, in one wild moment, as sudden as summer lightning, Thomas came. It was not an experience unknown to him, but whatever he had felt of it before was mere shadows. He was too gloriously lost in his own body for anything close to thought, but his heart instinctively understood the difference—this was not merely pleasure, it was given pleasure, the kindest, sweetest gift he had ever received, and from the most extraordinary man. His spinning world had found again its centre, and Thomas, no longer lost, felt safe and whole again.

Micha, his eyes as blank as glass, caught Thomas's spendings in his hand before he pulled abruptly away.

Thomas fell back, gasping, still pleasure-stricken though Micha no longer touched him, and waited for his breathing to steady, his heart to slow, and the world to return to some semblance of normality. But, no, his dazed eyes beheld the brightest sky, the reddest trees. And the light came down through the branches like spears of gold, as though it wanted to build a pagan temple to their desires. Micha had half-turned away, but Thomas, heedless suddenly of his earlier remonstrance, caught him in his arms and pulled him back down, so he could drown the last shudders of the ecstasy Micha had given him in the man's skin.

Micha's body was cold and unresponsive, except between his legs, where his cock burned and throbbed against Thomas's hip. Thomas slipped a hand between them, wanting to give Micha what Micha had just given him.

"No." Micha sounded so ferocious that Thomas immediately drew back.

Though he still refused to be touched, Micha did not pull away, so Thomas accepted that as well, whatever it meant, simply glad for Micha, as he was. The violence of completion was fading from his flesh. He sighed, shivered, bliss-wrung, grateful, and fragile. His beauty-dazed eyes blurred with a sheen of moisture, hastily blinked back, and he gave a shaky laugh. "You must think me the most callow of lovers. I can only apologise for . . ." Thomas did not quite dare to give the act a name ". . . so gracelessly upon your hand." He tried again for mirth, but it was hard to know how laughter sounded when his breath was suddenly so uncertain. "Perhaps I am in need of practice . . ." It was no use. He swallowed hard, but his eyes felt as painful as if knives had gathered in the corners. When the first tears escaped, if not for the shame that he wept, it could have almost been relief.

Micha jerked away from him as if scalded by their closeness. "Oh no. Don't do that. Don't you fucking dare."

Thomas sat up, trying to smother tears on his fingertips. "I'm so sorry."

Micha was kneeling on the leaves, like a vanquished knight, his head bowed to conceal his expression. "Look," he muttered. "It was just frigging. I'm sure God wouldn't count it."

"No," said Thomas hastily. "No. That is not what occasioned this foolishness. It was simply . . . the moment . . . I suppose one release led to another." It was too embarrassing even for words. He hid his face in his hands. "Please forgive me. My experience of these matters is limited, but I am more than reasonably certain that this is not the usual aftermath of physical intimacy."

Micha snorted. "You'd be surprised." Then he went on, in no kinder a tone, "But what is the matter with you, if not religious hypocrisy?"

Thomas moved across the leaves until he was kneeling as Micha knelt. He reached out a hand and, with careful, gentle fingers, lifted Micha's chin so that he had to look at him. "Micha, you must believe me when I tell you I have no guilt for this. No shame. I cannot. I can only thank you, with all my heart and soul."

Micha's eyes skittered away. "All right, all right. Calm down. It's sex, not the creation of the world."

"Yes, but I had no idea it would be like this."

"Wait. What? You've never . . . ?"

Thomas shook his head. "I have always tried to live in accordance with my profession. Until I met you, I did not even realise I was made this way." Micha was staring at him with utter incomprehension, so he kept on talking. "And it has been quite the loneliest discovery I have ever made."

"I don't understand."

"I felt so set apart. So lost. Knowing there was a part of me, an unchangeable part of me, that would make others hate me. You must know how terrifying that is. But today you showed me it need not be so." He smiled into Micha's frowning face. "I can't begin to tell you how it feels to know that you are as I am. And that you like me too."

Micha dragged his hands out of Thomas's clasp and sprawled backwards on the leaves, laughing. It was not a happy sound.

Thomas leaned over him. "Did I say something odd?"

But Micha kept on laughing, his whole body shaking with it. "Forget it," he said finally, somewhat breathlessly. "It's nothing."

Since Micha seemed disinclined to move, Thomas lowered himself onto an elbow at Micha's side.

"What are you staring at?"

Thomas flushed. "Just at you. I . . . I think you're very beautiful."

"Stop that. We fucked. There's no need to get sentimental over it." But then Micha rolled over so that his position mirrored Thomas's. They were face-to-face, breath-to-breath. And, after a moment, he slid a hand lightly over Thomas's flank and left it resting there. "It would have been different if I'd known. You should have said."

"I had no opportunity with your mouth on mine," said Thomas primly, earning a sour look from Micha. "Besides," he added, his voice softening, "it was perfect. And you are perfect."

"You've no metric to judge."

"I need none. I know."

"You're an idiot."

Thomas risked putting a hand over Micha's hand, and, although Micha glared at it, he did not shake it off. "How remarkable," Thomas murmured, "that in the vastness of the world, we should find each other. Some benevolence must have guided us together."

"I don't know about benevolence."

"It still feels like a miracle to me."

"You'll get used to it."

They were silent for a while. Thomas had no awareness of moving, and he certainly did not see Micha do so, but, somehow, their bodies slipped together. His head found Micha's shoulder. Their legs became entangled, their hands intertwined.

"How long have you known?" asked Thomas.

"You mean about me or about you?"

"Both."

"You, awhile now. Me, forever. Since I was eighteen at least."

"Since you were eighteen. My word, that is forever."

"I wish people would stop teasing me about my age. It's not funny."

"Do you know . . . I mean . . . are there . . . many . . ." Thomas made an uncertain gesture.

"Buggers?" offered Micha. "Mandrakes? Sodomites? Nancies? Perverts?"

"Men who love men."

"Plenty."

"How wonderful."

Micha sneered. "Why, do you want to fuck them too?"

"No, of course not. I just find it comforting to know they're there."

"Oh yes, you and your lonely universe."

"Mock all you wish." Thomas smiled dreamily and found himself unexpectedly rewarded by a trace of warmth in Micha's eyes. "I am too happy to mind."

"If you ask me, the universe is a bit too bloody crowded."

Thomas tucked his head beneath Micha's chin, his gaze drifting over his shoulder to the wood that seemed to him, now, an enchanted place. "Not here."

"No," agreed Micha, "not here."

Thomas closed his eyes, letting physical languor and the warmth of Micha pressed against him lull him into a drifting state that was not quite sleep.

"Micha," he murmured, minutes, years, or lifetimes later, "can I ask you something?"

Micha's eyes fluttered open. This close to him, Thomas could see greenish flecks floating deep in his irises. "You seem hell-bent on it."

"Do you remember when you were ill, and you told me that my dreams were terrible?"

"I remember."

"You never did tell me yours."

Micha was silent. His body tensed against Thomas. "I don't have any."

"But you must have once."

"What does it matter?"

"It matters to me."

Micha huffed out a sigh. "It's stupid. It was always stupid."

"No more ridiculous, surely, than a priest who wishes to see deserts and lie with men."

"You could lie with a man in the desert. That might bring about the apocalypse."

Thomas laughed. He reached out a hand and let Micha's curls run through his fingers. They twisted there like little snakes, as though they wanted to keep him captive. "Please. I won't insist. But I would like to know something of you."

"Access to my body does not give you any right to my heart."

"Are they not one and the same?"

"No."

"As you wish."

Thomas closed his eyes again and let the subject die. Unexpectedly, he felt Micha's lips on his.

"I wanted," whispered Micha, against his mouth, "I wanted . . . to be someone to come home to. That's all."

Chapter 14

Micha was in hell. It was not supposed to be like this. The opium was the barrier between his body and anything it might have to feel. And yet, somehow, he was breached. Thomas had barely laid hands on him, but he had given of himself so utterly that it had not mattered. Every sound he'd made was seared into Micha's skin like a brand. His mouth tasted of Thomas's mouth. The skin on his palms, where he had touched the untouched, felt raw. He'd drugged himself into a stupor, but still the memory would not release its hold on him. It was not a thing of the mind. It was a thing of the body, indelible somehow, written into him and onto him, as surely as Isidore and everyone who had taken Micha since. But Thomas was unblurring, the freshest, the deepest and brightest, as though he had drenched Micha in sunlight.

Micha lay in bed, waiting for the laudanum to help him, but it felt as though ants were crawling inside his skin. Edward's paintings swarmed across his vision. In a blur of too-brilliant colour, he saw Thomas's body arching red-gold under his own, his hair spilled across leaves only one shade lighter, pale hands clutching at nothing, gleaming like the moon. That night, for the first time in months or even years, Micha touched himself by choice. His flesh responded only distantly, like the bells that used to chime daily over the gables of Oxford. He wrapped a hand around his half-stirring prick, imagining it was Thomas's hand that touched him or Thomas's prick he touched, but his ardour was a guttering thing, and both hand and prick were too familiar to inspire anything beyond contempt. He raked his nails over the head of his cock until he hissed. That, at least, he felt.

He gave up. He wanted, but not this.

He wondered what it had been like for Isidore the first time they had lain together. If Isidore had watched the wonder dawn in Micha's eyes as today he had watched it dawn in Thomas's. And felt the power of it, so terrifyingly sweet. Micha tugged the covers over his head and curled in on the memories, trying to smother them in heat and darkness.

He did not want to want.

He had chosen his craving.

But Thomas had made him into a world. A whole universe, star-studded with kisses.

Micha could still not entirely untangle the impulse that had made him yield himself. Thomas's grief. The white horse. The empty palms of history. He had thought, grinding Thomas into the oak tree, forcing their mouths together, that he would take something from him. But all Thomas had done was give and give and give. Isidore had said there was no sin or shame in love. It was not until Thomas that Micha had come close to believing it.

The next evening, they attended the first meeting of the Nettlefield Reading Group, which was held up at Chalfont Manor, or "the big house," as most of the village residents called it. They walked there together through the evening haze, Micha slouching along, doing his best to appear as if nothing had happened, and Thomas practically bouncing. The man had an absolutely ridiculous glow about him and a smile that kept slipping onto his lips like a guest who refused to go home.

Micha felt annoyed and pleased and absurd. "If you turn up for an evening of improving literature looking like that, they'll think you've been at the communion wine."

"Like what?" asked Thomas, whose eyes brightened as they alighted upon Micha.

Micha made an ill-conceived gesture. "Like . . . that. All happy for no reason."

"Is happiness a sin now?"

"You tell me."

Thomas made a visible effort to contain himself. "I'm sorry. I just feel so very blessed."

Blessed? How could he possibly. "From one . . ." Micha made another ill-conceived gesture, and Thomas went pink to the tips of his ears.

"Not just that," he said, quickly, "though it was lovely. Everything. You. Being with you. Knowing I am not utterly alone. And feeling, for perhaps the first time in my life, truly myself."

"And how are you squaring this with your God?"

"I'm not."

Micha widened his eyes.

"It's so very strange. I've never felt so confident in the beauty and benevolence of the world, and its creator, but I suppose I must be very far from grace indeed, to be who I am, and do what I have done." Thomas shrugged. "I presume an answer will come to me in time. But, whether it does or doesn't, I must consider how to proceed with my life."

This had not been a conversation Micha had ever envisioned having. Certainly not less than twenty-four hours after a few kisses and a hand job. "Why? Can't you just go on with it?"

"Well, of course I shall go on with it. But I can hardly remain in the church, can I? I cannot preach duty, chastity, and obedience when I am neither dutiful, obedient, or"—Thomas smiled—"chaste." And, suddenly, he whirled round, right there in the lane, and pressed a swift, clumsy kiss on Micha's astonished lips.

"What the fuck are you doing?" cried Micha, looking wildly in all directions in case someone had seen them.

Thomas burst out laughing. "There's no one here."

"Yes but . . . yes but . . . you don't do that."

"Why not?"

"What do you mean, 'Why not'? It's obvious."

"The only sensible reason," said Thomas mildly, "that I can imagine for not kissing you is you not wanting to be kissed."

"There are lots of sensible reasons."

"Is that among them?"

"N-no but—"

So, of course, Thomas kissed him again. Micha froze, though his heart hammered wildly. This was stupid. Madness. Somebody would surely catch them. And then Thomas made a soft, yearning noise against his mouth, and Micha found his fingers had coiled into Thomas's hair and he was dragging him closer until their bodies met as intimately as their lips. Thomas, it seemed, was a swift learner. There was no hesitation in him, no anxiety. He shaped the kiss, but he did not control it, and he claimed Micha with painstaking care, and a thoroughness that made his knees shake. Thomas's tongue slipped lightly between Micha's lips, explored him, worshipped him, took possession of the deepest corners of his mouth. It was a sweet, certain communion, and Micha felt precious. Annihilated. He heard someone actually whimper and realised—with some bewilderment—it was him. He pulled away, pressing fingertips to his mouth, as though he had never been kissed.

"I love doing that." Thomas gazed at him with naked adoration. "I think about it all the time. I love the sounds you make. I love the way you look at me."

"Stop it."

If only it was more of an act. That might have made it bearable. It was what a whore did, after all. But this was neither entirely truth nor entirely fiction. It was something else, something both and neither.

"Sorry." But Thomas spoke so entirely unrepentantly that Micha had to bite back a smile.

"Stop looking at me like you want to propose. I told you, it's just sex."

"Oh," said Thomas, in the same giddy fashion, "if only we could be married."

"You can wear the gown."

"A small price to pay."

"Stop it. It's not funny."

"I wasn't trying to be amusing. I think it makes perfect sense. How could love ever be sinful, whatever form it took? So really our only wickedness is fornication. And that is only because we are denied an alternative."

Micha sneered. "Does this help you sleep at night, Father? Look at yourself in the mirror in the morning? It's still wrong. And pretending there's more to it makes you a hypocrite as well as a pervert." Thomas reached for his hand and Micha jerked away. "What the fuck are you doing now?"

Thomas made a gesture of surrender. "Micha, if I truly believed that what I did with you was wrong, I would not do it. That is why we are granted conscience. I am pretending nothing. I love you. It's very simple."

Micha's mouth fell open. Pure disbelief. A touch of horror. And a swirl of something else much less easily articulated. How could Thomas just say that? Out of nowhere. As if it was easy. Of course, Micha had said it to Isidore often enough, the words such meagre messengers of his fervour, and Isidore had always said it back. Always said it back. As light as his caresses. This was nothing like that. And yet there it was, something else Thomas had given unasked.

"Oh dear," Thomas went on, rather wryly. "I can see by your expression I have not pleased you. I know you're not in love with me."

"You can't love me," whispered Micha. "You don't know me."

Thomas smiled at him gently. "What has knowledge to do with love? Love is a kind of faith, is it not?"

Micha rolled his eyes. "Damn priests." But perhaps Thomas was right. What had he truly known of Isidore, after all, beyond his brilliance and his beauty? He might as well have been a stained-glass saint. And yet Micha loved him still, for loving Isidore was the last part of himself he did not hate.

"Anyway," he added, "if you want to practice the tenets of your newfound faith, I can think of some interesting things for you to do on your knees."

"Such as?" Thomas had the attentive air of a pupil at lessons.

"I'll . . . I'll show you later."

"I shall look forward to it."

They walked the rest of the way in silence. The smile was still glimmering at the edges of Thomas's mouth, but at least he managed to restrain himself from any further alfresco displays of his feelings.

Micha was enthusiastically welcomed to the Nettlefield Reading Group—which had already mostly assembled in one of the manor's larger drawing rooms—and plied immediately with tea and cake. The villagers greeted Thomas with a kind of wary courtesy that soon developed into eagerness. Despite Micha's warning, happiness was spilling out of the man like sunlight. And some long-abandoned, sensual part of Micha wanted to bask in it. To think to himself, *I did that.*

It was strange to see Thomas with other people. He had such a careful way about him, listening gravely to whatever was said and considering each answer before he gave it, a neat, prosaic figure in sober black, a point of stillness in the lively room. And yet Micha was also conscious of a prickling sense of unease. The parishioners treated Thomas with respect, and seemed happy for his attention, but he was so reserved. So much the dutiful servant of his Lord's people.

Thomas was the man who'd stood with Micha beneath the stars, the man who'd whispered shyly of his dreams, laughed at the absurdities of life, and wept over the death of his brother. The man who had kissed Micha breathless and spent against his hand. That was Thomas. He did not belong to these people. He did not belong to God. He belonged—

"So he came." Esther appeared at Micha's side, teacup in hand.

It was obvious to whom she referred. Micha had been staring. He shrugged.

"What's next?" she asked. "The knitting circle?"

"I don't want to join the knitting circle."

Esther cackled. "Spoilsport." There was a pause. "How do you feel about crochet?"

Micha spluttered.

"If you intend to stay all winter, you may rue the day you turned your nose up at crochet."

"You mean," he asked, "because the season gets very cold or very boring?"

"It *is* quite cold. Boredom's a matter of personal taste."

Micha tucked his hands into his pockets, his gaze wandering across the room, to land again on Thomas. He was too far away to hear anything but the vaguest snatches of the conversation—whatever the topic, Sophie Butterworth seemed very animated about it, and Thomas was listening attentively to her. But then he looked up, as though Micha had called out his name. His eyes flared warm, and his mouth curved almost imperceptibly into a smile. Micha flustered and stared at his feet. "Maybe I like boring."

"I very much doubt it, dear."

Ruff, it turned out, was also an honorary member of the book group. He ambled in with Ada, was thrown into paroxysms of joy at the sight of Micha, and demonstrated his pleasurable recollections of their first meeting by dashing across the room and knocking him over.

"Oh my," sighed Ada, looking down at where Micha flailed futilely on the rug. "And not a stream or a pond or a lake or even a puddle anywhere near."

"You are an obsessed woman." Esther shook her head, despairingly.

Ada dimpled. "But who can blame me?"

"Um," said Micha, as Ruff, wildly excited by this latest evolution of their game, nuzzled his nose wetly into Micha's ear. "A little help here? Any time now."

"Leave him alone, you bloody Cerberus." Esther hauled the dog away by the scruff of his neck. "I should sell him or shoot him or something."

"Yes." Micha scrambled upright and pulled his clothes back into order. "You should." Ruff immediately rolled over Micha's feet, snuffling lovingly. And Micha bent down to tug on his flyaway ears. "Stop trying to be winning," he muttered.

Ruff's tail thumped.

"I'm afraid he takes after his master," said Esther. "My late husband used to do that."

Micha glanced up. "Drool on your boots?"

"Hah. No. Act the donkey and then try to make up for it."

"I hope he was better at it."

"Mm, considerably. I did marry him."

"Oh, Michael." Ada tugged suddenly on his arm. "You will come and sit next to me, will you not?"

Esther shook her head. "Incorrigible."

"You aren't going to push me into a stream or anything, are you?" he asked.

She laughed. "Don't be silly, I just want to be near the best-looking man in the room."

Micha flushed, tried to stammer out a response, and realised he had no idea what to say. *Thank you? That's very flattering, but I like men, actually. You're scaring me, stop it.*

"That makes no sense." Esther came to his rescue. "You should arrange for him to sit on the other side of the room so you can have an unhindered view. I mean, heaven forefend you came here to read a book."

Ada huffed. "Don't sneer, dear, it doesn't suit you. And, anyway, there's no harm in it. Everyone will be green with envy, and Michael will be able to tell me all the gossip about Thomas."

"But . . . but . . ." Micha flapped his hands. "I don't have any gossip."

"Believe me," said Esther, dryly. "That will not stop her acquiring some."

"Also," added Ada, her eyes darting like hawks about the room, "we can claim that sofa by the window. It looks by far the best choice."

Micha had half-hoped, half-expected he would be next to Thomas, but now he realised what a ridiculous notion that had been. What had he imagined? That they would sit there like courting sweethearts, body to body, hand in hand?

Ruff was rolled away and Micha let himself be dragged onto the sofa, with Ada claiming his left and Esther his right. Ruff gambolled after them and tried to squeeze between Micha's legs, an intimacy Micha firmly declined. Finally, the endeavour was abandoned, and Ruff consented to laying his chin possessively over Micha's knees instead.

Esther had twisted round to look out of the window. "I don't like the look of that sky."

Micha also turned. Grey was amassing on the horizon, stained ominously pinkish by the setting sun.

"I thought it was 'red sky at night, shepherd's delight,'" said Ada.

"That's not red sky." Esther pointed at the clouds. "That's a storm coming."

"Oh don't, it's been such a beautiful autumn, I should hate to see it spoiled."

"I don't control the weather, Ada."

Micha hid a smile behind his teacup.

"I've never understood that saying anyway," went on Ada, entirely unrebuked. "I don't see what the colour of the sky has to do with whether it's sunny or rainy."

Esther shrugged. "It's probably just an old wives' tale."

"Actually," offered Micha, "it's because weather moves from west to east, so a red sunset in the west means good weather is coming towards you, and a red sunrise in the east means good weather is going away."

They stared at him. "And clever too," sighed Ada.

Micha shifted uncomfortably. "A friend told me."

Speaking of Isidore was a habit both compulsive and self-destructive. He knew he should let it heal, but without the wound, there would have been nothing. As if Isidore had never happened or never meant anything. As if he had not changed everything. Micha waited for the dull twist of pain, but it did not come. A strange panic flared. It was like reaching for something and finding it gone. He dug his fingers deeper.

"He liked knowing those sort of things," he went on. "The whys of the world."

Nothing. Nothing at all. An emptiness deeper than opium.

"Ah," said Esther, with an arch look that suggested she believed Micha was simply too modest to admit to his own curiosities, "but did this 'friend' know the Shakespeare reference. 'Like a red morn that ever yet betokened Wreck to the seaman.'"

"It goes back further than that," came a different voice. And, suddenly, Thomas was standing before them, light in his eyes, wearing a smile that Micha was sure could have only been meant for him. He wanted to catch it with his mouth. Hold it like a treasure somewhere safe inside himself where the world could not reach in and take it from him. "'When in evening, ye say it will be fair weather: For the sky is red.'"

"Oh, everything's in the Bible." Esther waved a hand dismissively, and Ada gave a small, shocked meep. "That's practically cheating."

"I was not informed there were rules," said Thomas so gravely that Micha knew he was secretly laughing. "I forfeit." He crouched down, his leg brushing briefly against Micha's, and stroked a hand down Ruff's silky throat. The dog made a sound of pure canine ecstasy and rolled over.

Oh fuck. Micha should have been committing himself to Bedlam. It was the only possible explanation. He should not—*should not*—have envied a fucking dog.

Thomas glanced up, his voice as gentle as his hands. "How are you, Esther?"

"I keep busy," she told him, rather grudgingly. "Ruff needs walking. Ada needs someone to stop her doing anything stupid. Young men need dragging out of streams."

Micha, startled by her manner, opened his mouth to speak, but Ada shook her head at him, and he fell silent.

Thomas was still watching Esther with steady warmth. It was a look Micha knew well. He had felt its strange power, like a touch upon his skin.

Esther's shoulders slumped. "But how many years for it to stop feeling like yesterday?"

There was a silence, and it was not quite comfortable.

"I don't know," said Thomas at last. And then, rather stiltedly, "You may be sure, though, that God understands."

"How generous of Him."

Somehow, Thomas had vanished in plain sight. All his passions, all his pains, all his kindness and his secrets, locked away behind words and a black coat. Micha wanted to take him by the hand and drag him back to them. Together, they could shake off Thomas's God as though he was nothing but a shadow.

"It's not a sin to grieve," Thomas was saying, "only to grieve as though we are without hope, or that we suffer our pain alone. Remember, when Jesus came to the home of Mary and Martha, he wept with them for their loss."

Esther said nothing for a very long moment. And then she gave a faint, dismissive smile. "How right you are, Thomas. I had not thought of that."

At that moment, someone called Thomas's name from across the room, and he climbed to his feet, brushing long red-gold hairs from the knees of his trousers. "Excuse me." A polite nod and he was gone. Micha tried not to watch him walk away.

Esther shook her head. "Hopeless."

"What do you mean?" cried Ada. "He was remarkably civil, even though everyone knows you are a complete raging harpy when it comes to Jack."

"As," retorted Esther, "is my inalienable right as a disgruntled widow. Mary and Martha, my arse."

"Is it not a comforting story?"

"Only in the sense the Lord casually resurrects their dead brother for them. For the rest of us, it's just adding insult to injury."

"I'm sure Thomas meant well." It was such a spineless, lovesick platitude that Micha was shocked to realise he was the one who had uttered it.

Esther gave him a look. "Of course he meant well, Michael. Why do you think I didn't spit in his eye?" She sipped her tea. "If nothing else, the fellow tries."

Micha wished he could pretend he did not understand, but he did. Where once he had looked at Thomas and seen only privilege, wealth, and ease, things Micha regarded with mingled envy and disdain, now he saw restraint, sacrifice, and duty. The price of being good carved straight from a man's soul. And Thomas was too honest, too clever, and too worthy not to know his own failings and suffer in that knowledge. Micha could have told him, *It is you they want to love, not your church. Love them as you would have God love them, and the rest will follow.* But he had abandoned love long ago, as love had abandoned him, and there were not even embers spread amongst the ashes of his heart.

"I wish he would try a little less on Sundays," murmured Ada and then covered her mouth with her hand, looking as shocked as if she had accidentally disgorged a live snake.

"God yes," agreed Esther, "and I do not take the Lord's name in vain. Those sermons."

Micha frowned, the inclination to defend Thomas so terrifyingly natural he barely realised he was doing it until he spoke. "He can't be that bad. I certainly can't imagine him being all hellfire and damnation."

"Nothing like that," said Esther, quickly. "He's just terribly dull. Most of us simply want to hear that God loves us and be sent home again. But Thomas, well, he discourses, as though faith is simply a matter of reason and good manners."

"Can't it be?"

"Sometimes. But what is intellect without passion, understanding without conviction?"

"If you ask me," put in Ada, "he needs a wife. Someone to love him and look after him. Make him happy like he is today. Why, I hardly recognise him."

The sky flooded iron, sweeping the room with sudden shadows. From the deep-grey distance came the sonorous crackle of thunder. Everyone scrambled to turn up the lamps and light the candles.

Micha was glad for the activity that surrounded him. He felt cold and floaty, as though poppy-drowned, as though he wasn't really there.

"I say." Laura banged her spoon against her teacup. "We'd jolly well better start this thing, before we get flooded out like Noah."

Those who had not already done so took their places. A couple of copies of *The Woman in White* were produced and passed round. Laura and Fred-Violet Mouseworthy sat side by side, sharing the book between them, their heads close as they leaned over the pages together.

Thomas was prevailed upon to read first. As the familiar rise and fall of his voice washed over the room, Micha remembered, in sudden, lightning-bright flashes, fragments of his fever. Isidore twisted round him like a serpent, naked skin and promises. And a stranger, reading to him through the long night, like a candle left to light his way back home.

Once again, the words flowed unheeded past him.

Instead, he thought, *He loves me.*

He corrected himself. *He believes he loves me.*

But, somehow, it reverted anyway. *He loves me.*

Everyone else was lost in the unfolding narrative and Thomas's attention was focused on the page, so Micha was at liberty simply to look at him. He watched the slightest movements of his lips. The ripple of his throat. The shift of his eyes beneath his lashes. Like a thief, wild with desperation, Micha stuffed his pockets with forbidden glances. And knew it was fairy gold. Nothing but sand. The lamplight was not kind to Thomas. It cast jagged shadows across his cheeks, sharpening all his angles and emphasising the lack of symmetry to his features. Stern jaw. Leonine nose. Deep-set eyes. Heavy brow. Wide lips. He had never looked less lovely. And Micha had never wanted him more.

The evening slipped away convivially. Even Micha was—at some point—drawn into the story. He took his turn with the book and acquitted himself creditably, winning not only laughter but applause for his wearily drawling Mr. Fairlie. Outside, the darkness deepened, the thunder rolled, and the wind howled, but nobody paid any heed at all. It was well past a civilised bedtime when the party, finally, began to break up. The reading itself had ceased nearly an hour ago, but the attendees had fallen on what was left of the cakes and let themselves be drawn into fervent speculation. Who was the woman in white? Was Mr. Hartright absolutely devoid of any mental acuity? What was Glyde's dastardly scheme? And would the author compare any other of his characters to vegetables?

But, eventually, they managed to extricate themselves, and Micha was filled with a terrible, shameful gladness to be alone again with Thomas and the secrets they shared. They were ten minutes down the road from the big house when the storm hit them. The world sheeted white, and then the sky broke open like a bowl, lightning cracking over the clouds. The downpour was immediate and merciless. They were soaked within seconds.

"Good grief." The wind ripped Thomas's words from his lips as though they were discarded rags.

Micha turned his face to the rain. It landed on his skin as cold and hard as thrown stones. He didn't know why but he laughed.

"We should run," cried Thomas, over the thunder and the deluge. "The last thing you need is another chill."

He caught for Micha's hand and pulled him down the hill, which was already well on the way to becoming a quagmire. Thomas lost his footing as the ground levelled off and skidded gracelessly forward in a flail of limbs and flying garments. Micha clutched for him, and they both nearly went over. They steadied—just—entangled and breathless, staring at each other through a haze of rain.

"Bloody hell . . . I mean . . . oh dear." Thomas's eyelashes were clumped together with moisture.

The thought came from nowhere, but Micha uttered it nevertheless: "The world rains curses."

"The world rains rain," said Thomas firmly. "Come."

But Micha shook his head. He put a hand—as soggy as the rest of him and trembling with, he hoped, cold—to Thomas's face, and Thomas stilled almost instantly.

"Micha?"

The weather raged around them, a forgotten creature in the grip of its own tantrum.

And, suddenly, Micha slanted his mouth hard over Thomas's, his fingers twisting into the other man's hair to hold him there. Thomas tasted of the rain and innocent things. Tea and lemon cake. But there was nothing innocent in the sound he made or the way he pressed himself into Micha. His lips were icy, but the interior of his mouth was impossibly warm. His tongue was a serpentine flame. Water fell from the curling tips of Micha's hair, trickling between the scant spaces of their kisses.

"Fuck," he gasped. "Oh fuck."

This was probably how it felt to be martyred. He was freezing and burning and dying all at once. He wanted it to end. He wanted it to begin. He wanted. He *wanted.* And he had forgotten how to take. How to ask.

He caught Thomas's hands by the wrists. His thumbs left brutal shadows over the pulse points, but Thomas did not pull away. In the gloom, his eyes—slightly wide—were nothing but pupil and the faintest edge of golden-brown iris.

"Touch me," Micha muttered. "For fuck's sake, touch me. Make me feel something."

His grip slackened, and, tentatively, one of Thomas's smooth gentleman's hands trembled at Micha's jaw. Followed the line of stubble down his chin into the rain-slick hollow at the base of his throat.

"I said make me feel," Micha snarled.

He was nothing but a beast, caged in his own opium-saturated flesh. For the first time he truly saw his prison and felt the weight of the chains he wore. The dream-bright horizon seemed as tawdry now as the painted backdrop of a twopenny circus. Despair rolled through him, thick as smoke. Wanting was nothing but a reminder of everything he couldn't have. What if he had met Thomas, not Isidore? What then, what then? What if the ghosts of six hundred other men did not stand between them? What if Micha had not already sold his soul?

He pulled Thomas's hand down his body, the palm skimming senselessly over his chest, leaving nothing in its wake but the memory of a ripple of cold, then forced it beneath the waistband of his trousers and against his half-stirring cock. Thomas's fingers opened like a flower, curling round Micha, clumsy and eager and kind. Warmth. Pressure. So much. So little. The rain pelted against Micha's back and slithered through his hair. The wind lashed at him and the cold numbed him. And Thomas stroked him like he was touching something beautiful. A gift, given to a recipient incapable of deserving it.

"Down." Micha's voice cracked like the lightning. "Get on your knees."

He put a hand on Thomas's shoulder and pressed. After the slightest hesitation, Thomas dropped into the mud.

"Get your hands out of the way."

One last, barely there caress, and they were gone.

Micha tore his trousers fully open, seized his cock, and dragged it across Thomas's lips in a smear of rain and pre-come. Thomas looked up at him from where he knelt. There was no alarm or revulsion on his face, just a terrible sort of trust. And, although Micha had told him to keep his hands out of the way, they were suddenly there again, embracing Micha's hips, holding him close and steady in the centre of the storm.

Micha made a sound that was almost a sob. Then, "Let me in."

Thomas opened his mouth and Micha shoved inside without kindness or finesse. Heat, slick and soft, engulfed him. A noise, a breath or a groan, caught at the back of Thomas's throat. Micha stared down at him, shaking heavy hanging hair and wetness from his eyes. Thomas was just a piece of bedraggled darkness, crumpled at Micha's feet, wavery through a grey veil. His gaze was intent on Micha's, even as tears pooled in his eyes and slipped from the corners, mingling with the tracks already left by the rain.

Micha looked away and thrust. His hands knotted in Thomas's hair. Thomas made another sound, pained, wet, and breathless, and Micha ignored him. The storm ran over them. Micha was sure he was cold, but he felt untouched and untouchable. It was like fucking the dark, a hot, deep void. He imagined running a knife across his skin. He would bleed dust and rust-red petals that would blow away in the wind. He had chosen his own god, and his body was its temple. He housed nothing else.

"Stop it. It's no use." He jerked himself away, fumbling with the fastenings on his trousers.

Thomas fell forward, catching himself on his elbows before he landed in the mud. He was a mess of rain and tears, spit and mucus. After a spluttering, gasping moment he sat back on his heels.

"I'm sorry—" he began.

"Don't. Don't. It's me, not you, I can't. I just can't."

Thomas came a bit shakily to his feet. His clothes had fared no better than the rest of him. He wiped his swollen mouth on the sleeve of his coat.

"Come." His voice was raw.

Micha could have stood there until the storm consumed him. Until the wind flayed him. Until he was nothing but water droplets lost in the torrent. Except Thomas took up his hand and led him home.

Ten minutes later, they staggered into the rectory. Thomas had to struggle to close the door in the face of the prevailing wind. Then, apparently unconcerned by the mess he was making and the mud he was tracking everywhere, he hurried into the drawing room and began building up a fire. As soon as it was lit, he sank to his knees in front of the blaze.

Micha stood in the hall, water streaming from his hair into his eyes and down his face. The rain felt as bitter as tears. His mouth stung with salt and shame. He yanked off his boots and made a dash for the stairs.

Thomas's voice pulled him back. "Micha."

"I . . . should . . . I don't . . ."

"Come here, please." It was not a command, nor really a plea, but it reeled Micha in like a fish upon a line, and, in truth, he had no wish to resist. He did not know if he could bear to see the disgust, recrimination, or, worse, the hurt in Thomas's eyes, but he deserved them. That, in itself, was absolution of a kind. Perhaps on the other side lay freedom. From Thomas and wanting and himself. How much easier it would all be now that Thomas hated him.

Micha stepped into the room like a convicted criminal going to his execution. The warmth of the fire curled around him in welcome, and the pleasure of it was both irresistible and incongruous. A long, deep shudder ran through him, his chilled flesh shaking itself awake. He peeled his sodden coat off and let it fall to the floor. "Listen. I'm sorry, all right? I . . . I'm sorry." He huddled down in front of the fire. Steam swirled up immediately from his clothes. And the heat reminded him of Thomas's mouth.

There was a long silence. The firelight gleamed on the arch of Thomas's cheekbones. "I have wanted," he said, finally, "to touch you for a very long time. But not like that."

Micha closed his eyes. "I . . ." he started. But there was nothing to say.

Thomas's fingers brushed lightly over Micha's.

"I don't want to be like this," Micha muttered. "I was . . . I used you . . ."

"That I would not mind."

Micha's eyes flicked open, startled. Thomas was looking directly at him, and it was now impossible to look away.

"I think," he went on, "I could have liked it. The act was not without power, not without beauty, and I do not fear to be the supplicant of your passion."

It had been a long time since Micha had found even a fleeting trace of beauty in the base mechanics of sex. Even clothed in Thomas's quiet conviction, the idea seemed absurd and impossible. "I brutalised you."

"And I will not allow you to touch me in that fashion again."

A cold, deeper than the rain, settled over Micha. Unbidden came the image of Thomas sprawled beneath him on autumn leaves, helpless, abandoned, and utterly his. Micha swallowed. "That's . . . fine."

Thomas leaned over and kissed his cheek with the ghost of a smile. "I said in that fashion. You may be as rough as you need to be with me, but I won't let you use me as though I were not there. As though you sought nothing but pain and ugliness and emptiness in our coming together. It seems to me almost a form of sacrilege."

"Sacrilege," repeated Micha, with a faint, mirthless laugh. "It's all sacrilege, Thomas."

But Thomas only shook his head.

"You are such a stubborn fucker."

He smiled. "In my way."

Micha turned his gaze back to the fire, and when he spoke, it was barely more than a whisper. "I wish . . . I wish I was different."

"You can be anyone you wish to be."

"Don't. It's not that simple."

"Well, as it happens, I have grown rather accustomed to you as you are. Even fond."

"Fond?"

Thomas gave him a mischievous look. "Very fond." He reached out and caught one of Micha's rain-damp curls between his fingers, pressing out the water and letting the hair spring back. "You may not be the easiest man, but you can be very kind when you wish. Very warm. Very clever. And very amusing. And I'm sufficiently superficial to find your beauty arresting."

Micha coughed, but he felt the heat rising to his cheeks. "I shouldn't have . . ."

"No," agreed Thomas, "you shouldn't. And now I understand better of what may be done between two men, you may be sure you will not do it again."

Micha dropped his head wretchedly onto his knees.

Thomas nudged his shoulder reassuringly. "I have as good as forgotten."

"Have you, uh, forgiven?" mumbled Micha.

"Forgiveness is, thankfully, a problem for the Lord. And I shall remember with great joy the tightness of your hands upon my hair. The taste of your—" Micha looked up in time to see Thomas flush scarlet. "Oh my word."

"Cock. The taste of my cock."

Thomas nodded. "Precisely," he said primly. "Which I hope to experience again, under more convivial circumstances."

For a moment, Micha felt almost like he could smile. But it was still a little too soon, and the more Thomas tried to comfort him, the worse he felt. "I'm so sorry." The words rushed out of him in a choked torrent. "I'm so sorry. If only there was something I could say or do."

There was a pause.

"There is." Thomas darted a sidelong look at him. "If you want. And only if you want."

Micha wished. But he had learned his harshest lessons well. "What is it?" he asked, narrowing his eyes.

"Perhaps you could," said Thomas softly, "ask me again what you asked in the rain."

"I can't remember what I said. I said all sorts of things."

"I remember. You said, 'Make me feel.'"

Micha remembered only bile and poppies. "Did I?"

"Yes. And I should like to try. If you will let me."

Bile and poppies and hopelessness. "I won't spend."

"That wasn't what you asked."

"Oh fuck."

Unexpectedly, Thomas gave a soft laugh. "You said that too."

Micha was so terrified he could barely speak. It was one thing to yield himself for money, but to do so by choice? Could he even recall how? Did he want to? And Thomas would surely be disappointed in him. This hollow shell of a man he found beautiful. "All right," he managed at last.

But still Thomas waited.

Micha's mouth had gone painfully dry. "M-make . . ." he croaked. "Make me feel." And in case that was not enough. "Please."

And the next thing he knew, Thomas was full-length on top of him, fire-warm, rain-damp, all long limbs, sharp bones, and clumsy eagerness. His lips were on Micha's lips, just long enough to make him breathless, then they were sliding down his throat, over his quickening pulse. Thomas's hands were tugging open the fastenings on his shirt, and Micha trembled in some awful combination of fear and reaction. It was all he could do not to reach up and cover himself. When he had been naked—far more naked—than this. Thomas leaned over him and kissed his collarbones, his tongue lashing like flames over the ridges of bone. His breath travelled over Micha's skin like the glow from a shot of brandy.

Micha stared blankly at the moulding on the ceiling, his hands clenching and unclenching in the hearthrug. "You," he said awkwardly, "you also said something."

"Hmm?" Thomas lifted his head. His expression was dazed, his eyes as hazy as a man's who had taken too much wine. His hand shook where it rested upon Micha's chest, rising and falling with his unsteady breaths.

"Say it again." Micha did not know if he was begging. He feared he might be.

"Say what?"

"In the lane. Say it again."

"Oh." Understanding flashed, bright as sunshine, across Thomas's face, and then he smiled, saying just as easily as he had the first time, "I love you."

"Again."

Thomas kissed him, right over his too-fast, too-hard pulse. "I love you."

The words enwrapped him like chains of silk, and Micha made a strange, mortifying noise. His hands came up to cover his face, but Thomas caught them and kissed his palms, his wrists, his fingertips. Micha's blood rippled like long-stagnant water, freshly disturbed. A tingle ran through the veins in his forearms all the way to his heart.

Thomas rose onto his knees, straddling Micha's thighs, the heat of his cock pooling against Micha's own, which stirred and ached, with dulled, half-forgotten desires. And Micha twisted, moaned, and dared—just a little—to want. Nothing more than this. No hope of more, no fears of less. Simply Thomas, the touch of his hands, the brush of his lips, the sweet prison of his weight not quite holding him down.

Micha eased himself from Thomas's grip. For a moment, he was at a loss for what to do with his liberty, and his hands hung between them like frightened birds. Then he brought them slowly to rest on the thighs that enclosed his own. Thomas was a lean gazelle of a man, surprising strength, a touch of gracelessness. Micha traced those long, wiry muscles, feeling the responsive flex, like a smothered gasp. A profane image came to him: Thomas wrapped round him in passion, the harsh embrace of his legs, the deep, secret heat of his body.

Thomas smiled suddenly, his eyes locked on Micha's, and murmured, "'Let him kiss me with the kisses of his mouth: for thy love is better than wine.'"

And Micha, closer to lost than he had ever been, arched up helplessly into Thomas's waiting arms until they were sitting, half-entwined, locked in each other's embraces, and that was how they kissed, sweet and desperate, soft sounds and broken breath spilling from mouth to mouth, endless and unending. In the deep darkness behind his eyes, Micha saw a world of undiminished stars.

"'Behold thou art fair, my love,'" said Thomas, as they broke apart. "'Behold thou art fair; thou hast doves' eyes within thy locks. Thy lips are like a thread of scarlet. Thou art all fair, my love; there is no spot in thee.'"

Micha shuddered and dropped his head into the curve of Thomas's neck, breathing in the scent of him, the warmth and the last traces of rain. His fingers dug desperately into the fins of Thomas's shoulder blades. "'Stay me with flagons,'" he muttered. "'Comfort me with apples.'"

He felt Thomas's lips against his temple and, between them, like an unbroken promise the steady thud of his heart.

"Please . . ." said Micha, asking mindlessly for something he hardly knew how to articulate wanting.

"'Thou hast ravished my heart,'" whispered Thomas, drawing Micha with gentle fingers into another kiss.

And then came a beating at the door.

Chapter 15

At first Thomas thought it was some idiosyncrasy of the weather or, perhaps, a dislocated tree branch beating against the rectory door. But it was too regular, too desperate, too human somehow, a noise.

Micha's hand coiled about his wrist. "Ignore it," he snarled, his eyes wilder than the storm.

Thomas could not have denied that it was a tempting idea, though not truly, not dangerously so. It was, in fact, an odd sort of pleasure, to have something—someone—so utterly worth wanting that delay was its own sweet pain. But Thomas believed a love that made him think only of himself was a poor tribute to lay at Micha's feet. Perhaps not even love at all. "Someone may need me."

"And I?" asked Micha, a peculiar note, almost anxiety, in his voice.

Thomas smiled as the other man's fingers slackened and slipped away. "Already have me."

A sudden sense of sheer, exhilarating joy bubbled up and possessed him at his own words. Micha did have him. And what was more extraordinary still, Micha wanted to. Thomas bent down and pressed his lips to Micha's with fresh urgency. Micha's mouth opened instantly upon a moan, and Thomas forgot everything but the kiss. The press of Micha's naked skin. The rain-sharp taste of his breath. His sudden and absolute surrender. Micha's hands clawed into his upper arms, needy, clinging, frantic, dragging Thomas deeper until he fell to his knees between Micha's spreading thighs.

Micha sprawled back upon the hearthrug, his throat sleek and bare, his eyes half-closed. His body arched in brazen invitation, vulnerable and vulgar, and undeniably, dizzyingly provocative. This was not like the broken fragments of himself that Micha had hesitantly offered up before. It was everything, and perhaps nothing, and Thomas knew something was different but his capacity for reason had all but abandoned him. His teeth grazed the edge of Micha's neck, and Micha made a low, feral sound.

"Yes," Micha murmured, and his voice was softer, more inviting than Thomas thought he had ever heard it. "Yes. Like this. Take me."

And that was when Thomas heard the silence amid the storm. The knocking had ceased. Horrified, he pulled clumsily away and scrambled to his feet. Micha pushed himself onto his elbows, watching him with sharp eyes, and Thomas was confused. He had the strangest sensation of having evaded something. Had Micha done that deliberately? But why? "Forgive me, I must go." Thomas made a hurried gesture. "I will close the door to ensure your privacy."

"Don't worry." Micha came to his knees, his mouth pulling into its customary sneer. "I'm a prof—" He snapped off the end of the sentence, and Thomas lacked the time to consider what he might have been about to say. "I can be discreet."

"Thank you." Thomas had no choice but to put aside his half-formed concerns. He ran his hands through his hair, put his clothing back into some sort of order, and hurried into the hall. He undid the lock and yanked open the front door to admit only the night, the wind, and a flurry of freezing rain.

"Hello?" he called, raising a hand to his eyes to shield them from the onslaught. "Is there someone there?"

Dimly, through the darkness, he saw a pair of figures, drifting away from him like grey ghosts.

"Hello?" he tried again, but the storm batted the words back in his face. He ran, hatless, coatless, into the downpour.

"Wait," he shouted. "Please wait."

Finally, they heard him, stopped, and turned. He could just about make out the smudged-charcoal outlines of a woman and a girl.

"Mr. Mandeville." The woman spoke so softly he hardly heard her.

He pushed forward a few more steps.

The wind whipped the woman's dark hair into wild snakes, and the rain deepened the anxious lines that scored her young face, but he recognised her at once.

"Mrs. Clark." Surprise rippled through his voice. "What brings you to—"

At that moment, she fainted. Not gracefully or delicately, but with the weight of sheer, hopeless exhaustion. Thomas darted forward and just about succeeded in catching her before she slumped onto the ground. She was as brittle as glass, as thin as moonlight, as though she would drift away on the wind. Thomas had never held a woman so closely. It was not like touching Micha. He was fire and fury; she was ice and shadow. He whispered her name and, when she did not rouse, gathered her gently into his arms. He looked up and found himself pinioned on the pale, luminous gaze of the girl.

"Mama," she explained, with all the solemnitude of childhood, "has not eaten today, and we have been walking for a very long way."

Thomas was, truthfully, not very accustomed to children. He encountered them in the course of his parish duties but rarely without the mediation of helpful adults. Mostly they treated him with wary, nervous civility, and—too self-conscious to show them warmth or understanding—he kept his distance. It was yet another matter in which his brother outstripped him. George adored children and they him, though there were few enough of them in their lives.

For a long moment, Thomas and the child regarded each other distrustfully while the rain pelted around them. He sought something to say—something that might lessen the outlandishness of standing in front of her, carrying her unconscious mother—but he found himself wordless and more than a little ridiculous.

"Please come inside." He led the way back to the house.

Micha was waiting in the hall, fully dressed and leaning against the banisters as though he had not less than five minutes ago been kissing Thomas as if he might die if he stopped.

"What the f-f-f . . ." he began, stuttering to a halt as soon as he saw the child. Then he saw Mrs. Clark and turned so pale that Thomas half-thought Micha might be about to swoon as well.

"Would you be so kind as to see if we have some hartshorn somewhere?" Thomas asked. "And I know there's a decanter of brandy in the library. Would you bring it, please?"

"Uh. Yes." Micha fled.

Thomas bore Mrs. Clark into the drawing room and laid her down on a sofa close to the fire. She stirred and mumbled something, already reviving in the warmth. After a moment of utter awkwardness, Thomas bent over and began to work free the sodden knots of her bonnet and travelling cloak. It felt like an unspeakable intimacy, and his fingers trembled. After a moment, a pair of small hands brushed his away impatiently, and the girl finished the task herself. She had already shed her own bonnet and cloak. The clothes beneath, though not stylish, were neat and practical and had survived the worst of the weather.

He cleared his throat. "Thank you."

She turned her mother's cool, pearl-pale eyes on him. "You are quite welcome," she said, in the refined accents of the carefully coached. She had a pale, narrow face, sharp and intent, and wishbone-yellow hair that had straggled lankly free from whatever bindings had once held it. There was a brief silence. Then her composure wavered. "Is Mama dead?"

"No," returned Thomas, quickly. "Oh no. She has merely fainted. She will come round directly and be quite well."

She swallowed. "Good. I should not like it were Mama to die."

Thomas gazed helplessly at Mrs. Clark and, because he had once seen Esther do it when Ada had taken too much sun, took up one of her hands and rubbed it vigorously. She was very cold, the skin as delicate as paper, despite the calluses that speckled her palms and fingers. The child watched him gravely, as though he performed some obscure miracle.

One that, against all reason, seemed to have some effect. After a moment or two, Mrs. Clark's eyes fluttered open, and she took in a startled breath.

"Mrs. Clark," said Thomas. "Please don't be alarmed. You're amongst friends. All is well."

The girl almost knocked him out of the way in her rush to get closer to the sofa. "Mama." She flung her arms around her mother's neck. The two embraced and Thomas glanced away, oddly confused by the ease of their familial affection. It was not something he had ever experienced, and it filled him with a strange wistfulness.

He had never before thought of children. But now he imagined himself with his own son or daughter, perhaps reading them stories as Edward had once read to him and George. Lifting this imaginary person, this girl, this boy, onto their first horse, never mind that Thomas was no horseman himself. Helping with Latin homework. But try as he might, he could not make it anything more than a moment of fancy. It was too impossible even for dreaming. He could not picture a wife. Only Micha, burnished in the firelight.

"Oh dear." Mrs. Clark broke gently into his thoughts. He met her eyes, and the faintest suggestion of a smile tugged wearily at her lips. "How wretched. I suppose it serves me right for boasting to you that I never faint."

Thomas, conscious that he was looming over her, lowered himself to his knees at the far end of the sofa. "Extraordinary circumstances. So we will not count it."

Footsteps sounded from the hall and Micha came in, just as they were laughing. "What a pretty tableau," he drawled. "I brought brandy, but I couldn't find any smelling salts."

Mrs. Clark looked towards him, surprise flashing on her face. Their glances locked like blades for a moment, and then broke apart.

"You remember Michael Dashwood?" asked Thomas, in some confusion.

He had grown so used to having Micha with him that he had forgotten the unlikely circumstances that had first brought them together. A few months ago, he would have thought nothing strange in two close male friends sharing an abode, but now he wondered if the truth was plain to see. The possibility filled him with dread, not because he was ashamed, but because he could not bear the idea that the most beautiful thing that had ever happened to him could become the subject of a stranger's scrutiny. That the world would see only sin and sordid things.

"Oh yes," whispered Mrs. Clark. "I remember Michael Dashwood."

Micha came forward and slammed the brandy decanter down so hard on a glass-topped table that a spiderweb of cracks skittered across the surface. The girl's pale eyes went wide as moons.

And when Thomas stood and crossed the room towards him, Micha shied away like an unbroken colt. Perhaps he, too, had just recognised the precariousness of their situation. Thomas wished he could comfort him somehow. He tried to catch Micha's eye, but the other man was resolutely looking away.

"For what is a man profited," Thomas thought, *"if he shall gain the whole world and lose his own soul." Micha, oh Micha, you are my soul.*

But Micha still would not look at him.

Instead, Thomas lifted the decanter and poured an inch or two of liquid into a tumbler. "Take this." He offered it to Mrs. Clark. "It will strengthen you."

She gave him one of the faint, wry smiles he remembered so well from his time in London. "It will likely just make me roaring drunk."

"How foolish of me. I was told you had not eaten today."

Mrs. Clark dropped her gaze to the hands that were folded neatly in her lap. A few tendrils of hair sagged wetly forward to hide her face, but he thought she blushed. She reminded him, just a little, of Micha. The same terrible pride, worn like a knight's tarnished mail. "I've made the most dreadful imposition of myself."

"No, not at all. But I must see if I can find you some food. I'm sorry, my Mrs. Allen goes home for the evening, and I'm a little bit helpless without her." He risked a smile of his own. "I think I know where to find the pantry. If not, you will have to send out a search party."

"We could eat each other," offered the child. "As explorers are sometimes obliged to do."

Thomas gave a startled laugh, which he tried ineffectively to conceal behind a hand. The girl gave him a look of mingled censure and astonishment. He could almost see the thought as it formed: *So this is the position of the Anglican Church on cannibalism.* Alarm rolled through him. She was going to carry this with her into adulthood, the strange priest who thought eating people was funny.

"I'm sorry." That was Mrs. Clark, clearly attempting to repair the damage. "I don't believe I introduced my daughter to you." She paused, her lips twitching with a trace of irresistible, private mischief. "This is Hope."

Hope nodded earnestly.

"This is Mr. Mandeville," her mother added. "And his friend, Mr. Dashwood."

Thomas, not really knowing what else to do, offered his hand. And, after a moment, the child shook it. It was, he thought slightly hysterically, more nerve-racking than meeting the bishop. From the other side of the room, Micha regarded this little ceremony with obvious derision.

"Will you excuse me a moment while I go to the kitchen?" said Thomas. "And please, under no circumstances, devour each other in my absence."

"It's all right." Micha jerked suddenly into motion. "I'll do it. I actually know where the kitchen is."

He sounded much as he ever did, harsh and careless, but Thomas could read him better now. Micha's expression said nothing at all, but there was a sick, greyish tinge to his skin and something that looked like real fear lurking in his eyes.

Thomas wished he could go to him, though Micha rarely allowed himself to be soothed. The intimacy of the past few days had slipped as easily as blossom into a habit, a need, he was loath to abandon. It was a deep, peculiar pain to stand so close to his lover and be unable to touch his hand.

"Thank you." Helpless and inadequate words.

Micha gave a brief nod and disappeared. The room seemed both emptier and lighter without him.

After a moment, Thomas moved a chair closer to the fire. Water was running freely from Mrs. Clark's hair, soaking the fabric of her dress, pooling on the floor behind her, and leaving silverish trails upon her neck like a gleam of starlight. "I hope you will not think it presumptuous, but will you tell me what has befallen you to bring you so urgently to Nettlefield in the middle of the night?"

"Presumptuous," repeated Mrs. Clark, with a rather hollow laugh. "It is I who presume. I must seem like a figure from a melodrama, emerging from the storm like this, but Mr. Mandeville, I am desperately in need of help, and I did not know to whom else I could turn."

He could not imagine what that admission must have cost her. "Whatever is within my power is yours."

Her eyes sought his and held them, tight as a hand clutching his. The desperation stood stark upon her face. "It's not for myself I ask. It is for Hope." Hope did not look very happy at that. She took in a deep, impulsive breath and would have spoken had not Mrs. Clark continued. "The truth is, I have lost my position, and I . . . I do not believe it will be possible to get another like it."

"You lost your position? At the London house? But why?"

"Because, Mr. Mandeville"—she still did not break from his eyes—"I lied to get it. I lied about my experience. I fabricated a reference. And I prevailed upon your father's secretary in a manner I"—her gaze flicked momentarily to Hope—"I would prefer not to mention."

Thomas knew that such things were done, but he was still a little shocked. Positions were correctly earned on merit, were they not? And all had equal need. It was the sort of calculated wrongdoing that hurt only innocent strangers and, as such, perhaps was more difficult to understand than crimes of passion, desperation, or ignorance. But, as a priest, it was not his place to judge. And, as a man, he was as stained by sin as any other. Perhaps more so.

"But why," he asked again, "would you do that?"

"It was the only way of securing respectable employment. I had to support my family."

"Could you not have sought assistance from—"

"My name is not Clark," she interrupted. "There is, and was, no Mr. Clark."

Thomas stared at her. He felt a little unreal, like a character in a book or a play. "Then, who are you?"

Again, a laugh that reminded him faintly of Micha. "My mother's name was Abbett, though she did not use it either. She called me Bathsheba. And this does not answer your question, does it?"

It did not. It only created more. Her name, he realised, mattered very little. Who she was—whatever that meant—was the woman before him. A woman who had shown him kindness, who had laughed with him and given him aid when he had needed it. A woman he had, in return, regarded so little that he had not even known she had a daughter. He had been too blinded by Micha, too lost in his own doubts and fears. What did it matter that she'd had a child out of wedlock? What did it matter that she'd lied? She needed his help.

"Mrs. Clark," he began. "I mean, Miss Abbett, why would you tell me this? What may I do for you?"

Her eyes did not flinch from his. They were like Micha's eyes, ancient and weary, but there was love there too, some shreds of brightness, a touch of hope. "I did not give myself to an undeserving man, Mr. Mandeville, or fall victim to an uncontrollable passion.

Before I was a housekeeper, I was a whore. As was my mother. My daughter will not have that life."

"I do not wish to be a whore," explained Hope. "I wish to be an explorer. Or a maharaja. I should like to ride an elephant." She turned to Thomas and went on helpfully, "They are great, grey four-legged beasts, with a prodigious proboscis. That means 'big nose.' I have seen pictures."

Thomas, once again, had no idea what to say to this.

"You must despise me, I know," whispered Mrs. Clark wretchedly. "But, whatever my own misdeeds, Hope is innocent of them. Please. I will not lose her to a workhouse, and I will get money, and I will send it. You must help her, Mr. Mandeville, you must."

"Well." Thomas spoke slowly, hardly knowing what he was going to say before he said it. "I'm afraid we are rather low on elephants in this part of the world."

Mrs. Clark dropped her head into her hands and made a strange sound half-laugh, half-sob. "Is this really a time for levity?"

And then Thomas knew exactly what he was to do and say. If he was wrong, the Lord could sort it out later. That was, after all, His job. And Thomas's was to do what he believed was right in accordance not with the laws of man, but with the conscience he had been given. That little spark of divine love. He reached out and took her hand, his longer fingers and her slender ones interleaving easily, like two halves of a pattern. "How can you expect me to be anything other than ridiculous," he said gently, "when you are yourself absurd? I have been a poor friend to you, and I could never despise you."

Micha came into the room with a tray and froze. "There's not much. Bread and cheese. I'm not cooking."

At any other time, this little revelation would have diverted Thomas tremendously. Why—and when—had Micha ever learned to cook? During his travels? His hard times? It was such a strange skill for a gentleman to have acquired. *And to think,* Thomas wanted to say, *you claimed to have no accomplishments.* Instead, he simply slipped his fingers free from Mrs. Clark's and went to take the tray from Micha's cold, white-knuckled hands. "Thank you."

Micha caught him by the wrist and held him there, just long enough to stare so fiercely at him that Thomas felt quite breathless. Whatever Micha was looking for, he'd found, because he pulled away abruptly and threw himself down onto the window seat, from where he silently watched the ravages of the storm.

Mrs. Clark and Hope fell upon the food with a gusto only lightly checked by decorum, and Thomas did not trouble them with further questions until they were done. He would have tried to draw Micha into the little circle by the fire, but he looked so remote, and so hostile, he did not dare. At the very least, it gave Thomas a little time to consider what might properly be done.

By the time she was done with the food, Mrs. Clark was still drawn, bedraggled, and a little too thin, but colour had returned to her cheeks. George had been correct, Thomas realised—she was a remarkably handsome woman.

"Would you be willing," asked Thomas at last, pondering aloud, "to consider taking some employment here in the village?"

Micha's head snapped round.

"Truth always catches up with you in the end," she said, "and your parishioners would not thank you for making me a part of their lives. Hope needs—"

"Her mother?" suggested Thomas, mildly.

"Yes," agreed Hope, stuffing the last hunk of bread into her mouth. "I do." There was a pause while she chewed and swallowed. "I do not know my father," she told Thomas. "I usually say he has died, but Mama says I am not to lie to you."

"I appreciate that." Thomas tried unsuccessfully to match the gravity of her tone.

"I know that it is a sin to lie," she went on. "But sometimes one must be prag-prag . . ."

"Pragmatic?"

"Yes. That means doing what is sensible. And besides," she continued, doggedly, "since I have never had a father, I do not count it any sort of loss. Whereas I love Mama dearly."

"Nobody will take you away from your mother."

Hope nodded. "Good. For I would take that very ill indeed."

Thomas flinched from her stone-cold eyes. "I think, perhaps, nobody would dare take you away from your mother."

And then, as sudden as sunlight, the girl smiled. This was something else Thomas had experienced but little, and it left him slightly dazzled and more than slightly gratified. He felt as though he had passed some test he had not previously realised was important.

"I'm sorry," said Mrs. Clark. "I'm afraid I have encouraged her to be wilful, and . . . she reads too much."

"That's nothing to apologise for." And once again, Thomas felt the unexpected, extraordinary warmth of Hope's approval. It had never before occurred to him children could be reacted to the same as any other sort of person. That they could be liked. Not that Hope, with her intense eyes and cold demeanour, was particularly likeable. But, somehow, he found he liked her regardless.

"I'm afraid"—he gathered himself—"something continues to trouble me. Did my brother dismiss you?"

Mrs. Clark said nothing. The fire crackled. The rain battered the windows with almost biblical fury. Finally, she gave a short, sharp nod.

Thomas frowned. "Because of your past?"

Another nod.

It made no sense. George had never shown any interest in domestic matters. Why would he go to such trouble to look into Mrs. Clark? And George was troubled, frustrated, careless. He was not truly cruel. Was he? Some instinct, perhaps one of self-preservation, made Thomas want to let the subject drop. Since Mrs. Clark was clearly reluctant to discuss it with him, it benefited no one to press the matter. But he also knew that it was cowardice that held his tongue and selfishness that made him seek excuses for doing so. "George is no man to stand in judgement of the conduct of others. What business is it of his? How did he know?"

There was a very long silence. Thomas felt, rather than saw, Micha's eyes upon them.

"I'm sorry," murmured Mrs. Clark. "I do not know."

Micha rose from the window seat, like a shadow blown by the wind, grabbed the untouched brandy Thomas had poured out earlier, and downed it in a single gulp.

"Could you not have reasoned with him?" Thomas heard himself speaking as if from great distance. There was a note of pleading in his voice that made it sound like the voice of a stranger. "I'm sure if he understood he would not have wished to ruin you or—"

"Please," interrupted Mrs. Clark, in a stifled voice. "It was simply not possible. Don't press me further."

And then suddenly, with a sickening kind of lurch, like stepping off a cliff, Thomas remembered. The gleam in George's eyes. *She's a stunner, man.*

"Did he . . ." It was all he managed to choke out.

"No," she said, quickly. "No."

"But he tried?"

Her hands twisted together and then apart. "This serves no purpose but pain."

"I want to know."

"He made it a condition of my continued employment, yes. And I refused." She ducked her head and then looked up again. Thomas caught the tension in the curve of her neck. "Not because I care so greatly for what is left of my honour, or my body, but because I would not trust your brother to have power over me. The man cannot govern himself."

George had always been headstrong. But that was no longer a truth that mattered. "There is some darkness in him. And I cannot always reach him. Not since our brother died."

"If he were my brother," said Mrs. Clark softly, "I would fear for him."

Thomas was suffocating on secrets. Edward. George. Himself. It was almost too much to bear. He wanted Micha. To be held. To know, if not comfort, pleasure as deep as oblivion, sins sweeter than paradise. Micha was not an analgesic, but Thomas was almost sure that if someone didn't touch him, he would shatter like glass.

The worst of it was, the deepest betrayal, the most unspeakable thing, the wrong beyond all others, was that nothing Mrs. Clark was telling him was a revelation. Nor even a shock. In some fashion, with his heart, if not his mind, Thomas had always known. But he had done as he was bidden: kept his peace, kept his silence, and turned away from truth in the name of duty. He had sensed something of his own nature. Just as he had realised the George who returned to England in 1855 was not the same man who had left it two years before. If he were only a little braver, if only he dared look a little deeper, he would surely understand why Edward had shot himself the day after his honeymoon. The answer, long denied, was waiting for him too. And still, always, just out of reach.

Mrs. Clark's hand came down on top of his, cool and ghost-light. "I'm sorry to bring this to you. I did not know where else to go."

"No, I should be the one who's sorry. I am. For my brother." *And for myself.* He took a breath. His lungs hurt as though he had been drowning. "And of course you were right to come here. I will think of something."

"I'm not your responsibility, Mr. Mandeville," she said, tightly.

"No." He spoke to the hand upon his own. "You're my friend."

At last, something in her seemed to give way, and she nodded. "Very well. And thank you."

It was, frankly, something of a relief for Thomas to be able to think only of practical matters. Things that could be done. It was an illusion, of course, but it was enough to temporarily quell his inner tumult. "One thing at a time. I must find you somewhere to stay for tonight, and we can consider the future tomorrow."

Micha spoke sharply from the edges of the room. "You're protecting the reputation of a whore?"

"Micha," Thomas gasped. "That is unnecessary."

Mrs. Clark, however, did not react. "I am a whore. The word does not frighten me."

Thomas made a convulsive, awkward "There's a child present" gesture, and Hope glared at him. "I am not afraid of words either." She jerked up her chin. "A whore means a person who does something for money. A bastard is a child without a father."

And I, thought Thomas with a deep and terrible clarity that brought with it a strange sort of freedom, *am a sodomite.* What a party they made.

"What you were, or how you have lived, is not important," said Thomas. "Do you both feel ready to brave the storm? Let me get an umbrella."

He would take them to Esther. For all the sharpness of her tongue, he could not imagine her turning them away. He even half-hoped she might welcome them, unorthodox though the whole situation was. Despite the gravity of Mrs. Clark's circumstances, Thomas could almost have smiled at his own. For a man who lived the quietest of lives, he seemed to have discovered a talent for finding the unlikely and extraordinary.

"They'll think she's your mistress." Micha came after him, sullen as the rain-sodden earth. "They'll say the girl's yours."

"I would hope they know me better than that."

"How can you be so fucking naive? You can't just show up with some strange woman and a fatherless brat and expect people to accept it."

"Why?" asked Thomas.

"What do you mean 'why'?"

"These are kind people, Micha. Do you have no faith in simple goodness?"

"No." Micha curled his lip. "And neither would you if you had any sense."

Thomas reached out to him, but Micha knocked his hand away and went back to the window, where he stood, staring out at the night. "You'll never choose me, will you?"

"I have chosen you."

But Micha just shook his head. "You choose goodness every time. No matter what I offer. Even if I beg."

"Why do you place yourself in opposition to what is right?"

"Because that's what the world does to people like me."

"People like *us*," Thomas reminded him gently.

"We're not alike."

The words were a wall. Unbreachable. The Micha who had opened himself, surrendered himself, there with Thomas in the firelight seemed suddenly a dream. An impossibility. A moment too fragile to survive beyond its instant. Thomas didn't know what to do, what to say, how to make Micha his lover again. And Mrs. Clark and her daughter were waiting for him.

"I'll be back soon," Thomas tried, half-pleading with Micha's rigid back.

But Micha only shrugged.

In the hallway, Mrs. Clark was helping Hope back into her travelling cloak.

"Are we having another adventure?" asked the girl.

"Only a very small one." Thomas buttoned his overcoat all the way to his chin.

"There is no such thing as a small adventure. If there was, it would not be an adventure."

"Then, I suppose," he agreed, "we are having an adventure."

He shoved the door into the face of the wind, stepped into the storm, and tried to put up the umbrella. Within seconds, it was inside out.

"Not one of my better ideas." He dropped it onto the doorstep.

Hope came up beside him and, to his surprise, slipped her hand into his. "We cannot all be men of genius."

"Is that supposed to make me feel better?"

And then, almost lost to the weather, came a soft, shy laugh.

She nodded. "Perhaps you have. I don't think it's a kind thing, this love of yours."

"Don't pity me."

"Don't flatter yourself. I have no interest in you, Micha, for good or ill. And I was not the one to break my promise."

"I wish you hadn't come," he said, with sudden fury.

"I didn't come to ruin you," she replied.

"But you still can." He couldn't stop trembling. "Will you?"

Again, she was silent. Across the fields, detached, drifted the laughter of the girl. Then, "No."

It was what he needed to hear. What he had pleaded for. But it felt too easy. Far, far too easy. "Why?"

She shrugged. "I suppose I've seen enough of ruin. I'd like to be done with it."

"But . . ." he protested, against his own interests, hardly knowing what words were going to fall from his lips. "But I would deserve it," he finished wretchedly, hating her and hating himself still more ferociously.

"Indeed." Her look was cool and wry. "Fortunately, I'm a better person than you."

His lip curled bleakly. "The whole fucking world is a better person than me."

To that, she offered no answer.

"Do you mean it?" he ended up asking.

"That I'm a better person than you?"

"About . . ." Micha stumbled over Thomas's name. It was like he had lost whatever right he'd ever possessed to utter it. "You really won't say anything?"

"No."

"How can I trust you?" His voice cracked. He had intended to be firm with her. But he just sounded . . . desperate.

She shrugged. "That is not my problem." She looked at him with cold eyes. "And if the uncertainty torments you, I'm afraid I'm not quite enough of a better person to lament it."

If he had believed for a moment he could get away with it, Micha would have thought nothing, right then, of murdering her. Anything that would return things to the way they had been a day ago: a closed world of nothing but Thomas. Thomas and laudanum, usurper and king.

"Micha," Mrs. Clark said, softly. "You know there are things you should tell him for yourself. Things you must."

"That I'm a whore?"

"That you take laudanum."

He shook his head. The colours of the meadow smeared in his vision, so he closed his eyes. He tangled his fingers through his hair. "I can't," he whispered. "I can't get out. I try but I can't."

And there it was. The truth he had barely dared admit to himself, spoken instead to a stranger who had every reason to hate him.

"Enough of that." Mrs. Clark pulled his hands out of his hair.

"I try to stop." Still, he was speaking. Against his judgement. Against his will. Poison flowing out of him. "Every day, I try to stop."

"You must reduce the dosage gradually."

"I try that too. But I don't. And . . . and the moment I feel anything I just take more anyway."

Mrs. Clark rose from the stile and lowered herself into the meadow. "This isn't my problem either."

"You're the one who fucking brought it up."

"For Thomas's sake." She shook some clinging clematis blossoms from her skirts. "Now I'm going to join Hope. Stay away from us, Micha. It's the least you owe me."

She gathered up her skirts and, with a step as light as a girl's, ran through the flowers towards her daughter.

Micha watched them only for a moment and then turned for home, Mrs. Clark's words echoing unwanted in his mind. He tried to imagine the future she had half-suggested could be his. If only he were strong enough to take it.

A few weeks of hell. And then a lifetime. A lifetime without opium, with Thomas.

It felt, in the last balmy evening of autumn, possible.

Though, of course, his resolution faltered in the silence of the house, when the first shivery cravings crept upon him. A little more, a little more, what could it hurt? Reduce gradually. He could start tomorrow.

He would start tomorrow.

Chapter 17

Thomas arrived in London very late that evening, having ridden some forty or fifty miles as though pursued by the devil himself. George was neither at the lodgings he kept on Half Moon Street nor at the townhouse. Brimstone was near to dropping from exhaustion, so Thomas saw him stabled and, on the hope rather than the likelihood of finding his brother, set out for the Army & Navy Club in Pall Mall.

The hour was beyond merely unsociable by the time Thomas stepped between the Corinthian columns and richly decorated arches of George's club. The interior was as lavish and ornate as the exterior, and Thomas, travel-stained and dishevelled as he was, was not well received. He waited in the echoing hallway, at the foot of the sweeping stone staircase, until George, at last, came sauntering down it. He was with a couple of rakish-looking young men Thomas vaguely recalled from his brother's regiment.

"Thom!" cried George, with an expansive gesture. He was clearly the worse for drink. "Tell me you bring good news. Is the marquess dead?"

Thomas had barely slept. He had ridden all day. He had prepared a speech. Prepared it a hundred times, a thousand, with every mile that fell to Brimstone's hooves. And then he had abandoned it, for what could he say, what use were words, when all he had were questions?

Why? What happened to you? Who are you?

And now even they were lost in the scalding rush of pain, fury, love, and loss. Was this careless, brittle stranger really all that remained of his brother George? The boy who had broken his arm trying to rescue the stable cat from a tree. And had broken the other one, taking a fence too hard and too fast on a horse too big for him.

It was one thing to grieve the dead, but the living too?

Thomas stepped smartly across the entrance hall, his footfalls echoing upon the marble, opened his mouth to speak, and, instead, found himself delivering a straight left to his brother's face. Thomas had boxed for Cambridge in his youth, and though he had not practised in years, his skills had not entirely atrophied. There was a horrific crunch of cartilage. George staggered back, cursing incoherently through a rush of blood, his hands coming up to shield his nose.

There was a ripple of shock and outrage through the attendants. Somebody dropped a tray of drinks. George's friends just gaped.

"What the deuce?" snarled George. "Are you deranged?"

Thomas was, if anything, even more appalled. He had fallen, instinctively, into a guard position, and now he dropped his hands. "I . . . I'm so sorry. I don't know . . . why I . . . I'm so sorry."

George glared at him through blood-smeared fingers. Then, still clutching his face, he ducked low and charged, tackling Thomas about the waist. Thomas might have boxed, but he was unprepared and undefended and the army had taught George efficiency and brutality. The two of them crashed heavily to the floor, Thomas underneath. The impact, coupled with his brother's weight, knocked the breath from his body. For a moment, he was too dazed to react. George straddled his chest, bracing himself on an elbow. Thomas flung up a hand to protect himself, but it was too late. His brother brought back his arm and slammed his fist into Thomas's face, once, twice, three times. A dull rust-coloured pain billowed through Thomas's head, his vision blurring bloody, then black. Struggling under George, he managed to get his arm between them, just enough to ward off the worst of the blows.

"George," he gasped. "Enough. Please."

But Thomas knew of old that it would do little good. His brother, in the grip of any strong emotion, was not easily restrained or subdued.

He showed absolutely no sign of having heard Thomas or even that he still recognised who he was. Thomas could have been any assailant, from any battlefield. There was no time to think, and George was lost to reason. Thomas caught his brother's other arm by the elbow and twisted up with his hips, flinging George to one side.

Through the smudges of pain that muted all his senses, Thomas could hear, albeit distantly, a commotion. Voices. Running feet.

He staggered upright, only to have George rush him again. In desperation, Thomas swung a right hook, caught his brother ineffectually against the side of the head, and went down under him again. George shifted his weight forward this time and, when Thomas tried to shove him away, pinned him to the floor with one arm across his throat and one knee upon his upper arm. George pressed down hard, Thomas struggled hopelessly and choked for breath, his head full of lights and splinters, and then George's friends were dragging him away.

Thomas drew in a mouthful of air, and it burned his throat like liquor. The commotion was louder now. It was all around him. He tried to stand, but the effort made him instantly dizzy. He dragged a heavy, swollen hand to his face, and it came away bloody. His jaw, his cheek, his brow, all throbbed sullenly. His knuckles and his mouth stung. His soul wept.

"Come on, old man, hup, there's a good fellow." One of George's friends grasped his hand and yanked him upright, then caught him by the waist as he swayed.

The other one, as far as Thomas could tell through the blood and tears, seemed to be soothing the situation with money.

"Just a misunderstanding," he was saying. "High spirits. We're just leaving, aren't we, chaps?"

Thomas opened his mouth to speak and spat blood onto the pristine marble at his feet. Someone stuffed a handkerchief into his hand, but his fingers refused to close, and he saw it fall, turning over and over like a white flag.

Time was acting strangely. He kept losing pieces of it. The next thing he knew, they were on the street. George looked ghastly in the oily gaslight, but he seemed otherwise unhurt.

"So that was jolly." That was the man who supported him. "What next? Tenter Street for a whore?"

"Not tonight." George. His voice still thick. "I need to see to my brother. And my nose."

Laughter.

More words. Spinning around senselessly like May dancers. Thomas's head fell back. He blinked at a sky without stars. Fogged like breath across a dirty glass.

Farewells.

A hackney cab, painfully jolting.

Time slipping away again and Thomas letting it.

"Here, drink this, you stupid fucker."

George's rooms smeared gradually into focus. Bachelor lodgings, well furnished and surprisingly well kept, given the way George had always been careless with his things when he was younger. Thomas gingerly took the glass from his brother's outstretched hand and took a sip. The whisky seared his still-bleeding lip and made his eyes water.

"I can't believe you broke my nose." George flung himself into a wingback chair and held a cloth to his face. He had made some effort to clean the blood, but he still looked a little monstrous. "Was there a reason, or did you just feel like it?"

Thomas tried to pull himself out of the sprawl into which he had fallen. "I don't know." He touched his mouth again and winced. "I only wished to speak to you."

"What is it then?" asked George. He leaned back in his chair and stretched out his long legs, looking surprisingly at ease for a man who had just fought with his own brother in the entrance hall of the Army & Navy Club. "You've clearly got a bee in your bonnet about something."

Now the moment had come, Thomas felt entirely inadequate to the task. Wrong though it was to go around punching your brother, it was sometimes by far the easiest course of action. "It's about Mrs. Clark," he tried, carefully.

"Who?"

Typical that George could idly come close to destroying a woman's life and not have noticed. "The housekeeper, George."

"Oh her. Uppity quim's done a runner actually. I had to charge the marquess's steward to find another one."

"Yes, because you threatened her. She's staying with me."

"Is she now?" George's eyebrows twitched tauntingly upwards. "Didn't think you had it in you, old boy."

"Not improperly." Thomas's head ached, inside as well as out. "Must you be a . . . an arse? Have you no sense of shame? No regrets? No morals at all?"

"Ever the prig, Thom." There was a whisky decanter on the table at George's elbow. He poured himself a liberal measure and knocked it back. His mouth twisted. "As it happens, no, I don't. Why should I?"

"Because," said Thomas patiently, "what you did was not only wrong but cruel."

It seemed utter hypocrisy to speak to another man of moral ill, and Thomas heard the lack of conviction in his own words. That touch of self-righteousness his brother had always disparaged.

"You came all this way to read me a lecture?" drawled George. "Reminds me of the marquess when he had his health. I suppose I should be flattered."

"I didn't—"

"Spare me, old boy. She's a whore, what does it matter?"

"She was under your protection, that is all that matters." Thomas leaned forward. His brother was far drunker than he had initially realised. There was a hollow glitter to his eyes. "I can hardly believe you would do something like that. I sometimes think I don't know who you are anymore."

George mirrored Thomas's pose mockingly, his empty glass hanging limply from one hand. "Then you had better take a good long look, oh my brother. Because this is who I am."

"A man who would force himself upon a woman?"

"Why not?"

Thomas shook his head and immediately regretted it. Lightning cracked beneath his skin, new-forming bruises flaring hot. "I know you to be better than that."

George gave a strange laugh, sat back, and poured himself another drink. "You always did have the heart of a spaniel. But don't delude yourself on my account. Why shouldn't I have a woman if I want her? I've done worse." His gaze drifted from Thomas to the liquid sloshing in his glass and then away to nowhere. "Far worse."

"What do you mean?" Thomas swallowed, blood and whisky acrid in his mouth.

It was a long time before George answered, and then he spoke so softly Thomas barely heard him. "'Thou shalt not kill.' It makes no difference what I do or don't do. I'm already damned."

George had a medal from Crimea. Thomas remembered, suddenly, his brother's homecoming. *Bad news, Pater, but I'm not dead yet.* And then the medal, arcing through the air, spinning silver. The marquess, of course, had not flinched or moved, the bruise livid against his pale cheek for weeks. George had been thin and dark-eyed, but whole. The ladies had found him quite dashing, a hero in a scarlet coat. "Any priest would tell you that the commandment is against murder. A premeditated and wilful act. You fought for your country, for a cause, against enemy soldiers. It is a different matter entirely."

"What the devil do you know, Thom?" George gave a weary sigh. "Everyone looks the same on a battlefield. At Balaklava the fog was so thick, you could barely recognise your closest friend. Half the time, I didn't know who I was fighting. I don't think anyone did, that whole bloody war. You heard they sent the cavalry straight at the Russian artillery?"

This was more than George had ever spoken of Crimea, at least to Thomas. But George had always been far closer to Edward than to his unwanted, unlike twin. "I read of the charge. The noble six hundred. 'When can their glory fade?'"

"Don't quote that bilge at me." George reached for the decanter and poured himself another measure.

"Those men were patriots. We should honour their sacrifice."

"Patriotism is a tattered flag flying over a field of corpses. They died in a foreign land, fighting someone else's war, because somebody couldn't relay an order, and for what? To secure our trade routes to India. A land not ours to begin with." He lifted his glass in a derisive toast, brought it to his lips, and swallowed without pleasure. "Nobility indeed. A glorious sacrifice, for Queen and Country."

Thomas watched him helplessly, unsure what to say or do. Edward would have known.

"And to think," George went on, his words slurring, "if our father had bought me that commission in the Eleventh as I wanted, it would have been me. Amusing, isn't it, that one of His Lordship's little games saved my life? I would have died that day with the rest of them." He paused. "I sometimes wish I had." He poured himself another drink with shaking hands, the liquid spilling down the sides of the glass and onto the table. "But instead, I lived. And I kept on living, while everybody else around me died. Even Edward."

"Well," said Thomas, unsteadily, "I, for one, do not wish you had died at Sevastopol. And given how many soldiers did, I think it shows a certain lack of respect that you would say you wish to join them."

George dropped the glass onto the table with a dull clatter. He leaned forward again, hands clasped loosely between his knees, and stared at Thomas with a wild light burning in his eyes. "But don't you see? It was punishment. For everything I did, for all the lives I took, for all the lives I couldn't save."

Thomas moved to the edge of the sofa, but the small space of floor between them seemed endless, as though it stretched all the way to Sevastopol. "What was?"

George gestured impatiently. "Edward, of course."

Horror and pity sliced through Thomas's heart like cold steel. "No, George, no. That was an accident. And you must not think like this. It's madness."

If George heard, or if the words meant anything to him, he gave no sign. Instead, he stared unseeing into a far corner of the room and kept talking. "They all said I had the devil's luck, you know. I'll never forget that winter. The storms, the snow, the constant rumble of the guns like we lived always the end of days. The tents were as good as rotten. Nothing could keep the cold at bay. Even the officers were crawling with vermin. No fuel, no heat, no food. My best friend died of dysentery. How glorious do you think it now?"

Thomas said nothing. He had known little of this. And it was still slightly beyond his power of imagining. How old had George been, then? Twenty? Twenty-one? Watching his country squander its youth while Thomas had laboured over dusty tomes at Cambridge, safe inside his golden cage of learning.

"I still remember it was beautiful." George reached again for his glass. "That white city curling round the glittering turquoise bay. While we sat in our muddy trenches, shivering and starving in the dark, and died in droves."

"George." At his name, George's head jerked up as though he had forgotten where he was and to whom he spoke. "That you lived while so many died is a blessing, not a curse. And God would not punish you for it."

"You don't understand anything, do you? Edward was the price, for my sins, for my survival. He used to write to me, you know. Not like you. 'Dear George, the weather continues clement.'" The ghost of his old smile curled on George's lips. "You were so boring it was a wonder I didn't fall on my bayonet."

Thomas coloured. "I'm so sorry. I'm a poor correspondent. I didn't know what to tell you or even if you wished to hear from me."

"Of course I wanted to hear from you, you bloody fool. I kept trying to write back, but what could I say? 'Weather continues inclement, everybody dead, I remain your loving brother.'"

"I would have preferred truth to silence."

George gave a great bark of laughter. "Not the family way, old boy, not the family way. It should be our motto. 'Sub silentio.'"

"What about, oh who was it again, St. Erth's second daughter. Rosa, was it? Everyone thought you would marry her."

"Oh yes, I liked her well enough. Too well to marry her. I was grateful for her letters, though. They were pretty things. Smelled of flowers. So did she. But it was Edward who kept me sane." He finished his drink. "Or some approximation thereof. He made me believe the world was waiting for me. Except it wasn't. He lied, though I can't hold it against him." George came to his feet and spread his arms wide. "This was the illusion all along. In truth, I never left Sevastopol."

"You're drunk." Thomas was pleading and he did not care. "You don't know what you're saying. You're here, with me, and you're safe and good and you're still my brother. And . . . and . . ." It was not something spoken in their family, but he said it now. The words learned, not from God, with all His promises and mysteries—and the endless, endless silence—but in Micha's arms. "I love you."

"Yes, I'm drunk," said George mildly, ignoring the rest. "And I know exactly what I'm saying. It's been ten years, Thom, and I still dream of it. I still see the bodies. The mud and the blood and the glittering sea. I still hear the guns in every carriage that rattles down the street. Drinking helps but not very much." He looked down at his hands and the scraped knuckles. "I haven't touched a woman I haven't paid for in over a decade." He crossed to the window and stood looking out at the shadow-sloshed street below. "It's why I wanted that bloody housekeeper. She looked untouchable. As though you could never hurt her."

"That does not excuse your conduct."

George sighed. "I know. I'm not fit for human company. It's true what they say. 'Any hussar who is not dead by the age of thirty is a blackguard.'"

There was a long silence.

"George," said Thomas, at last, "you need to know something."

"Oh?"

"Well, a lot of things. But this is about Edward." Thomas took a deep breath. His heart was pounding like hoofbeats. "It's not your fault he died. It was not some divine retribution for your actions in the war. The gun did not discharge by accident. He chose to take his own life. He . . . he killed himself."

George's back went absolutely rigid. "What?"

"The marquess made me keep the secret. To avoid the disgrace. And I didn't take much convincing because I wanted to see our brother buried well."

"And why," asked George very softly, "was this kept from me?"

"I . . . don't know. He insisted, and I was not strong enough to gainsay His Lordship. Perhaps he thought it would upset you."

"Whereas being lied to is something I particularly enjoy."

"I'm sorry."

"You always are, Thom. You always are." George turned slowly. The moonlight bleached his face to bone. "I used to hate you for being so much our father's creature. But now I see that none of us were any different."

"You do at least understand," Thomas insisted, "that you cannot blamc yourself for Edward's death. I should have told you. I know that."

"By his own hand, or another's, it makes no difference. Our brother is lost."

"Not lost, just waiting. We will see him again."

"Not I. I know what awaits me." George came back to his chair and lifted the empty decanter, watching the dregs careen back and forth, in shades of amber and gold. "Do you know why he did it?"

"No, but I feel I should."

"As do I." George's face hardened. "I'll find out."

"How? The man is dead."

"I don't know. But, for now, I'm going to bed. I'm very drunk, and I'm tired of talking."

Thomas nodded. "As you wish."

"You're still a prig, old boy."

"I know."

"You can stay here if you don't want to use the townhouse."

"Thank you. I should return home as soon as I can, but I'd probably fall out the saddle."

"Get a few hours' sleep. Just don't wake me when you leave." George ran a finger round the rim of the decanter and licked it clean. "By the way, what happened to that mongrel of yours?"

"Micha? He's still with me."

George frowned. "I don't trust the fellow. He's using you, and I have no idea what game he's playing."

"I don't think he is," said Thomas quietly. "I think he's a good man who has had a difficult life. He changes a little every day. And he makes me happy."

"For a supposedly good man, he was quick enough to betray a friend."

"Pardon?"

"Your housekeeping harlot. He sold her out to get me off his back."

Thomas's eyes widened. For Micha's sake he wanted to dissemble—pretend he already knew—but he was under-practised in dissembling, despite his father's best efforts. "What? Why would he do that? And how? I don't believe they even know each other."

"Something to think about, eh?" drawled George infuriatingly. "Good night." He tipped an imaginary hat and staggered from the room, taking with him any hope Thomas had of sleeping.

Thomas fidgeted away a couple of hours on George's sofa, as plagued by doubts and questions as he had been the night before and prepared to depart in the early hours of the morning. He cleaned himself up as best he could, considered taking the train, but, impatient to leave, he borrowed one of George's horses and set out a little after dawn. It was another long, gruelling journey, made considerably worse by yesterday's aches and his newly acquired collection of bruises. He did not push his mount, stopped often to rest, and was already too weary to give much thought to anything beyond the man who waited for him at the rectory.

He arrived in Nettlefield close to midnight, saw to his horse, and let himself into his house. Thinking Micha would most likely be sleeping, he took care not to make too much noise, but then he heard the sound of footsteps upon the stairs, and there was Micha, half-drowned in shadows, clad only in his trousers and a very rumpled shirt.

"Thomas." Micha rarely spoke his name, except in mockery, and now it was uttered not so much with something that was recognisable as gladness but something else, something deeper, something raw.

And Thomas forgot all of George's cryptic warnings in the simple pleasure of homecoming, when home was no longer about a place, but a person. He opened his arms, and Micha rushed into them.

"How ridiculous," he muttered into Thomas's neck. "Two days and I turn moonstruck."

Thomas clutched at him.

"And you should know you smell like a dead horse." Micha pulled back a little. It was hard to see in the gloom, but his brows dipped into a frown. He caught Thomas by the chin. "Wait. What have you been doing? What happened?"

Thomas winced as one of Micha's fingers brushed against the tender place on his lip. "Nothing, really."

"'Nothing, really'?"

"Well, George, but . . . I hit him first."

Micha made a sardonic gesture. "Oh well, that's fine then."

Thomas stifled his amusement, not entirely successfully.

"It's no laughing matter." Micha took Thomas by the hand and dragged him into the library, where he lit a lamp and then let out a low hiss at the sight of Thomas's face.

"It looks worse than it is," offered Thomas, awkwardly.

"It better," growled Micha. "Or I'll fucking kill him. Now sit down and let me clean it properly."

Thomas was all too glad to cast off his sweat-stained coat and sink into the nearest chair. He must have dozed because, when next he opened his eyes, Micha was there with a cloth and a bowl full of water. He put them down, unceremoniously pushed Thomas's legs apart, and dropped to his knees between them. It was strange, for Thomas had kissed this man's lips, held his cock in his mouth, but this seemed an entirely different intimacy. It abashed him, somehow, even as it pleased him. "You don't have to do this."

Micha's upturned face looked starkly beautiful in the lamplight. Lucifer before his fall. "I'm going to," he snapped. And then, more kindly, "I want to."

He took Thomas's hands and spread the fingers. His touch was surprisingly gentle as he cleaned the scraped and swollen knuckles.

"An ill-advised right hook," explained Thomas.

Micha said nothing. His head was bent over his task, a curl of dark hair falling forward across his brow. When he was done, he leaned forward a little more and lightly kissed Thomas's fingertips.

"I'm so sorry I smell like a dead horse," whispered Thomas, freshly dismayed by the state he was in and Micha's tenderness. "That cannot be very attractive."

Micha glanced up with a rare grin. "You're wearing clothes you've slept in, you're covered in blood, and your face looks like you walked repeatedly into a wall. Attractiveness went out the window some time ago."

"Well, my face was not much to celebrate to begin with."

Micha pushed himself to his feet. And then he was in Thomas's lap, heat and solid strength, and the sweet shock of his closeness. "I happen to like your face. So don't go getting it punched again."

Thomas smiled and split his lip open.

"I can't believe what an idiot you are," muttered Micha as he dabbed up the blood and cleaned the wound. His words were angry, but his hands were careful. Even loving. And what little pain they caused was salved almost immediately by the proximity of his body.

"You should see George."

"Gave him what for, did you?" asked Micha, with a wry look.

"Absolutely. I did some serious damage to his fists."

Micha actually laughed, and Thomas half-suspected he was being humoured, but he was too warmly contented to care. He closed his eyes and let himself be tended. When he opened them again, Micha had put the water bowl aside and was simply looking at him, his expression softer than usual but typically unreadable. "There. All done."

He would have moved, but Thomas caught him and held him. "Don't go."

Micha cleared his throat. "This isn't terribly comfortable, you know," he grumbled. But he stayed.

Finally, he asked, "Does it hurt? I think . . . I might have some laudanum somewhere?"

Thomas reached up and touched his lips to Micha's. "How good you are, but I'm fine."

"Not good. And I hope it was fucking worth it."

"Not really." Thomas sighed. "My poor brother. I grieve for his pains and can do little to alleviate them." He reached out and ran the rough fold of his fingers across the edge of Micha's cheekbone. Micha's lashes fluttered, and he let Thomas touch him, without protest. "How little we truly know of other people's lives," Thomas went on. "We think we understand, but we don't. We just see the crudest shadows."

Micha shrugged. "Maybe it's better that way."

Thomas was silent. Perhaps Micha was right. Perhaps there were some things that were better left unknown. But Thomas had kept his peace for years, and it had brought him no closer to happiness. "Micha?"

"What?"

"George told me something . . . about you." Thomas felt the tension that suddenly rolled through Micha's body, as though he had slipped a blade between the man's ribs. "He said you knew Mrs. Clark? In her previous life."

"I haven't fucked her." He sounded as sharp and brittle as glass.

Given how reluctantly Micha spoke of anything to do with himself, or his past, Thomas had half-expected a denial, though not of this particular familiarity. "It would not trouble me if you had," he said gently. "I have no claim on you." He paused. "What concerns me is that you would betray her to my brother, knowing full well the likely consequences."

Micha turned his head away, showing just the shadow of his profile. "I didn't think he'd try to force her."

"But you must have seen the precariousness of her position."

Micha was trembling now, with some volatile combination of anger and fear. He untangled himself from Thomas, the convulsive movement rousing from temporary slumber a jangling collection of bruises and minor scrapes. "What do you want from me?" he snarled, almost stumbling in his haste to get away. "Contrition? 'Oh forgive me, sweet benefactor, for my moral lapse'?"

Thomas stared at him, shocked by the sudden change, the loss of the care he had sacrificed for his question. "Of course not. And I'm not your benefactor. I am your—"

"My what? What are you, Thomas? My keeper? My patron?"

"Your lover? Your friend? Am I not these things?"

Micha's whole body hunched. "I don't know. It seems to depend on whether or not you like my behaviour."

"Do you not think," asked Thomas, "I have some right to know what might drive you to such an act of wanton cruelty?"

"Oh you have rights now, do you? To judge my actions. To know whatever it is you want to know about me." Micha's voice climbed to something that was too ragged to be a shout. "You think because I let you have my body that you can take whatever else of me you want? How does that make you better than your brother?"

Thomas rose painfully to his feet. "My words were ill-chosen. And I apologise. But I thought . . . I don't know . . . a little bit of truth sometimes might be something lovers shared. Something you wished to give."

"Well, it isn't."

There was a deep and endless silence, like tumbling into a dark chasm. "Do you have no faith in me?"

"I have faith in nothing."

"You can't live that way."

"You know nothing of me, or how I live."

Thomas put a hand to his brow and squeezed the bridge of his nose, as if that could lessen the pounding in his head. "I have heard that a lot, lately." He took a breath that hardly seemed to fill his lungs. "Micha, this is no use."

"Of course not," said Micha, viciously. "I haven't pleased you, so you're done with me."

"For God's sake—"

"And leave Him out of it."

"For fuck's sake, I love you. How can you say this to me?" Thomas closed the distance between them and put his hand over Micha's thundering heart. "'Whither thou goest, I will go and where thou lodgest I will lodge: Thy people shall be my people and thy God my God.' I love you but you would have me love nothing but shadows."

Micha's hand came up and closed over Thomas's, his fingers curling into frantic claws. "Shadows is all I am."

"No. I know who you are; you show me sometimes. I love that man and this man, and every shade and shard of you. But I cannot fight against you for you."

"Can we not . . ." Micha's voice trailed away a moment. "Simply go on? As we are?"

"Which is what? You said yourself that I'm not your friend or your lover." Thomas leaned a little closer, letting the now-familiar warmth of Micha's body brush softly against him like the memory of a touch. "What would you have me be?"

Micha twisted away but only slightly. "I spoke in anger," he muttered.

It was, as ever, not quite an apology or an explanation, and, for once, Thomas did not let it be enough. "Then tell me, Micha," he pressed, "what am I to you? A friend in whom you do not confide? A lover you do not love?"

"Please don't make me do this." Micha's voice softened unexpectedly, though his eyes were bleak. "You've given me something close to peace, something close to happiness."

"I would give you everything," said Thomas simply.

Micha's lip curled into its familiar sneer. "And your price?"

"It's not a transaction."

"It's always a transaction."

Desolation swept through Thomas like winter. It was hopeless. Micha was as unreachable as George. As Edward. "Let me love you," he pleaded. "Let me be your friend. Sometimes you make me think you must feel something for me too."

There was a brief silence. "You are the best man I've ever known," said Micha, as though the words were wrenched from him. "And I have done nothing to deserve you. But I can't." His voice was steady and without inflection. "I can't." And, all the while, something frantic flickered in the darkness of his eyes, like an unheard scream. The hand that still rested atop Thomas's hand was icy. And then he was pushing Thomas away, silence and emptiness filling the new-made space between them. Micha's chin came up. The coldness settled over his face. "So what now?" he asked. "You will want me gone."

"No but—"

"Surely you cannot want me to stay?"

It was all so swift and so sudden. Bewilderment flared into anger. "What I want," snapped Thomas, "is for you to think about this. Must you simply react, like a beast with its leg in a trap? Take a day, take a week, but, at least, think about it. If you care for me at all."

"Yes," returned Micha dully. "I care."

"I don't know what holds you back. Fear or mistrust or doubt or pain. But is it truly worth keeping? Come to me, or fly from me, but choose. Do not let your demons drive you."

And then, wearily, sore in body, heart, and soul, Thomas walked from the room into the darkness, and he did not look back.

Chapter 18

Micha sat on his stile, trying to sketch the meadow and failing. Instead, he had drawn Thomas's hands, the tendons standing out on his wrists as he clutched in helpless passion at a scattering of new-fallen leaves.

Micha slipped the page to the back of the book and forced himself to concentrate on the landscape instead. Autumn was dying around him. The green in the meadow was fading to grey, the wildflowers were curling in upon themselves like heartbroken lovers, and stripped-back trees stood stark against a sunless, opalescent sky.

He made a half-hearted attempt to stop the pond looking as though it floated about three feet above the landscape and then went back to Thomas, lightly detailing his forearms, exposed in ecstasy, and then the interior crease of his elbow. The bunched-up sleeves of his dark coat. Narrow shoulders. He had barely seen the man for the past few weeks; how could he remember him so vividly? How could he draw him, with such surety and ease, when his pencil would not delineate the scene right in front of his eyes?

And why was he still here?

Since he did not know how to begin giving Thomas what he wanted—what he deserved—it was simply another deceit to remain.

But leaving seemed equally impossible.

He had nothing, and nowhere to go. Nowhere he was wanted and nowhere he wanted to be. Except here. With Thomas.

A bark in the distance broke into his reverie, and he hastily shoved his drawing out of view as Ruff came tearing through the grass like a fireball and slammed into Micha's knees.

"For fuck's sake," growled Micha, trying to hold on to his sketchbook and preserve his modesty as Ruff's nose delved eagerly into his crotch. He had just succeeded in dislodging the dog as Ada and Esther rounded the corner, and by then, it was too late to pretend he had not seen them. Ruff was tugging lovingly at one of his boots in any case, so flight would have been impossible.

"Oh Michael," cried Ada, as soon as she was close enough for speech, "you weren't at book group."

"I haven't been feeling very well. Sorry."

"But the plot thickens. It is tremendously exciting."

"It is possible," said Esther dryly, "to read privately as well as publicly. Michael can catch up. I will lend him the book."

"It's fine. I might . . . might not have time, anyway." He bent down to tug at Ruff's ears so he did not have to look at the Nettlefield ladies, a tactic that worked only for as long as Ruff was capable of standing still, which was about ten seconds. The dog wriggled under the stile and dashed away into the meadow, leaving Micha undefended.

Ada climbed up beside him and sat down, hustling him over to make space and tucking her feet neatly onto one of the slats of the fence. "Sheba read beautifully," she sighed. "That's Thomas's friend from London. She's staying with Esther."

"How kind of you to point that out to me, Ada," murmured Esther. She folded her elbows on the wall and stood at her ease, watching Ruff chasing his own tail.

"She is very lovely," Ada went on. "Do you not think so, Michael?"

"Sure," he said, wanting to die. "I mean, yes. Yes, she is."

Ada's brows flipped up artlessly. "Are you acquainted with her?"

A hundred possible answers tumbled through his mind, as ugly as toads. "I've met her. But I would not say we were acquainted. I know very little of her." There. A wrong put right? But the words tasted sour.

It was a meaningless gesture; all the damage he was capable of causing, he had already done. And it had made no difference, no difference at all.

"Yes, but are she and Thomas very close, do you know?"

Micha gave Ada a furious look he found he had no power to conceal. "What are you suggesting?" he snapped.

"Ada," said Esther, soothingly. And then, "She's shameless, Michael. She has decided, on the basis of no evidence, that Thomas is in love with Sheba."

"Not no evidence," protested Ada. "They enjoy each other's company. I know they walk together nearly every day. He is terribly attentive to her."

"He is attentive to everyone, dear."

Ada flicked her curls. "Well, if he is not in love with her yet, he very soon will be, mark my words. It is about time Thomas was thinking of marriage. He must be so lonely up in the rectory all by himself." She patted Micha's knee. "Of course he has you, Michael, but a gentleman friend does not count."

"He's not lonely," he said, again unable to prevent himself.

"I am sure he must be." Ada ignored him. "He has such a melancholy look."

Micha looked to Esther for help, but she only shrugged. "Perhaps."

"I have given the matter a lot of thought," Ada continued. "They are soulmates, I am sure of it."

"Friends," whispered Micha. "They are friends."

"For now. We must bring them together, help them recognise the strength of their true feelings for each other." Ada's eyes glinted. "The depth of their passion."

Esther gave an unladylike snort. "I knew it was a mistake to let you read a book. It has addled your mind."

"You may pour scorn on me if you wish, but you cannot deny it is a lovely idea."

"They do seem well suited," admitted Esther. "I have rarely seen Thomas smile as much as he does in her presence. I think she makes him laugh. That is a vitally necessary quality when it comes to a life partner."

"And what a handsome couple they will make. What lovely children they will have. I can see them with five or six, at least."

"I'm surprised you have not already picked out their linen and silverware."

"That," said Ada, laughing, "they may do for themselves." She sighed happily. "How romantic. Even you must admit it is romantic, Esther."

"It is quite romantic," said Esther. "I have already admitted it."

"And what else are we to do this winter?"

"You could try," snarled Micha, "minding your own fucking business."

He jumped off the stile and fled. He could not go back the way he had come, nor across the meadow, so he struck out randomly, blundering through the fields without direction or purpose. He felt ridiculous and guilty and sickened all at once, and it somehow helped to keep walking, as though it could prevent him from having to think or take any note of his feelings. But eventually he came to the limits of distance and had to stop or accept that he had run so far from himself that he had run away from Thomas as well.

Micha had been alone in the world and without means before, but at the time, he had not understood how hopeless his situation was or how far he had to fall. He had, in short, not known enough to be afraid. But the memory of the toil and privation, the uncertainty and despair, was enough now to fill his heart with dread and halt his footsteps.

He had come to the outskirts of a small wood, little more than a cluster of naked trees, and he stood ankle-deep in leaf mould and mulch. Against the far horizon, he caught a gleam of white against the grey-green hills.

Was this . . .

He brushed his fingertips against the bark of the nearest tree. Had he pressed Thomas here and kissed him? Had he lain with him here, on this bare earth? With only the sky as witness to the sin and the beauty of it? Was this where it had all gone wrong? The moment Micha's soul had cracked, and Thomas filled up the spaces like sunlight.

He dropped to his knees into the dirt, and that was where Ruff found him some time later. He pushed his face into Micha's, and, for once, he was neither rough nor boisterous.

"Oh fuck." Micha buried his wet face into Ruff's silky fur.

Eventually, he stood up, made a futile attempt to brush off his trousers, and sheepishly accepted the handkerchief Esther was holding out to him. "I shouldn't have said what I said. I'm sorry."

Esther shrugged. "We all occasionally fall subject to the urge to curse at Ada."

"Is she upset with me?"

"She'll be fine. It was a bit of excitement for her. And she's sorry too. As am I. It was thoughtless of us. I should have guessed."

"Uh . . ." Micha gave her a look wild with mingled hope and panic. "Guessed? I don't—"

"You love her too."

Micha burst out laughing. It wasn't the slightest bit amusing, but it was the only socially acceptable sound he felt capable of making. And then, just as suddenly, he couldn't bear it, not for another minute, not for another second. Not another lie. He was drowning in them. He would die of them. "Him," he said. "I'm in love with him."

There was a long silence. Oh fuck, what had he done? The village was going to rise up against him like he was Mary Shelley's monster.

"I beg your pardon?"

It was too late, really, to take it back or try to deny it. And some part of him, some confused, destructive, utterly infatuated part, did not wish to. He would fling his wretched fragments of love into the teeth of the world. Let it flinch. "I'm in love with Thomas."

There was an even longer silence. Esther's face had gone completely still around her wide eyes. "But he's your cousin."

Not the first potential objection Micha would have raised, but he supposed it was human nature, sometimes, to take refuge in inconsequentialities. "He's not my cousin, all right?" he said shakily, still clinging to the solid, slightly wriggling warmth that was Ruff. "We're just . . . friends, I suppose."

"And," Esther asked slowly, "you . . . you love him?"

"Yes." His voice steadied. As much as he had shocked himself with his own confession, there was a kind of liberty to it too. "Yes. As a wife loves a husband. As a husband loves a wife."

"But he's a . . . you're a . . . oh, you poor boy."

He had expected disgust. He was not sure he preferred pity. "Why would you say that?"

She frowned but in thought, not in distaste. It might have been comical, had it not been his life she was trying desperately to understand. "Well, it cannot be comfortable for you to entertain such feelings for another man."

"It's just the same," he said. "Just the same as loving anybody. Uncomfortable and terrible and, you know, wonderful."

She nodded, something of her customary manner creeping back into her tone. "Yes, that does sound like love."

The bitter-edged wind swept between the trees, making the bare branches twitch like severed fingers.

"Can something not be done?" Esther asked, into the silence.

Micha glanced up, startled. "What?"

"Can it be put right?"

"Oh, you mean me. Can I be put right."

"I didn't quite—"

"Right or wrong, I don't think I can change it." He paused. "I'm not sure I would, even if I could."

"Even for a wife and a home and a family of your own? Even for a normal life?"

"I want those things desperately. But not at the cost of"—he had no other word for it—"my soul."

Assuming he had any soul left. He had bartered it piece by piece, year by year. He looked up at Esther, half-wishing he had not spoken but knowing he would not have been able to hold his silence any longer.

The worst of it was liking her. She had been kind to him, when he had only just begun to remember what kindness was. She had reminded him what it was like to be human. And to have a friend. One he had thrown away in a single moment of excessive honesty. "Say something." His voice rang harshly, even in his own ears. "Call me unnatural. Scorn me. Turn away in revulsion. Tell the village."

"Oh, Michael, I'm an old woman, my back would play up something chronic. I can't turn away in revulsion like I used to."

He stared at her, too disbelieving to yet dare to be hopeful.

"I confess, I cannot begin to understand," she went on. "And perhaps it is best I don't try, but if you truly believe this is who you are and what you wish, then so be it."

"'So be it'?" he repeated, incredulously.

She shrugged. "So be it."

The breath rushed out of him, bringing with it, to his mortified horror, another flood of tears. He tried to hide them in the dog, but the whole experience was far too reminiscent of a bath for even Ruff's loyalty to withstand, and he pulled out of Micha's arms with a betrayed whine.

"Fuck," said Micha, shielding himself with his hands. "Fuck. Sorry. Fuck."

"Um." Esther patted his shoulder. "There there?"

He half-laughed, half-hiccoughed. "'There there'? Is that the best you can do?"

"I suppose I could give you a hug, if you'll stop crying."

"I'm not crying. I'm just . . . I'm not crying."

Micha stood, and Esther enfolded him in an embrace that was far warmer than he would have expected.

"I'm sorry I imposed on you," he muttered. "And made you listen to that."

"Don't talk nonsense, Michael."

"Sorry."

"And stop apologising."

"Sorry."

When they stepped away from each other, Micha was almost composed.

"Come." Esther shook out her skirts briskly. "We must be getting back. It gets dark quickly these days."

"I can find my own way. You don't have—"

"For heaven's sake. I will not have an apoplexy. You have given me something of a shock, I cannot deny it. I had no idea such things were even possible. But I have always been a strong-minded woman, and I fully intend to come to terms with this." She put two fingers into her mouth and gave a short, sharp whistle, and Ruff came bounding out from between the trees. "And I will expect to see you at book group next week."

He gave her a sharp look. "You will, will you?"

"Yes. You and Thomas both."

"This sounds like blackmail."

If he had been attempting to discourage her, the attempt was not sincere, and doomed to failure regardless. "Precisely," she said. "Really, my dear, you have no idea how dangerous it is to share your secrets with me. I will be quite merciless. Before you know it, you'll be holding my yarn and carrying my shopping."

"Don't count on it."

She smirked at him.

"But I might consider it if you ask me nicely."

She slipped her arm into the crook of his. "Whatever others may think, or you may believe, you're a fine young man, Michael. Now, let me fill you in on what you missed in *The Woman in White* . . ."

They walked at Esther's pace back towards Nettlefield as the temperature dropped and the sky darkened. The conversation was mostly dominated by Wilkie Collins, which Micha appreciated because it meant he did not have to concentrate. He felt as though his footsteps barely landed on the ground. As if he had stepped off a cliff and not fallen.

"Michael," said Esther, as the first thatched rooftops appeared in the distance, "may I ask a question?"

Micha eyed her warily. "You can ask."

"Does Thomas reciprocate your feelings?"

Yes. Yes. He loves me. And it is the only worthwhile thing in my worthless, wasted life. "No."

Esther nodded. "Forgive me. I should not have pried. I was wondering if it was a common thing."

"Not uncommon. But he does not know, and he is not like me."

"It seems to me a difficult thing to love as you love and even more so to love unrequitedly."

"My love may not always be unrequited." He gave a half-smile, half-lost in the shadows of dusk. "And I used to dream it would not always be difficult."

He walked Esther to her door and then hurried up the hill to the rectory. Thomas was not there. Micha wandered restlessly through the empty rooms. A faint itching buzzed beneath his skin. The world was starting to grate against his eyes. A little laudanum would help. He could reduce the dosage tomorrow.

No. Now. He would reduce the dosage now.

He pressed his fingernails into the palms of his hands. His heart was beating too fast. Unspecific anxieties gathered inside him like carrion birds. He paced. He trembled. He paced some more. He started weaving a pattern between rooms, counting his footsteps as they resounded against the floorboards.

The walls pressed in around him, like a crowd, like an unwanted lover, squeezing the air from his lungs. Sweat broke out across his skin. He reeled to one of the windows in the garden room and tried to yank it open. There was not enough air in the world to let him breathe.

And then he saw.

Thomas outside. In the last of the light. A man caught between twilight and starlight, delineated in the deepest silver and the faintest gold. He was in his shirtsleeves, armed with a wooden sword, teaching

Hope to fence. They danced back and forth across the grass. Madame Defleur's daughter sat curled on a nearby bench, watching them with amusement.

Though Micha had lost the will to struggle with it, the window perversely swung open, and the room filled up with the clack of swords and distant voices.

"En garde, varlet."

"Hope, please do not call Mr. Mandeville a varlet."

But Thomas was laughing. "A challenge. On my life."

"And I will answer it!"

They met again in a clash of blades, Hope coming at him with far more aggression than technique, and Thomas falling back, Micha thought, because he was the sort of generous idiot who would do that.

He caught for the window and slammed it shut again.

Then he went to his room and took some laudanum.

Took more than he had intended because when next he stirred from his dull, dreamless stupor it was full dark. He pulled himself upright on the bed and tried to shake off the aches and the lethargy. There was just enough opium still in his system that Edward Mandeville's paintings glowed through the gloom like gemstones.

It was too late, and Micha's mind was too disordered for it to be remotely sensible for him to seek out Thomas. But he went anyway, stumbling his way through the dark towards the faint gleam beneath Thomas's bedroom door.

Thomas answered his knock swiftly. He was clad in a startling multicoloured cotton print dressing gown. His expression was somewhat guarded, but hope flashed in his eyes, as bright as spring.

"A present from George," he explained, gesturing at himself in response to an expression Micha had not quite been swift enough to conceal.

"It's ghastly. And now I really do know all your secrets."

There was an uncertain pause.

"Did you want something, Micha?"

"Yes." He stepped forward and Thomas stepped back and it was just like in their forest except this time everything was different. Micha kicked the door closed behind him. "Yes." He caught Thomas's face between his palms and claimed his mouth. "Yes."

Thomas put his hands on Micha's shoulders, as though he was not sure whether he wanted to push him away or pull him closer. But then Micha kissed him, as he had once been kissed a lifetime ago on a golden afternoon in Oxford. All the dreams of youth and hopes of age, promises spilling from his silent tongue, worlds and lifetimes spun on a thread of breath. Since leaving London, Micha had seen Isidore in only half-dreamed fragments.

But he felt a trace of him now, an echo in the kiss that connected them—Micha, Isidore, Thomas—like a gift, or a curse, or a whisper rippling across the years.

And Thomas yielded, just as Micha had yielded, with only the softest of noises, spilled wanton as communion wine against Micha's mouth. It became an embrace then, two bodies melting together like new-made shadows in the flickering lamplight, lips clinging to lips, hands to hands, as they learned on instinct alone the deep lessons of each other's flesh. Micha shuddered, half-lost, half-found, and so very afraid. Then he closed his eyes, and everything was gone, drowned in the dark, sweet Lethe of Thomas. All the faceless hands and the nameless faces, ghosts, and reflections of nothing, as hollow as Micha's poppy-drenched self.

"Micha, I—" Words, pressed breathless to his mouth.

Micha's fingers curled into Thomas's arms, the harshness mirrored in his voice. "You want this."

"Yes but—"

"You want this."

There is no sin or shame in this. This is what Isidore tells me.

He calls it Mesopotamia, this secluded island where the Cherwell splits, sun-dappled and dreamy with celandines and willow trees. The sky is a cerulean Aegean, the river a snake of silver. And Isidore holds strawberries to my lips. The juices run in damp garnets down his fingers.

His eyes are greener than the grass, as bright as diamonds. He is an angel of alabaster and gold, and he kisses me, he kisses me, and I think I might die on the wonder of it. Sunlight and strawberries. But there is a roughness to his mouth that thrills me in the deepest, darkest ways. When his tongue pushes between my lips, it is a shudderingly perfect violation, and I moan, I moan so wantonly he kisses me harder, until his mouth shapes mine, forces mine, until I feel the strength of him like a shadow in all his touching. And it is the sweetest shame I have ever known.

Thomas's head dropped in defeat against Micha's shoulder. "You know I do."

"Then say it." Micha dug his hand into Thomas's hair and pulled until Thomas gasped and looked up again. His eyes were wide, lust-drowned, faintly golden in the dim light. Micha put his mouth against the other man's throat, silk and stubble and the beat of his blood, and branded kisses into his skin. "Say it." Micha felt the catch of Thomas's breath beneath his lips, the quick, wild flutter of his pulse, strong and fragile at the same time. Thomas's skin tasted clean, like nothing, like his mouth, pure and perfect. He arched into Micha's hold, shameless and heedless, a dazed moan slipping into the silence.

The utter ease of Thomas's passion filled Micha with a kind of despair. It was too innocent, too unrestrained, much as his own had been before he had learned different lessons. He wanted it, knowing he did not deserve it, and knowing also it was not enough, for it was not the surrender he craved. "Say it." But Thomas's only response was a shuddering gasp that blossomed into a cry when Micha, lost to his own savage needs, bit him.

Micha jerked his head up and would have pulled away, but Thomas would not let him, his arms warm and tight around Micha's body. There was a dull red mark pressed into the soft skin just above Thomas's collarbone. Micha brushed it with a thumb, and Thomas quivered in response, an expectation of pain transformed into the beginnings of pleasure. *I leave those on your soul,* Micha thought, with a twist of utter self-loathing. But he wanted that as well: to imprint himself on Thomas like a plague. To leave bruises on his skin and footsteps on his heart. To change someone else, as he had been changed.

A slight push was all it took, and they tumbled onto Thomas's bed in a breathless collision of bodies, Micha still clinging like a vampire. He nestled a knee between Thomas's spread legs and yanked hard enough on the dressing gown to send the buttons scattering to the corners of the room. Thomas, unconcerned at the fate of his clothing, brought his hands up to rest lightly on Micha's hips. The delicate curl of his fingers reminded Micha of a potter at work, the touch at once protective and assured, as though Micha could perhaps be fashioned afresh in kindness at the centre of the world's ever-spinning wheel.

He shuddered, for a moment suspended there between Thomas's hands, and then he grabbed both wrists and bore them down against the quilted coverlet. "Say it." His voice shook and then broke on a note of pleading. "Why won't you say it? You want this. Not them. This." With every word, he shoved Thomas's hands harder against the bed, the bones grinding beneath his thumbs.

"Micha." The other man spoke so gently that Micha only stared at him, his own name having become briefly incomprehensible. Then Thomas pushed against him, the movement so swift and sudden that Micha did not even think to fight against it. He sat up on the edge of the bed, and Micha went tumbling unceremoniously to the floor between his legs. Leaning down, Thomas cupped his jaw, his hands as soft as his voice. "Micha, what I want is not in question."

I know what you want.

Isidore strips me slowly beneath the turquoise sky in the golden light. His mouth and his fingers caress every fresh discovery, every little piece of me, as though he is Raleigh, and I am El Dorado. I am claimed by his touches, mapped and made precious. I tremble for him because I cannot help myself and because it makes his eyes spark like green fires. His kisses are breathless things against my shivering skin.

I know I should not want this, should not allow it, but the wanting and knowing are their own incitement. And the more my mind resists, the more my body surrenders, the more it makes itself an instrument for his playing, the more it twists and turns beneath his hands, the more my throat makes music, music just for Isidore, profane and lovely, its notes thrown only to the unwatching sun.

He lays me out like a maiden. The willow fronds cast shadows in the shapes of fingers over everything that Isidore has laid bare, my body, my heart, my soul, the truth of me.

Micha was shaking helplessly with some terrible mixture of fear, desire, and memory. Tremors, hot and cold, rushed across his skin and buried under it like worms. He turned his face into Thomas's palm and closed his eyes. He belonged here, vanquished and in pieces, at Thomas's feet. But, after a moment, Thomas slipped down beside him, his long legs folded around Micha's as though they knelt in mutual prayer, his body bringing with it a deep and solid warmth. The only certainty in a universe otherwise as random as petals upon the breeze.

They sat there a long time in silence. Then Thomas leaned in and brushed his lips over the stubble-rough edge of Micha's jaw. "I missed you."

Micha let out a breath he did not know he had been holding, the heat of it dissipating in ripples over Thomas's hand. "Why?" he muttered. "Why must you make me defenceless?"

"You aren't."

It had all seemed so simple that day in the woods, in the shadow of the white horse. A mere seduction of the skin. An exchange of services: sex for power. But, perhaps, even then it had been too late, the damage done, the wound too deep for cure, for the moment they had begun to touch each other, Micha had wanted Thomas, and the knowledge had shattered him utterly. As it shattered him now. He kissed the soft, secret interior of Thomas's palm and slowly opened his eyes. "I'll give you everything." He paused. "But you won't want me."

Thomas's fingers stroked lightly over his skin. "I do."

Micha took a deep breath and hurled his confession like a spear. "I read your journal. I always knew."

Thomas stilled.

"About Edward. And about you. And the way you felt about me. It wasn't some great mystical fucking confluence of sodomites. I knew."

"But in the woods you . . . the way you . . ." Thomas put the hand that had once touched Micha over his mouth. "Why would you do that with me? To me? And I thought—God, what a fool I am."

"You liked it well enough."

"I loved it. It was beautiful. And you were different that day."

It was so typical of Thomas. He did not even try to shield his heart. He loved fearlessly and utterly, and it made Micha ache with longing. He pushed himself away and moved restlessly, almost mindlessly, to a corner of the room, like a beast at bay. "I don't know why you can't be just like everyone else. You could have fucked me, and it would have been fine. But you had to make me feel everything. You had to fall in love with me. Why can't you just leave me alone?"

Thomas had not moved. "I don't understand. If you didn't want me, what did you want?"

"I don't know. Power. Control. Proof that you were human, weak and wicked." Micha put his head in his hands. "But all you did was make me want you back. It's all you've ever done, and I hate it. I hate you."

Love me. Give yourself to me.

He opens me with slickened fingers, and the shock of it makes the breath catch behind my teeth. He murmurs to me over the rushing of the river and the rustle of the willow. His shadow falls over me first, then his kisses, like sun dapples on my skin. His mouth is a circle of warmth, full of words and promises, and his fingers glide, press, twist, glide, press, twist until I learn to want them. Until I am mad with wanting. I spread myself soul-wide upon the grass for Isidore. The flush stands bright upon his pale face. Sweat glimmers at his brow and on his upper lip. And he watches me as though he cannot look away. As though I am the brightest star in his vast and dazzling universe.

By the time he presses into me, I am breathless with begging for him, senseless with pleasure. Our bodies join like our tangled hands, like they were made to fit together, and there's no pain, no uncertainty, just the closeness of his body, and the rough rhythm of his breath, and the slowly building furnace of our desire.

Isidore sheds his poise like a selkie's skin. He is savage and glittering and desperate. He kisses me like he wants to drown in my mouth. He fucks me like my body is a shrine he wants to desecrate. And it's beautiful. He's beautiful.

I love you. I love you. I love you.

Yes, he says, yes. As he pours himself into me.

"Oh Micha, really? All this time? Everything you have done for me was done in hate?" Thomas was silent a moment. "I don't . . . I can't . . . understand it. How could you have been so kind, if you hated me?"

Micha shuddered, self-loathing trickling through his veins as thick as poison. "Kind? I've never been kind. I've done nothing but use you and lie to you."

"But I lied to you. I lied to you about Edward, and I tried to pretend I did not desire you and that my heart was pure. I am every bit as corrupt as you would have me be."

"But you're not," cried Micha. "That's the fucking problem. I wish you were, but you're not."

"Those are not the words of a man who could hate me." The sharp edge of pain was fading from Thomas's voice, but Micha could still not bring himself to face him. "I am no saint, Micha, and I would not wish to be. I tried to carve myself into the image of one, but you showed me what a hollow man it left me."

"Please. Please, stop it. I've done nothing for you."

Suddenly, Thomas's arms were around him. Micha tried to resist and then to pull away, but he lacked true conviction and his body betrayed him. He leaned into Thomas as if he could not have stood alone for another second, his head falling back against Thomas's shoulder. And when Thomas spoke, his lips moved against the edge of Micha's cheek like an ever-forming kiss. "Nobody has ever asked me about my dreams before. Nobody has laughed with me. Nobody has told me the names of the stars."

"God," muttered Micha. "Does your life so lack for love?"

"I don't know. Mostly yes, I think. But I cherish what you have given me, Micha. I adore the world through your eyes."

"How could you?"

"You see so much beauty. I was blind before I met you."

Micha shook his head, his hair tangling with Thomas's, like strands of shadow. "Don't talk like this. It's pathetic. This isn't love, it's barely the shadow of it."

But Thomas would not be silent. "You comforted me when I grieved. You tended me when I bled. If these are the actions of a man who hates me, I want nothing of love."

Micha had thought himself immune to shame, but now he felt its sting as deeply and bitterly as he ever had. It was strange, and oddly painful, to see the moments he had cast away as carelessly as grains of sand made precious in another's eyes. Regret stirred in his heart like ashes. He had wanted Thomas's love as a thief desires a trinket, a thing coveted but not earned. He turned slowly in the yielding circle of Thomas's arms. "I don't hate you. I couldn't. I can't." He pressed his face against Thomas's neck. "I'm sorry, I'm sorry."

Thomas's fingers coiled lightly in his hair. "There's no need to apologise, my dear, dear friend. Can't you see how much you mean to me? How much you've done?"

"But it's so very little," whispered Micha brokenly. "And you think it so very much. I wish . . . I wish I was different. I wish I was better."

"That's not the first time you've said that. I would have you as you are." Thomas lifted Micha's head. He slipped a hand between their bodies and let it rest against Micha's pounding heart. "This is the man who saved me. This is the man I love."

"But you don't know the half of it."

"Then tell me, and I'll listen, and love you still."

Micha nodded and met Thomas's eyes. "I'll teach you the names of all the stars," he said unsteadily. "You'll be so fucking sick of them."

"Never." Thomas's lips curled into the faintest of smiles.

Micha's fingers clutched at him clumsily. "You can beat me at chess. All the time. I'll fill your house with flowers. I'll draw you terrible landscapes. I'll learn how to knit and make you a scarf for the winter. And I'll . . . I'll lie in your arms all night, I'll wait for you all day, I'll . . . I'll—"

"Micha." Thomas silenced him with the sweetest of kisses. "Micha, please, it's all right, I understand."

Micha was breathless from his own babbling. "Understand what?"

Thomas's smile grew radiant. "That you love me too."

There was a long silence. Then Micha nodded. "With all my ruined heart."

Isidore, oh Isidore, oh please, please.

His body is a trembling velvet weight on mine, and I am as wild as a trapped lark. He stirs, heavy-eyed, his hair falling over his face in damp, golden rivulets, smiles, and kisses my helpless mouth.

He turns me onto my side, our two bodies nestled together like a pair of quotation marks in one of the texts I'm supposed to be studying. His hands idle across my body, ships at the mercy of the wind, trailing a wake of pleasure that gathers on my skin with the sheen of sweat. I writhe into all his touches, breathe only in gasps and pleas, unravel and am remade. His teeth graze my shoulder and his hand closes hard about my prick until I'm driving myself mindlessly, shamelessly against his ink-stained fingers, lost in the moment of his making. He cries out my name and I shatter into starlight in his arms.

Afterwards, when our lips are sore from kissing and our bodies weary from coupling, we lie beneath a sky swirled pink and gold by the setting sun. And Isidore says, come away with me.

And I say yes.

"It all began with Isidore." Micha sat hunched on the edge of Thomas's bed. He glanced up with a faint, sardonic smile. "We fell in love at Oxford, and, when he left, I went with him."

"You travelled together?" After a moment of hesitation, Thomas reached out and took his hand, and Micha did not pull away. His cold fingers lay quiescent, enfolded by Thomas's.

"Yes. On his money, for I had none. We never intended to return to England. Isidore said we would take a villa in Naples, live out the rest of our days together beneath a kinder sky." Micha swallowed. "He always loved the sea."

"Oh Micha, you were so young."

He nodded. "Boys playing at being men. But he loved me, I know he did. I think that's what I find hardest to bear." Thomas's fingers stroked and squeezed. "And, of course, I loved him too. How could I not? He was beautiful, brilliant, extraordinary in many ways." Again Micha's eyes sought Thomas's. "He was not like you."

"Well, no," said Thomas gently. "I am none of those things."

"You see people. Isidore saw only the horizon. I admired him terribly, but it was like staring into the sun. I should have known I couldn't keep a man like that."

Thomas frowned, just a little. "It was very wrong of him to make you promises he did not intend to keep."

If only it had been that simple. A villain, a victim, a betrayal, and a broken heart. "It wasn't like that. We truly believed we could be together. We thought love was enough."

"What happened?"

"His father died unexpectedly, and Isidore inherited everything. That was the first time we truly understood the choice we'd made. It was easy enough for me to give up my world; it was such a narrow thing. An education. A respectable career. A wife from a good family. Fuck." He leaned lightly against Thomas, his head resting against the other man's shoulder. "But Isidore, he had ambition, intellect, and a whole shining future waiting for him back in England. It was me or everything else. So we parted ways at Dover. It was the greyest day I'd ever seen, and I had absolutely nothing."

"He gave you no assistance?"

Micha's head jerked up. "I was his lover, not his whore."

"I didn't—"

"And, anyway, I was too miserable and too proud to tell him the truth."

Thomas smiled rather sadly. "That sounds so very like you."

"It's not real pride. I lost that a long time ago."

"Had you no friends to turn to? What of your family?"

"Our friends Isidore and I shed together. And my family I lost when I left Oxford. I should never have told them. I don't know why I did. Perhaps they would have forgiven me, but I didn't dare go back."

Thomas drew in an unsteady breath.

"What's wrong?"

"I'm sorry, it's absurd, I can't protect you from your past, but I hate to think of all you must have suffered."

"Don't weep for me." Micha pressed a kiss against Thomas's cheek to take the harshness from his words. "It carried a heavy punishment, but I saw the world. I knew love. How many people can say that?" He paused. "And it seems to have brought me to you."

"Yes. You are world enough for me."

"Let's not make promises. I'd rather just—" He broke off. Thomas raised his brows quizzically, and Micha laughed, surprising himself. "Have faith," he finished.

Thomas's hand tightened on Micha's. "That I can do."

"I may test you yet."

"I'm ready. How did you make your way in the world without money or friends?"

"I . . ." Micha sighed. "I fell upon hard times. I'll tell you, if you ask me, because I don't want to lie to you anymore. But please don't. I don't want to speak of it."

"Then I will not ask," said Thomas, at once.

"Are you sure?"

He nodded. "I have faith in you too, Micha. I don't need to hear anything you don't wish to tell me."

Micha pulled Thomas with him onto the bed, so that they fell together, entangled. "I don't deserve any of this," he muttered, relieved and humbled and perilously close to happy.

Thomas gave a small, breathless laugh, all but smothered by Micha's body pressed against him. And suddenly they were kissing, clumsy and frantic, scrabbling and struggling to get closer to each other, as though flesh itself had become a barrier.

"Oh hell," growled Micha, dragging himself away before he lost any power to do so. "Thomas, there's something else. Something I need to . . . change. Somehow."

Thomas's hands stroked languorously up and down his spine. "What is it?"

"While I was . . . that is . . . during . . . when I was . . ." He stuttered into silence. Micha's habits were well known at Madame Defleur's, but he had never spoken of them. It had not been necessary. Survival, in whatever form it took, was simply unquestioned. But he hated to lay such wretchedness bare before Thomas. "I can't remember when I started, only that it helped." Thomas was nodding but without comprehension. Micha took a shuddering breath, the word clogged in his throat. "Opium. I lived for it. I always knew it was treacherous, nothing but smoke and madness and empty dreams, but a beautiful falsehood is better than an ugly truth."

"How lost you've been," whispered Thomas, tears thick in his voice again.

"Beyond rescue, or so I thought. And I've been using laudanum since my illness."

Micha felt the scrape of Thomas's eyelashes across his skin as he blinked. "Sheba thought so, but I saw no sign of it."

"I hid it from you. I was ashamed. I still am."

"Why? Is it harmful?"

"Maybe. Maybe not. But it drives my actions, and I want to stop except I can't, I just fucking can't." Thomas held him and gentled him while Micha raged. "It's why I did what I did. I made your Mrs. Clark bring me laudanum. And then she knew all my secrets, so I wanted her gone. Please . . ."

Micha faltered, despising his own weakness but unable to deny or suppress it. "Please don't hate me. I've committed so many wrongs, but I was desperate."

"All this," said Thomas, softly, "for a remedy?"

Micha could only nod. "Or for my own frailty. I can't tell where the one begins and the other ends."

"You know I would have given you anything? Helped you however I could."

"I know. And I know that makes it worse."

The seconds moved slowly, landing as heavy as rain upon Micha, until Thomas finally spoke again. "Thank you, at least, for telling me. And for trusting me."

Micha gave a soft, tight laugh. "I think I was in love with you, even then, but in such a twisted way it barely deserves the name." He cringed from the remembrance of himself, so wanting and so afraid. "I was monstrous. Most likely I still am."

Arching up, Thomas kissed him, pressing a denial into his mouth, like a bite without teeth. "I cannot lie. I wish you had behaved differently, Micha. But it's not for me to judge you."

"Because"—and here Micha's tone grew sardonic—"that's reserved for your damn God?"

"Because I love you."

"Even after . . ." Micha couldn't finish the sentence.

"Even after," Thomas confirmed.

It was exactly what Micha needed to hear, but it crushed him nonetheless. He sheltered his face beneath his arm. "I don't deserve—"

"Let's not speak of what is or is not deserved." Thomas cut him off gently. "I doubt you deserved your hard times either. May we go back to the laudanum?"

"Why not?" Micha huffed out a sound that was not quite a laugh. "I always do."

"If I am to understand you correctly," Thomas began, his voice careful, the words deliberate, "you've been using laudanum since your illness, and opium before that, and now you wish to stop?"

It was not the right term. *Wishing* implied more volition than Micha truly possessed. But still he nodded.

"And stopping is difficult?"

Another nod.

"I hate the thought of you suffering more than you already have." Thomas's gaze was stricken. "Must this truly be done?"

"It must be done." It was not until he'd said the words aloud that Micha discovered something perilously close to conviction. "It comes between us. It stops me feeling and I want to feel. And, with you, I want to feel everything."

There was a long silence.

"Then what do we do?" asked Thomas.

"There's no 'we' for this. It's simply something for me to endure." For Thomas's sake, he mustered what boldness was left to him. Micha had experienced a little for himself, and witnessed in others, the ravages of opium withdrawal, and he was not so lost to dreams of love that he did not fear them. He doubted his own strength, but he did not doubt Thomas. If this was to be the price, he would somehow find a way to pay it. If it was punishment, for old sins or newer ones, or for all those he wished to commit, he would bear it. He would fight this dragon of his own making, cut it from his flesh, and vanquish it. He would prove himself worthy. Gods be damned. He would have Thomas. They would have each other.

Micha was shaking slightly with the knowledge of what lay ahead, and Thomas held him tightly, body to body, heart to heart. "There must be something I can do to help you."

"No," Micha snapped. "No." And, gentling his tone with difficulty, "I don't want you to see. It's miserable, Thomas. And repulsive. I still don't know if I'll even be able to do it."

"I believe you can, if that's what you want."

Micha shrugged. "Maybe not for myself, but for us, I can try."

"I don't know if I'll be able to stay away from you."

"You have to promise me. Please."

But Thomas shook his head. "I can't give you that promise, but I'll try to honour your preference."

"You're a stubborn fucker."

Thomas smiled. "Yes."

Micha groaned, love, despair, and surrender tangled up inside him, almost indistinguishable from each other. "It'll take a while. Maybe a month or two."

"A month?" repeated Thomas, so dismayed it was almost comical.

And suddenly a month felt like an unbearably long time to Micha too. He pressed himself against, or perhaps into, Thomas's grasp. "Just kiss me. Like you did in the wood."

Thomas's lips twitched into a smile. "You mean, without any idea what I was doing?"

"Like you knew me."

Thomas leaned over him and took Micha's mouth in a deep, sure kiss. And Micha arched up into it, breathlessly moaning, his abruptly uncertain hands clutching at nothing. "Will you . . . I want . . ." It was ridiculous, but heat rushed suddenly to his face, and he was blushing like a virgin. "I want to be with you. I want to feel you."

Thomas's sharp hips were pressed into Micha's, but it was a welcome ache. "Whatever you want is yours."

"Oh." Micha twisted a little, tormented by a longing so rare and unexpected it felt almost sweet. "I wish I could fuck you, but I don't think I can."

"We could try?" Thomas ducked his head shyly. "Or I could find some other way to please you." His free hand traced a somewhat hesitant path between their bodies.

Micha's breath quickened, sheer hope and instinct, and then he reached his arms above his head, offering . . . yielding himself to Thomas. "Fuck me. I'll show you how."

Thomas was silent a moment. "Is this something we share or something you give?"

"Both, and something I take." Micha curled a leg around Thomas, drawing him closer, feeling the hot, hard pressure of the man's cock against his own, even through two layers of clothing. Thomas's body jerked, a deep tremor running through him, like he was a bow Micha had drawn tight with a single, simple action. Micha made a mindless, needy noise, his fingers curling over his exposed palms. "Tonight," he panted. "Whatever happens, give me tonight."

"And every night that follows. Every day."

"No promises, remember? Just fuck me. Let me feel something before tomorrow."

When Thomas eased them apart, Micha ached with loss. He struggled semi-upright and yanked the shirt over his head.

"What?" he asked.

Thomas was simply looking at him.

"What?"

"You're so remarkably beautiful, Micha." Thomas splayed a hand across his chest, his fingers carding lightly through the coarse hair that gathered there. "Like Blake's tyger." He traced a band of shadow across Micha's torso, then a band of light, and Micha shivered helplessly, responding less to the sensation than the intent within it, the care and reverence.

He fell back onto his elbows, the uncertain light spilling like liquid over his skin, shifting with his quickened breath. Thomas followed him, his lips catching at the pulse beating in Micha's neck, then tumbling in tiny kisses across his collarbones and shoulders. The tip of his tongue pursued the flickering patterns of light, leaving new ones, silver-bright amidst the gold, a ripple of silken warmth that did not entirely fade.

Micha's chest heaved. His head fell back. Thomas's tongue swirled across one of his nipples, and his back arched wildly. "Fuck, oh fuck. Oh Thomas."

"Magnificent," whispered Thomas, the word flaring white-hot like a brand. He glanced up with a rather wicked smile. "'Did He who made the lamb, make thee?'"

"I don't bloody care. Take your clothes off."

Thomas laughed, sat back on his heels, and let the dressing gown slip from his shoulders, pooling on the bed behind him like a rainbow cast from the sky. He started to work on the knot in his cravat.

"Today, if you don't mind?" Micha reared up like an avenging valet and yanked the linen free from Thomas's collar. Then he began to tear at the shirt, his hands slipping between skin and fabric until, at last, a very tousled Thomas emerged, shaking the hair from his eyes.

He was pale, even in the glow from the lamp, though rather than making him appear fragile, it gave him a deep clarity, like a single perfect note, played on a perfect instrument. If Micha's composition tended towards a certain baroque extravagance, Thomas embodied a pure, and striking, simplicity. Long-limbed and lean-flanked, he was all precise, clean lines and the subtle promise of strength.

Micha's fingers trembled too much to be useful, so he braced himself one-handed and brushed the knuckles of the other against the ladder of Thomas's ribs. His skin was raw silk and sun-warmed marble, flawless, and only lightly stippled by pale, gold-tipped hair.

A flush, like the fairest dawn, rose to the surface of Thomas's skin. "I'm not—"

"Don't. I love you."

Somehow, tugging and pulling, wriggling and laughing, they shed the rest of their clothes, and Thomas, sleek as a seal, slipped naked into Micha's waiting arms. And, suddenly, everything was skin. They gasped in muddled unison, Micha's harsh obscenity entangled with Thomas's softer, gentler groan.

"I have dreamed of this." Thomas sounded half-delirious as he pressed his body to Micha's, sliding between his legs, against his chest, moving with him, as sensuous and shameless as a cat in catmint.

"I . . ." Micha found himself breathless, wordless. Thomas's erection was nestled against his thigh, insistent enough to stir his own into temporary arousal. He parted his legs and arched his hips until they met, a rough-sweet clumsy-tender intimacy that made Thomas cry out in startled wonder. That was its own pleasure, warm as whisky on a winter day, and Micha buried his hands in Thomas's hair and dragged him into a finesse-less kiss.

Sex had long ago shed its mysteries for Micha. There was little that had not been done to him over the years, but, even with Isidore, it had not been like this. He had been an assured, imaginative lover, passionate often, tender sometimes, occasionally cruel, a man of incalculable erotic refinements. And Thomas was simply Thomas. There was nothing remarkable in the way they touched each other and moved together, but there was no restraint and no uncertainty now, just a deep mutual joy that Micha thought perilously close to a kind of innocence. It swept across his skin with Thomas's hands, like the brush of sunlight. And Micha unravelled, not artfully or even entirely consciously, just blissfully and completely, moaning open-mouthed against Thomas.

Finally, he pushed away, and Thomas pulled back, dazed and dreamy-eyed, bruise-lipped and shaking slightly with arousal. The play of shadows made his patrician English features stand out more starkly than ever, but Micha knew all their secrets now. How to coax the stern mouth to playfulness, draw warmth from those plain brown eyes.

"Give me your hand."

Despite the abrupt order, Thomas did, without hesitation. Micha took it up—that pale gentleman's hand he had, caught between yearning and despair, once imagined touching him—and closed his lips over the slender fingers, drawing them deep into his mouth.

The breath stuttered out of Thomas in a broken sigh, and his eyes fluttered closed.

"Someday soon," said Micha, somewhat muffled, "I'm going to do this to your cock."

Thomas answered only with a delirious noise.

Releasing Thomas's fingers, Micha nudged him into position between his knees and tipped up his hips, throwing wide his legs. He would have felt utterly absurd if not for the look on Thomas's face. Thomas stroked his free hand up the inside of Micha's thigh, not quite gently, and the intimacy of the touch, the hint of possession, made Micha's heart thud hard with instinctive pleasure.

"Here." Micha seemed to have lost the ability to converse in more than jerky monosyllables. "Like this." He spread himself and pressed Thomas's fingers awkwardly to the entrance of his body.

"Will I hurt you?"

"No."

But, in this, Thomas would not be controlled. He twisted Micha's hand free from his wrist and did the deed himself, his damp fingers fluting so lightly over the muscle that it made Micha writhe in helpless anticipation.

"Fuck's sake." Micha's head tossed restlessly against the covers. "I want to feel y—"

The words were consumed in a cry as Thomas parted him with deft fingers and pushed inside. There was little to feel, the laudanum saw to that, but there was still the warm stretch, and the pressure, and the fact it was Thomas, to light tiny sparks behind Micha's eyes. He rocked himself against the fingers inside him, wanting more, far more. Wanting everything.

"I could spend just watching you do that," breathed Thomas.

"Well don't."

Thomas experimentally curled his fingers upwards, and the tiny sparks ignited into a silver-white inferno.

"Ahh, fuck, oh fuck." Micha clawed at the covers, then at Thomas, grabbed for his hand and pulled it away, hard enough to feel the shock of withdrawal. He flipped onto his stomach, twisting his head so he could still see Thomas over one shoulder. "Like this."

Thomas covered him, smooth heat and supple strength, and Micha just . . . groaned. Ground his hips back. And Thomas answered with a kiss, pressed sweetly into the nape of his neck. A ripple of response ran all the way down Micha's spine.

Micha drew in a sobbing breath of sheer, frantic need. "Please. Will you fucking . . . please."

Thomas's hands moved over him, soothing his burning, trembling flesh, and Micha dropped his head onto his folded arms, lost in the waiting and the wanting. Then came the flutter of Thomas's fingers and the darker, deeper pressure of his cock. Micha hissed out something that might have been "yes," struggled onto his knees, and shoved back hard. A brightness that might once have been pain flashed briefly across his vision, but it stirred his dulled senses, and that was, in itself, a kind of pleasure.

Thomas steadied him by the hips, his ragged breath gusting across Micha's skin in harsh benediction, but he would not move. Micha thrashed futilely, trying to force his own body's yielding, incoherent obscenities tumbling from his lips. Thomas leaned over him, running kisses and love words up and down his spine like climbing roses until the tension went out of him. Thomas's hands pressed Micha flat, and then came the muted burn and the rough-smooth glide of Thomas coming all the way into him.

Thomas managed something that might have been Micha's name, transformed into a breathless prayer. And Micha spread his legs and arched his back, ceding himself to Thomas, in this, as in everything. He turned, as best he could, just enough to see Thomas's face, strained and flushed with ecstasy, the slender muscles standing out on his upper arms as he braced himself above Micha. His eyes snapped open as though in answer, and, for a moment, there was nothing but the act of looking, their eyes and bodies locked together, like pieces of pattern, links upon a chain. Then Thomas caught him under the chin and kissed him, their mouths jostling clumsily, words and breath and tongues tangling together into a profane and private glossolalia.

At last, when shivers were chasing each other across Micha's skin and his every breath was a smothered moan, Thomas released him. His hands covered Micha's where they were clutching frantically at the coverlet and smoothed them out, spreading the fingers wide so Thomas could interweave his own between them. Hesitantly at first, and then with growing assurance, he began to move, claiming Micha's body with thorough and powerful tenderness, just as he had kissed him that day in the woods near the white horse.

Their mouths found each other again and clung like their hands.

The ghosts of physical pleasure stirred shyly from within the prison of Micha's flesh, but love was its own, still wilder bliss. And that was Thomas, all Thomas, only Thomas. Thomas's body driving into his, Thomas's tongue deep within his mouth, Thomas's fingers curled around his own. The words themselves seemed meaningless. They were written into his skin and upon his soul, with every touch, and every breath.

Thomas's thrusts were turning as ragged as his kisses, his body heaving with incipient culmination. And Micha wanted the other man's pleasure, as desperately as though it was his own he sought. Something given, taken, shared. And perfect.

"Please," he gasped, rough against Thomas's mouth. "Come for me. In me."

Thomas's fingers tightened on Micha's, a shudder shook him, and then his head dropped into the crook of Micha's shoulder as he surrendered himself to the moment. Micha wished he could have watched his face, but he felt the echo through his own body and in Thomas's muffled moans. Thomas was a damp, heavy weight, but Micha welcomed the closeness and the sweat-studded heat that blossomed between their still-joined bodies.

Thomas, however, was too considerate to linger like that for long. He slipped free of Micha and collapsed onto his side, still breathing hard. Micha tucked his hands beneath his chin and rested a cheek on them, feeling well loved and languid.

Thomas reached out and smoothed the heavy curls that fell across Micha's brow. "Oh Micha."

"Well," he returned softly, "now we're both damned."

Thomas did not flinch, did not stop touching him. "No, my love, that was a sacrament, not a sin."

Micha let his suddenly heavy eyes fall briefly closed. "If that's what you need to believe."

"We are fashioned in His image, Micha. To love each other is the most intimate communion with Him."

"Can we leave God out of it for once?"

"I'm sorry."

Micha sighed. "It's like we're having some kind of divine ménage à trois."

"There's only you in my eyes, in my heart." Thomas's fingers caressed his cheek, the edge of his jaw, warmth trailing in their wake.

Micha's eyes drifted closed again, and, when he spoke, there was too much dreamy pleasure in his voice for his words to have any sting. "I thought He was supposed to be a jealous God."

"It's all connected. There is no shame in love." Micha felt motion beside him. And Thomas's hands moving between his legs, cleaning him with . . . something. He blinked. "That better not be my shirt."

"Mine, I think. And not likely wearable, regardless, since you tore it off me."

Micha smiled, just a little, feeling absurd and impossibly content, even knowing the hell that waited for him on the other side of dawn. Thomas cast the shirt aside and lay down again, elegantly and unselfconsciously naked, his sweat-sheened skin shining as softly as the moon. Micha hesitated a moment and then sidled closer. He put his head on Thomas's chest, over his steadily beating heart, and Thomas slipped an arm around him, drawing him closer still.

For a long time, they were silent.

Thomas's fingertips traced idle curlicues over Micha's back. "That was beautiful, Micha."

"Oh, yes, sodomy's great. No wonder they keep outlawing it."

"You know"—Thomas's eyes flared with sudden mirth—"your manners improve considerably during coitus."

"My what?"

"You become quite polite, if insistent."

"Fuck off." Thomas laughed, and the sound wrapped itself around Micha's heart like Mayday ribbons. "It's bad form to mock a man for the things he says in the heat of the moment."

"I would never mock you."

"What's this then?"

"Teasing. And, besides, I liked it. I liked it very well indeed."

Micha felt heat rise to his cheeks again. "So did I."

Silence claimed them once more. The lamp had burned low. The room filled up with shadows. Outside, the world was dark and cold, sunrise a still too-distant promise, yet the possibility of morning pressed against Micha's heart, heavy as an iron bar. He was tired, but he feared sleeping and the loss of these few scant hours.

"Don't stop touching me." His voice broke the stillness like a stone dropped into a well. "Please."

Thomas's arms tightened around him. Their legs entwined. The fingers that had so lightly caressed Micha's skin became a palm instead, moving across his back as strong and inevitable as waves against the shore.

But it was not enough. He was falling helplessly into the future. "Thomas. What . . . what will become of us?"

There was a pause. "What do you mean? I will not abandon you, as Isidore did."

Micha sighed. "He didn't abandon me. I just became a choice he couldn't make. Is it so different for you?"

Something Micha could not quite interpret flickered across Thomas's face. "You know," he said softly, "the strange thing is that I feel closer to God than I ever have, in ways I would never have understood before we met. But I can't remain a priest. Not now."

"Because of me?"

"Because of me. It wouldn't feel right, attempting to guide others to the grace of God, when I would be seen as excluded from it."

For someone who had felt so little for so long, Micha was now feeling far too much. And much of it was guilt. Shame. Terrible relief that Thomas would still be his. "There's nothing in the Bible against what we are, you know. Isidore told me."

"He's not wrong," agreed Thomas. "And neither are we. But I would be living in sin, not because we're both men, but because . . ."

"Because we're violating the sacred covenant of marriage, I know."

"I'd marry you in a heartbeat, Micha. If I could."

Micha tried to laugh it off. It was, after all, an impossibility and, therefore, not worth squandering either thought or dreams upon. But it was something that Isidore—either too practical or less romantic than he seemed—had never said to him, never offered. Even as an impossible dream. "Fuck," he said. "I hate that you have to give up everything just to be with me."

"Not everything. I mean"—Thomas gave a pained smile—"in the spirit of honesty, I've never been much of a priest."

"That's not true." The modes of giving comfort had long since been lost to Micha. But he was rediscovering them now. For Thomas. "I think you're so concerned with being a priest that you forget to be a man. Or a human being rather."

"But it's my job to—"

"To obliterate yourself?" Micha asked sharply. "To strip away all that's good and kind and true in you in order to fulfil some duty, meet some standard, that only you decided was right or necessary?"

"Is that how you see it?"

Micha shrugged. "Am I wrong?"

"No." It was a simple admission, but the sorrow of it struck what remained of Micha's heart. "I think I thought that if I could become the priest I was supposed to be, it would make up for . . . for all that was lacking in me."

"There's nothing lacking in you."

Thomas cupped Micha's face gently. "With you, I can almost believe it. But there's no escaping the fact I'm a poor son. A poor brother. And even by your reckoning, I'm a poor priest."

"That's my point, though," Micha protested. "You don't have to be. You love it here. And you love your parishioners—no matter how much you tell yourself you shouldn't."

"That's immaterial. I can't serve them and lie to them. Nor will I give you up."

Micha had heard such promises before. What was wrong with him that—even after everything—he ached so deeply to believe them? "Then what do we do?"

"We'll need to stay here awhile. Until you're free of your laudanum dependency. Until I've put my affairs in order and done what I can for Nettlefield."

Micha had heard promises like these too. Promises that were little more than compromises. But he just nodded. "And after?"

"Whatever we want. Perhaps"—and here Thomas offered a sweet, uncertain smile—"I will finally see my desert. And you could show me Venice. Or Prague. Granada. The whole world."

"And while I'm showing you the whole world, how do we live?"

"I have a small inheritance from my mother's side of the family, and I'm sure I could supplement it with teaching or . . . or . . . something."

"But what will I do?"

"Again, whatever you want. Draw. Keep house. Take in an urchin."

Micha said nothing and hid his face against Thomas. He knew he was making exactly the same mistakes all over again—trusting everything to love, and the vaguest of hopes—but he lacked any power to turn away from it.

"We'll be fine," said Thomas, sounding like he meant it. And then, teasingly, "Are you not better than a sparrow?"

But Micha was not in a humour to be teased. "For fuck's sake, God isn't going to provide for two sodomites on the run."

"The Lord loves the lost, and we'll provide for each other. I believe in that. I believe in you."

"I wish I believed in myself," Micha muttered. "And I wish . . . I wish we had no future."

Thomas drew in a sharp breath. "How can you say that?"

"No, I mean. Not because I don't want one. But because it's complicated and uncertain. I don't know who I'll be without opium. Even assuming I can give it up. You'll be an exile, from your family and your friends, and even your God. How can we—"

"Stop." Thomas untangled himself from Micha, rolling him onto his back. And all Micha did was moan as Thomas's long, lithe body stretched out, hot and perfect, over him. Thomas folded Micha's hands together and pinned them gently above his head. "Those are questions for tomorrow."

"I'm scared of tomorrow," Micha admitted, wrenchingly. "Tomorrows have never been particularly good to me."

"Then let's make *now* last for as long as we can."

"How?"

"Tell me about Venice again." Thomas released Micha's wrists, but it was only to draw him into an embrace. And they held each other, lovers trying to hold the night as well. "I always love hearing you talk."

Micha lifted his head, pushing the hair back from where it clumped over his brow. His memories had lived inside him, neglected things summoned only by opium, for so long that he did not really know how to begin to share them. But he wanted to please Thomas, and to give him something simply because he had asked for it. "I . . . I don't . . ." he began and stopped. It was not a story. There was no natural beginning.

Thomas's eyes were upon him, a gleam of hope through the gloom.

Micha met his gaze, gave up thinking, and simply spoke. "The railway bridge had been rebuilt after the Revolution, so that was how I first saw it, a city rising from the mirror of the water. It wasn't what it once was, silenced somehow, to the heart of itself, but still beautiful. A dimly dreaming city, of azure and dusty gold."

And so Micha talked, and Thomas listened, and time—ever the thief—slipped slowly away from them.

Chapter 19

Had Thomas allowed Micha to extract the promise he'd wanted, it would have been broken within two days. The next week cast them both into a hell the like of which he could not have imagined, and nothing on heaven or earth would have induced him to let Micha face it alone. Even though Micha had become a demonic creature—one who hated Thomas, cursed at him, and sometimes came at him in violence—he was too weak and delirious to be able to cause any real harm. But holding at bay the man he had previously held in his arms was its own particular pain.

That first morning, Micha surrendered to Thomas's hands two bottles of laudanum, one from London and one purchased from the village druggist. The next day, crying and shaking, he had offered up a third bottle, and then flown into a fury when Thomas had refused to return it. Rage, at last, had exhausted him, and Micha had huddled on the floor like a broken bird, his hands curled painfully tight into his hair, and his body streaming with sweat. By then he'd been close to incoherent, choking out a tangle of apologies, self-hatred, and bile. Thomas had sat at Micha's side trying, without success, to calm him or aid him, until—in a fresh bout of frenzied despair—Micha had banished him from the room. So Thomas had crouched in the hall outside, head in his hands, listening helplessly as the man he loved wept and suffered on the other side of the wall. Then, he prayed, at first without much thought, just forming words made smooth as seashells from long habit.

It got no easier.

Micha's health deteriorated. His body seemed to take violent antipathy to itself, tearing apart in a manner as painful as it was undignified, and his mind offered little refuge from the physical torment. Within a mere handful of days, Micha no longer seemed able to recognise, or remember, who Thomas was. He saw only nightmares, phantasmal monsters from his past, and Thomas could neither understand nor vanquish them. Sometimes he caught Isidore's name through the tumult, but even that brought Micha no comfort. Lost to the cruel chimeras of his affliction, Micha cowered and wept, shook uncontrollably and clawed at his own skin. He had become unreachable, untouchable.

When Thomas tried to comfort him, Micha would cringe away, as mindlessly fearful as a beast. When he became so great a danger to himself that it was necessary to physically restrain him, he would struggle wildly, and then plead with Thomas and the ghosts who lay beyond Thomas's reach, *Don't touch me, please, please don't touch me*. At last, he would fall utterly quiescent, and Thomas, close to tears himself, would search his blank eyes desperately for a trace of Michael Dashwood, and find nothing but an empty darkness.

In these moments, Thomas would pray again, but not to his God.

I love you. I am waiting for you. I love you. Come back to me.

Thomas had told Mrs. Allen that he had fallen afoul of some slight indisposition and needed to rest. The possibility of contagion had not been enough to keep her away—and soup was accumulating in the kitchen at an alarming rate—but he had managed to persuade her to moderate her hours, at least, and Ellen, the maid of all work, had gone to stay with her family in the next village. So the days and nights passed indistinguishably in a blur of anguish. A mere handful of months ago, Thomas knew he could not have borne it. He would have exhausted himself in futile questioning. His soul would have shivered in the cold vastness of the universe, and he would have believed himself alone.

But he knew now what it was to love, and be loved, and he was not afraid. He was not forsaken. And he knew this pain would pass.

At last, Micha began to have patches of lucidity, but all he wanted was laudanum. He demanded, he bargained, he begged. His damp, trembling hands would curl around Thomas's as if in mockery of every touch they shared: *Help me, Thomas, please help me; if you loved me, you would help me.*

If Thomas could have lashed himself to the mast and stopped his ears with wax, he would have done it.

No matter how gentle his refusals, the demon would return, his words an excoriating tangle of truth and lies. This Micha knew terms so obscene that Thomas barely understood them, and they fell upon his heart like drops of acid. There were many such scenes, each a little more unbearable than the last.

Bowed but not broken, at least not quite, Thomas was sitting on the stairs, where he had once sat with Micha and grieved for his brother, when there came a knocking at his door. Such was his weariness that it took him a moment to recognise the unfamiliar sound. The hour had grown late and the shadows long, but the dregs of his lamp offered a faint, butter-yellow light that would have rendered unconvincing a pretence of absence. Thomas put a hand to his unshaven cheek and then tried to smooth his tousled hair. He had not washed in days. He was not fit to be seen.

On the other side of the door, there surely waited a parishioner in need.

And Thomas could do nothing. He would not leave Micha's side. He would, instead, betray his calling, betray himself, for love and for Micha, and the deepest, darkest truth was this: It was no choice at all.

It was why he could not be a priest, if he had ever truly been one. Once a dutiful servant, he was now not even that. He was a man, wholly and imperfectly a man.

Another flurry of knocking. "Thomas? Are you there? It's Sheba."

Thomas lifted his head. Her voice was so unexpected, so utterly welcome, that he had staggered to his feet and flung wide the door before he had even articulated the wish to do so.

She was a grey shadow against the grey evening, her eyes touched by the colour of the fading sky. She took one look at him and held out her arms with instinctive warmth. "Oh Thomas."

And he tumbled heedlessly into an embrace. It was not like holding Micha, for she was slight, and soft in ways a man was not soft, but there was no frailty in her either. Her body pressed to his was as strong and subtle as a flame. Thomas had little experience of being touched in compassion, and it quite undid him. It was as though it healed a hurt he had not even known was there.

After a moment, Sheba gave him a little shake, the swift transition from tenderness to pragmatism reminding him strangely of Micha. "You should have asked for help."

He pulled back in sudden awkwardness. "How did you know . . . that is . . . I don't think Micha—"

"For yourself. Damn Micha's ridiculous pride."

"It's all he has."

Her callused fingers lightly traced the scratch marks that crisscrossed the backs of his hands. "And what of you?"

Thomas gazed at her, too exhausted for deceptions and too unravelled by her kindness. "He is everything to me."

He waited for surprise or confusion, but she simply nodded. "May I come in?"

He stood aside to let her pass into the house. His body felt like little more than a mound of insensate flesh in which his mind stirred only sluggishly. She nudged him towards the drawing room.

"Sit. Rest."

He was too tired to protest. Moments passed untethered from each other, and, at last, Sheba returned, bearing tea things.

Thomas stirred guiltily. "Oh, please don't . . . it's too much. You don't work for me."

"No, but I am a woman, and is not the need to serve and minister inherent to my sex?"

"Yes but—no but—" said Thomas hopelessly.

"Thom," she cut into his flailing. "It's a cup of tea, a small gesture of care from one friend to another. Please drink it."

He drank the tea. It warmed him, though he had not realised he was cold, and steadied him just a little. Like her touch, it reminded him of a world beyond the walls of his own home and the future that was waiting for him with Micha. But, for the first time, hope came swirled with something that felt like grief, for Micha had taught him to see beyond the trammels of his life and shown him a world that was beautiful and full of joy. Nettlefield, with its honeyed summers and deep winters, its fields and meadows, its star-wild sky, and its parishioners, their lives all entangled like strands of bright yarn. And Thomas had been so very blind, so very lost. Unrepentant sinner though he was, he almost thought he could, at last, have been worthy of them, capable of loving and caring for them as they deserved. Yet he was leaving.

And what of Sheba, dear Sheba, and the strange, dour daughter who smiled so radiantly? Friendship had not previously played much part in Thomas's life, nor, for that matter, in Sheba's. Duty had restrained his nature; experience had subdued hers. But, equally wary, they were also equally grateful, tending together a shared sense of warmth, a mutual desire to trust and be close. They exchanged small absurdities, shy smiles, delicate confidences, building their intimacy slowly, like children with a jigsaw they did not quite understand. And that, too, he would lose. There would be no more walks from the big house. No more quiet evenings of silence and conversation. No more Saturday afternoons with Hope. No more elephants. No more pirates.

Thomas had been staring somewhat absently into the depths of his cup as if an answer might be curled for him among the dregs, but now he glanced up, wordless, weary, and bewildered. Sheba sat a little way across from him, calm and prosaic, her hands folded neatly in her lap, her beauty undeniable and inextinguishable, as hard and bright as a pearl in that gloomy room.

"How is he?" she asked.

"He sent me away. It's been . . . difficult." Thomas sighed, trying to speak pragmatically, but unable to banish either the fear or the pain, or the burning remorse that had lately begun to consume him. He knotted his hands together. "Sheba, I think I torture him."

"It's not you. It's the laudanum."

"I truly had no notion of its power."

Her eyes held his steadily, reflecting a depth of understanding that chilled him. "Opium is a jealous master."

"He will hate me for what I've done to him."

"He's doing it for you."

Thomas put down the cup and then buried his head in his hands, his body shuddering in helpless sympathy for another's remembered torments. "For me? I would not wish this on any man, let alone the one I love."

"But he wished it." He heard the rustle of her skirts as she leaned towards him, her voice low and urgent. "He chose it."

"I don't know anymore, I don't know, I simply don't know." He dragged his head up, cutting himself off abruptly. "And I should not have spoken of this. I must have shocked you."

The faintest of smiles curled across her lips. "You forget the life I have lived. Very little shocks me." Like a pale ghost, she slipped across the space between them. "I know well the effects of opium, and I know that there are women who prefer the company of women, and men who prefer the company of men."

He flinched, on some old, still-unforgotten instinct, to hear such things from the lips of a woman.

"And now," she said, with a wry look, "I am the one to have shocked you."

"I think, perhaps, I shock myself." He had not expected to speak of this with anyone but Micha, and he lacked the words. "The reality of the sins I have committed."

"It's simply an act of the body." She shrugged, and it was one of the few careless movements he had ever seen her make. "There are many such acts."

Thomas shook his head. "It is more than an act of the body. Far more." He paused and then plunged on. "I . . . it . . . that is . . . I've told him we'll leave. When we're ready. Find somewhere we can have a life together."

"I see." Sheba sank slowly back onto the sofa, her shoulders slumping. "Actually, no. I don't see. Why?"

"I cannot lie with Micha and call myself a priest."

Her voice cracked like glass. "Why not? No one would know."

"I would know. God would know."

There was a long silence.

"I'm sorry," she said at last. "I cling too tightly to you. It's just, you're the only friend I've ever possessed."

Thomas reached out a hand and caught hers. She was still and cold, like a woman carved of ice. "I truly wish I didn't have to leave." He faltered. "Leave you."

"Don't think of it. You deserve your happiness. You deserve every happiness."

"Come with us." The words came in an impulsive tangle.

She blinked, opened her mouth, and then closed it again. And then laughed, though it was not quite mirthful. "An unattached woman with a child, travelling with two gentlemen not her relations? Even in the darkest recesses of Europe that would be a scandal."

"Would it matter?"

"Perhaps not for me." She looked thoughtful. "But it is not the life I wish for Hope. And"—a twist of a smile—"I cannot imagine Micha would thank you for the invitation."

Thomas blushed. He had spoken entirely from the heart, heedless of anything else. "You do seem to trouble him," he admitted.

"I care little for him, but he is a far greater enemy to himself than I could ever be."

"He is better than he believes."

"Since he's the man you want, I hope for your sake that he is."

There was another silence. Sheba's fingers stirred restlessly beneath Thomas's. Then she whispered, "Stay."

It was what some part of him had been desperate to hear. But could he? Could it work? It would seem odd, not to marry. Yet no one would suspect his relationship with Micha anything more than the natural affection of two gentlemen friends. Could they live that way? Always pretending? Always hiding. Always hypocrites. Always sinners. "I cannot."

They gazed at each other, equally torn, equally decided.

Sheba nodded sadly. "I think Hope and I could have a life here. She wants adventures, of course, but if I can give her stability now, she might someday find her own."

"I would have loved to be part of that life. To make things less precarious for both of you."

"You've done more than enough. Enough to have earned that cup of tea, at least."

He tried to smile.

"I have somewhere to live. I have a job."

"You're a servant."

"Yes, but a respectable one. It does not pay so well as harlotry, but the hours suit me better." Another of her wicked smiles to ease the harshness of the words. "And perhaps one day I will rise again to housekeeper, through merit this time. I may even have a home of my own."

"If only I could give you that home. If it lay within my power, I would give you the world, so you might give it to Hope."

"You've given us kindness. And now you must think of your own life. Your own future."

Thomas cast his anxious gaze at the ceiling. "I should go to him."

Sheba gave his hand a brief squeeze and then rose, shaking out her skirts. "If I may, I will come again tomorrow."

"I . . . yes, would you?" He shifted self-consciously. "I don't know what I would have done if you had not been here tonight."

"How many days has it been?"

Thomas stared at her blankly. It had all become such a blur he had lost track. “Six or seven, perhaps.”

“It will turn, I promise. It will become easier.”

Thomas nodded and tried to believe her. And, when she had gone, he climbed the stairs to Micha’s room and went inside.

Micha was curled up into a shaking, gasping ball. His face was wet with sweat and tears, but he half-raised his head to look at Thomas, and his bruise-dark eyes were almost clear.

“F-fuck,” he said. “F-fucking kill me, Thomas. I want to f-fucking die.”

It was the most coherent thing he had said for days, and he sounded almost like himself.

Thomas flew across the room, dropped to his knees, and drew Micha gently into his arms. The other man groaned weakly.

“I s-said kill me, not f-fucking hug me.”

Micha smelled, frankly, appalling, sickly-sweet and sour at the same time, fetid and human. Thomas covered his face with kisses. “Micha, I’ve missed you so much.”

“Ow, ow, ow, stop it. It h-hurts. Everything f-fucking hurts.”

The next day, he was considerably worse, delirious again, restless and self-destructive, but it was still a turning point. Gradually, though not consistently, less-bad days began to creep amongst the bad days, and then, at last, came good days. Micha’s body began to right itself, the pain lessened, and he was able to keep down some sustenance. Thomas was once again able to take up the mantle of his neglected duties about the parish, but he knew he performed them ill. His mind never left Micha. Micha, who was still so weak he could hardly stand, who could not sleep and could barely eat, and who was, in many ways, little more than the shattered remains of a man. But Thomas could see him, day by day, moment by moment, putting himself back together. Sometimes it was nothing more than the faintest tug of his mouth, half-smiling, half-sneering, or the glitter of his eyes, but Micha was still there, still fighting and coming back to Thomas, piece by piece.

Nights were the worst. Thomas spent them at Micha's side, holding him close, whispering love words, and telling him stories, but Micha was disordered through lack of sleep and terrified of the nightmares that still haunted him. He wouldn't tell Thomas what he dreamed, only that he hated it, and that was all that mattered. In time, however, they began to fade, and, even if he did not sleep, Micha was able to pass some hours untroubled within the circle of Thomas's arms.

"Fuck," he said, one night, his voice cutting harshly through the darkness. "I'm a fucking wreck."

Thomas kissed the back of his neck, offering lightly, "Much less than you were."

"Oh, that's fine then." Micha twisted his body around. "Am I some sort of fucking charity case to you now?"

Thomas winced. "You never were."

"Ah, yes, because you wanted to fuck me."

"Micha."

"Sorry." His head dipped into the curve of Thomas's shoulder. "Sorry. I just . . . I think I've spent our entire acquaintance being repulsively ill."

Thomas slipped his fingers into Micha's messy curls. "I seem to recall a brief space in the middle where you did and said many wonderful things."

But Micha was clearly not of a mood to be teased or comforted into better humour. Although he did not pull away, his body was tense against Thomas's. "Every time I think I can't fall any lower, I do, and it's always in front of you." He sighed, his breath hot and slightly stale against Thomas's skin. "How can you possibly still want me?"

"For better or for worse, in sickness and in health."

"Yes," snarled Micha, with something of his old ferocity, "but it's always fucking worse, isn't it?"

Thomas tugged lightly on his hair until Micha lifted his head, and then he kissed his scowling mouth. "You put yourself through hell to be with me, when you could easily have made another choice. How can you say that's the worst of you?"

Micha was silent a moment. "I love you. I want you to look at me and feel pride, not pity. And," he added despairingly, "I've just spent the best part of a month lying on your floor, weeping and babbling, covered in my own shit and vomit."

"It was the bravest thing I think I've ever seen anyone do."

"I don't feel brave, I feel . . . bestial. Less than human."

Thomas caught Micha's thin, ravaged face between his hands. "Don't talk like that. I love you. I want you. I'm proud of you. I'm proud for everything you've suffered and everything you've done, and that you want to be with me."

Micha drew in a shuddering breath. "I feel too fucking much. Everything hurts."

"The pain is back?"

"N-no. I mean . . . being alive. I'm nothing but new skin. I'm happy and angry and ashamed and frightened and so in love with you I don't know how I'm supposed to stand it without opium."

"Is it so dreadful?"

Micha made an odd noise. Not quite a laugh, not quite a sob. "Yes. And no. I suppose I can learn."

"I'll be with you, every step of the way."

Slowly Micha relaxed, the lines of his body yielding, his hand gliding over Thomas's hip, slightly protective, slightly possessive. But, when he spoke, his voice was bleak. "To tell you the truth, I don't think I'll ever truly be done with it. I think I'll always carry this weakness."

"This weakness," whispered Thomas, "and this strength."

"You're my strength. I think I could do anything for you. Anything." But before Thomas could say anything, he went on, sleepily, "Now tell me again just how terribly fucking brave I am."

Thomas smiled, even though he knew Micha would not be able to see it. “Like a knight of old.”

“I did slay a dragon.”

“And you rescued me, Micha, from a prison so cunningly wrought I could not even see the bars.”

But Micha did not answer. He had slipped effortlessly into sleep.

Chapter 20

Midway through December, Nettlefield was blessed by a few days of snow. Thomas managed to acquire a sled from somewhere, and he and Hope spent the afternoon careening down the hill that ran from the rectory to the village. Micha, wearing so many layers he looked like twice the man he was, could not be dragged into such indignities, but he watched them from the garden with Madame Defleur's daughter. Thomas's laughter, heedless as a boy's, unravelled like a rainbow.

"Oh fuck," said Micha. "Will you look at him. The idiot. He belongs here."

Madame Defleur's daughter shrugged. "He belongs with you."

~

"My word." Thomas leaned over Micha's shoulder to look at his painting. "That's quite . . . extraordinary. What is it?"

Micha glared.

"No, wait, don't tell me, don't tell me. It is quite self-evidently . . . Is it a cake?"

"What the fuck are you saying? A cake? Where are you getting cake?"

"Well, those ripples there." Thomas's fingertip tapped the page. "They look like pastry. And are those not raisins?"

"It's the village, you prick," snarled Micha, though on his lips the insult became an endearment, which became a caress, which brought the heat rushing to Thomas's skin as surely as a touch. "Those are roofs."

Micha's finger slid alongside Thomas's, making his breath catch. "And the raisins?"

"Windows."

"Of course. My mistake."

"Damn right it is. You're misunderstanding my genius."

And then, suddenly, somehow, they were kissing, hands tangling like their mouths, the sketchbook falling disregarded between them.

~

"Oh yes." Micha thrust a triumphant hand into the air. "Will you look at that? I won. I fucking won."

Thomas sat on the other side of the chessboard, his head thrown back, his face contorted in some unbearable combination of torment and rapture. His breath came in shallow pants. "I think," he managed, "you . . . cheated."

Beneath the table, Micha's stocking-clad foot was nestled between Thomas's legs. His toes nudged in a rough caress against Thomas's cock, and Thomas arched his back, thrust his hips, and groaned.

"You could have told me to stop at any time," said Micha in his most dulcet tones.

"Oh no. D-don't stop. Please don't stop."

Micha laughed and withdrew his foot. Thomas gave him a wide-eyed, bewildered look. Pushing back his chair, Micha disappeared beneath the table. He pressed his mouth against the fabric that covered Thomas's straining erection.

"Oh my," came Thomas's breathless voice from above. He made a convulsive movement, and Micha heard the rata-tat-tat of falling chess pieces. "I should lose more often."

~

Thomas was labouring over his sermon when he heard the clatter of hooves on the path outside. He glanced up in time to catch a glimpse of Micha as he flew by on Bucephalus, his hair already tousled by the wind and his cheeks flushed by the chill. Thomas propped a chin on his hand, all thoughts that were not Micha dissolving like ice in sunlight. Isidore had taught him well. He had far more natural grace and ease in the saddle than Thomas had ever possessed, and he'd been riding since the age of eight.

At the top of the hill, where Laura was waiting for him, Micha wheeled suddenly round, Bucephalus's mane and tail streaming behind him like banners. He was too far away for Thomas to be able to see much of his expression, but he performed an unmistakably knightly bow and then cantered into the distance.

After a moment, Thomas turned back to his sermon. But he was smiling now.

~

The floor of the library was awash in papers, books, and maps. Madame Defleur's daughter's daughter was sprawled out at the centre of it, her ankles swaying behind her in a manner no lady would have countenanced. Thomas sat cross-legged beside her, an absurd configuration of angles. They conversed in low, urgent voices, pausing occasionally to throw a book at each other or gesticulate at one of the maps.

"Uh," said Micha, uncertain in the doorway. "I made tea."

The girl had previously paid almost no attention to Micha. He was little more than a fly in her universe of elephants, sword fights, and Thomas. But now she turned her extraordinary eyes in his direction and did not dismiss him. "Thank you. This is thirsty work."

Madame Defleur's daughter looked up from her book. "They are planning an expedition to discover the source of the Nile."

Once this cosy circle would have filled Micha with a bitter, burning envy. It was still not entirely easy for him to witness, for it was just a little too close to a life Thomas could or should have had, one that held no place for Micha.

He put down the tray, still clinging close to the edges of the room. "I thought that was already found."

"Yes, but not proven." Hope braced herself on her elbows. "It is not enough," she explained, "merely to believe a thing."

"Hope, you heathen." That was her mother.

"Sometimes it is enough." Thomas. But his eyes were on Micha.

"There was to be a debate on the matter at the Royal Geographical Society," Hope went on. "But Mr. Speke happened to die the day before it took place. I think that quite suspicious."

"He's dead?" Micha blinked. "I had no idea."

"You were quite ill at the time," said Thomas. "I did not realise you would be interested."

Micha frowned, momentarily lost in the cracks between his fractured selves. "I wouldn't have been, but . . . once I think I might have. I don't know."

"Will you join us, Mr. Dashwood?" asked Hope. "It is a most perplexing problem. Mr. Speke claims to have solved it but leaves us little scientific evidence. And Mr. Burton talks an awful lot but has never even examined the lake or the falls that Mr. Speke discovered."

"So, as you can see"—Thomas's smile was for Micha, only for Micha—"it is up to us."

~

Thomas woke to an empty space beside him. He wrapped himself in his dressing gown and found Micha huddled on the floor of the garden room, his nails gouging the skin of his bare, shivering arms. He looked up, his eyes red-rimmed and hollow.

"I'm sorry," he said, "I'm sorry, I'm sorry."

Thomas went to him, catching at his hands. Micha was freezing cold and clammy with drying sweat.

"I can't sleep. I can't think. Everything hurts."

"It's all right." Thomas drew him into the garish folds of the dressing gown.

"It's not all right. I want some fucking laudanum. I really do." He pressed himself against Thomas, trembling. "I just wish I could sleep."

"It takes time."

"It's the waiting. The night lasts forever. I hate it. Fuck."

"Then," said Thomas, smoothing the curls back from Micha's brow, "we shall defy the night."

"How?"

"If you cannot sleep, we shall not sleep. Let's do something else."

"Like what? Play chess? Dance the waltz?"

"Whatever you wish, but, I warn you, dancing is not one of my talents."

Micha was silent a moment. Then, almost shyly, he asked, "Can we go out? Away from the walls?"

"Of course."

They dressed in the half-light, struggling into whatever garments they could most easily find, and stumbled outside together. The world was only just beginning to stir, the sky a pale mirror reflecting the fog-drenched fields. Everything was frost-limned, brittle and silver, and the breath left Micha's parting lips in a coil of smoke.

"It's like it's just for us," he whispered.

Unthinking, Thomas took his hand.

And Micha did not pull away.

They walked in silence through the meadows. The nascent light gleamed gently on the grass that crunched beneath their footsteps, and the mist curled the bare trees in gowns and garlands that formed themselves anew with the passing moments. The pond had become a cast-down moon, as still as an unblinking eye, staring back at the heavens.

Micha went carefully down to meet it. He tapped the frozen surface with his boot and then edged out onto the ice.

"Micha," Thomas murmured. "Think how foolish you will feel if you fall into the water twice."

He looked up, grinning, his eyes shining like pieces of polished onyx. "But how can you resist?"

"I confess I do seem able to find that power."

Micha glided a few steps, his arms flung wide for balance. "But look. It's fine."

Thomas covered his eyes, peering between the slats of his fingers. "The ice will break. I know it will."

Micha swooped into the middle of the pond, twirled, slipped, righted himself, and spun in a giddy circle, breathless and laughing. "Thomas, Thomas, I'm walking on water!"

Thomas spluttered.

And Micha came flying back to him, hair streaming, hands outstretched. "Come on."

"Oh no. Certainly not."

"It's safe, I promise."

"'O'er ice the rapid skater flies, with sport above and death below, where mischief lurks in gay disguise, thus lightly touch and quickly go.'"

"It's a very small pond. There's absolutely no danger of death."

"I'm not reassured." But, somehow, Thomas was taking Micha's hand again and he was being drawn, step by reluctant step, towards the ice. As soon as his foot touched the glassy surface, he flinched. "Oh God." As soon as his other foot landed, "Oh God." He tried to move, slipped, and clutched at Micha. "Oh God."

"Are you taking the Lord's name in vain? A lot?"

"No, I'm genuinely praying."

"Don't you trust me?"

"Of course I trust you. I just—"

There was a cracking as loud as gunfire, and they plunged straight through the ice into cold, brackish, ankle-deep water.

There was a long silence.

"Whoops," said Micha.

And Thomas began to laugh.

~

On a bright, cold Sunday, Micha sat on a tree stump in the churchyard, his sketchbook open but untouched. The service had finished some time ago, but Thomas had, as ever, been waylaid by his parishioners. At last, he managed to detach himself, and Micha rose to greet him, smiling because he simply couldn't help himself.

"There's no need for you to wait, you know," said Thomas.

Micha shrugged. "I like to."

"You could come inside next time."

"Hah. No thanks."

Thomas's hand brushed the sleeve of Micha's coat. "Do you expect to be struck down? Turned into a pillar of salt?"

"No, I just don't like God very much. And I can't imagine He thinks much of me for stealing one of His ministers."

A shadow of something that was not quite sadness darkened Thomas's eyes. "You can't steal something already given."

Chapter 21

They spent Christmas Eve up at the big house, which was apparently a tradition of long standing. Micha, unwilling to trespass, had evinced reluctance, but Thomas had given him the irresistible look and said "please," and, truthfully, Micha desperately wanted to be there—part of something, even if it was only pretence. Of course, he had been warmly welcomed. And it had all been lovely, or perhaps that was the mulled wine talking. But it was an evening Micha would never forget: the laughter ringing through the marble halls, and the golden glow that spilled like pirate treasure from the ornate fireplaces. And Thomas, made beautiful in that generous light, smiling at him, his eyes bright with messages only Micha could read.

The hours slipped away, unheeded as sand, lost to the simplest of pleasures. Conversation, parlour games, dancing, and songs. Laura and Violet were proven unconquerable at charades. Thomas was hopeless, and Micha even worse, and they soon fell to arguing with the sort of amused ferocity known only to lovers over matters of no consequence. They played Adjectives and perpetrated unspeakable atrocities on the works of Charles Dickens, which Esther particularly relished. And, later, with military precision, Ada manoeuvred Micha under the bough of mistletoe that arched over the main staircase, where she kissed him soundly on the cheek.

Then, as midnight was approaching and Thomas had to prepare for Mass, there came an exchange of small gifts. Micha's last Christmas had been lost to opium dreams, the ghost of a man who used to love him, and a silent city that unravelled with his mind into countless iridescent threads. The one before to some unremembered drudgery. Now he sat among friends he suspected he did not deserve, abashedly receiving presents he was sure he did not. Esther rather wickedly gave him a copy of *Wuthering Heights*, solely because Ada had once compared him to Heathcliff. From Ada came several pots of her "world-famous" port-and-damson jam. From Laura, a vast, multicoloured hand-knitted object that was, she thought, either a scarf or a shawl or, perhaps, a blanket. Hope solemnly presented him with a new set of pencils, and Violet, with one of her rare, mysterious smiles, gave him an exquisitely embroidered sampler which read *Love worketh no ill to his neighbour: Therefore love is the fulfilling of the law.*

Thomas had warned Micha of this particular Christmas Eve custom and had even suggested they combine their gift-giving efforts, but Micha had been quite adamant that he would manage for himself. It was, therefore, with more than a trace of awkwardness that he distributed his sketches. But he need not have worried—he was far more skilled at portraits than he was at landscapes, and everyone was delighted. For Laura, there had been a picture of Violet at the piano, for Violet a picture of Laura on her monstrous horse. For Sheba, a picture of Hope, riding an elephant, and for Hope, a pirate ship, herself as captain and Thomas as first mate. For Esther, an attempt to render Ruff at full speed—which was, truthfully, not much more than a hairy orange blur, but Esther said it conveyed his spirit splendidly. For Ada, a picture from the book group: herself and Esther, deep in conversation, the moment caught so perfectly upon the page that Ada said one half-expected to hear what they were saying.

They concluded with a toast.

"To Christmas?" offered Ada.

"To friendship?" Esther.

"To love." That, surprisingly, was Thomas, slightly flushed but otherwise resolute. "To the multiplicity of love, in all its manifestations."

After that, the party broke up for church, and Micha, weighed down by presents and mince pies, staggered home. He could have gone to bed, but his sleeping patterns were still somewhat irregular. And, besides, foolish or not, he wanted to wait for Thomas. He tucked himself into the window seat where he used to doze away his laudanum-soaked days and stared out into the darkness. It was a cold, clear night, and the stars were flung across the sky in the same wild abundance he had seen on his first night in Nettlefield. They gazed back at him, gleaming steadily in their private spheres.

Thomas woke him a few hours later with a kiss.

Micha uttered an absurd, disorientated noise and then remembered where he was, and with whom. He eased the cold and the stiffness from his limbs and smiled. "How did Jesus like his birthday?"

"Probably not as much as I did. I had such a wonderful evening. Though"—Thomas's eyes flashed—"I still can't believe you failed to identify 'artichoke.'"

Micha swung round in mock outrage, laughter wavering in his voice. "How the hell was I supposed to? I had no idea what you were doing."

"Yes, but 'ear cravat'? What on earth is an ear cravat?"

"Well, I don't know. You were pointing at your ear, then at your throat. I didn't have a clue what you were doing."

"I was signifying 'sounds like,' you . . . you . . . cabbage."

Micha swept to his feet, bringing his height to the debate. "How," he demanded, with magnificent scorn, "does 'artichoke' sound like 'ear cravat'?"

Thomas actually stamped his foot. "No, sounds like 'heart.' Why do you think I was touching my chest like that?"

"I thought that was just non-specific frustration."

"No," cried Thomas, in quite specific frustration, "I was trying to tell you sounds like 'heart.'"

"And the cravat thing?"

"'Choke,' of course. 'Choke.'"

Micha digested this. "That's the most ridiculous thing I've ever heard."

"Not as ridiculous as 'ear cravat.'"

"Well, you're an idiot."

"No, you're an idiot."

They glared. Then laughed. And Micha shoved Thomas up against the wall and kissed him. "Artichoke my arse," he muttered, when his mouth was not otherwise occupied.

Thomas made a soft, tender sound and rubbed his cheek against Micha's.

"And," added Micha, "you just called me a cabbage."

"I should not have said that."

Their breath mingled in the scant space between their mouths, like a sigh of mutual longing.

"I'll forgive you." It was impossible for even Micha to sound harsh at such a moment. He dipped his head, and they kissed again, as gentle as summer rain, as though they lived in a world without time.

"Oh." Micha drew back, just enough for words to slip through. "I forgot. I have something for you."

"Hmm?" Thomas blinked love-dazedly at him.

"For Christmas. A gift."

That, at least, seemed to break the sensual haze. "Micha, really, there was no need."

"I wanted to. Here." Micha stepped away and picked up his sketchbook. He slid a page free from the very back and handed it to Thomas.

Thomas, who had peeled himself away from the wall, looked at the drawing, froze, and turned a deep shade of scarlet. He swallowed and, if possible, went even redder. "You . . . you seem to have given me a naked picture. Of myself. For Christmas. I-I don't know what to say."

"Well, 'thank you' has quite a tradition behind it."

"Yes but—oh but—it's lovely, skilfully done, but . . . I surely do not look like that?"

"You did and you do." Micha slid his arms around Thomas's waist from behind, resting his chin lightly on his shoulder, and Thomas leaned instinctively into the embrace. They looked together at Micha's handiwork: Thomas, half-naked, sprawled on a bed of gold-red leaves, head thrown back, eyes closed, utterly lost to a profound and private ecstasy.

Thomas gave a shy, uncertain laugh. "You have been most generous with my . . . proportions."

"I enjoyed drawing them. Your beautiful cock." Micha's own stirred in memory and reaction, and Thomas's body pushed back against him. "That," he went on, desire deepening in his voice, "was when I first knew for certain I was in love with you."

Thomas stroked his fingers over the lines, as though he was imagining Micha's hands drawing them, and Micha's hands touching him. "Because of my . . . beautiful cock?"

"Hah. No. Because of everything you are."

"Thank you." Thomas's head fell back against Micha's shoulder, and Micha slid a caressing hand about his exposed throat. Thomas moaned, sweetly helpless, and his pulse jumped beneath Micha's palm. Micha leaned down and claimed his lover's mouth, and they kissed, body straining to body, the vulnerable curve of Thomas's neck pressed without hesitation against Micha's palm so that he felt every quivering breath before he tasted it.

With his spare hand he caught the drawing before Thomas's fingers entirely forgot their purpose and released it. Thomas murmured a largely incoherent apology which Micha kissed away as he tossed the page onto a nearby table. He fumbled with the fastenings on Thomas's waistcoat and then the shirt underneath, dragging aside silk and cotton until he met skin. Thomas's chest heaved beneath his hand and Micha slid downwards, over slender crests of bone and muscle, planes of velvet. Lower still, beneath the fine worsted of Thomas's trousers, to the solid heat of his cock through his drawers. Thomas made a rough, exquisite sound, his hips thrusting gracelessly, his mouth slackening against Micha's.

Micha broke the kiss and turned his head. He wanted to see Thomas's face, the unabashed yearning, the pleasure burning in his half-closed eyes. The man looked as he had in the woods, as he did in the picture, lost and fearless, stripped to the truth of himself. Micha had wanted him then, and he wanted him now, but this time tenderness was woven through the instinct to possess like a glimmer of gold. He tormented Thomas with the lightest of caresses until Thomas was moaning softly, twisting against him, his hands clawing at Micha's hips.

"Oh Micha, please."

"Fuck, I love it when you beg." The words were little more than a groan.

Thomas's breath stuttered. "You m-make it so very sweet to beg."

"Tell me what you want."

"Anything." Thomas's eyes flared hot beneath the shadow of his lashes. "Everything."

And Micha made another mindless, savage noise. It was ludicrous to feel so powerful, and so utterly undone, at the same time. Once his own frailty would have infuriated him, but now the contradictions of his desires found their own harmonies in Thomas. He slid his hand to the other man's jaw, turned his head and pressed his mouth to the side of Thomas's neck, a kiss, a bite, a brand, a promise. Thomas gasped, arching into the touch and, inadvertently, against Micha's cock. And the pleasure of it rushed over him, as raw and bright and harsh as flame. He had forgotten. The sharpness of it. The purity. Almost unbearable, like staring into the sun, or standing insignificant beneath a cathedral's vaulted sky. Micha's control unravelled like yarn, his knees buckled, and he clung to Thomas with trembling hands.

"Micha?" Thomas turned in his arms. Their bodies had long since found familiar patterns, the pressing of thighs and nestling of hips, an instinctive fitting together that felt more natural than standing alone. "What's the matter?"

He had no idea how to even begin to articulate it. The nakedness of being simply and only Micha. Opium had been both his protector and his master, but now its rust-red chains were broken, and he was alone, with nothing to hide or give except himself. The world crashed against his unprepared heart, his newly vulnerable soul, and the body that, at last, was remembering how to feel. Micha opened his mouth to reply, but all he managed was "I need you."

Thomas met his eyes. "I'm yours. Have me."

"Yes," Micha whispered. "Yes."

He pushed Thomas back a few steps and Thomas yielded, their bodies moving together effortlessly, as though they were dancing. And to think Thomas had claimed it was not one of his talents. Their mouths met, rough and urgent, the kiss unbroken as Micha tumbled Thomas onto the window seat and began tearing at his clothes. Thomas curled his legs over Micha's flanks, pulling him close, and Micha, who had wanted this before his body had even remembered how to want, went a little wild. He thrust himself against Thomas, crushing him into the narrow space, tangling his hands in his hair, covering his exposed skin with deep, desperate kisses that left dusty red roses blooming in their wake. And Thomas simply spread his hands across Micha's shoulder blades and urged him on, soft cries falling from his lips as abundantly as coins from profligate fingers.

"Oh fuck," gasped Micha, tearing himself away. "I need to get something."

Thomas's eyes fluttered comically. "A cup of tea?"

"No . . . I . . . I'll be back in a moment."

Micha ran from the room, shedding clothes as he went. His stockinged feet slithered on the tiles in the hall as he threw himself upstairs, seized what he needed from his room, and came rushing back. Thomas was sitting primly on the window seat where Micha had left him, his hands holding his shirt closed across his chest. With his ruffled hair and kiss-dark lips, he looked thoroughly, delightfully debauched.

Putting the flask down, Micha shrugged off the rest of his clothes, and his abrupt nakedness seemed to alleviate some of Thomas's bewilderment. His attention lingered, instead, on the contours of Micha's body, and Micha—who had been uncaringly unclad before more men than he now chose to remember—was conscious of a sudden, absurd shyness. There was ugliness here too, stark and undeniable in the cold moonlight, the ravages of illness and opium withdrawal, wasted muscle and the knotted bones of his rib cage. But Thomas was gazing at him as though none of it mattered, and Micha, who was as accustomed to being looked at as he was at being naked, shivered with a new kind of pleasure in it. There was nothing possessing or acquisitive in Thomas's regard, but it made Micha feel loved, wanted, safe.

"I went to get a preparation," Micha explained, a trifle awkwardly. "It will ease—I don't want to hurt you."

He dropped to his knees at Thomas's feet and began to tug off his boots, followed by stockings, trousers, and drawers.

Thomas reached down, his fingers moving softly through Micha's hair. "I want to be with you. I want us to be one."

"You make everything sound so fucking romantic." Micha nudged Thomas's legs apart and pressed between them, turning to drop a light kiss against the inside of one of his thighs. Thomas put his hands behind him for balance, his fingers pressing into the cushion, a tremor of response running all the way down his body, and through the long, lightly muscled legs that wrapped Micha in a tight embrace. He groaned and kissed Thomas again, sweeping his tongue over this secret, silken skin, towards the crease at the top of his thighs. Thomas caught his breath and stuttered out something that sounded like "oh my." Micha slid his hands up to Thomas's hips and pulled them against the edge of the window seat, tipping him back in a graceless flail of limbs. But, before Thomas could protest the indignity, Micha pressed his open mouth to the tender diamond of flesh he had exposed, and Thomas did nothing but gasp. The sound, so shocked, so naked, sent a jolt through Micha, like a hand upon his cock.

He parted Thomas like a fig, his breath and his mouth swirling together over the forbidden places of the other man's body. Thomas made another delirious, frantic noise, his legs falling wide like the fronds of a profane flower, a hand reaching back to thunk against the glass of the window. And Micha worshipped him, pressing soft kisses to the entrance of his body, circling him delicately with the tip of his tongue until every breath Thomas drew was a helpless moan and his hips were jerking uncontrollably beneath Micha's hands. He tasted simply like Thomas, like his own skin, but stronger, darker somehow, and the power of having him like this, in defiance of everything believed to be right, natural, or sacred, was as sweet and rich as honey. Micha's cock ached with raw longing. He wanted to claim Thomas, his heart, and their own private paradise.

He pressed his tongue past the tight, quivering ring of muscle, deep into the secret darkness of Thomas's body, and the man arched desperately, a shameless, untempered cry ringing out through the silent room. Micha's answer was in the digging of his fingers into Thomas's skin, the wild beating of his heart, the tender violence of his mouth as it coaxed the most primal of yieldings from Thomas's flesh. At last, when Thomas was shuddering and close to senseless, Micha withdrew, soothing him with kisses and long caresses.

Thomas trembled, sweat-studded, star-scattered, his body a chiaroscuro of broken shadows and moonlight, his gleaming cock straining towards his stomach. Micha ran his tongue up the length of it and Thomas cried out again, the sound caught somewhere between pleasure and pain, almost a sob.

Micha pushed himself to his feet, and Thomas pulled him down into something that was as close to a struggle as it was an embrace, skin sliding over skin, as they fought against the limits of flesh. Micha, groping blindly, unwilling to draw back from his lover, fumbled with the flask, unstoppered it, slicked his fingers, and thrust them into Thomas, swift and certain. There was a moment of instinctive resistance, and the breath hissed from between Thomas's teeth, his body suddenly rigid against Micha's.

Micha leaned over him, kissing the tightly knitted brows, the compressed line of his mouth, crooning nonsense. "Darling, darling, it's all right. Relax for me. Let me inside you. It won't hurt for long. Please don't let me hurt you."

Thomas's eyes flicked open, a faint smile curling beneath Micha's mouth. "Not hurting," he said, soft as a waking dreamer. "Just strange, passing strange."

"I'll make it good, I promise. I'll make it wonderful."

Thomas's hands swept the sweat-damp planes of Micha's back. "I believe you." He uttered another small gasp as Micha stretched him with another finger and writhed anxiously against him. "But do get on with it, if you please."

Micha gave a shaky laugh and pulled himself free. He doused his cock in the unguent, arranged Thomas's legs around his waist, and eased himself inside, as carefully as he could. Heat and pressure engulfed him, Thomas's body yielding, inch by inch, moment by moment, the pleasure of it so intense that it left Micha dazed, humbled, and terribly, nakedly in love.

"Oh fuck, Thomas." He blinked the sudden moisture from his eyes and slid a little further.

They groaned in unison, but Thomas's voice was tinged with strain, and Micha stilled at once.

"Hurting?"

"N-no . . . just . . . just . . . I don't know."

Thomas's breathing had turned swift and shallow. His head fell back, and Micha bent over him, kissing the bared curve of his throat until he felt the other man's pulse fluttering in response. He wrapped a hand around Thomas's fading erection and stroked it lavishly, drowning unfamiliar violation in familiar bliss. Fresh perspiration gathered, moon-silvered, in the hollows of Thomas's body, and he began to moan softly, pressing against Micha's cock and his hand. His eyes had fallen closed, leaving his face open, and as unprotected as his heart had ever been.

And, at the sight, Micha came a little bit undone. Rough desire, long stifled by opium, rushed over him, driving him hard against Thomas. "Oh Thomas," he muttered, fighting himself and the uncontrolled selfish urges of his flesh. "My love, I need you so." His voice broke on a note of desperation. "Please, darling, please."

Thomas reached up suddenly, flung his arms about Micha's neck, and pulled their bodies together until Micha was fully sheathed inside him, one flesh, as close as breath and their beating hearts. Micha babbled out a stream of obscenities that were their own caress, and Thomas clung to him, panting and trembling. For a long moment, they were still, accustoming themselves and each other to the intimacy of their entwining. It had been so long since Micha had felt anything like it. He thought he might break from the joy of it.

He pressed his head against Thomas's shoulder, pouring clumsy kisses over his skin. "You feel like fucking heaven."

"Are you using that as a verb or as an intensifier?" Thomas's voice shook a little, and he shifted him against Micha, as if trying to become comfortable with new sensations. "Because . . . it works . . . either way."

"We'll make our own heaven."

Thomas's fingers dug into Micha's back. "Oh . . . oh good."

Micha unhooked Thomas's arms and lowered him onto the window seat. Very gently he began to move, a slow, gliding rhythm that made Thomas's eyelashes flutter dreamily. Sliding a hand beneath one of Thomas's knees, Micha adjusted his angle and drove in deep—

And Thomas's eyes jolted open. He arched like a wildcat in the moonlight. "Oh my God . . . I mean—" Micha repeated the motion. "Oh . . . my . . . oh . . ." Thomas's hands flailed and landed, helpless as wind-buffeted birds, against Micha's chest.

"My name," growled Micha, "say my name."

"Oh Micha."

"Yes."

"Can you—oh yes. Oh Micha. Yes."

Micha was half-laughing, half-crying, undone by the sheer pleasure of pleasing. It was like knowing all the secrets of the universe. A glimpse of the numinous that brought him not into an awareness of some abstract deity but into perfect and complete communion with another person. His lover. Thomas.

They fucked with increasing urgency, entangled in each other's arms and learning together the patterns and rhythms of how to move with each other, their responses mingling and echoing, like the touch of body to body and skin to skin, to drive them into deeper, wilder ecstasies. Micha pushed Thomas's legs back, bracing himself with a slipping hand upon the windowpane, his other curled around Thomas's cock, stroking it clumsily to mirror his thrusts. Thomas threw back his head, starlight speckling his throat and shoulders, gave a shattered gasp threaded with Micha's name, and climaxed.

Micha was left, shuddering desperately on the brink of release. The pleasure was pain-bright, clawing like a trapped thing in his flesh. Sweat streamed from him, sparkling silver over Thomas. He closed his eyes, but bodies, other bodies, were twisting in the darkness, and his mouth was sour with the memory of laudanum. He was falling, too lost, too ruined, traitor to himself, even to the last. "F-fuck, oh fuck, I can't."

Thomas reached up, cradling Micha's face between his hands, whispering his name, calling him back.

And then, like a forgotten, impossible miracle, it happened. He was caught by Thomas, caught by the moment, not falling but flying, and he was free. Micha opened his eyes, drove himself into Thomas, into the blissful, sinful heat of him, and claimed himself, his past, his future, and the body he chose now to surrender entirely to pleasure. Culmination rushed over him, ferocious as fire, annihilation and renewal, eternity in a handful of seconds, and Thomas held him through it, still murmuring softly. Micha fell against his lover, utterly spent, still shaking, but unafraid, unbroken.

They stayed like that, crushed together, for longer than Micha thought was, strictly speaking, polite. But he could not move, and

Thomas, of course, did not push him away. Eventually, though, they untangled, their bodies sticky and reluctant. Micha groped for one of their hastily shed garments and began to clean up some of the evidence of their exertions.

"That better not be my shirt," said Thomas, smiling sleepily at him.

They dressed themselves just enough for decency. It was cold without a fire, but Micha barely noticed. His body felt alive with heat and satisfaction, and the closeness of Thomas, who was curled up between Micha's legs on the much-abused window seat. His head nestled against Micha's shoulder, his face in shadow, his breathing slow and even. Micha thought he slept, but then he tilted up his head and whispered, "Happy Christmas."

Micha kissed the curve of his bare shoulder.

From the slowly greying sky, a few haphazard snowflakes began to swirl in restless spirals, gleaming softly through the gloom like fragments of fallen stars.

Micha drifted, not quite awake, not quite asleep, and when he next opened his eyes, Thomas's face was turned in to the breaking dawn.

"How lovely it is," he said. "So much unheeded beauty in the world."

"But you're heeding?"

"Yes. Now I am. For most of my life, it would never have occurred to me." His fingers drifted lightly across Micha's forearm. "I love these moments with you. They make me feel so close to God."

"I'm not sharing you with Him," Micha growled, not entirely jesting.

"You don't. I give myself to you."

"And how do you think He feels about that?"

"My choices hurt no one, nor do they take me from Him."

"Fuck," whispered Micha, burying his face in Thomas's tangled hair. "Your faith is fucking unshakeable."

"On the contrary, I have been assailed by doubt my whole life."

"What changed?"

"I understood love, Micha. Simply that."

They were silent for long moments. The intricate traceries of frost that had crystallised upon the windowpanes during the night were weeping silver tears.

"You know what I don't get?" said Micha, at last. "Why does all the good stuff get dumped on the doorstep of the Lord, but the bad stuff is always our own bloody fault. I mean, you look at the stars or the sky and it's always"—he mimicked Thomas, rather cruelly—"'Oh look, how lovely, there must be a loving God.' But you don't see a dying child or a family starving in a tenement and say the same thing."

"Human misery is caused by humans."

Micha waved a hand in the vague direction of the outside world and the pearl-pink dawn. "And that is caused by the rotation of the earth." He took a breath. "And if you say the rotation of the earth is caused by God, I'll . . . I don't know . . . fuck you senseless."

"Are you trying to persuade me to accept your position, or to refute it?" But the playfulness faded from Thomas's voice as Micha made no reply. "I can't explain the workings of the universe to you. A sunrise isn't a piece of rhetoric. The mind is only one part of faith, just as it's only one part of love."

"I'm not just going to believe something because I need the consolation or because I'm too scared not to."

"Of course not, my love."

Micha tightened his arms around Thomas. "I'm taking you away from everything you care about."

"It was you who taught me how to value it. I came here for duty, and I shall leave for love. Because I belong to God, and I belong with you."

"If He loves you as you say, He wouldn't make you choose."

"He didn't. I chose."

"And I'm still your choice?" Micha touched his lips to the tender nape of Thomas's neck, making him shiver. "Even with so much to lose?"

"We don't have to lose anything yet," said Thomas. "You need to recover your strength. And my parishioners—"

"Will never not need you, Thomas. Surely you can see that."

"Nonsense." Thomas's tone was brisk and certain. "Another priest will serve them just as well."

Micha could never quite tell if Thomas was humble or naive—possibly he was both—but, in this, he wanted to be reassured. Convinced. So he simply nodded and settled back into the recesses of the window. Thomas snuggled a little closer, turning his face once more into the sunrise, which touched his hair and the tips of his eyelashes with the promise of gold. Looking down at his lover, Micha felt something terrifyingly close to happiness sweep through his heart like the light across the sky.

Chapter 22

One bright, cold afternoon, a few days into the New Year, George arrived. As ever, he burst into the room without ceremony, the scent of mud and horse clinging to his clothes, and frost gilding the edges of his overcoat.

"Thom, I need to talk—" He paused, gazing about the room, his expression disdainful. "Well, isn't this domestic."

Thomas half-rose, his eyes darting in some alarm from George, to Micha, to Sheba.

But then Hope looked up from the map she was studying and said sternly: "It is not domestic. It is the Isla Tortuga, a den of iniquity."

There was a long silence, filled with far too many tensions, and, surprisingly, George was the first to break it, some hint of a man Thomas had not seen since Edward's death stirring in the shadows of his eyes. "Is it now?" He unbuttoned his coat and tossed it aside. "And who might you be, to frequent such a place?"

"Nancy Blood. Captain Nancy Blood."

Micha coughed to cover something Thomas was sure had to be amusement, tore the top leaf from his sketchbook, and displayed it to the room. *WANTED,* it said, *for treacherie ypon the high seas, piracie, iniquitie and sundrie other villanies too vyle to mentioune.* And then a picture of Hope, delineated in heavy black lines to look like a poor-quality woodcut.

"Hope," said Thomas, with another anxious glance at Sheba. "This is my brother George."

"Known in these parts," added George quickly, "as Blackhearted George."

Hope eyed him appraisingly. "Anyone could be *known* as Blackhearted George."

"No they couldn't." George dropped to his knees on the rug beside her. "Because it is a name earned through black deeds, and I would gut like a rabid cur any who crossed me."

Hope looked impressed. "Oh. Tell me of your black deeds. Thomas will not allow me to commit any. I have been a pirate since December, and not a single prisoner has walked the plank."

"Then I say we keelhaul the lubber, strike the Jolly Roger, and begin plundering the Spanish Main at once."

Sheba sent Thomas a small, private smile and went back to her book. "Ousted by my own brother," he said, reassured and laughing a little. "How very typical."

"Do you mind terribly?" asked Hope.

"Not at all, I don't think I was cut out for piracy."

"You can be the local governor," she offered, magnanimously.

"Why, thank you."

"And then we shall capture you and hold you for ransom."

"Ah." Thomas's face fell. "Must you?"

"Yes, I am sure you are deeply corrupt."

Thomas looked to his brother for help, but George was busy turning over the coffee table and dragging it into the centre of the room. "Was there something you wanted to talk to me about?"

"Later, old boy, later. The tide waits for no man. And bring grog!" He lowered his voice. "Or tea, as I believe some people foolishly call it." George, Thomas realised with sudden joy, was looking far better than the last few times he had seen him. His face was still marked by weariness and dissipation, but his eyes were clear. "And hardtack."

"You mean . . . biscuits?"

"Aye!"

Thomas surrendered with good grace and nodded at his housekeeper, patiently standing nearby. "As you wish, but please be nice to poor Mrs. Allen. She is not to be menaced by pirates."

Poor Mrs. Allen told them, in no uncertain terms, she thought they all belonged in Bedlam, and that they were not to break anything.

They broke a few things, a vase, a chair, and a table leg, but George dismissed these as inevitable casualties of the pirate life. They terrorised the high seas for most of the afternoon and a good part of the evening, captured the Spanish silver train, unearthed buried treasure, thwarted a mutiny, overthrew Thomas, and turned Port Royal into a republic and pirate haven.

Micha, who had watched the adventures unfold from his window seat, his pencil long stilled over his paper, at last threw his sketchbook aside, joined the navy, rose through the ranks sufficiently to claim command of the HMS *Dining Room Table*, and came to Thomas's rescue. Thomas, who had been sitting quite contentedly in the bilge, writing Sunday's sermon, found himself the subject of several hairsbreadth 'scapes and sudden reversals of fortune, and came very close to being forced to walk the plank over shark-infested waters on no less than six separate occasions. Following a pitched sea battle with an entire pirate fleet, ably led by Captain Nancy Blood and her loyal minion, Blackhearted George, Commodore Dashwood and Governor Mandeville found themselves marooned on a desert island, and the saga came to its natural end.

"What happens after?" asked Hope, pink-cheeked from the exertions and dramas of piracy. "Do you expire slowly of privation and tropical disease?"

"Of course not," said Micha. "I build us a cabin, of wood and leaves and . . . things. Like Robinson Crusoe."

"I learn to catch fish and hunt wild game," added Thomas.

"We eat mangoes that taste of dusty sunlight."

"Drink from mountain streams as clear as glass."

Hope glanced between them, her expression a little bit quizzical. "You could be rescued?"

Micha laughed, lost in the moment, and Thomas, heedless, was laughing too. "We don't need to be rescued. We live happily ever after."

"That seems fair," said Hope, into the sudden silence.

She and her mother departed not long after, as the hour had grown late, and Micha, George, and Thomas attempted to return the rectory to something like proper order before Mrs. Allen came back in the morning and saw the mess. The nonsense that had made them comrades through the afternoon had fled, leaving them strangers again. Thomas tried desperately to think of something he could say that would bridge the chasm between his last remaining brother and the lover he could not acknowledge.

George smoothed his hair back into civilised order. "Charming child. I suppose you'll wed the mother?"

"Well . . ."

"The marquess won't like it, of course, but he fades with every passing day. Do what you will—there's nothing he can do to stop you." His hand came down on Thomas's shoulder, warm and steady, but heavier than Thomas found entirely comfortable. "Take your happiness, Thom. And the devil can take our father."

"George, I—"

"I should go." Micha's voice cut through him like a blade. "I have things to do."

George's eyes flicked his way, as if he had only just remembered the other man was still present. "Yes, you should."

Thomas opened his mouth to protest, but Micha simply nodded and fled, the door crashing closed behind him.

George crossed the room to the sideboard, where there was a decanter of brandy, almost two-thirds full. He poured himself a glass, and then merely stood staring at it, tilting the liquid back and forth, lost in thought.

"George," said Thomas. "George. I do not intend to marry Sheba."

His brother's eyes lifted reluctantly from the glass, as if they had trouble focusing on anything else. "But you're not a man to keep a mistress. Is it because of her past? Or because I tried my luck with her?

She'd have none of me, Thom. And if it's a question of money, when the title's mine, you can have all you want."

Thomas drew in a steadying breath. "I care for her, very much, but I have no wish to marry. She has no such expectations."

"Women always have expectations."

"Not in this case."

George lifted the glass, then sighed and put it down again. "I shouldn't drink this. I want it too much." He strolled back into the centre of the room. "Apologise to her for me, won't you? It don't mean a damn, of course. I'm a beast, I know I am, but maybe she'd like to hear it."

"You are no beast, but I'll gladly deliver the message."

George made an abstract gesture of gratitude and slumped into a chair. "You might want to take that drink, old man. I have some things to tell you."

"Are you well, George?" Thomas had no wish to drink either and perched anxiously on the edge of the sofa. "You seem to have found some measure of peace."

"Some measure of it, perhaps. I don't know. Trying not to drink. Hell on bloody earth." George reached into an inner pocket of his coat and pulled out a tattered bundle of papers. "I found this among Edward's things." Thomas reached out to take it, and George pulled his hand back. "It's going to shock you, Thom. I'm sorry."

A chill crept over Thomas's skin. "Show me." George let him take the book, which was little more than a bound pamphlet, printed on cheap paper by a careless hand. The blurred frontispiece read: *The Gentlemen of London, for the Year 1862*. "I don't understand? What is it?"

"Read it."

Thomas let the pages fall open where they would and cast his eyes, somewhat uncertainly, over the words that appeared before them. *Mr. B. Wils-n, No. 27 St. Giles. This pretty gentleman is somewhat plump, but fair of face, and possessing every requisite to make an agreeable bedfellow. He performs all paces in a pleasing manner.* Thomas glanced at his brother, still bewildered, a faint sense or premonition of sickness swirling within him. "I still don't understand?"

But George only exhorted him with a wave of his hand to read on.

Thomas turned the page. *Mr. K. R-ssell, Titchfield Street. An impressive stallion, near thirty years of age, a Yorkshireman by birth, rather lusty, with the strength to perform whatever labour may be requested. It is a pity he has received no education; however there are some who derive great relish from a certain coarseness of manner and vulgarity of expression that may be well served in his arms. He is also celebrated for the dexterity with which he yields a birchen rod for the gratification of those gentlemen who have occasion for this activity to raise the fire of Alexander in their veins.*

Thomas could read no further. The little book slipped from between his cold, shaking fingers and landed on the floor at his feet, splayed wide like a broken dragonfly.

"So," said George.

Thomas stared blankly at the thing on the floor. "There are men who . . . sell themselves . . . to men? As women do?"

"Well, of course there are. Don't be a fool, Thom."

"I'm sorry. It had simply never occurred to me." He was silent a moment. "That must mean there are a great many men who desire to lie with men."

"For God's sake, yes, there are a lot of sinners in the world. As a priest, this should not surprise you. But you see what this means?"

"I'm not sure—"

"Edward, our brother, this was his. He was a frequenter of such creatures."

"He loved men?"

"He committed sodomitical acts with them, yes."

"Oh God." Thomas put his head in his hands. All those terrible words were buzzing like wasps behind his eyes. He could not think. And he felt nothing but a kind of sullen despair. George, who had at some point risen, shoved a glass of brandy at him, and Thomas took it, and drank it, and it burned and did not help.

"Sorry," George said brusquely. "But better to know, eh? Better to know what he was."

What he was? "He was our brother," Thomas whispered.

"He was a liar, a pervert, and a coward. And I'm done wasting grief on him."

Thomas glanced up, dismayed. "George, how can you say that? This changes nothing."

"It changes everything. All this time, wondering and . . . and hurting, feeling less than him, less without him, and the marquess was right all along. He was no fit heir. No fit man." Some of the savagery faded from George's voice, and he dropped his hand heavily to Thomas's shoulder. "Come, brother. No more tears for him."

Thomas scrubbed the moisture from his eyes with the back of his wrist. In truth, he was weeping as much for himself as Edward. "He must have felt so unbearably alone. To take his own life like that."

"Best thing for him. Filthy beast."

"Oh no." The brandy roiled in Thomas's stomach, and for a moment he thought he might be sick. "I can't believe that anyone truly deserves death."

"Unrepentant criminals. Vicious murderers. Those who fornicate with children."

"It's . . . it's not the same," Thomas protested, weakly. But there was no understanding, no mercy, in his brother's eyes. He pressed on. "You would conflate tendencies that harm others with tendencies that harm no one. You would equate acts of violence with acts of love."

George passed a hand across his brow. "Christ, you're such an innocent. Do you even know the unnatural deeds you're trying to defend? There's no love in"—he pointed at the publication that still lay at Thomas's feet—"that."

"Not in that, no." Thomas glanced away from *The Gentlemen of London* with a shudder. "But do you not think that the men who seek such consolations are forced to it because they are denied everything else? All hope of home and family and companionship? The needs of their hearts and souls reduced solely to the needs of their bodies?"

George made a noise of frustration and contempt. "No, I do not. I think they're criminals, I think what they do is disgusting, and it shames me to know our brother was like them."

"But he loved you." How lacking those words seemed just then.

"Of what use to me is the so-called love of a sodomite who lacked even the strength to control his depravities?"

A kind of bleak and unyielding cold had settled over Thomas, cutting through his skin, turning his blood to ice and water. Silence, he knew, would serve him far better than truth. But at what cost? What betrayal of self? Of Edward. Of Micha. Of everything he had come to believe.

He closed his eyes for a moment, full of a deep and extraordinary pain. Having lost one brother, he did not know how he would bear the loss of another.

He tried to remind himself of his old doctrine: "God never afflicts us with more than we can endure." But his desperate thoughts—his prayers—contained little of reason. Instead, he begged for an impossible boon. *Please. Don't demand this choice. Don't take him from me.*

"I don't know," he said, at last. "But I am . . . the same."

For the moment, George's only reaction was bewilderment. "You what?"

Oh, why did it have to be so difficult. "I am like Edward. I . . ." How was he to explain it? *I am a sodomite* seemed an entirely inadequate description of something that was at once complex and simple and ordinary. "I love men. Well. A man."

There was a long, awful moment of something deeper than silence. A profound stillness. And then George jerked away from him, all bewilderment banished. "Of course. Why didn't I see. Michael whoever he is . . . he's your"—his lip curled in revulsion—"catamite."

"Friend. Lover. Husband."

"Have you no shame?" George was staring at him as though he no longer recognised what he saw. "How can you talk this way?"

"I suppose because I believe I've done nothing that shames me."

"But you're a man of God—"

The words were exploding out of George. Yet Thomas, discovering a reserve of conviction he hardly knew he possessed, cut over him. "No. I was never a man of God. Only a man of duty. And now, thanks to Micha, I'm simply a man."

"You're sick or mad or both."

Thomas shook his head. "Please. Can't you try to understand?"

"I don't want to understand." George pulled in a shuddery breath and took a few restless turns about the room.

That was when Thomas realised, beneath all the rage and scorn lay sorrow. And that hurt most of all.

"Don't do it." George sounded close to pleading. "You don't have to . . . be like this."

Thomas's eyelashes were clogged with tears. "It's not a choice. Or if it is, I would not choose differently."

"Why did you tell me this? What purpose does it serve but to ruin us both?"

"I suppose I was tired of lies. I've been lying for Edward at our father's behest for so long. Now you ask me to lie for myself. Is who I am really enough to make you hate me, George?"

George said nothing for what felt like a very long time, his eyes moving back and forth over Thomas's face, searching for something that must have eluded him. "You're no brother of mine," he said, and walked out.

The door closed behind him with the softest imaginable click.

Thomas sat, staring at an empty room, stunned with anguish.

After a moment, perhaps from a habit of tidiness or simply for something to do, he leaned down and picked up *The Gentlemen of London*. His eye passed over the page without curiosity, then snagged on a familiar configuration of letters. *Mr. M. D-shw-d, No. 12 Church Lane, Whitechapel.* And he read on instinctively, almost without understanding what he saw:

And such as knew he was a man would say / Leander, thou art made for amorous play. Here a connoisseur of classical temperament may satisfy his most ardent longings. Mr. D is a fine, tall gentleman vigorous and well formed, with a captivating countenance and striking dark eyes that inflame the senses. A genteel companion, clearly of some breeding and education, his nature is not spirited but he is quite obliging and submits himself to all pleasures requested of him.

Oh Micha, he thought, *Micha.*

He let the book fall into his lap. Then he picked it up again, ripped away the meagre binding, and began methodically to shred the pages until they littered the floor at his feet like corrupt petals. Finally, he gathered up the pieces and fed them, one by one, to the fire until there was nothing left.

It was sometime later that Thomas climbed the stairs to the room he no longer thought of as being solely his. Micha was curled up on his side on the bed, Thomas's dressing gown spread over him like a blanket. Thomas tugged off his boots and his coat, and joined his lover, sliding a hand over his waist and pressing his face into the familiar place between Micha's jutting shoulder blades. Micha stirred and eased his body closer to Thomas, engulfing him in warmth.

Thomas parted the soft curls that gathered at the nape of the other man's neck and kissed him there. Micha gave a deep, luxurious shiver, and Thomas tried not to think of the words of strangers. He let them go, letter by letter, until they were nothing but the memory of a shadow, fragments of a fading past, as insubstantial as withering leaves. Powerless in the face of the future they would have together.

"For an arse," Micha murmured, "your brother can sometimes be almost endearing."

Where once that might have made him smile, now it recalled Thomas to everything that had just transpired, and he uttered a soft sound of pain.

Micha tensed against him. "What's the matter?"

"I . . . I . . . told him. About me. About us."

"Fuck, why?" Micha rolled onto his back, hands tangling into his hair, a low groan escaping him. "He could see us imprisoned."

Accustomed always to the protections of wealth and privilege, Thomas had given very little consideration to the legal reality of their transgressions. But now understanding settled over him like cold mist. He had endangered Micha—threatened what was already a precarious life—with nothing but a handful of careless words and misplaced hopes.

"Do you have any idea what they do to men like us?" Micha was saying, all the old ferocity in his voice. "Even before they send you to the wheel."

"Don't—"

"They'd make you a public and medical spectacle, the property of any learned doctor summoned to examine you for signs of sin. Dilation of the fundament. Elongation of the penis. Details, naturally, to be published in the scandal sheets the very next fucking day. Is that what you want?"

"Micha," Thomas whispered, "please stop."

"Oh God." Micha turned and came suddenly into Thomas's embrace. His face, nestled against the side of Thomas's neck, was damp. "I'm sorry. I'm so sorry. I don't mean to be monstrous. I'm . . . fuck . . . I'm scared. It's frightening, to be who we are, and want what we want. Even though it's no fucking different to what they take for granted."

Thomas held him tightly, understanding for the first time the kind of fear Micha had lived with, and not quite sure what to say.

"I can't bear the thought of anything happening to you." A shudder rippled from Micha's body into Thomas's. "I hate that you have to think about these things now. What kind of world am I dragging you into? You used to be safe, and now it's all secrecy and shame and—"

"Stop." Thomas stilled him with a light finger to his lips. "I would not trade this life with you for any other sort of life imaginable. And I promise to be more circumspect in future."

Micha muttered something about Thomas being romantic and ridiculous, but he had stopped trembling.

"Besides," Thomas went on, "George won't risk the disgrace. To expose me would be to expose the family. We have nothing to fear from him."

"Well." Micha huffed out a sigh. "All right. I don't trust him. But I trust you."

Thomas lay for a while, pressed up against Micha, not speaking. He loved everything Micha had taught him, the storms of passion and the wickedness of shared laughter, but he cherished the quiet too. The intimacy of small touches when the world felt very far away.

Then, haltingly, he told Micha what he had learned about Edward, which was, perhaps, something he had always known, and Micha turned in his arms to hold him. It did not, and could not, make it better, but it made it bearable, and that was enough.

"Do you think it's true?" Micha asked. "Do you really think that's why he did it?"

"I'm not sure," returned Thomas, after a moment's thought. "It's hard to really know anything for certain. But it's almost unimaginable to me, the despair and desperation that would lead one to such an act."

"Perhaps he was being blackmailed. It happens."

An old and helpless fury, carefully suppressed, stirred like a demon in the chains Thomas had forged from acceptance and filial piety, and the forgotten power of it flooded him now, bitter as wormwood. "He was being blackmailed his entire life. George's duty was to join the army and die a heroic death. Mine was to join the church and be quiet. Edward's was to live precisely as our father determined. To bear the title, to marry, to procreate." He sighed, rage fading to pain. "His future must have felt impossible."

"I'm so sorry." Micha sounded young and a little helpless in the face of all that deep and distant hurt.

"I think George hoped understanding would make a difference—help somehow—but loss is simply loss. It doesn't come with an answer."

There was a small pause, and then Micha muttered, "You should have said that to Esther. Instead of telling her a pointless story about Jesus."

That startled a laugh out of Thomas. Perhaps it was wrong, just then, to be laughing, but all he felt was relief, the tangled knot of his heart unravelling sweetly. "You heathen. Also, is this really the time to critique my priesting?"

"You're right." Thomas could feel the upward curve of Micha's lips against his skin. "It's just there's so much . . . understanding in you. So much love. I wish you wouldn't hide that from the people who need it most."

"How can you see so much good in me when I have spent my whole life in costume?"

One of Micha's hands stroked lightly over Thomas's flank, spreading warmth and a lazy kind of pleasure. "Because I love you."

Thomas was silent a moment. "I'm going to do better by them."

"Who?" asked Micha, sleepily.

"Esther. My parishioners. Everyone."

"I thought we were leaving."

"Yes but . . . until then."

"As you say," returned Micha, and Thomas did not have to be able to see him to know the sardonic half-smile that accompanied his words.

"I just wish," Thomas admitted to the trustful dark, "I knew how to express what I feel, not merely what I've been taught."

Micha kissed Thomas's shoulder. "You seem to do all right with me."

"So when I stand there, at the front of the church, I should speak as though to you?"

"Why not?"

As was occasionally the case, Thomas wasn't sure if Micha was joking or not. But perhaps it didn't matter. The idea settled over him like starlight—insubstantial when he reached for it too hard but present, nonetheless. It was not, however, something for now. He was already too exhausted from the day's unsought revelations and wanted only to be safe and selfishly happy in Micha's arms.

It was enough and, for a while, he slept. But then he awoke, agitated and anxious, in the bleak indigo hours after midnight and could not find his peace again. Rather than stare at the dark, he crawled out of bed, lit a candle, and tried to draft a letter to the bishop. But the words wouldn't come. He hadn't lost his faith. He'd found it. And the truth proved simply inexpressible.

I have fallen in love. It is a love I hold dearer than my love for my God. It is a love I put above my duties. It is a love that makes me careless of the love of others. It is a love that makes me selfish. It is a love that saved me.

Before long, papers scattered the floor at his feet like the pale wings of fallen butterflies.

Eventually Micha stirred, rolled into the empty space Thomas had left, and sat up with a start. "Thomas?"

"Sorry. I'm here."

The shadow of Micha pushed a fall of sleep-tumbled curls out of his eyes. "Thinking about Edward?"

"No. Maybe I should be, but I'm not. I'm thinking about myself."

"What's the matter?"

"I'm trying to, I suppose, resign." Thomas sighed. "Except you can't really resign from the church. A defrocked priest is still a kind of priest."

"You're also a man, with the same rights as any other."

"I'm not sure the two are extricable."

Micha threw back the covers and padded naked across the room, the scents of sleep and sex clinging to his body. His hands came down warmly on either side of Thomas's neck. "You don't have to worry about this now."

"I know, but it's important."

"Come back to bed." Micha's thumbs kneaded a knot from just under the wing of Thomas's shoulder blade, his voice deepening to a husky purr. "I can take your mind off it."

"I . . . I'm sure you can."

He went to extinguish the candle, but Micha prevented him, a hand upon his wrist. And Thomas—unwritten letter already as good as forgotten—turned, just to look at him, this man who was his, illuminated in gold. He was so beautiful. So exquisitely, so undeniably male. Those austere curves, his legs with their rough dark hair, and that strong, lean back, all dips and planes and the groove of his spine, where the shadows gathered like ink.

Idolatry, thought Thomas, with a wry smile. *And licentiousness.* For his admiration of Micha was as carnal as it was loving, and his gaze was wont to linger in wicked places, like the dimples at the top of his buttocks and the dark crease between them. Thomas knew well the tenderness of the secrets within. All the ways Micha could yield.

Releasing Thomas, he returned to bed, sprawling out, still naked, his body arched and spread and brazen. His eyes were full of dark promises, his mouth a kiss waiting to be taken.

They had barely touched, and Thomas's desire was already an inferno. The truth was, Micha had his tricks. He knew how to inhabit his skin, how to seduce and inflame with nothing more than a look or a gesture, how to present his loveliness as a chef might a dish to be sampled and devoured. Thomas had always taken it for granted that it was natural to him. This shamelessness. This sensuality. Now he knew it was learned.

Part of him wanted to say, *You need not do this for me. I only want you.* But he feared such a truth might hurt Micha past the point of recovery. So he let himself be plied and beguiled and chose to see not the blandishments of a whore, but the gifts of a lover.

Chapter 23

Micha was starting to resent Sundays. Thomas was busy most of the time—so much for that old joke about a clergyman's working hours—but there was no escaping the fact that on Sundays he belonged to his parishioners, to his God, to everyone but Micha. It was absurd to be jealous—could one even be jealous of something so abstract?—but Micha had no other word for the ugly feeling. It was a little bit like loneliness and a little bit like loss, and it made him scratchy and desperate, like a feral cat, locked out in the cold.

Of course, he need not have stayed away. He could have attended any of the services, joined the gossip in the churchyard after, gone along to lunch, or tea or dinner, and been welcomed as lavishly as any biblical prodigal. The residents of Nettlefield were too polite to mention such things, except to make the occasional joke about Micha's wild and heathen ways, but he knew his godlessness troubled them. Depending on his mood, he found it some combination of officious and strangely charming that there were people who cared about him enough to extend that concern to the state of his soul after death. As if all that was standing between him and eternal glory at his divine Father's side was his poor church attendance.

Probably they consoled themselves with the thought that he was young, and the Lord was infinitely forgiving, but the truth was, Micha simply did not like God. He could not believe in Him the way Thomas could: with unshakeable trust in his goodness, His understanding. The truth was, Thomas had been changing. Was changing still. Not in essentials but in small ways that nevertheless accumulated, each a blade of grass. And, one day, Micha would open his eyes and see a whole new landscape.

Though he was as grave and softly spoken as ever, Thomas's newfound certainties shone like polished glass. Very little trace remained of the painfully dutiful servant who had first brought Micha to Nettlefield. And Micha rejoiced for him, was entranced by him, and did his best to lock away his bitterness. For he was the one to show Thomas passion, and yet it seemed God had claimed that too.

They had never discussed it, but Thomas seemed to have made some pact, come to some arrangement with his other beloved, that the seventh day was His alone, and he would not touch Micha at all. Sometimes he would barely even look at him. Micha had accepted it with good grace, then bad grace, and finally rebelled. He told himself he would have been satisfied with the smallest acknowledgement—a kiss, a touch, a loving look, anything to remind him he had a place in the heart of this suddenly uncomfortable stranger. But Thomas was marble, cold and shining and splendid. So now it was open warfare, a battle of flesh and spirit, God and man, that Micha was losing. Even so, it was somehow easier to have his seductions ignored, and physically rejected, than to hear Thomas say he didn't want him. And easier still to make this an external struggle than one rooted in Thomas's own conscience.

Sundays were nothing, however—mere inconvenience—compared to Thomas's occasional summons to the Episcopal Palace. It was a world to which Micha had no access and in which he had no place, and Thomas always returned to him, restless and subdued, and then it would be Sunday for days, sometimes weeks. And Micha could not even bring himself to be righteously indignant because Thomas was so unhappy. Eventually he would find his peace again, and crawl into bed with Micha, and he would be too relieved, too joyous, to do anything but welcome him.

And then, one winter evening, Thomas came back from dinner at the palace, and, instead of creeping about like a penitent ghost, he shed his clothes with something close to violence and flung himself straight into Micha's arms. It should have made Micha happy—and it did, it did—but he had resigned himself to the pattern of their lives, with its peaks and troughs of closeness, and this change was too sudden. It was everything he would have wished for, but Micha did not believe in miracles.

Thomas kissed him, the faintest tang of salt and brandy on his breath, his naked body sleek, and warm, and familiar against Micha's. More than familiar, intimately known, all its little imperfections and hidden beauties, the texture of the skin of otherwise untouched places. He loved the trembling softness of Thomas's belly, the chalice of his armpit, the pearly smoothness of his inner thighs, everywhere he was precious and open and vulnerable. But he also loved more carnal things: strong legs wrapped around him, a hard cock driving into him, hands that could—and did, when he willed it—pin him down, leave their bruises, like promises upon his flesh.

And Thomas knew him too, and that was its own wonder. He roused Micha now with a few urgent touches, the clumsiness its own provocation, because it was so full of need. And that was like an iron bar prying his ribs open, leaving his heart naked to the world. Thomas reached between them, wrapping a hand around Micha's cock. This, perhaps, he knew too well. Exactly the rhythm and pressure, the long drag and little twist, to make Micha spend. Sometimes Thomas liked to tease, to hold Micha breathless and half-sobbing, blissfully helpless on the edge of satisfaction, but not tonight. Tonight he sent Micha soaring towards climax with all the defiance of Icarus chasing the sun. He neither enticed surrender nor demanded it. He simply took it as his due, claiming dominion over Micha's pleasure, his body and soul. And Micha came within moments, with a harsh cry and almost without volition, spilling hot over Thomas's fingers and his own stomach.

Thomas leaned over him to lick up his issue, his tongue tracing the shuddering grooves of Micha's stomach, as he kissed his way back up to his mouth. Now he tasted of Micha, but his lips were wet with fresh tears, and when he pulled away, he whispered, "He knows. The bishop knows."

Micha jerked partially up, all the languor of gratification leaving him. "What? How?"

"I don't know. Perhaps George told him. But perhaps he simply guessed. He's a worldly man. Ironically, you don't get to be a bishop in the Church of England if you're not."

"Fuck me," muttered Micha. "That must have been quite the confrontation."

"I wouldn't say it was a confrontation. More a conversation."

"A conversation about your preference for men?"

"Essentially." Thomas gave a little shrug. "He told me tonight. He took me into his study for a private talk, poured me a brandy, and said, as calmly as you please, 'I understand you're a sodomite?'"

This time there was no unseemly, selfish joy in Micha. Just a cold dread. "He's got no proof. And making something like this public would do as much harm to the church as it would to you individually."

"Yes, but I couldn't deny it," Thomas protested.

Micha stared at him. *"Why?"*

"Because . . . it would have meant denying you."

"Fuck's sake." Groaning, Micha fell back against the pillows. "What's going to happen to us? To you?"

"As it happens," said Thomas, sitting up, "nothing very much." He wiped his eyes with the heel of his hand. "The bishop cares more about maintaining his connection to my family than he does about . . . personal immorality. Mainly he's disappointed I'm not political enough to be a useful archdeacon."

Micha was having trouble listening. He felt too cut open and left raw, and Thomas's words were coming at him as if from a great distance. "So it's fine then? Just like that?"

"Well . . ." Thomas finally met his eyes, his own little more than shadows in the moonlight that crept from between the curtains. "I'm supposed to be more discreet."

"'More discreet'?" repeated Micha. "What does he mean, 'more discreet'?"

There was a long silence.

"He suggested I should marry."

Micha sprang out of bed, the heat of the covers suddenly overwhelming, the smell of their bodies in pleasure swiftly turning sour. "You what? You've actually been considering it, haven't you? And this is how you tell me, with your hand on my cock and my come in your mouth?"

"Oh Micha." Thomas looked stricken.

"Don't 'oh Micha' me." He was angry, furious, rightfully so, but his eyes had betrayed him with tears. "I don't fucking believe this."

"It needn't change anything between us?"

"Thomas," Micha cried, hating the broken sound of his voice in the quiet room. "You'd be married. To someone else. How could I be with you, live with you, then?"

"We'd find a way. We could—"

"What? Fuck each other when your wife is out teaching Sunday school?" Micha dragged a blanket from the bed and wrapped it round his waist. The conversation was already verging on unendurable, but standing there naked, with his spent prick sticky between his legs, was making it infinitely worse.

Thomas visibly flinched. "God, no. It wouldn't be like that. We would find someone with . . . with understanding."

"Understanding. Of course." Micha sat slowly on the edge of the bed. He hurt. Everything hurt. "You've done more than consider this. You've thought it all the way through. You're going to marry her, aren't you? Your other whore."

He glared at Thomas, daring him to lie, to dissemble or insist that the idea hadn't even crossed his mind. And, this time, Thomas didn't flinch. "Yes," he said softly. "Yes. I . . . I wondered. It would be some measure of protection for all of us. And it would secure Hope's future."

"But"—and Micha cringed from the bewildered hurt in his own voice—"you're mine. You've said so, time and time again. Were you lying?"

Thomas gasped like Micha had physically struck him. "No. Never."

"Except now you want me to watch while you become someone else's?"

Thomas gazed at him pleadingly. "In name only."

"You say that as if it's nothing. But it's me who'll be nothing."

"That's not true. You're everything to me. You know that."

Micha's anger was fading fast. And when it was gone, it would leave him bereft, just like Thomas had. "There's only so much of you. There's a piece for your God, and a piece for your flock, and a piece for every lost soul who crosses your path. A piece for your woman and a piece for the child. Even a piece of you for the brother who won't speak to you because of who you are. What's for me, Thomas? What part of you is truly mine?"

"My heart?"

"What use is that when you give your life to someone else?" Micha's lip curled into a sneer that felt as familiar to him as the bitterness of laudanum. "You coward. You fucking coward."

Thomas's head snapped up. "You have no idea what it's like. I have a calling, Micha. You would have me cast that gift aside because you have a pretty arse?"

Micha nearly said *Because you love me*. But he closed his lips over the words. "No."

"Oh God." Thomas's voice broke, and he dropped his head into his hands. "I can't do it anymore. I can't. It's too much. I'm to minister to these people and help them live with God and His church, when I myself do neither. I'm a hypocrite, the w-worst of sinners. I d-don't deserve to be their priest. I deserve to be in hell. I am in hell." And then he began to weep, soundless, terrible sobs that made his whole body shake as though he might shatter at a touch.

It was unbearable. Micha had believed hearts only broke in fairy tales. He pushed away from the bed and dropped to his knees at Thomas's feet. "Please," he whispered, half-crying himself. "Please don't. I'm sorry. I love you. I love you. I'll always love you."

At last, Thomas let him peel his hands from his face and kiss away the wetness from his eyes. "I don't know what to do. I don't know what's right anymore. I just don't know."

"We'll think of something. We will. Just don't cry. Please don't cry." The reassurances fell in a babbling stream from Micha's lips, though he barely believed one word in ten. "Come back to bed with me?"

Thomas stared at him, with hopeless, red-rimmed eyes, and then his lips turned up in a smile Micha had never seen before. "To coin a phrase, 'What use is that?'"

And their laughing was weeping inside out.

"No use at all," admitted Micha, when they were lying together. "But I'm always happiest in your arms."

"As am I," Thomas agreed. "And I'm sorry, Micha. I'm so sorry. I've been such a fool. I think I must have . . . panicked in the moment?"

Micha made a soothing, forgiving noise and drew Thomas closer. It wasn't that he disbelieved him, for Thomas's distress certainly hadn't been feigned. But while he may have spoken to Micha impulsively—while whatever the bishop had said to him might have spurred him to it—Micha could not shake the conviction that these were thoughts Thomas had previously entertained. Had, in fact, probably been entertaining for some time. And that should not have felt like a betrayal. But it did.

Not a grand one. Except this was worse.

This was betrayal like grains of sand, flung carelessly into his eyes.

When Thomas slept, Micha slipped from the bed and paced the hallways of the rectory, with Thomas's dressing gown wrapped loosely around him. Even the fact it smelled of Thomas—the slightly medicinal tang of Pears soap—was less comfort than usual. It was at once a relief and a torment to Micha that he had no laudanum. He would have mixed himself a draught and swallowed it down without hesitation. Instead, he wandered through shadows and empty rooms, and shuddered, and ached, and was suddenly so very afraid.

He should have expected, if not this, then something like it. They were fortunate it had only been Thomas's "worldly" bishop. But hadn't Micha tried to warn Thomas? How many times had he told him that they needed to be careful? That someone would, at some point, discern who and what they were. And that destruction would inevitably follow.

But Thomas hadn't quite believed him. And somehow—lulled, distracted, hopeful—Micha had let himself stop believing too. He had forgotten to be fearful, and, at some point, they would both pay the price for it. They'd been stupid, careless, complacent in their settled lives. And they'd taken their happiness for granted. Somehow convinced themselves they had a right to it. That they could be free. Was it idealism, or pride, or the simple lunacy of love, which felt too much like invincibility sometimes?

Now, though, there could be no more hiding, no more recklessness and self-deception. Because the truth was this, and it had been their truth all along, and all the love in the world could not change it: They lived on the edge of ruin.

Chapter 24

Spring came swiftly that year, flooding Nettlefield in ice-bright sunlight. The trees bedecked themselves like debutantes, spilling their raspberry-and-cream blossom endlessly down the village streets and across the flower-strewn meadows. In the churchyard, where Micha waited for Thomas to give his service, the grass had given way to a carpet of snowdrops, crocuses, and daffodils, as brash and joyously chaotic as children at play.

Micha rested against a crumbling, ivy-coiled obelisk, its inscription long lost to time. The sky arced over him, endless, infinite, and almost cloudless, shining like the sea. Blossoms kept tangling in his hair. The world was silent, but for the faintest movement of the breeze through the softly sighing trees and a trace of birdsong in the distance.

He felt like the only man left on earth.

But soon, Thomas would be done, and they would walk home, as close to arm-in-arm as they dared, and, perhaps, one of these Sundays would be the Sunday. The Sunday they went in search of that impossible future Thomas had promised and Micha had chosen, as some chose to put their faith in plaster saints, to believe in. Of course, that would also mean leaving. They would leave misty mornings in the meadows, long evenings by the fire, wild nights of secret carnal embraces, lemon drizzle cake and reading groups, fluff-brained dogs and white horses that granted wishes, in search of other beauty, other happiness, as if this was not enough. As if Thomas did not belong here, among these gentle greens and golds, where he had, at last, learned to be loved.

Not for the first time, Micha wondered how his love alone could be enough to replace a whole world. To become one.

The doors to the church stood open, flung as wide as arms, and Micha paused outside as music and voices raised in song came flowing over the threshold. "Tears for all woes, a heart for every plea. Come, Friend of sinners, thus abide with me."

Micha's lip curled. It had been a long time since he had felt any desire to enter a church. In truth, he felt no desire to do so now.

But then the music died away, and he heard Thomas begin to speak. "'Beloved, let us love one another: For love is of God; and every one that loveth is born of God, and knoweth God.' John 4:7." A pause, and then Thomas went on in a more conversational tone, "I've had occasion recently to think back on all the sermons inflicted on you over the years"—a ripple of gentle, if slightly knowing laughter—"and I realised I've never once spoken of love."

Micha, who had been about to retreat, paused. And then, unable to help himself, came slowly, reluctantly, into the church. It was a plain building, white walls and wooden beams, high arched windows and a few simple stained-glass scenes. This was English country Anglicanism at its most traditional and austere, but for the lavishness of the light that swept the little room, silver-gold and butter-soft, and the flowers, oh the flowers, riotous in their abundance, brazen in their beauty, as invincible and perfect as the secret laughter of lovers.

"In my life," Thomas was saying, "it's always been a word both over- and underused. I know I've said on far too many occasions that I love my first cup of tea of the day." He smiled so delightedly at this very small, and not very amusing, joke that Micha wanted to run up the nave and kiss him. Then cringed, internally, at the direction of his thoughts. But no lightning came to strike him down.

"And yet," Thomas went on, "if you have never known love, the love of your father, the love—as a parent—you will feel for your child, or even the love for a sweetheart or a spouse, how can you even begin to understand the love of God? A love that's as gentle as it is strong, as tender and as intimate as a lover's embrace, as warming and wonderful as that first sip of tea. It seems impossible to comprehend, but it's the nature of love to be all these things, all these things and more, both in heaven and in earthly counterpoint." Thomas paused, his eyes shining like the sky. "And that is what I wish to think about today. The miracle of love, in all its multiplicity."

Micha cared little for God, but he loved Thomas and so he listened, believing not in the benevolence of the deity but, instead, in the conviction of the man who stood before them.

"Love is not a . . ."—for the first time Thomas stumbled, seeming to search for words—"a static thing, like a piece of wood you can hold in your hand, and say, 'There, that is love.' It's fluid, changeable, endless; it grows, and we grow with it. I think of Philippians 1:9: 'And this I pray, that your love may abound yet more and more in knowledge and in all judgement.' The more I live, and the more I love, the more I know that this is what I want. It's what I pray for, above all else. Simply, that I may grow in love." Thomas was silent a moment, then continued. "When I was writing this sermon, I thought about everything I've done here and I asked myself, 'Is this love? Is this a work of love?' And I think this is how the Lord answered me. That loving Him, and loving the world, is mediated through the ways we love the people around us, as partners and parents and lovers and friends. All love flows together, from Him and to Him. The multiplicity of love keeps multiplying."

Thomas's quiet voice filled the little church, rich as the light, as sweet as the scent of flowers. Micha was more than half-entranced. The man at the pulpit was still Thomas, still very much Thomas, diffident of manner, careful with his words, but surety infused him like flame. And there was such passion in his eyes.

Oh fuck, Micha thought, understanding at last, *oh fuck.*

That's how he looks at me.

He heard nothing more until the very end.

"I shall simply leave you with this," said Thomas, smiling. "1 Corinthians 16:14: 'Let all that you do be done in love.'"

Micha stumbled out of the church, into harsh sunlight that burned his eyes and a sky that suddenly seemed a vast blue nothing. He had not been smote, or turned into salt, but he might as well have been. For love had vanquished him, as it always did, and the pain of it was as deep and sharp as the spring.

Once he'd loved Thomas without recognising it, in fear and need and desperate avarice. Now, though, all that was gone, and all that remained was the love, stripped down to some bare, pure quintessence, bright as an unquenchable flame.

He had told Thomas these were his decisions, faith or love, Nettlefield or Micha, when, in truth, they were Micha's decisions too. Unused as Micha was to having choices of his own, it had perhaps been easier to let Thomas bear the burden of their future alone. Yet he knew now, with a terrible certainty, that Thomas would never leave Nettlefield. Of course, he believed he would—he sincerely thought that he could—but asking him to give up his small quiet future was no better than asking Isidore to give up his brilliant one.

Then again, unlike Isidore, Thomas would insist he wasn't being asked.

But how could he take Thomas from Nettlefield? Because it would be taking. And it wouldn't be love. It would be selfishness.

Limiting, not multiplying.

If Micha had been a braver man, a better man, he would have slipped away quietly. No tears, no protestations, no goodbyes. Let Thomas think him faithless. But he couldn't do it. He had, almost without noticing, learned to stop counting. The kisses and touches and love words had gathered between them, innumerable as grains of sand, as precious as opals. But there were not enough of them. Not nearly enough. There would never be enough.

Every day he woke with the same thought. *One more kiss. Just one more kiss. Tell me you love me. One more time.*

One *last* time.

He sat down on the edge of a sarcophagus to wait, fingers playing idly over the moss-riven surface of the gold-grey stone.

And, finally, came Thomas, an angular figure in sober black, picking his way through the snowdrops, smiling the smile meant only for Micha.

Micha tried to contain the longing that rose up inside him like it wanted to choke him. "I think," he managed, "if I believed in your God, I'd love Him too."

Thomas reached out and curled his fingers—those smooth, perfect gentleman's fingers—around Micha's wrist, though only for a moment. This was how they touched, like traitors sharing a conspiracy. "I thought I saw you at the back. Then I thought I must have imagined it."

"No, I was there. For a little."

A trace of pink warmed Thomas's cheeks. "I was thinking of you." He pulled himself onto the sarcophagus, next to Micha, aligning their shoulders, their thighs, the edges of their hips. And Micha tried not to imagine sitting like this, together in some other place, beneath a different sky. After a moment, Thomas reached into the pocket of his coat and drew out an envelope, addressed to the bishop. "I managed to . . . find the words. And today seems as good a day as any to tell our friends that we may soon be leaving them."

Micha stared at the envelope, and at the precise, modest script that was as essentially Thomas as his anxious hands, his lean, pale body. When he spoke, his voice sounded unfamiliar even to himself, as eerie as distant brass. "You're not going to send that letter, Thomas. And we're certainly not going to speak to our friends."

Thomas's eyes flew to Micha's, searching them for answers and finding none, for Micha hardly knew them himself. "What do you mean? This is what we want, isn't it?"

"More than anything." A breath he did not realise he had been holding rushed out of Micha, roaring in his ears. He knew he should have lied and made it easier on both of them. Unfortunately, he had lost the habit, along with his other dependencies. "But you . . . your faith . . . I didn't understand before. It's as real to you as I am. It's who you are. It's—"

"It's who I've become," interrupted Thomas gently. "Because of you."

Micha laughed, with a trace of his old bitterness, swiftly whisked away with the cherry blossom on the breeze. That, too, had faded with the lies, the laudanum, and the memories of hands and bodies and strangers. "I'm so fucking in love with you." His eyes stung, the light pressing against his eyelids like needles. "And this is bloody typical."

"Micha, please don't talk like this. Something has changed and I don't understand what it is, and"—Thomas's voice twisted in sudden uncertainty—"you're worrying me."

Thomas had told him once: *It's all connected.* Micha hadn't understood at the time, but he did now. Him, and God, and love and faith, and Thomas and Nettlefield, inseparable and impossible. "You can't give up everything for me. And I don't want you to."

There was a long silence. Thomas's hand closed desperately over Micha's, trapping his fingers between flesh and stone. "I'm not Isidore."

"I know. He left me for his world. You gave me faith in yours."

"My love, you are my world. Without you, I would still be lost."

Micha swallowed. There were hooks in his throat, catching his words, making them hurt. "And you've changed me too. I was base metal before you found me."

"You were always gold," whispered Thomas.

"Only in your eyes." Micha lifted the knot of their hands and kissed across Thomas's fingertips. "But I'm not the man I used to be. I want to love as you love, with my whole heart and what little goodness I possess. I want you, almost past bearing, but I can't—I won't—be the villain in your story. I'm not going to take you from your faith, and your home, and the people you care for."

"Do I have no say in this?" Thomas's voice trembled like the grass at their feet. "I chose you."

"Yes." Micha smiled, jagged as the cracks in his heart. "And I chose you. So I'm leaving."

"No. I . . . no. Please. Please."

The despair in Thomas's voice seared Micha to blood and ashes. "Don't," he choked out. "Don't. You know you're needed here. I love you, but I don't need you. You've already saved me."

"No." Thomas's hands struggled in Micha's, as if he could hold him forever with something as simple as the touch of skin. Perhaps, had everything been different, he could have.

Micha gazed at him helplessly, but Thomas's attention was locked on the writhing muddle of their hands. "Thomas," he pleaded, "you have to understand. You made me believe. I believe in you. I believe in this love of yours, this boundless, endless love, and I cannot keep it for myself alone."

"You think this life is so important to me?" Thomas had gone as still as the carved monuments that surrounded them.

For long moments Micha was silent too. Then, "Tell me truly, Thomas, if I was to say, 'Very well, let us go and post that letter now,' would you?"

"The post office is closed," Thomas whispered, for he was hopeless at dissembling.

"Would you?" Micha asked again. And when Thomas said nothing more, he plucked the envelope from his hand.

"What are you—"

Without another word, Micha tore the letter to pieces.

"Micha, I worked hard on that."

"I know you want to send it. I know you wish you could. But I also know you can't."

Thomas tried to frame some kind of answer and, instead, uttered only a noise of bewildered, incoherent misery. He pulled himself sharply from Micha's hold. "Without you," he said, "how can anything else mean anything to me?" Then he leaned in and kissed him, right there in full daylight, in the middle of the churchyard. Micha tried to protest, but beneath the sweet, familiar pressure of Thomas's lips, his words became a gasp, which became an offering. He unspooled beneath spring's careless sun in threads of amber and gold, love and loss and an ever-restless wanting.

Thomas pushed him down and stretched full-length over him, locking them in an embrace so shockingly, undeniably carnal that Micha forgot himself. The stone was cold beneath his shoulders, but Thomas was all heat and strength, pinning Micha beneath him and grinding their bodies together, rough and relentless, upon the harsh edge of pleasure, the sweet edge of pain. Micha writhed, moaned, and clutched mindlessly at Thomas, driving up against him, surrendered to the madness of a moment, and a kiss made raw with the salt of tears.

Suddenly he could think of nothing but Thomas, the way their bodies moved together in love and passion, and lay together in sleep. All their smiles and touches and little jokes, as countless as the stars. He turned his head, tearing his mouth away from Thomas. "What the fuck are you doing?" There was no answer. Just the movement of Thomas's lips over his throat, a string of savage little kisses that made Micha's pulse crackle like fireworks. "Someone will see, and it will ruin you."

Thomas glanced up, wild-eyed. "If that is what it takes to keep you, I will be ruined."

Their mouths met, urgent and hopeless, Micha helplessly caught between pushing Thomas away and pulling him closer. If only there was not a world beyond the closed circle of their bodies. If only there were no other people who mattered. If only there were no choices. If only someone would come and take everything else away. "Don't do this."

"Don't make me stop."

Micha shuddered, waiting, almost hoping for the rustle of footsteps, the indrawn breath, the outraged cry. But there was nothing, just an enclosing silence, and an envelope of sky. "Please stop."

Thomas gazed at him, truly stricken now, the hollow centres of his pupils as deep as wounds. If Thomas touched him again, Micha knew he would let him. Welcome him, yield to him, never let him go. They would fall to ruin, laughing and together. He wanted it so much he ached and burned and could barely breathe, but he did not hope for it, because he knew Thomas would never force him. And he was right.

Thomas rolled clumsily away and crumpled into the long grass that wreathed the base of the sarcophagus. He drew his knees tight against his body and wrapped his arms around them, as graceless as a felled albatross. "Stay," he said, at last, whispering not to Micha but to the mud, the weeds, and the snowdrops. "If you won't leave with me, stay with me instead."

Micha, bereft upon cold stone, hauled himself up. "As what?"

"As we are. As whatever you wish to be."

"And your church?"

"I can . . . I will . . . oh, I don't know, Micha." Thomas blinked tears from his lashes. "You know I cannot find iniquity in love, but the world would make it so. How do I live that lie? How do I serve the Lord while I do?"

"If we leave, you can't serve Him at all."

"And what of us, Micha? What of love? What about"—Thomas's voice was almost lost to anguish—"*me*."

Micha slipped off the sarcophagus and knelt in the grass beside Thomas. "If that's what you wish. Let's put ourselves above the whole world, abandon those who need you and everything you believe. Let's live for nothing but each other. Come away with me now. I'll give you everything I am, and I'll never leave your side."

He held out his hand, steady as stone, and Thomas lifted his eyes to Micha's.

Reached out.

And hesitated.

Micha's lips quirked into something too painful to be a smile. "This is why I fell in love with you, Thomas. I wouldn't change you, not even for forever."

"Oh God." Fresh tears had gathered like fleeting diamonds upon Thomas's lashes. "I can't bear this. It will rip me apart."

"In some ways, it changes little."

"How can you say that?"

Again, Micha tried to find a smile. And, this time, he almost succeeded. “I don’t need to be with you to love you. I always will.”

“But where will you go?” It was half-question, half-protest. “What will you do?”

Micha cast his mind to the banknotes George had thrust upon him what felt now like a lifetime ago. “Don’t worry about me. I’ve some resources to fall back on, since your brother tried to pay me off—”

“He what?”

“He was trying to protect you. He thought I had some nefarious purpose. Which, I suppose, I did.” He shrugged. “In any case, I could never bring myself to use his money. Now it seems fair enough that I do.”

Something rather cynical fleeted lightly across Thomas’s face. “He does seem to be the only one of us getting his desired outcome.”

“You have your path, Thomas. And I will find mine.”

“If you ever need anything,” Thomas said, pleading, “you will come back?”

Micha reached for his lies and, this time, found them easily. “Of course.”

“And you will not fall prey to . . . hard times?”

“No. I’ll even wrap up warm, eat green vegetables, and always carry an umbrella.”

Thomas gave a hopeless, shattered laugh.

“I promise you”—Micha firmed his voice—“I will be quite well. I was thinking I could be a drawing master.”

“But you can’t draw.”

“Or, a secretary, I could be a gentleman’s secretary, don’t you think?”

“No, I don’t. I think you’d be a terrible secretary.”

And now they were both laughing, clutching for each other as though it could make a difference, until, at last, there was nothing left but impossible promises and already-uttered words.

Thomas made a convulsive movement, his hands coming together almost in prayer. “Please, Micha. Please, don’t leave me. There must be—”

"Uncle Thomas, Uncle Michael?" The cry rang through the churchyard, like the peal of Sunday bells. Micha tore his eyes from Thomas to see Hope, bounding with unladylike vigour, towards them, her hair and her bonnet strings flying. "Why are you both sitting on the ground?"

Thomas could not find his words quick enough, so it was left to Micha to gather himself and perform a hollow charade of playfulness. "We can sit on the ground if we want to."

Hope considered this gravely. "Yes," she conceded, "I suppose you can. Esther sent me to fetch you because the tea is getting cold and there will be no plum cake left."

"That would be tragic."

"If you were excessively attached to plum cake, yes. Which I am not. I think it brings out the worst in plums and the worst in cake."

"But it's Thomas's favourite," murmured Micha.

Hope nodded. "Which is why Esther thought you should hurry."

Micha nudged Thomas gently, and he climbed to his feet, as jerkily as a puppet. He looked dazed, like a man lost in someone else's dream.

"Are you coming, Uncle Michael?"

He smiled. It was the first time he had faked a smile for so innocent a purpose as reassuring, and it came to him with surprising ease. "Soon."

Hope tucked her hand into Thomas's, and Micha saw the way his fingers tightened around hers, as though she was the last real thing left in the world.

"I have been reading a most edifying book," she said.

"Oh?" Thomas's voice sounded rusty but was otherwise steady. "What about?"

She gave a little skip. "Cannibals."

Micha watched them as they walked away, the man he loved and the girl with a thousand futures spinning in her eyes like stars. The sun cast its capricious eye upon them too and, in a moment of idle kindness, fashioned them each a crown of gold.

Volume III

After

"For you see your majesties," cried Count Malodorous, "this lady is not who she says! Why she is no lady at all! She is none other than Euphrenadora Hussington, scourge of Europe!"

With that ungentlemanly ejaculation he tore off Euphrenadora's mask and stamped it to dust beneath his boots.

A terible hush fell across the ballroom.

Euphrenadora shook free her magnificant mane of flame red hair now making everyone gasp and some of the gentleman feint clean away in an excess of passion. "It is true I am indeed Euphrenadora Hussington but I come here today to warn you of a dark plot against your majesties plotted by none other than this man! Count Malodorous!"

Everyone gasped again.

"What is the meaning of this!" roared the King.

Count Malodorous had gone the colour of pea soup which was not becoming at all. "She lies!" he roared back. "You cannot trust her! Everyone knows she is the daughter of a snake charmer and who knows who else and moreover she has a child out of wedlock!"

Nobody gasped because as the Count had already said this was not new information.

"You are wrong!" cried Euphrenadora. "I have twenty six children out of wedlock and they are all very happy. I enjoy having children out of wedlock very much. But I could have a hundred twenty six bastards and it

would not change the fact you came here tonight to murder Crown Prince Krystian and seize the throne of Lithandria for yourself!"

Now Count Malodorous was the colour of pea soup left to turn cold and go lumpy and unpleasent. "You have no proof of this."

"Oh contrair!" Euphrenadora darted forward and pulled a jewellry box from where it was hidden in the Count's pocket.

He snatched for her but it was already too late. "Nooooo!" he howled.

Euphrenadora opened the box and showed the King and the Queen and Prince Krystian and the Chamberlain and the nearest guests who were all craning their necks the stolen blue diamond cravat pin. "Count Malodorous meant to return this to his highness but it has been treated with a undetectible and deadly poison."

"I say again," said Count Malodorous again, "you have no proof of this."

"There is a very simple way to check."

Before the Count could stop her Euphrenadora lunged at him and cut him on the back of his hand with the sharp tip of the cravat pin.

And at that moment you could have heard a cravat pin drop in the ballroom.

Everyone stared at Euphrenadora. Had she made a teribble mistake?!

Then Count Malodorous gave a wet gurgle, bloody foam spurting from his nostrils as he writhed about in hideous agony and then fell to the floor where he thrashed in his death throes for along time. At last he was still, contorted in a pose of unspeakible anguish, his mouth frozen in a crimsun O.

"I rest my case," said Euphrenadora.

Then there was a shriek of outrage from somewhere among the guests and Lady Nightsbane rushed at Euphrenadora wielding a bone dagger. Euphrenadora immediatly pulled the rapier from her stocking and stabbed Lady Nightsbane through the heart and she fell down dead next to her former lover.

So the Crown Prince was not poisoned by the blue diamond cravat pin, all the bad people were summerly dispensed with, Lithandria was saved and it was all thanks to Euphrenadora! The King and Queen and all the people of the kingdom were very grateful to her and made her a Knight of the Realm.

Prince Krystian however was very sad because he had truly fallen in love with Euphrenadora when she was in disguise as Lady Dominika.

"I'm sorry," she said, patting his hand gently. "But you must marry and stay here to look after the kingdom because you are the Crown Prince and that is your job and it is also what you are suited for."

"But I love you, Euphrenadora!" he cried his eyes, which were exactly like the famous and now no longer stolen blue diamond of Lithandria, filling up with tears. "You are the bravest and most beautiful woman I have ever met and so clever and your skills with both small sword and rapier are unparallelled."

It was all true but Euphrenadora was not one to boast. "We will always remember each other" she said. "But you must also be a good husband to your wife."

"I will," promised Prince Krystian. "But may I first have a kiss to hold in my heart forever?"

"You may," said Euphrenadora and they kissed and it was a very nice kiss and nearly as good as all the other exciting things Euphrenadora had done in her life.

Then she said goodbye to Prince Krystian and left Lithandria for her next adventure.

Chapter 25

By moonlight, the church looked cold, washed away to nothing but greys and shadows. Of course, Thomas had been here after dark before, at Midnight Mass for many years, but there was candlelight for that, all a-glitter, and voices raised in joyful song, bodies pressed together to warm so much old stone. Now, though, it was simply a room. One that, as Thomas paced its confines, felt empty.

He wasn't sure he'd truly slept in days, possibly even weeks. Mornings, evenings, afternoons, they could have been anywhere, anywhen, and he had stumbled through them, smiling when it was required he smile, nodding when it was required he nod, offering words by rote, like the psalms he had learned as a child, with no reference to their meaning. The nights, though, the nights were interminable. In the rectory, the ticking of every clock had become a blade, cutting his life into a thousand scattered pieces of *after Micha*. It was mostly a need to escape the noise, and the silence, and to pass the time, the too much time, that had driven Thomas from home. Once he might have believed that the fact his steps had led him to the church meant he was seeking guidance, or even comfort. Now he did not know what he sought. If anything.

He paused before the altar but did not ascend the steps. He was not, in this moment, a priest, and he had never felt less of one. When had he learned to find joy here, purpose, a kind of peace? And how had he lost it just as swiftly, just as inexplicably?

Where are you, he wondered.

And could not have clarified who he was asking for.

Thomas had been taught, and fallen naturally into, a brisk, practical English Protestantism. He'd found little use for what he thought of as papist effusions and discouraged his parishioners from anything even slightly resembling them. There was, after all, enough in life already to demand your supplication. No truly loving Father should want that from His children.

Nevertheless, tonight he knelt. The flagstones were ice-cold, but he barely felt them. He barely felt anything. He couldn't remember the last time he had. Slowly, he lowered himself further. To his elbows. Then full-length, his cheek in the dust of so many footsteps. Closing his eyes, he waited. Waited for something to change. Then realised nothing was going to.

Because it was still there, the soft tug inside him, that delicate fishhook, embedded in the tenderest sinews of his heart, the deepest places of his soul, drawing him as inexorably to God as life to death. As lover to lover.

Had he known how, he would have ripped it from himself. Left it there on the church floor, like a silver worm in a bloody pool. Walked away and never looked back. Except it had been part of him since before he had known how to recognise it.

It was what made him believe in kindness over cruelty. What made him find hope for tomorrow. For the day after tomorrow. It was what made him want to be a better man, even if his power to be so was enacted on the smallest imaginable scale. It was what helped him accept that this could be enough. Not only for him, but for any who chose—in the face of an often-indifferent world—even a little goodness.

The salt of his own tears stung his cracked lips.

Thomas had written once, in the journal he had found no reason to continue, that God never subjected you to more than could be endured. He had repeated those words as rote consolation more times than he could remember.

But he understood them now. The truth of them.

Because he could endure this. He could.

"It's just"—he lifted his head, moonlight spilling down his cheeks, illuminating nothing—"how am I to forgive you?"

And God had no answer. For He did not need to give one.

At some point, Thomas rose and moved to one of the pews, where he waited not quite awake, not quite sleeping, barely thinking, neither wanting nor able to pray, as the hours passed. The light swept through the church, grey-tinged at first from the fading night, then flame-bright with the sunrise. It was the colour of meadow primrose by the time Sheba came and sat next to him.

"How did you know I was here?" he asked, his voice raw from tears and unspoken words.

"I didn't," she admitted, smiling. "But you scared the life out of Sophie Butterworth when she came with fresh flowers."

Thomas searched himself for the capacity to interact like a reasonable person. "It's surely not so unusual for a priest to be found in a church."

"You're not generally here so early. She was afraid you might have been here all night."

"And this made her flee the building?"

"She was worried about you. And she thought you might speak more easily to me—a friend." She paused. "Was she wrong?"

"Just at present," Thomas admitted, falling back on honesty in the absence of anything more useful, "I'm not certain I recall how to speak to anyone."

Sheba's hand came to rest lightly, affectionately upon his knee. "What happened, Thomas? Between you and Micha?"

For some reason, it felt almost impossible to say, even though it was the simplest of all possible answers. "He left."

"Why?"

"Because"—Thomas swallowed, his mouth full of ashes—"I couldn't leave with him. I thought I could. But he was right. I . . . I'm where I'm meant to be."

She was silent for a long time. "I don't think I understand?"

"God placed me here."

"Did not the bishop place you here? To appease your family?"

Thomas made a sound that, at another moment, could have been a laugh. "Earthly machinations may sometimes reflect heavenly intent."

"That's rather convenient, don't you think?"

Thomas dropped his head into his hands. The light was making his eyes ache. "You're very like him, you know."

"We have a lot in common," she agreed, mildly. "More than enough to dislike each other for it, at any rate."

"I never understood his antipathy."

"Oh." She flicked her fingers dismissively. "He wishes he were better than me, but fears he is not. On some days, simple jealousy."

"Why would he be jealous?"

"Don't be foolish, Thomas."

"I gave him no cause."

"The world gave him cause. He would be jealous of any woman to whom you showed the smallest favour, simply because she could offer you what he cannot."

Thomas blushed beneath the shadow of his own palm. "There are things I would not wish a woman to offer me."

"A woman could marry you. Give you a child. Live a life openly by your side. With a woman, you could keep your God, without qualm or question."

"My God?" repeated Thomas. "Is He not your God also?"

"I very much doubt it." Her tone was a little wry, but not bitter. "He is a man's God, after all. I'm honestly rather surprised He still feels like yours."

"It's not God who holds my love a sin. But to love, I must live in sin. And what kind of priest would that make me?"

"Priests are just people, aren't they?" she asked. "Are you saying no priest has ever sinned?"

"It's not the sin. Everyone struggles with sin." Thomas sighed. "It's the persistence of the sin. Are you familiar with Saint Paul's letter to the Romans. Chapter seven?"

Her lips twitched. "Clearly not."

"I won't quote it to you—"

"My thanks."

That drew from him an unexpected half-smile. "Paul, as is rather typical for him, I will admit, is wrestling with what it means to understand sin, and believe in God's law, and yet continue to fall short of doing what is right."

"I see."

"He concludes," Thomas went on, giving voice to thoughts that lived inside him like rats, feeding upon him endlessly, "that mistakes are to some degree inevitable because, unlike God, we aren't perfect. And that as long as we recognise God's goodness, and hate the ills that we do, we can trust in His grace to save us from the worst of ourselves."

"And what does that have to do with you?"

He sighed, the taste of dust in his mouth, his tongue as cumbersome as stone. "I could never hate being with Micha. I would be choosing sin, day in, day out, knowing always I was in the wrong and refusing . . . unable . . . to repent."

"I thought you said"—Sheba's voice was gentle, in contrast to the needle-prick precision of her words—"love wasn't sin in the eyes of the Lord?"

"Love isn't. Fornication is, and for good reason."

"It's not as though you have another choice. If you were to act as married, forsaking all others, until death do you part, et cetera, would it still be fornication?"

"Well," said Thomas, rather hopelessly, "yes. Not all religious laws are secular laws, nor are all secular laws religious. For that matter, it's not always the case that what's morally right is upheld by either religious doctrine or legal precedent."

Sheba's look was wry enough to remind him, painfully, of Micha. "This all sounds very convenient, Thomas. Convenient for people who are not us."

"Even so"—on this, at least, he could be firm—"it is not for me alone to decide what holds weight and what doesn't. I can only live as best I can, in accordance with what is right under the church, right under the Crown, and right to my own conscience."

"Your own happiness can't be right also?"

"Not if I want to stay a priest."

"And you do?"

"I must."

"Forgive me for what is probably a foolish or insensitive question, but *why*?"

"I know it sounds absurd to feel . . . called, I suppose, to so small a life, and yet I do." He managed the faintest of smiles, for the wretched absurdity of it all, if nothing else. "I thought it was one father who demanded this of me, but it turned out to be another who truly drew me."

"How can you be sure?" she asked, her tone more curious than it was sceptical, though it was not devoid of scepticism either.

"I wish I could tell you. Like all love, it's simply there. And it will be until the day I die."

There was another long silence. It swept through the little church, heavy as a peacock's tail. "I'm sorry," said Sheba finally. "I came to comfort you, but I don't know how."

"I'm sorry too. I'm afraid I don't know how to be comforted." Thomas half-turned on the pew so he could look at her directly. "And it's not that I don't appreciate the effort, but why do you speak on Micha's behalf?"

Her eyes widened, flashing silver. "On Micha's behalf?"

"It seems as though you would have me be with him."

"I speak on *your* behalf. Because you want to be with him."

"I'm not quite free to want as others are. I have been given other gifts."

"Your vocation?"

He nodded.

"Well," she said, and he could tell he had left her at a loss, "it's your life."

"In many ways, it has been a very fortunate one. I've never been hungry or impoverished or desperate. And the losses I have suffered . . ."

"Perhaps need not have been suffered," she suggested, "had circumstances been otherwise."

"That's a road to madness, Sheba. We live with what is, and what has been, not with what could be. And besides"—he did his best to reassure her—"while some futures are impossible for me, there may be others I am now at liberty to offer."

Her expression grew, if anything, more perplexed. "You think you could fall in love again? With a woman, perhaps?"

"No, nor with another man. But not everyone wants that."

"You . . . you think not everyone wants to be loved?"

"I think a home of one's own is not to be undervalued. Security. A safe environment to raise a chi—"

"Do you speak of me?" Sheba's voice cut over him, too loud for the quiet church, sharp as ice.

Thomas flushed, realising he'd said far too much, far too soon. "Am I wrong?"

"Not wholly and yet nevertheless completely."

"I'm confused."

"What on earth"—there was a note of betrayal in her voice that startled him—"suggested to you that I might be willing to marry a grieving man for 'security' and a 'safe environment.'"

"I didn't mean immediately," he tried, as if that would somehow make the situation better. "I will not always be grieving."

"Grief is like love, Thomas. Like your faith. It is simply there."

"But unlike love and faith, it will loosen its grip on me." At this point, he could no longer tell if it was Sheba he was trying to convince, or himself.

"I'm still not going to marry you," she snapped.

"Do you think I would make so poor a father? So poor a husband?"

She softened slightly. "I think you would make an excellent father. And an excellent husband—to the man you're in love with."

"I'm sure I could be a good husband to you too." Oh, why was he persisting? She had made her wishes plain enough. But loss had made him fearful of further loss. And, in that moment, he could not tell who felt more distant from him, God or Micha, and who he needed most. "I care for you deeply, Sheba. I could give you a home, financial comfort, ironclad respectability. And there are things I would never want from you."

She rose, her skirts whispering softly against the flagstones where he had lain, furious and despairing, last night. "Thomas," she said, with more exasperation than he was used to seeing from her, "has it not occurred to you that I might *prefer* to be with a man who wants those things from me?"

"I'm sorry. I've been thoughtless. But I hope you know I would not stand in the way of anything you—"

"Oh please." Once again, she cut him off. "Do you really think a vicar's wife who, forgive my language, fucks around, would be any more acceptable than a vicar's wife who is a man?"

Of course she was right. This was the wildest nonsense and, on some level, he had always seen it as such. Yet he still couldn't let it go, this whisper of a future that looked almost like the future he wanted. The one anyone could have but him. "And Hope?" he could not help asking.

"What about Hope?"

"You don't think she—"

"If you try to tell me she should have a father, I will be very inclined to slap you."

"No," protested Thomas, weakly. "I simply thought she might benefit from the protection of my name."

Sighing, Sheba put a hand to her brow, the gesture unexpectedly expressive for someone he thought of as naturally rather restrained. It made him realise how well he knew her but also how little, the woman she had been, the lives she had lived, who she was deep inside, free from the world's judgement. "She might, Thomas. She very well might. And perhaps I have not always made the right choices when it comes to her. Maybe I should have become your brother's mistress rather than cast us both into uncertainty. But I don't want the only thing I teach my daughter about the life of a woman to be that it must be one of sacrifice." She smiled an oddly fragile smile. "She may wish to be a mother herself someday."

Thomas opened his mouth, then closed it again. "I'm sorry," he said, at last. "I'm so sorry. I've been—I'm being—a very poor friend to you."

At last, the rigidity left her posture. "I understand you're not yourself. And why would you be?"

"I just . . ." His voice cracked. "I feel so terribly alone. What's wrong with me?"

"Nothing's wrong with you," returned Sheba, only slightly impatiently. "You're heartbroken. That's one of the most ordinary things in the world."

The tears were spilling down Thomas's cheeks, and he was too consumed by shame to even think of brushing them away. "But how can I have found all this faith and certainty and understanding, for it to still be insufficient? Am I so selfish, so covetous and greedy and flawed, that God's love will never be enough for me?"

"I'm not the expert here, but if it was supposed to be, would He have bothered to create a companion for Adam in the first place?"

"I . . ." Thomas pressed the sleeve of his coat to his eyes. "I don't know. I think myself in circles until all I am is lost. Why has this been asked of me?"

Her mouth thinned. "Maybe it hasn't."

He gazed at her, temporarily shocked from his grief. His tear-dimmed gaze had transformed her into a pale watercolour, all greys, like the night she had come to him in the rain. "What?"

"Maybe your God is perfect, as you say." She spread her hands in a helpless, frustrated gesture. "Maybe His love is also perfect. Maybe His understanding is infinite, and His mercy as boundless as the sea. Maybe all this is true. But we live in an imperfect world. And there is only one way to live in an imperfect world, whether it's His will or not."

"Which is?" asked Thomas.

Those mirror-cool eyes held his for a long time. "You find a fucking compromise."

Chapter 26

Micha had found a white rock close to the tide line, rising from amidst the brown-grey pebbles like the back of a whale. Perched on the edge of it, he watched the waves as they rolled, blue-green and silver-capped, beneath those familiar ghost-pale cliffs. In his hands he held a brown glass bottle, purchased that afternoon from a druggist he had passed in Dover. He had paid for it, not with George's money, but with coins passersby had offered in return for quick portraits he had sketched of them. Sailors mostly, only too happy to have some memento they could send back home or offer to a sweetheart in the hope that a sweetheart she would remain after long months at sea. While Micha had started drawing mostly to distract himself, he had in the end almost come to enjoy it. He had certainly not intended to ply any sort of trade. *But better this one,* he thought, *than the alternative.*

As for the laudanum, he wasn't sure if it was weakness, desolation, or even a kind of sick defiance that had impelled him. Maybe it was simply habit. Closing his eyes, he turned his face into the sharp edge of the wind. It was easier, infinitely easier, to ache for laudanum than it was to ache for Thomas.

After a moment or two, he stood and hurled the bottle out to sea. Hard enough that he heard it smash before the tide swept over it.

"Fuck," he whispered. "Fuck."

Sitting back down, he curled his fingers into his hair and wrenched at it, wanting to feel anything—*anything*—that was not this loss. This emptiness. This endless fucking pain.

It was then that he heard the crunch of footsteps behind him.

"Forgive me but . . ."

The voice was refined but wrong. Not the one he'd dreamed of and wept for. Micha whirled around to see a man, well dressed and stately, some twenty years or more his senior. "What?"

"Are you—do you need some assistance?"

"I'm not for sale."

The stranger flushed. The fact he did not recoil or retreat, however, was an answer all of its own. "That was not the proposition I intended."

"So there *is* a proposition?" Micha leaned back on his hands, caught somewhere between hostility and intrigue, wanting to be left alone and also terrified to be.

"No." The man's flush deepened. "I'm sorry. I'm not in the habit of—I saw you this morning."

"You better not be following me."

Wisely, the stranger made no answer, seeming to recognise that any he could make would be damning.

Micha thought about walking away. There was nothing to stop him. Instead, he said, "Scant few reasons for a gentleman to be hanging around the docks."

"I was bidding farewell to my youngest son. He's spending the spring and summer travelling with his tutor before he goes to university. Not quite the grand tour. But he's ready enough to have his own life, I think. As . . ." There was the slightest of hesitations. "As am I."

"And what does that have to do with me?" asked Micha.

The man offered a self-deprecating smile. "Very little."

"Yet here you are."

This was a familiar conversation to Micha. Not the words exactly. But the cadence of it. The dance that was not a dance. The fencing match where nobody knew if the foils were tipped. If they would come away bleeding. Except Micha wasn't sure if his companion was quite so familiar. Despite his air of elegance, there was something unexpectedly open about him. Or Micha was himself too open—had been left that way, defenceless in the wake of love—when he should have been wary.

"Well I . . ." Another hesitation. "I thought you were . . ."

"What?"

The man glanced away. "Beautiful."

"You should probably be careful," Micha said finally. "Going around telling strange men you think they're beautiful."

The gentleman turned back to him. There were threads of green in the gold of his eyes. Threads of grey in the brown of his hair. "Do I need to be careful with you?"

It was not a question Micha knew how to address. "I've been a whore, you know."

"Haven't we all," returned the stranger, with a lemon twist of irony in his refined voice.

"Some of us more literally than others."

"Perhaps that just makes you more honest."

"I suppose"—Micha stirred the pebbles beneath his feet—"you'd like to fuck."

"I think I'd like to know your name first."

"Oh, you're one of *those*."

"What does that mean?"

It had been old bitterness that had spoken on Micha's behalf. "Ignore me," he muttered. "My name is Michael. Michael Dashwood."

"Mine is . . . well." Once again, the man blushed very slightly. "It's Galahad, but in my defence my mother is Welsh. My friends call me Gale."

"Are we to be friends then?" asked Micha, half-curious, half-wary.

"I would not care for us to pursue further intimacy, if we were not."

"Doesn't that rather limit your opportunities?"

Gale shrugged. "I haven't touched another man since I was at university. That was twenty-seven years ago."

"Then you must be bad at making friends."

"I had a wife. For that matter, I still do. But she has her own lovers, and all our children are grown."

"Was it worth it?"

"My wife is a good woman. And I love my family with all my heart."

"And now you're . . . what? Trawling the streets of Dover looking for . . . ?"

"I wouldn't say I was either trawling or looking." Reaching out a gloved hand, Gale gently pushed a lock of hair back from Micha's brow. It wasn't how a client would have touched him. And it wasn't like Thomas. But he felt warmth nonetheless from that promise of skin. "Then again, one never knows what the tide brings in."

"Or washes out."

Gale made a sound so soft and lost it was almost lost beneath the rustle of the waves. "It's probably not fair on those I care for, and who care for me, to say I'm lonely, Michael. I can't make a mockery of the life we built together by claiming to be unhappy. But the years keep passing and I . . . there are so many pieces of me I have put aside. For safety. For convenience. Sometimes out of sorrow. Sometimes in shame."

Impulsively, Micha caught Gale by the wrist and drew his hand back, folding their fingers together. "The thing is, I'm only fucking pieces. But"—and here he smirked—"I'll show you mine if you show me yours."

~

It's been a very long time, he tells me, gazing up at me with such trust in those green-gold eyes. And then he asks, can you . . . can you be gentle with me?

I can be anything you want, I promise.

And, to my surprise, I can. It's easy to take care of him, the way I might want to have been taken care of myself, in a different life. And it feels good, not the best it's ever felt, but good enough, my body belonging to nobody but me.

Afterwards, though, I cry, and he shushes away my apologies, and holds me, and I let him. He doesn't press me for more than that. For an explanation I'm not ready to give and wouldn't know how to even if I was.

The truth is, love has taken so much from me. I'm just relieved it's finally given something back. Even if it's only myself.

Chapter 27

Thomas had been in Dover for the best part of a week. Why Dover, he hardly knew, only that it felt right. He was sure Micha would not have gone to London, not after his previous experiences there. And this was where the last man Micha had loved had left him. It made sense he might return here, on being left again. Or on being the one to leave, though Thomas had not helped him stay.

It was on his second day of walking unfamiliar streets without direction that Thomas had realised that he had no real hope of finding Micha. But he kept wandering, kept looking, his heart stumbling in his chest for dark curls glimpsed at a distance, the certain set of a spine, every profile that could have been Micha's. He enquired at boardinghouses and cheap hotels, scoured the manifests of departing ships. And, after dark, followed less reputable paths to dank rooms, full of smoke, or the moving bodies of men. Everywhere he went, memories of Nettlefield and Micha clung to him, intermingling with desperate fantasies of a future that, even now, he knew could not be theirs. Soon it all began to feel like the same dream, one he could never fully wake from and, like Caliban, would weep for all his life.

At some point, his steps would take him down to the shore, to the beaches, and coves, and bays, where the waves churned themselves through shades of grey and blue and green beneath the equally protean sky. With the horizon unbound like a ribbon from a dancer's hair, and the vastness of the world laid softly at his feet, it was easy to feel God, but Thomas didn't pray. He just searched and waited. And, eventually, one day, he did see Micha, sitting on a rock, looking out to sea, his hair ruffled by the breeze.

It was impossible. A miracle. Everything Thomas had not dared to hope for. And, yet, in the moment, he felt no surprise at all. And, from the expression on Micha's face as he turned towards him, neither did he.

"I can't do this." The words came from Thomas without thought or even volition.

Micha's gaze was sharp and unreadable. "Do what?"

"Anything. Without you."

"You can't do anything with me either."

"Then let's do it anyway."

With a clumsy, convulsive movement, Micha was on his feet, his face as grey as the sky and his curls as wild as the waves. "We've tried this, Thomas. Fuck knows we've tried. You won't, you can't, come away with me. And I won't, I can't, stay with you. Play housekeeper and whore while the world calls me your friend. And eventually, when the bishop escalates from suggesting to demanding, someone else your wife."

"I'll never marry, Micha." Of this, at least, Thomas knew he was certain. "The worst the bishop can do is look askance and tut."

"What about your Mrs. Clark?"

"I don't think she's much for tutting."

"She'd marry you in a heartbeat."

For the first time since Micha had left Nettlefield, Thomas felt calm. Felt like himself. "She wouldn't. And she'd be right. As would any woman."

Micha's lip curled. "You sell yourself and your pretty parish too short, Thomas."

"Were I to wed anyone, it would be adultery. Because in my soul I am married to you. And I will be until death do us part."

For long moments, Micha just stared at him. Then he lifted his wrist to dash away a glitter of tears. "For fuck's sake, Thomas. Don't do this to me. Not when . . . not when I'd almost begun to bear being without you. Besides, I know you want to be a father. I see the yearning in your eyes every time you look at that girl."

"What do you see in my eyes," Thomas asked gently, "when I look at you?" And then, when Micha seemed unable to hold his gaze, he went on, "Nobody gets everything they want in life. We all pay prices, make choices, accumulate regrets. There will always be paths we didn't, or couldn't, take. But I fell in love with you. I wouldn't change that, even if I could. Even for every other dream in my heart."

"And your God?"

Thomas's lips twitched. "My God made me. He'll work it out."

"He may," Micha conceded. "But will Nettlefield? Will your family?"

"I suppose we'll see."

Micha's face was a mess of raw hope and pained disbelief. "This is madness. You know it is."

"I don't care," Thomas told him.

"There'll be rumours. Potentially a scandal. Fuck."

Micha curled his fingers into his hair, the gesture achingly familiar. Thomas reached out and caught him by the wrists, and, suddenly, they were embracing, frantic for each other, as they stood ankle-deep in the icy surf.

"It'll be the ruin of you," Micha muttered. "*I'll* be the ruin of you."

Thomas clung to him, breathing in salt, tears, the scent that was only and forever Micha's skin. "Then take whatever steps you must. Come when you can. Depart when you wish. Return when you're able. I'll wait for you. I'll never stop waiting for you. Just . . . don't leave me."

"And what do I do," asked Micha roughly, "when I'm not with you? Scratch the days off on my cell wall?"

Lifting his head, Thomas pinned Micha with his eyes. "You live as freely and truly and with as much love when you're without me as when you're with me."

"Thomas, no. That isn't—"

Possible? Reasonable? Right? Fair?

Thomas didn't know what word Micha might have chosen. But it didn't matter. "I wish I could give you everything I want to give you," he said. "And I wish I could ask you to give me everything in return. That's the life I'd have chosen for us, Micha, if it was up to me. If I had the power to create it. But I don't. So this is what we have. What we can have. If we . . ." He swallowed, remembering the church at night, and Sheba, who had brought him answers after all. "Compromise."

Above them, a seagull wheeled against the endless canvas of the sky, its widespread wings flashing a black as defiant as Micha's eyes.

"Please," Thomas tried. "It's better than—"

"Nothing," Micha finished for him.

Thomas nodded. Suddenly, it seemed a small and paltry offer. Love like a handful of pebbles when he held a world of it inside him.

But then Micha smiled. One of his slow, rare, entirely unpractised smiles, intended neither to disarm nor to deflect, but simply to express what he was feeling. It was a little lopsided, a little cynical, because Micha always was, but tender too. "Well," he said, "if it was good enough for Persephone, I suppose it can be good enough for me."

"I'm not sure I have much in common with Hades."

"Oh, don't you?" asked Micha, still smiling, his eyes at their most gleaming. And, seeing the understanding in them, Thomas shivered, soul-bared, because he suddenly realised how well Micha knew him. Better, perhaps, than Thomas would ever know himself.

In ways only a lover truly could.

And then Micha embraced him and kissed him, heedless of any who might be watching, and the sky enfolded them both in the vastness of its forever.

Epilogue

1890

My dearest,
I think Thomas would have wanted you to have these letters. They're full of you, but also of him. Some of the drawings might surprise you. I'd be a little careful with those—they're probably not a side of him you're entirely ready to see. But everything else, these words, this love, are as much a part of him as we are. I hope you will understand.

Do you remember the week we spent together at the seaside? You, me, Thomas and our friend Micha. I think that was when you lost interest in piracy and highway robbery and fell in love with geology. We were all very relieved. It was Micha, you know, who found you that spiral ammonite, the one Thomas would later have made into a necklace—I think it's still among your things in the rectory, with the sea glass and the cockleshells.

We were all very happy that week. I think of it often, especially now. I have so many memories of Thomas, all of them precious, but these are my favourites. I remember your cold little hand in mine and your eyes as wide as the horizon. And I remember two men in love chasing each other through sun-bright shallows.

All my love,
Mother

~

She had forgotten England's muted beauties, the pearl-pale iridescence of the sky and the deep, golden softness of the light. Her world was full of harsher glories: nights of amethyst and emerald, rolling oceans as black as ink with moonlight glistening upon the waves, deserts where the stars fell like rain, lost lakes, brighter than mirrors, hidden high among white peaks, waterfalls so deep within the rainforest they shimmered in shades of silver and jade, falling into pristine pools the colour of her husband's eyes. And now she walked briskly through the village guided by an instinctive familiarity that ran deeper than mere memory, and she felt neither homecoming nor alienation, for hers was a restless heart that lived in all places.

Few would have thought to call her beautiful, but she cut a striking figure nonetheless. She looked to be a little beyond her thirtieth year, her movements energetic rather than graceful, her skin honeyed by exposure to the sun, and her pale, coarse hair streaked with bronze. She wore an open-weave linen walking dress, beaded in an almost military style and trimmed in maroon velvet. It could not have been the work of any London seamstress, for it clung to the long, lean lines of her body's natural form.

She paused a moment when she came to the church, her cool rainy-day eyes sweeping a building that seemed as much a part of her childhood as Thomas's gentle voice or the silly orange dog she had chased so often through the meadows. She had done her weeping in Ian's arms, beneath unfamiliar constellations, but these reminders of moments lost to time plucked the scabs from her grief and left it raw again.

In the churchyard, the fallen leaves tumbled brightly this way and that at the whim of the breeze, whisking through the gold-tipped grass like a serpent with a scarlet tail. There were conkers gleaming in the undergrowth, and she bent to pick up the largest she could find. It nestled against her palm, warm and smooth, like a living thing, a little piece of English magic.

Thomas had loved the autumn. The crunch of leaves beneath his feet would turn him as playful as a boy. Together, they would comb the churchyard for conkers, fighting over the most promising of them. They would bear their prizes proudly back to the rectory, where they would bore holes through them and thread them on strings in preparation for battle.

It did not take her long to find the grave. It stood on a slight rise, in a glitter of sunlight. The soil was freshly turned and heaped with flowers, so many flowers, in all the richest hues of autumn. She had come too quickly for tokens, but she wished she had some flowers of her own to cast among the multitude. It seemed beyond comprehension, somehow, to witness all the intricacies of a man turned into a piece of earth.

She would also have liked some moments alone, to readjust her universe about this new-made hollow, but there were already mourners here, two men she did not recognise, one kneeling on the grass, the other with his hand resting lightly on the first man's shoulder. Something about the way their bodies inclined, the ease of their touching, suggested a deep familiarity. At her approach, they both turned, the intimacy of their tableaux still, somehow, unbroken.

The kneeling man was perhaps some fifteen years her senior, and remarkably handsome, despite the grey that laced his spill of wayward curls. The younger of the pair was not as well favoured, but his eyes were quick and merry, his mouth generous. And there was something about the other man. He tugged upon her memory, like an echo of something not quite forgotten.

An anxious silence hung between them like a veil. And then . . .

"Hope?" he said.

It should have startled her, to hear her name on the lips of a man she thought she did not know. But she did know him. He had sat with her in the garden one clear winter night and named the stars for her. His pencil had given form to all her fancies. And he had loved Thomas, an idea partially grasped with a child's understanding she had only later understood. "Micha."

He gave a harsh, uncertain laugh. "I'm surprised you can remember me."

"You remembered me."

"I know all about you." He smiled, and the beauty of it would have turned anyone breathless. "Thomas wrote of barely anything else. He was so proud of you. As am I." Suddenly he seemed to recall the hand upon his shoulder. "Forgive me, I've always had terrible manners. Sam, this is Hope Bannatyne. Hope, this is Samuel, Viscount Larcombe."

"Bannatyne?" The viscount's sandy brows flicked upwards. "The geologist?"

She recognised his name too. It had been associated with a scandal in the seventies. Arrested with two other gentlemen in a public convenience, he had been charged with conspiracy to commit an act a gently raised young lady should not have been able to comprehend. His family had intervened, and he had been released with only a fine, but his reputation was tarnished beyond repair, and he had fled to the Continent. She regarded him a little curiously, never having met an affront to civic decency before, but she saw only a man, a rather sweet and earnest one.

"My husband," she explained. "I left him in the Amazon basin and shall rejoin him at the Indo-Australian Archipelago next year."

The viscount inclined his head politely. "I'm so very sorry for your loss."

"As am I." She caught then Micha's smile, a very sad and private smile, and she went on, "I believe it was a hereditary indisposition my father suffered."

He nodded. "We came as soon as I received your mother's letter. It struck him swiftly, and he did not linger, as his father did."

"By the time I even learned he was ill, it was already too late. I'm glad you were with him."

Micha drew in a breath, but it shuddered between his lips, and then his fine, dark eyes flooded with tears. He gasped out an anguished obscenity, and, suddenly, he was in Larcombe's arms, the two of them clinging together, like twin vines.

Hope found she was not particularly disconcerted by the sight of two gentlemen embracing, and her decency—such as it was—remained staunchly unthreatened, but she stepped away to give them the privacy of each other. She studied the headstone, which was a smooth piece of stone, simply carved: *All he did, was done in love. Thomas Edward Mandeville 1831–1890.* And she wished for Ian, that she might weep, and be held, also.

"All right." Micha's voice was rough with tears. "You can come back. I've finished making a fool of myself now."

Hope turned to them. They were still partially entwined, hand in hand. "It's no more foolish to mourn than it is to love."

That made him smile. "You might not be his daughter, but I can tell he raised you."

And that made her smile. "I'm proud to bear such a legacy."

They were silent awhile. A breeze rose up and gently stirred the flowers on Thomas's grave, bearing away a handful of scarlet and gold petals that soared into the pale sky like a flotilla of tiny kites.

Micha rose to his feet. "Perhaps we should not linger. Your mother will surely want to see you. And various of the Nettlefield ladies who, I swear, must be immortal. Oh, and there's children. I've no idea who they belong to, but there's about twenty-seven of them."

Larcombe grinned, showing slightly crooked teeth. "There are three of them, Micha. Three."

"Are you sure? They seem innumerable."

"I am quite sure. Unlike you, my darling secretary, I can actually count."

Their laughter warmed her, as did the prospect of her waiting family, but Hope was not ready to leave Thomas to his sunlit silence. "In a moment."

"I . . . you know . . . I think I should go back." Larcombe's fingers brushed the inside of Micha's wrist, before he released his hand. "I can tell them you're coming. There's no rush." He strolled away through the churchyard, a slight, rather dandified figure, light-gilded among the swirling autumn leaves.

"He seems to take great care of you," offered Hope, noting the way Micha's eyes pursued the viscount into the distance.

"Yes." He smiled his brilliant, heart-stopping smile. "I care for him very deeply."

"I'm so glad you're happy, Micha."

He ran an idle, caressing hand over the top of the grave marker. "Thomas deserves nothing less. His letters were always full of joy. He loved you and your mother very much."

"Yes, I know. He loved you too."

"And I've never stopped loving him." A shadow swept across his eyes. "I don't suppose I ever will."

Hope was too much a scientist to care very much for a divine presence she could neither see, nor prove, nor analyse, but she would not have denied solace to a grieving man. "Perhaps you will see him again."

"Do you really believe that?" Micha's lip curled into a sneer so familiar it made her ache a little for all the lost possibilities of life.

"Well . . ." But she was too like Thomas to countenance a lie, even a soothing one. "Well . . . *I* do not. But people believe and disbelieve all kinds of things. Some people do not believe in evolution. It does not mean they are correct."

Micha laughed suddenly, a touch of bitterness, and a touch of mischief. "Oh Hope, you haven't changed."

"I am quite a bit taller, thank you."

After a moment, he said, "But what does it mean, if there's nothing? Where does that leave us?" His voice cracked. "Here we are, parting from each other all over again, and I can't even visit. He can't even send me letters. He's simply gone."

"Some cultures," she suggested gently, "believe in continuance."

"Reincarnation? Past lives? All that spiritualist shit? Fuck, no." The sneer was back. "One life has been quite enough for me. I'm not doing this again."

Hope gazed at him, in mingled sympathy and bewilderment. A thousand lives would not have been enough to satisfy her curiosities or diminish her passions. Though she grieved with him, she wished she could offer him some comfort. Thomas would have known what to say. "Perhaps it is more abstract than that. Perhaps there is continuance through time."

"There's what?"

"I'm not much of a philosopher, and certainly no theologian, but it seems to me all lives, all actions, all choices have their consequences."

"And death is the most inevitable of all consequences? That's not very reassuring, my dear." But Micha was trying to smile, and it softened his words.

"I just meant that everything changes, with everything we do. And the world itself reshapes itself not from the upheaval of great continents, but in the tiniest of ripples, so the slightest movement of the most inconsequential archipelago has meaning beyond calculation or prediction."

"I thought we weren't supposed to be islands."

"Connected islands, like ideas passed from mouth to mouth, or book to book, or people holding hands." Hope looked again at her father's modest, flower-strewn grave. "Perhaps, this is not the end of anything. Perhaps there will be other lovers, who know greater freedoms and can make other choices, all touched in some small, indefinable way by the lives around them, and before them, leading all the way back to us, and the lives that have touched ours."

"That's scant fucking consolation, forgive my bluntness."

"It is," she agreed, "but it's some."

He smirked and saluted her like a fencer acknowledging a hit. Then he sighed. "We never did see Venice. Or his damn deserts." He shrugged. "But maybe someone will. Someday. Maybe that'll do."

Hope reached out and tucked her hand into his. And they waited with Thomas until the sun slipped beyond the horizon, and his grave turned slowly from gold to silver in the fearless light from the first scattering of stars.

About the Author

Alexis Hall is determined to marry into money, as his grandfather drank half the family fortune and gambled the rest. He lives in a tumble-down mansion in a fictional county, and his valet doesn't even have a humorous name.

Keep up with Alexis and his latest endeavors by visiting his website at www.quicunquevult.com or subscribing to his newsletter at www.quicunquevult.com/contact. You can also find Alexis on Instagram (www.instagram.com/quicunquevult).